THE

BIG

FIX

by

Jill Morris

First published in Great Britain by Jill Morris Author, 2021

Copyright © Jill Morris, 2021

First edition.

The Big Fix is a work of fiction, with a completely fictional plot, generated by the author's imagination. This fictional dramatisation, however, *is* based around actual football clubs and the top divisions in English football. This includes actual matches that occurred, mainly between April 2017 and April 2018. There is no suggestion whatsoever that any of the actual named (or implied) clubs, club officials, leagues, players, referees or league officials would undertake any of the illegal activities featured in this work. With regard to any fictional characters, any resemblance to actual persons, living or dead, is entirely coincidental.

Set in 11 Garamond/12 Gill Sans MT

A CIP catalogue record for this book is available from the British Library

Paperback ISBN: 978-1-7399478-0-4

www.JillMorrisAuthor.co.uk

For my mam and dad

x

To Megan

THE

BIG

FIX

From one football fan to
another, I hope you enjoy
my debut book.

Best wishes
Jill Morris
x

PROLOGUE

It was just a normal matchday. A big matchday, but still a normal one. Or at least, that's what most of the 75,000 plus people at Old Trafford thought on a typical spring day in April 2017.

Both teams had a lot to play for. Manchester United were desperately trying to reach the top four, with just a handful of games remaining. Meanwhile, Chelsea were aiming to cling onto top spot for the rest of the season. They'd hit a blip a couple of weeks ago, which had given Spurs some hope of catching them.

Matchday commander for Greater Manchester Police, Mark Yates, was keeping a close eye on the throngs of home and away supporters converging on the stadium. Today was, not surprisingly, a sell-out crowd and there was a lot at stake. Tensions would be high.

In the control room, the club's safety officer allowed him access to cameras that covered every aspect of the ground, inside and outside. They even covered the players' tunnel and the entrances to the dressing rooms. This was more from a security perspective, although there'd been a few unsavoury incidents in that tunnel over the years. The police had shown a passing interest in them, but it was generally left to the football authorities to penalise those involved. Sadly, the infamous 'stray boot' incident involving Fergie and Beckham was behind closed doors in the changing room. Yates would've liked to have seen that and have it recorded. For posterity of course.

Yates had briefed his team a couple of hours ago. Their intelligence suggested there wasn't any planned disorder at today's game. So they were mainly on alert for any sporadic clashes or drunken behaviour. Building up to kick-off, they'd also have to ensure both teams arrived at the ground safely. During the game, they'd protect the dugouts and prevent any pitch incursions. And depending on the result, post-match they'd be watching out for any situations that could lead to disorder.

All in all, the policing was relatively straightforward for such a big game.

Yates could remember the 80s as a football fan and they were different times. In fact, as a Man City supporter, he'd seen more than his fair share of bother. But these days, with a few exceptions, fans were generally well-behaved.

"Guv, I'm keeping an eye on this group of Chelsea fans in the car park."

One of his officers pointed out a bunch of lads that looked like they were up to no good. It was a camera from one of the nearby retail parks. Although the club's safety officer was responsible for surveillance within the stadium's footprint, the police monitored their own CCTV in the surrounding area.

Yates watched them, trying to work out what they were doing. They headed into Currys/PC World, about half a dozen of them, beer bottles in hand, barging into anyone in their path. His colleague radioed for officers to get to the store. As if by magic, four PCs arrived within seconds, having been positioned a matter of yards away. They both watched the monitors, satisfied to see their men escort the lads out of the store moments later. They'd be warned to behave and the officers would keep an eye on them heading up to the ground. They hadn't committed any crime. Not yet, anyway.

At that moment, Yates's eyes were drawn to the tunnel area, where the referee's changing room was located. There was security posted outside the door at all times, for several reasons. Two men were lurking almost opposite the closed door. They had Man United scarves on, but he had no idea who they were. Although one of them looked vaguely familiar.

Yates asked the safety officer to zoom in on the men. He was convinced he'd seen one of them before, but couldn't place him at all. They looked a little menacing, all dressed in dark clothes, save for the red and white striped scarves. The man that had jogged some sort of memory in Yates had a fairly prominent scar above his left eye. Apart from that, there were no other distinguishing features.

After a few minutes, the two men began chatting to the security guy. Things seemed very amicable and the men appeared to pose no malice. Probably some rich corporates he thought, expecting to get into every area of the ground. Yates relaxed at that point. The safety officer switched to other camera angles, moving swiftly through the various vantage points.

So far, so good.

What Yates didn't see, once he'd moved on to other viewpoints, was the two men flashing some sort of ID to security. The guard knocked, poked his head inside and announced the visitors to the officials within. They were only in the room for a matter of minutes; they didn't need to stay any longer. Just long enough to emphasise their message. After all, they wouldn't want to have been caught by any cameras, opposition officials or players. A few minutes was all it took.

A couple of hours later, a 2-0 win for Man United had thrown the title race wide open. Yates was skimming through the monitors as fans streamed out of the ground. It had been a strange match. Chelsea seemed out of sorts and there'd been a contentious decision for Man United's first goal. How the referee had missed a blatant handball in the build-up was beyond comprehension. If the Man United fans were honest, they knew it should have been disallowed; Chelsea fans were raging.

His team was on high alert, as ever, following the final whistle. Their eyes and ears wide open, ready for the slightest hint of trouble. Once the fans were on their journeys home, the responsibility passed to the British Transport Police or adjoining forces. But that could be at least an hour after the end of the game. Their work wasn't over yet.

Yates had a mischievous sense of humour about the possibility of bother on the trains. The away fans, for London teams, were generally outnumbered by the southern contingent of Man United followers. "Support your local team!" he always thought to himself. Many a time he'd wanted to shout that out loud at them, especially when they were kicking off or being dickheads. But he hadn't risen up the ranks by acting unprofessionally. And being in charge of match-day policing was his dream role. So he kept his true feelings inside and got on with the job.

The same sort of bandwagon jumpers had invaded Yates's club these days. That was the only real downside with his team in recent years. Since the oil money had come into the game, the influx of glory-hunting fans supporting Man City had grown inexorably. The game was worse because of them, although he felt his club retained a fair bit of its heritage. There were still plenty of proper Mancs who'd been there through thin and thinner. Back in the day.

Despite the downsides, Yates wouldn't change the experience of winning something after all these years. He'd been far too young to appreciate the only other silverware in his lifetime, the League Cup of 1976. Now he had to admit he felt spoilt, as trophy after trophy was being lifted.

You'd think it would shut this lot up, he thought, focusing back on the job in hand. Yet they still went on as if they were the greatest team on the planet; despite the evidence suggesting otherwise. As the trophy conveyor belt of their Salford rivals was grinding to a halt, the blue half of Manchester was gaining real momentum. They now had arguably one of the top global managers and Yates could see the building blocks being put in place. The future looked bright.

"Arrogant pricks!" he thought, as he shook his head at a group of goading, chanting Man United fans. They were squaring up to their Chelsea counterparts, as they headed towards the cricket ground car park. "Do they not realise Chelsea are top of the league and they're outside of the Champions League places?" he mused.

Still, he kept those thoughts to himself, as he radioed his officers on the ground to keep a watch out in that area.

He glanced through the various camera angles once more, pausing as he came to the players' tunnel again. At that very moment, he noticed the door of the referee's changing room open. He was about to move his gaze onto the next screen. It would no doubt be the referee or one of his assistants coming out. It could even be one of the opposing managers, in there for a moan about one decision or another. Let's face it, most managers these days weren't happy with the officials no matter what the result.

Yates stopped in his tracks when he saw who actually appeared from the inside of the dressing room. It wasn't the referee. It wasn't any of his assistants. It wasn't Jose Mourinho or Antonio Conte or even any of their backroom staff.

It was the two men from earlier.

As calm as you like, they acknowledged the security man on the door as they departed. A couple of minutes later, the referee did appear from the dressing room, his assistants following him in close succession.

Strange, he thought. I don't remember seeing that before.

And then, before he could consider what may have happened, one of his officers broke the silence.

"Guv, we've got a couple of groups kicking off near the Kelloggs car park. Looks like they're smashing up some cars."

"Shit. Send a couple of vans down sharpish. And get patrols down there straight away."

For the next hour, Yates was tied up with handling the fracas, directing his officers from the bank of monitors. There were a few cars damaged, mostly windscreens caved in. And a few cuts and bruises amongst both the perpetrators and his officers. It was the only real skirmish of the afternoon; and, whilst totally unnecessary, it wasn't a major incident. The worst bit would be all the paperwork it would cause. But at least that was one for his subordinates to sort out. His responsibility was completing the overall match report.

Yates didn't include the mysterious characters from the referee's changing rooms in his report. It wasn't really his place to question their presence unless they'd caused some sort of incident. But, as he sat down to watch Match of the Day 2 later that night, he did wonder who they were. And what they were up to.

And, more importantly, where had he seen them before?

PART ONE

- I -

24 August 2017

Today was the day he was going to end it all. Put a stop to all the unhappiness. Today was the day he'd finally be at peace and his loved ones would be better off.

He couldn't go on. He'd let everyone down. Sure, he'd had a lot of bad luck, but his actions had made everything so much worse. He was in debt up to his eyeballs. His wife was working so hard when she should be on the sick. And his son wouldn't know a treat if it smacked him in the face.

He couldn't see any other outcome to his situation. Everything was completely overwhelming as if he was sinking in quicksand and couldn't get out. The more he struggled, the more it enveloped him, pulling him down. And down. And down.

At times it felt like a volcanic eruption, the lava creeping menacingly towards him. When things got even worse, it was more like a tsunami, the speed of the creeping destruction picking up pace. Either way, it destroyed everything in its path. If he wasn't being burned alive, consumed by the heat of the lava, he was drowning in a powerful, devastating wave.

His financial affairs had become all-consuming. As each week passed, the dark cloud got darker and darker. It hung over his every waking hour. He didn't have a life anymore. He couldn't afford to go for a beer with his mates, couldn't meet them at the match, couldn't even buy his own son a ticket for his first game. He literally just worked, paid a few bills, ignored other bills, and desperately tried to pay off what he owed. Yet his debts were mounting all the time and the final demands just kept on coming. It was futile.

And now the final straw. He'd lost his job.

So, here he was. Sat on the edge of a bridge, waiting for the 20:58 train to approach. Waiting to jump.

He'd been sat here for over half an hour already. He hadn't leapt in front of the 20:34 train. That was too soon after he'd got into position. He had to build up to this after all.

But now he was ready.

He glanced at his watch. It was 20:56. Not long now. It'd soon be over. He hoped it would be instantaneous. That the pain would be fleeting and he'd know nothing about it, as his body was smashed to smithereens.

Five agonising minutes passed. Typical he thought. The trains are always bloody late.

What if it had been cancelled? When was the next one? He hadn't checked to see how late the trains ran on this track. Oh, God, what if he'd missed his chance? He couldn't bear the thought of having to live through another day. He'd have to come up with another way to end it all.

As he pondered his options, he heard the distant sound of a train approaching. Thank Christ for that.

He edged forward on the ledge of the bridge, catching his breath as he almost slipped in the process. He didn't want to fall off before the train arrived. It might not be final if that happened. It could be horrifically painful, life-changing in the worst way possible. That would be just his luck, the way things were currently panning out in his life.

The rumbling sound of the train was getting closer now. He began to see its lights in the distance. Not long now. Not long at all.

His life suddenly flashed before his eyes. He hadn't expected that. His wife. His son. His parents. His brother. His sister. His mates. His life. And then he realised that tears were streaming down his face.

Oh, God! This was so tough. But he had to do it. His family would be better off without him.

He wasn't religious but said a quick prayer. It was almost time.

The lights were getting brighter now. The noise of the train was getting louder.

Now or never. He moved forward. He was right on the edge. He was ready to let go.

As the train came in full view, he made to jump. Here. We. Go.

He thought he'd jumped. He had. He *had* jumped! But at that very moment, someone had grabbed hold of him. Someone had pulled him back. Back from the brink.

"Whoa! I've got you, mate. I've got you."

As he collapsed into those comforting arms, Liam both despised and felt eternally grateful to the person who had seen him about to jump. And who had been strong enough, quick enough and brave enough to save his life.

Liam and Callie had known each other virtually all their lives. They'd gone to the same schools, had the same circle of friends and drank in the same pubs.

Having joined the army at the first opportunity, Liam finally asked Callie out three years later when he was home on leave. And for the next four years, they survived a long-distance relationship, while he completed his army stint.

Liam proposed to Callie during his final year in the forces. It was romantic. For him. He'd been thinking about doing it ever since he'd put his notice in. He was apprehensive about returning to civilian life. But he'd become disillusioned with the army after nearly seven years. Seven years of seeing some of his best mates blown to pieces. Or suffering life-changing injuries in lands that were poles apart from their own. Seven years of putting his life on the line for an employer that didn't truly value that sacrifice.

They were both twenty-three, with a bit of money put by for a deposit. But they couldn't afford anywhere in the area they'd grown up in. And if they hadn't bought during the property crash of '09, they'd never have got on the ladder. The thought of shelling out all that money to rent somewhere for the rest of their lives filled them with dread.

For once though, luck seemed to go their way. Property prices were falling, just as they were looking to buy. They managed to get a two-bed flat within budget on Uxbridge Road, close to both Shepherd's Bush and White City. They'd had to mortgage themselves to the hilt, it was on a busy main road and not in the best of areas. It was poky at best. But it was theirs.

They almost regretted it on completion day. It was in a barely liveable state. The place needed re-wiring, re-plastering and re-decorating throughout. Never mind the lingering patches of damp and mould from a leak in the bathroom. But Liam was handy enough and he could count on his mates to help out. By the time they got married in late summer 2009, their home in Hanover Court was ready to move into.

It was just as well. Callie's parents had been great in letting him stay since he'd left the army a few months earlier. But it was never easy moving in with the in-laws. They longed to have a space of their own. Plus they'd be needing more room. Especially now they were expecting a baby.

They'd always planned on having kids. But it still came as a shock in the build-up to the big day to find out Callie was pregnant. They'd been pretty careful and living with her parents had dampened their sex life somewhat. While the timing could've been better, their joy at the thought of becoming a family was profound.

"Will we be ok for money though?" Callie had asked Liam at the time, the worry evident in her eyes.

"Yeah, we'll survive," he said positively, not knowing one way or the other. He'd had a bit of a payout from the army on leaving, via their resettlement grant. Having served as an electrical engineer during his time in the military, he soon picked up work as an electrician, although it was only a temporary contract initially. They'd managed to sort a mortgage thanks to his dad acting as a guarantor, but their finances were still precarious.

Right now, his soon-to-be wife needed his reassurance. She didn't need any extra worries. And he'd do anything to make sure she stayed calm and relaxed throughout her pregnancy.

How crap life is sometimes. When the initial joy of becoming parents is overshadowed by thinking you can't afford to bring a little life into the world.

As it turned out, they were fine for the next few years. Liam's contract became permanent. His occasional overtime went towards extra spending on the baby. And though she took the minimum maternity leave, Callie glowed throughout her pregnancy.

Robbie was born the following March. 6lb 3oz. A shock of red hair at birth and light blue eyes like glistening rock pools. They were truly blessed. It was scary as shit being responsible for another human being. Liam was shaking the first time he cradled Robbie in his arms, he seemed so tiny and helpless. But his heart felt as though it would explode. Unconditional love. He was a dad. He had a son!

All was well with their little family. Callie was enjoying working for London Fire Brigade as an emergency call operator. Liam was relatively secure at work and hadn't suffered an 'episode' in a long time. Robbie was a happy, healthy boy, who loved football, rockets and anything to do with Spiderman. They'd even started thinking about having another baby, now they were on a sounder financial footing. They weren't well off by any means, but they were managing.

Last year, everything started to unravel.

It began with something as innocuous as the service charge for their flat and then the bad luck kept on coming. They only owned the leasehold; a new company bought the freehold and doubled the service charge overnight. Liam doubted it was purely to cover the claimed maintenance costs. He suspected they were looking to force out some of the residents, make the flats more upmarket and charge even more. Yet, no amount of appeals could stop their payments being increased. It was a lot of extra money to find every month, but they cut their cloth accordingly.

Two months later, the next hit left them reeling. Their boiler broke down. They didn't have the savings to pay for a new one. So Liam made the fateful decision to take out a payday loan. Just for a couple of months, he thought. Then we'll pay it off.

Months passed and they were still struggling. He maxed out the credit card on their joint account. Another bad choice, made out of desperation.

It was the thin end of the wedge. Now, they were on a downward spiral money-wise. Every month that went by, they were racking up the debt. It was impossible to pay back.

And then the final straw came.

Four months ago, Liam was on his way home from work after an overtime shift. He'd been volunteering for a lot more hours, one of the reasons he'd recently switched jobs. But it was starting to take its toll. He was well and truly knackered. He didn't see the fox run out into the dual carriageway. Only woke up from his drift when he hit it. Then, in his dazed state, he swerved and careered across the carriageway. He overturned and finally came to rest by smashing into the central reservation.

He'd had to be cut out of the van. All things considered, he wasn't too badly injured. But the trauma of the crash triggered his PTSD. For the first time in a few years, he'd started having some episodes again. His employer was more supportive than he was obliged to be. But when Liam couldn't return to work for over two months, he'd had to let him go.

By now, their financial situation was perilous. They'd been able to get some help from their parents, but none of them were exactly well off. Liam's pride stood in the way of being completely honest about their circumstances.

Meanwhile, the debts mounted. And mounted. And mounted.

By September of 2017, Liam was at least back in employment. It was an uncertain role, with split shifts and the demands of being on call. But he was back on his feet and contributing again. His physical injuries had healed and his mental ones were almost coping. Having had some counselling, his episodes were happening less and less. Just the stress of a £30k debt to try and manage now…

Callie knew they were struggling, but didn't know the full extent of their debts. He hadn't wanted to worry her. Especially as she was trying to cope with her own demons these days. Because on the night he crashed his van into the central reservation, she was having the worst night of her life. And that was before she found out her husband had had a serious road accident.

14 June 2017 would be etched on Callie's mind forever. The night that Grenfell Tower burned.

-3-

There was nothing unusual about Callie's night shift on 13 June.

At least, not until about 1:30am the following day. Even when the initial call came in, just before 1:00am, her colleague had followed standard procedure. Engines were dispatched to deal with a kitchen fire on the fourth floor of a tower block. They all thought nothing of it, to begin with. These things happen from time to time.

This time was different though.

Callie had been on shift since 7:00pm and was due to finish at 7:00am. After working four nights in a row, she was looking forward to four days off to recover and reset her body clock. It was tough doing this shift cycle, your body never seemed to adjust to the constant upheaval. No wonder she never knew what day it was or whether she should be awake or asleep.

Around 1:15am, Callie and her colleagues began to receive calls from residents in a burning tower block. It was the same address as the kitchen fire. One of her colleagues checked in with the unit at the scene, to get an update on the situation. The others issued the standard 'stay put' advice for high-rise buildings.

Less than ten minutes later, they were informed that the Met had declared it a major incident. The shift team moved into emergency mode. Tension spread across the room. No one liked to be involved in this sort of scenario. But still, they believed everyone would be safe.

Quarter of an hour later, the London Ambulance Service declared it a significant incident. By now, the whole team was concerned. They were keen to calm down callers, especially those from in the tower itself. They couldn't yet see what was unfolding at the tower. They didn't know the fire had spread to the outside of the building, up to the top and all around. How it was engulfing the people they'd advised to stay put. They were working blind.

It was now 2:00am and more calls were coming in. Callie picked up the phone from someone high up in the building, alone in the flat with her young child. It was the second call the woman had made that night. She'd been relatively calm during her first call, half an hour earlier, but now she sounded frightened.

"Please help us, we need help. Urgently! There is fire in the main corridor, blocking the emergency exit. I can see flames down below when I look out of my window."

"Our units are there at present ma'am and they're working to extinguish the fire. You should stay in your flat. It's safer than trying to escape when there could be other outbreaks of fire on your way down."

"My daughter is only six years old. Please don't let us die here. Please."

Callie was concerned. What the hell was going on? "We won't ma'am. Is there smoke actually in your flat at the moment?"

"There isn't right now, but it won't be long before it is. How long will it be before the firemen are here to rescue us?"

"I'll find out for you and call you back."

"No! Please don't hang up. I beg you."

"Okay, I'll stay on the line, but bear with me while I get an update."

A sigh of relief at the other end of the phone. A whispered "thank you" as she was put on hold.

The update wasn't what Callie wanted to hear. The building was now fully ablaze and firefighters were battling to contain the fire. They were attempting to reach people on the upper floors. Still though, they were told to maintain their 'stay put' advice.

She re-connected to the frightened woman from the tower block and relayed the information. Help was on the way. Stay where you are and they'll be there as soon as possible.

"How long will they be? The smoke is coming under the door now! Please, please, I don't want to die in here." Callie was scared now. This was turning into the most perilous situation she'd had to deal with in her time as an emergency call operator. But she had to remain calm for the benefit of this poor woman.

Callie spent the next few minutes giving the woman advice on how to minimise the smoke ingress. Put damp towels at the bottom of the door. Get damp towels for you and your daughter, so you can cover your mouths if need be. Stay down low on the floor.

"I'm at the window. Can they see me? Do they know which flat I'm in?"

"Yes they do, don't worry, they shouldn't be too much longer."

"I'm so scared. I don't think we're going to get out."

"They'll get to you, please believe me. You'll be safe. Just do your best to stop the smoke and wrap those other towels around your faces."

"My daughter is struggling to breathe," the woman herself was coughing now too. "It's so smoky in here. Are they still coming?"

"Yes, they're on their way. Please try and stay calm and do everything I told you."

Callie couldn't bear to leave the call now. She had to make sure the woman and her daughter made it. She couldn't believe an innocuous kitchen fire was turning into this major incident. What on earth had happened?

By now the woman was panic-stricken. "I don't think we're going to make it. Please. Please help us, I beg you," she sobbed down the phone. Her tone was one of both fear and despair. And she was clearly choking.

A short while later, as the clock showed 2:35am, the control room commander rocked the team to the core. The operators were ordered to revoke their 'stay put' advice. Anyone calling 999 should be advised to get out, to leave if they could find a safe exit route.

A shocked silence fell upon the room before the team quickly re-focused.

Callie spoke to her caller, fearing the reaction.

"Yes ma'am, the advice now is to get out, as quickly as you can, if you can find a safe way to exit."

She could barely hear the response, it was overtaken by uncontrollable coughing and wheezing. A feeling of dread swept over her. How was this woman supposed to escape? It sounded like a wall of flame was right outside her door. Unless the firefighters reached her, it seemed like a hopeless situation. Callie felt complicit. Tears pricked her eyes, but she brushed them away. There was no time for emotion, she had to focus on this woman.

"I'm going to put you on hold again ma'am. I'm going to try and get the firefighters there for you as soon as possible. Please hold on. Please."

Callie connected to the unit's commander. She relayed the information again and underlined the urgency. She was now begging for a woman and her six-year-old daughter to be rescued.

Before it was too late. The commander assured her they were doing everything they could to try and reach people on the upper floors. He noted the flat number again and advised they'd report back if they made it there.

As she switched back on to the woman, Callie struggled to stop the emotion from taking over. She couldn't raise a response.

"Hello? Hello ma'am? Ma'am are you still there?"

Her superior was wandering over to her desk.

"Ma'am? Ma'am? Are you still there?" Her voice was getting louder, more desperate by the second.

Her team leader looked at the screen in front of her and scanned the conversation.

"She may be trying to escape, Cal. If you can't get a response in the next minute or so, you should hang up. There may be other calls you can deal with."

She was desolate. She didn't think the woman was trying to escape. Not now. Not an hour on from her first call. An hour ago she may have been able to get out. An hour ago, her escape route may not have been blocked by fire. An hour ago, her flat wasn't filled with smoke. An hour ago…she was still breathing. Callie had a feeling in the pit of her stomach that the lady couldn't escape, that she was no longer breathing. She'd failed her. And her daughter, almost the same age as her son.

She tried, desperately, to raise a response. Finally, her superior took control and gently ended the call.

"Do you need a few minutes?" she asked her, conscious of the emotional toll.

"No, I'm fine. I'll get on another call."

"Callie, go and grab a coffee or something. This is going to be a long night."

She didn't argue. Julie was more experienced and knew when colleagues needed to grab a breather. She could spot the signs a mile away.

By the time she returned to the control room, Callie was feeling ready to take on more calls. She knew her team leader would keep her updated, so she had to try and focus on anyone else needing her assistance.

While she'd been away, the screens in the room had been turned on and tuned in to Sky News. Normally the control room was a sterile environment. Free from outside interference, it allowed the operators to focus on calls from a variety of incidents. This wasn't a normal situation. The ability to see what was going on at Grenfell might help them. As Callie wandered into the room, she wasn't sure it helped. The footage was shocking. Heart-rending. She almost had to walk straight back out.

She forced herself to sit down and plugged back into the system. Ready to receive calls. Not sure she was ready for the conversations.

And then she saw it.

Earlier footage from the blaze now appeared on screen. It would be around the time she was on the phone to the woman with the young daughter. There she was, on the phone at the window, waving to anyone who could see. Begging for help. Begging for someone to save their lives. It had to be her. Callie was overcome. The flames were everywhere around her. Christ! How could anyone survive that?

She unplugged again.

Her team leader gave her time to head into the toilets. Allowed her time to let it all out, to cry for a woman and her daughter who had most likely perished in a terrible fire. Having made sure everyone else was coping, she was about to check on Callie when her phone rang.

By the time Julie eventually made it into the toilets, Callie had almost composed herself. Her face still had giveaway signs of the tears that had flowed for the last ten minutes. But she had pulled herself together, prepared herself to get through the rest of her shift. There could be other people that needed her help, whether it was at Grenfell or elsewhere.

Julie had already made the decision that Callie had finished her shift for the night.

"Sorry Julie, I… I think I've just seen that woman on the TV coverage. And there's no way she could've survived that."

"I know, Cal and I know it's hard. It sounds like there's gonna be quite a few fatalities, to be honest. It's awful."

"I'm ready to get back to work now though. I'll stay a bit longer at the end of my shift if it's needed."

"Actually, you're done for the night."

"No honestly, I'm fine. I'm okay to carry on."

"Callie, I've just had a call. It's Liam."

She looked confused. What did Liam have to do with anything?

"There's been an accident. He's been rushed to hospital. Apparently, it's serious. You need to get there straight away."

Callie gasped. Reached out to hold on to something. Anything. Julie caught her just in time.

4

Gavin looked ten years older than Liam. His border collie, Jack, was on its hind legs, front paws on Liam's knees and head resting between. If Liam had bent his face towards Jack, he was convinced the dog would try to lick him to death. With affection of course.

The two men were sat in Gavin's local pub, having a pint, not yet confronting what had happened twenty minutes ago. Liam was sure that moment wasn't far off.

To his surprise, Gavin began with small talk.

"So, do you have a partner, any kids?"

"Erm, yeah, I've got a wife and a little boy. He's seven."

"Ah, lucky guy. Me and the missus would have loved to have had kids, but it never happened. We got Jack a few years ago as a substitute. I dunno what I'd do without him now, he's like our baby."

Liam looked down at Jack and smiled. He was a handsome dog and it was therapeutic stroking his head.

"D'you follow football?" he asked.

Liam nodded as he sipped his pint. God, it tasted good. "Brentford. I don't go much these days though, money's tight."

Gavin spotted the pained look in Liam's eyes as he spoke. "Yeah, I'm the same. I'm a Fulham fan. Gave up my season ticket a couple of years back. My wife got ill, so I had to care for her."

"Is she… ok now?" Liam asked hesitantly.

"Yeah, she's in remission, thankfully. But you get out of the habit of going y'know? I get to the odd game, but it's not the same as it used to be."

He nodded, understanding the sentiments. "I'd love to take my lad though. He's getting really interested in football, especially the Bees. It's a family thing; my dad took me to my first game when I was seven, so between the two of us we've brought him up on Brentford."

"Brought him up well," said Gavin light-heartedly. "Kids these days just seem to want to support the so-called big clubs. Drives me round the bend. Where's the enjoyment in that? Nah, much more fun seeing your club plummet through the divisions and fight its way back up. And then yo-yo for evermore."

Liam laughed at Gavin's sarcasm, for what felt like the first time in a long time.

As they enjoyed another pint, shandy this time, the two men carried on their small talk, getting to know each other better. Gavin pulled a dog-eared photo out of his wallet; a young couple stood in front of a VW camper van, carefree and happy. Tanned. In love.

"That's me and my wife when we did the Great Ocean Road in Australia a while back," he explained. "I was terrified when she got her diagnosis, but touch wood," he tapped the table, "so far so good. Anyway, it's made us re-evaluate our lives. As soon as we save up enough for our own camper van, then we're off. We're gonna travel around the UK, Europe too, and take Jack with us. It's a few years off yet, but we'll get there."

Liam realised as they chatted that he wasn't the only one with problems. He began to feel guilty for what he'd just tried to do. His face gave the game away.

"Mate, you know that ending it all isn't ever the answer?"

Liam nodded, feeling his eyes well up. Immediately he tried to suppress the emotion.

"I know. But I'm in such a mess money-wise. I can't see any solution. The debt just keeps getting higher and higher."

"Have you spoken to anyone for advice?"

He shook his head. Of course he hadn't, other than taking the wrong routes via payday loan companies and credit cards. And while he'd spoken to his family to try and get help in a small way, he hadn't told them the full story of his debt.

"Don't be afraid to open up to people. You can't get help if you don't let anyone know you need it."

Liam nodded. He knew he had to start fronting up to his problems and asking people for help.

"Listen, if you ever need to talk, get in touch." Gavin reached into his wallet and pulled out a business card. "I work from home, so that's my home address on there if you're in the area. Or drop me a text, give me a call. Whatever. If you need to talk, about anything. Do it."

He put the card in his own wallet. It felt weird, having such a strong connection with a perfect stranger. But this stranger had quite literally saved his life. Brought him back from the brink.

He still had all his money worries. He didn't yet have a plan to solve them. Yet already he was feeling much more positive.

They hugged as they parted, Liam's eyes welling up once again.

"Hey, hang in there, mate. Think about all the things you'd miss if you ever feel like that again. Imagine missing your little lad growing up for one thing. And taking him to his first Brentford match."

"I know, I know. I can never thank you enough for saving my life. But I want you to know that I'll get myself sorted. Thanks, Gav. I really mean that."

He walked back to where he'd parked his van a few hours ago. As he slumped into the driver's seat, the reality hit him like a truck. What the hell had he been thinking? What had he almost put Callie and Robbie through? Not to mention his parents, brother, sister, his mates. All because of money. What Gavin had said was true. Suicide wasn't the answer. It would be hard to get through this, but they would get there. Even if they ended up homeless, that would be preferable to him missing out on life completely. They'd start over. They'd have each other. They *would* make it.

At that moment, Liam vowed he'd never get to that point again. He spent the next half hour letting all his emotions flood out. Sobbing his heart out wasn't something he did as a rule and he felt a strange sense of release. He knew he'd find it tough to open up and ask for help. He was a hardened ex-soldier. But one way or another, he'd fix this.

5

"Prick! Arrogant prick!" Danny thought to himself, as he overhead his client on the phone. He assumed he was on to his assistant, Emma. The way he spoke so dismissively and with such little respect really riled him. Who the hell did this guy think he was?

"Get me that room sorted, for crying out loud. I can't miss this meeting and I'm not driving back from Liverpool at that time of night," he was saying. "I don't *care* if it's already booked. I want the Presidential Suite. Just get it *sorted*."

Danny assumed he'd hung up, but no, he still had the phone to his ear. His face was beginning to redden, so Danny averted his eyes as he heard him say, "Yes, it's the night of 28th November, Emma. Do I have to spell it out for you all the time? Don't you think I have more important things to concern myself with?" A brief silence hung in the air before he said, through gritted teeth, "I don't care how you get it, just get it." He hung up abruptly.

Danny was pleased this job was almost over. He'd had a few weeks mostly avoiding Mitchell Roberts, whoever he was. If he'd had to put up with him the whole time, he would've happily walked off the job. Just like the last guy had.

That should've been more of a warning sign, but he'd been quite keen to get more work over this part of town. Maybe get some recommendations from Mitchell, get a few more well-heeled clients put his way. They spent a lot more on house renovations than his average customer, without batting an eyelid.

Now that he'd met this charmless bloke, however, he no longer wanted his endorsement.

When he first rocked up at the townhouse on Elystan Place, a couple of months ago, he'd met Mitchell's personal assistant, Emma. She talked him through the requirements of the job, apologising for the unfinished work left by the previous builder. She was elusive about the reason he'd walked out.

Emma told Danny that Mitchell wouldn't be there much during the day. So he could come and go as he pleased, as long as he stayed on schedule. And on top of the premium price on offer for the job itself, there would also be a completion bonus. A couple of grand, if he hit the deadline and the house-owner was satisfied with the work.

It seemed too good to be true. He couldn't turn it down. He'd have to find a way of juggling some of his other jobs while getting this one done. Get a labourer working for him here on the simple stuff. Keep an eye on his number two at the other big job he had on. And then do some extra hours on an evening, to keep on top of things elsewhere.

It was a dream job. Until he met Mitchell.

For a couple of weeks, before he encountered the owner, things had been running smoothly. He'd had the flexibility of having a set of house keys, plus the alarm code. Emma had carried out a CRB check on him and his business. But as he'd been clean for fifteen years, his old convictions were spent. These days he had nothing to hide. His criminal past was exactly that, behind him.

He'd struck lucky with the new labourer he'd taken on. Paul was a grafter. He'd made light work of knocking down the internal walls and ripping up the rotten decking on the roof terrace. He was skilled enough to do a few building jobs too.

Danny had already decided to keep him on when this job was over.

They were basically remodelling the entire first floor of the house. The huge drawing room with a pointless, tiny conservatory, would be converted into a bedroom with adjoining study and ensuite. The study would lead onto a refurbished roof terrace, a feature that had seen better days, but with amazing potential. Emma stressed to Danny that the study was the most urgent part of the job. The furniture was due to be delivered less than three weeks after they'd start work.

He did the usual builder's breathing through pursed lips when she mentioned that. "To be honest, it's better to do it all at once, but if you insist, we can work around it. We won't have it decorated by then though. That would be madness when we've still got other building work to do around it."

She agreed to the compromise. Poor girl, she looked so nervous about anything that might hold up the job or veer from the exact specifications. Yet the rest of the time, she came across as intelligent and resourceful. Definitely a bit of an enigma.

He was about to find out why.

Danny and Paul arrived at the house around 11.30am one Tuesday in September, having paid a trip to the builder's merchants first thing. As they began to unload the van, Emma appeared at the front door, looking on edge.

"Oh hi, love," greeted Danny, surprised to see her there.

"Hi, Danny," she responded. "Mitchell's here today; he's not happy that the study won't be decorated before the furniture arrives on Friday. He wants a word."

"Fine, I'll explain to him, don't worry." He thought nothing of it. The reason for leaving the decorating until the end was

30

obvious to anyone with half a brain. "We'll get this stuff in first and I'll talk it through with him."

She looked unconvinced but retreated into the house.

As they carted the building materials up to the first floor, Danny became aware of a pair of piercing eyes at the top of the staircase. A ruddy-faced, reasonably handsome, shorter-than-average figure was looking down on him. Dressed in a very expensive-looking suit, the dark-haired man didn't have the charisma to quite carry it off.

"Alright, mate? We'll get this little lot unloaded and then Emma says you want a chat about the study."

Still glaring at Danny, Mitchell replied, "I don't want a chat about it. I just want it done. As specified. No arguments. Are we clear?"

Unperturbed, he responded with "I'm Danny by the way, nice to meet you. You must be Mitchell," extending his hand out to shake, a much friendlier greeting than the homeowner warranted. Danny got on with most people, regardless of whether he liked them or not. He would find some thread of humanity, even if they didn't share any common bonds.

He was about to discover that Mitchell wasn't most people.

"I said no arguments." He stabbed his index finger backwards, pointing at the emerging study. "If you can't get this room finished by close of play Thursday, then you might as well pack up your stuff now and get out. But don't expect me to pay you a penny more; you're the one who's failed to deliver."

With that, Mitchell Roberts shoved past Danny and Paul, strode downstairs and yelled at Emma. "C'mon, get a move on! We're going to have to go into the office. I can't work here now with those idiots upstairs making a racket."

The two of them left, leaving Danny open-mouthed in shock and Paul about to comment on what he'd just witnessed.

"What an absolute dickhead," he said, as the front door slammed.

Paul wasn't far wrong.

6

"Well, I guess that's us told," said Danny, still reeling from the sheer rudeness of his client, as he'd stormed out of the house.

He scratched his head, as Paul laughed in agreement.

"Just as well we've already got the paint in, but I need to clear my head and rejig our schedule. Tell you what, son, nip out and get us both something for lunch, while I think it all through." He chucked Paul a tenner.

"What d'you fancy?"

"We can only afford a Maccy D's round here, lad. So whether we want it or not, that's what I'm treating you to."

Paul's eyes lit up. "Cheers, boss. Two Big Mac meals coming right up," he said, saluting Danny, sarcastically.

Later that day, they'd given the study a full first coat of paint and undercoated all the woodwork. Danny would have to put a few extra hours in now. The paintwork would inevitably need retouching at the end of the job. But as long as he got his bonus, he could live with that.

By the time Friday came, the study was finished and the two grafters were back working on the bedroom and roof terrace. Danny was creating some built-in wardrobes, while Paul was laying the new decking outside.

They'd had a few hours of peace in the morning but by midday Mitchell appeared, awaiting his furniture delivery. Emma had warned Danny he was on his way, but as he heard him walk through the door downstairs, his heart still sank. He was surprised

Mitchell hadn't left this task to one of his minions; it seemed way below his perceived level of importance.

As he rattled about in the kitchen downstairs, Danny hoped he'd stay down there until the delivery turned up. He couldn't be doing with making polite conversation with someone who didn't know the meaning of the word.

Damn! He could hear him now making his way up the stairs.

Mitchell's phone rang as he appeared on the landing. He grunted acknowledgement to Danny and turned away to answer it.

"Hello? Yes, it is. Uh-huh. Uh-huh. Uh-huh."

Danny felt like turning his drill on, to drown out the annoying one-sided conversation. But he knew that Mitchell would most likely go ballistic.

"Can you turn that racket off? I'm on the phone," came a sudden unexpected request.

"Oh, you're talking to me mate?" Danny thought to himself. Without even looking up, he turned the knob on his radio to off. Just who the hell did this bloke think he was?

Mitchell returned to his conversation.

"Yes, that should be fine. I'll make sure the builders keep out of your way. No, I've got to be out by 4 o'clock, so it'll need to be in place before that. Okay, see you then."

Blimey, who was that, thought Danny? That's the most polite I've ever heard him. It still wasn't friendly, but it was an improvement on the brusque, rude way he appeared to talk to everyone else.

As Mitchell hung up, he turned round to Danny once again.

"This furniture is due any minute, so I need you and the other lad to help the driver get it in and upstairs. And I've got a safe coming at 2 o'clock, so you'll have to keep the access clear.

They've got specialist lifting equipment to get it up here. Study seems ok by the way. Right, I'll be downstairs until they turn up." Mitchell turned and headed back down before Danny could muster a challenge.

~~~~~~

The deliveries were working like clockwork, driven by the demands of a certain Mitchell Roberts. While the driver sneaked a few crafty fags outside, Danny and Paul got lumbered with most of the heavy lifting. And it was heavy. A large black and walnut desk, two black filing cabinets, two black leather chairs, plus a solid oak bookcase and sideboard. Not part of my estimate, Danny thought, rubbing his aching back.

Now that the safe had turned up, Danny breathed a huge sigh of relief they didn't have to get involved with moving this monster. He'd never seen such a large, personal vault like this before; it was enormous.

He couldn't bear to watch the removal guys manoeuvre it up the dog-legged staircase, into the newly-decorated study. As professional as they were, he'd curse them if they caused any damage. He was almost a day behind schedule as it was.

As they spoke to Mitchell downstairs, explaining how they'd move the vault, Danny made his way out onto the roof terrace. Paul was making good progress with the decking. There weren't many more lengths to put down and then they could crack on with staining it. If they put their backs into it, they could get it finished today and let it dry off over the weekend. Mitchell hadn't deigned to tell them whether there was any garden furniture on the way. If there was, he had a good idea which mugs would be responsible for moving it up here.

"You've done a cracking job here, mate," he said, checking the slats up close.

35

"Ah, cheers, Danny. It's looking decent innit?"

"Yeah, looks great. Gimme a shout when you've finished laying it and I'll come and give you a hand with the staining."

"No worries. Hey, chuck me that screwdriver will you?"

He tossed the driver over to Paul and headed back into the house. As he made his way into the bedroom area to carry on with the wardrobes, he heard footsteps on the staircase. Mitchell.

Danny stayed completely silent, pretending to measure up, in case Mitchell came into the room. He was keen to avoid any other unplanned work. Instead, he heard him speaking to someone from the study.

"It's Mitchell. Yes, it's here now, they're just getting it up the stairs."

Silence. He was on the phone again, listening to someone on the other end.

"So everything's already inside? What do I do to open it?"

Silence once more.

"No, they're downstairs, they can't hear me. And the builders are outside. Twenty, twenty-nine, ninety-two. Ok. So I put that code in, wait for a double beep and then turn the lever? Ok, that sounds easy enough. Right, I'll see you next week. And you."

Danny heard Mitchell going back downstairs. He was almost polite as he passed the safe delivery guys, about to start their ascent with the vault.

"Thanks. I'll be in the kitchen. Let me know when it's all in place."

Danny poked his head around the bedroom door opening, looking into the now empty study. He'd heard Mitchell come upstairs this time, but he was unaware he'd nipped up a few minutes earlier. Having seen the coast was clear, Mitchell had assumed Danny was still outside with Paul when he came back up to make the call. He hadn't bothered looking out onto the terrace to check.

Danny had clocked the code; numbers he was now putting into his phone, so he didn't forget. He just needed to sneak outside, make a big noise coming back in and Mitchell would be none the wiser.

Chances were, Danny wouldn't do anything with the code. He'd made a note of it for the time being as an insurance policy, in case Mitchell fucked him over. All being well he'd finish this job, get paid in full and then forget all about the eavesdropped conversation.

But sometimes things didn't go to plan. And old habits die hard.

7

21 October 2017
Brentford vs Sunderland
Griffin Park, London
Kick-off: 3:00 pm

The first game Liam took Robbie to turned out to be a goalfest. Brentford didn't win. But to a wide-eyed seven-year-old, seeing 'his' team live for the first time, it was enough to get him hooked.

Robbie had managed to get a couple of free tickets from school, so it was like a win for Liam before the game even kicked off. His son had been badgering him for ages to take him, but money was so tight they couldn't justify spending precious cash on football tickets. So when he ran out of school the Monday before the game, with a grin from ear to ear, Liam was as excited as he was at the thought of fulfilling his dream.

With a tenner from each set of grandparents, Robbie could enjoy the full match-day experience, without impacting his parents' finances. Not that he had a clue about money or debt of course. At seven, you don't know about any of that sort of stuff. But also, what you don't know you don't miss either. So, there were no expectations that this could be a regular thing. It was simply the most exciting moment of his life so far.

The day began with the two of them jumping on the bus to Brentford, which took around 35 minutes each way. Liam would have preferred to get the train and halve the journey time, but the bus fare was so much cheaper. The bus ride passed quickly though, with Robbie chatting away the whole time, wondering which of his heroes would be playing today. He'd become quite knowledgeable in recent weeks and knew the names of most of the first team. His dad was impressed.

It was quite a big game for Brentford, with Sunderland having been relegated from the Premier League the previous season. As it stood, Brentford were actually above them in the table, despite an indifferent start. They were beginning to get into their stride and Liam hoped they could get something from today's game. Losing would probably take a bit of gloss off the occasion for Robbie.

It was an easy ten-minute walk from the bus stop to Griffin Park for the two football fanatics. There was a growing throng heading in the same direction. Brentford's capacity was around the 12,000 mark, yet it could still feel like a much bigger crowd on certain matchdays. This was one of them.

As both teams played in red and white stripes, it was difficult to distinguish between the two sets of fans, except for two things. One was the language barrier. To a born and bred Londoner like Liam, it amused him that both sets of fans hailed from the same country, yet spoke so differently. He had some lifelong mates from his army days who spoke with a similar twang, so at least he understood their shouts and songs better than most. The second difference was the level of drunkenness. It was all good-natured. But like their Geordie rivals the season before, these northerners did seem to put it away much more than their London counterparts. Or maybe it was because it was an away day. It had been so long since he'd been able to do one of those that his memory had faded.

Walking together up Ealing Road, Liam told Robbie about the time his dad took him to his first game. It was in the old

Division 3 he said, which was now League One, and Brentford were in fourth place with six games to go. Like Robbie, Liam had been begging his dad to take him to the match. Like Robbie, he was also seven and had discovered a love of football. He was hoping Brentford could stay in a play-off spot and win promotion that way. He had no idea they were about to win ALL of their final six games and be promoted as Champions.

Robbie's mouth opened in awe at the thought of promotion. And Champions too!

As they approached the ground, Liam looked wistfully at every pub they passed, filled with fans from both teams. They were bouncing. But there was no chance of meeting up with his mates today. Robbie's £20 would have to stretch a long way if he was to get the full match-day experience. It wouldn't go as far as a pint and he couldn't risk getting stung for a round.

Walking past the Princess Royal pub on the corner, he looked at his son's face as they approached the club shop.

"Ah dad, are we going in here?" asked the expectant boy.

"On one condition," replied his dad, prepared for this situation.

Robbie nodded.

"You've only got your money off the gramps and you want to do all the proper football stuff too, so you've got about £10 left to spend in the shop. Ok?"

He nodded again, even more keen. Ten whole pounds! That was loads of money.

He smiled as he watched his young son dive into the shop. Robbie was wearing Liam's old Brentford scarf and in turn Liam's dad had lent him his. Wearing the scarf didn't just keep Robbie warm on a chilly autumn day. It made him feel like he belonged, he was one of them, a true Bees fan. And the fact it was his dad's, meant it had history behind it. He'd been ecstatic when Liam had put it on him this morning and Callie had taken a photo of them together before they left home.

Following him into the shop, Liam felt a lump in his throat when he spotted Robbie looking all around him, like a kid in a sweet shop. He didn't know what to look at first, so Liam guided him over to where the gifts and accessories were, avoiding the out-of-reach kits. Out of reach for Robbie in both hanging height and spending money. Even the smaller items in the shop were pricey when you only had a tenner to spend. But he was a good kid. He'd be happy with a key ring, even though he had no keys of his own.

"What about this dad?" he asked, holding up the latest scarf.

"Don't you want something different? You've got my scarf to wear for as long as you like. What about one of these hats?"

He glanced around and saw that Robbie was no longer beside him. He'd spotted the thing he really wanted. Liam's heart sank at the thought of it being out of his price range. It was a drawstring gym bag. Quite smart. When he saw the price tag, he closed his eyes and sighed with relief. It was a tenner. Get in lad! He ruffled Robbie's hair and asked "Is that definitely the one you want?"

He nodded, a little uncertainly at first, not knowing if he had enough money. But when his dad said he did, the doubt went out the window. "Yes, I love it. And I can use it at school and for swimming and everything."

The sheer happiness on his face made Liam's heart melt. Robbie excitedly told the girl behind the till that this was his first Brentford match. She smiled back at him and said she hoped they got a good result for him. His eyes even lit up when she put it in a club shop carrier bag. Liam chuckled to himself, as he reminisced about his own first game. How every single thing was special.

Having bought a programme from his match-day fund, Robbie was hopping with excitement, gripping his dad's hand, as they made their way into the ground. Their tickets were for the Ealing Road end, Liam's favourite part of the ground. It was still terraces, unlike any other club in the top two divisions. It should've been an all-seater ground by now, but Brentford had had special dispensation from the authorities. They were due to move to a shiny new ground a mile away, so they'd been allowed to keep a section of terracing in the meantime.

In such a tight ground, the atmosphere at Griffin Park could be electric. Not always of course. But on the right day, it was brilliant. Liam prayed that today would be one of those days.

He led Robbie through the turnstiles, along the concourse and up into the stand. He watched his son's face light up as he took in the pitch, the stands and the terrace he'd be watching the game from. It was a special moment and one he remembered vividly from his past.

A bit too early to stand on the terrace, he tapped his mesmerised son on the shoulder. There was still one more thing to buy.

Neither of them had eaten since breakfast, so the obligatory match-day pie was a welcome treat. Chicken balti for Liam, minced beef and onion for Robbie. The aroma from the balti pie was unreal and Liam wolfed it down. Partly because he was starving and partly because Robbie was now starting to spill half of his pie filling down his front.

Liam quickly tossed his own rubbish in the bin and began to clean up the mess. By some miracle, Robbie had managed to miss hitting his scarf with any of the fallen mince. And in another stroke of luck, he hadn't scalded his mouth. Liam realised he needed to train his son in some of these matchday rituals.

By the time Robbie had finished making a dog's dinner of the pie, it was almost 2.30pm. The players would be out on the pitch warming up. Time to head out to the terrace. Robbie was just as awestruck emerging the second time, now spotting his idols on the turf. The occasion was becoming ever more real.

Liam found them both a good spot to watch the game from, taking care to avoid where he knew his mates would be. It wasn't worth the grief of having to explain why he hadn't seen them in so long, hadn't been to the games, hadn't even had a pint with them. Lifting Robbie up to sit on one of the crush barriers, he stood behind him, holding on to him loosely.

Liam almost lost his grip when Brentford took an early lead after eight minutes. He was delighted; Robbie was ecstatic. Even after Sunderland equalised a few minutes later, his young son was entranced. He kicked every ball, clapped or cheered every good piece of play and oohed or ahhed when they almost scored. He listened to the crowd singing their songs and, after a while, tried to imitate them. Liam hoped he didn't hear too much swearing, but what the hell, this was part of growing up.

And then, just before half time, Sunderland tried to spoil the occasion. It began when they took the lead in the 40th minute after the Bees keeper fumbled a corner into the net. Then with virtually the last kick of the half, they extended their lead with a penalty.

Half-time: Brentford 1 Sunderland 3

Liam felt a bit flat when the half time whistle blew, but his mood soon changed when Robbie turned round to face him.

"This is brilliant!" he exclaimed. "Isn't it fantastic, dad?" accompanied by the widest smile imaginable. The innocent and unadulterated joy almost made Liam long to be a child again.

Despite his son's obvious happiness, he hoped his team didn't cave in during the second half. Getting spanked at home by a team in the bottom three wasn't how he'd imagined Robbie's first game to turn out.

As it happened, the second half was close to perfect. Close, because they didn't quite sneak the win. But perfect because they did come back to earn a draw. The fightback began just after half time with a stunning goal from man of the match Jozefzoon. He was rapidly becoming one of Robbie's favourite players. And then, finally, in the 78th minute they got their equaliser.

Late goals were brilliant for football fans, as long as it was your team scoring. Anything in that last quarter of an hour that had an impact on the result. The combined roar of the crowd, the hugs with your loved ones or your mates when celebrating that moment. It wasn't even restricted to people you knew. One old guy turned and hugged Liam when the ball hit the net. Such raw but wonderful emotions. Nothing else mattered. The feeling was euphoric.

They walked back to the bus stop, beaming. Robbie's joy was infectious.

Today was one of those special days, but Liam had had to catch his breath, keep a lid on his emotions. It wasn't just the fact he was taking his son to his first game. It was that he'd almost missed this completely. Not just Robbie's first game either, but the rest of his son's life. How could he have thought that the solution to his problems was to end it all?

After such a momentous day, they were both shattered by the time they got home, although Robbie would never admit it.

He bounded into the flat, threw himself into Callie's arms and exclaimed "That was the best day of my ENTIRE life!"

You never forget your first time.

Full time: Brentford 3 Sunderland 3

8

Danny's annoyance levels were rising.

It was almost a fortnight since he'd finished the job at Elystan Place and he still hadn't had full payment from a certain Mitchell Roberts. He'd had to spend a further day finishing off in the end, but he'd done that at no extra charge. And yet, Mitchell hadn't settled the final half of the bill or the two thousand pound bonus.

And now, he was wasting even more time chasing the payment.

"Emma, I know this isn't down to you, but I want that payment in my bank account today, or I'll be taking more direct action. We did that job in good faith and I've got other lads to pay. If he's gonna try and give me any bollocks about the deadline, I'll swing for him. The only reason we went a day over was because of him messing us about. It's cost me an extra day's work, so I expect the completion bonus as well. No arguments."

"I'm so sorry, Danny. I'll try and get hold of him now and get it sorted." The poor girl sounded terrified.

He hung up and thanked the lord that he'd insisted on half of the estimate being paid upfront. Even so, he needed the rest of the money to be transferred today. It was Friday. He didn't want another week to pass before getting paid for a job that he had started almost two months ago.

A few hours later, Danny had a quick look at his bank account. He was shocked to see Mitchell had transferred the money for the work. He was less surprised to see that he hadn't paid the completion bonus.

Progress. Still some way to go, however.

He rang Emma back. It went straight to voicemail, so he left a message. He thanked her for sorting the payment but reminded her that Mitchell still owed him the bonus. He had until next Tuesday to settle, or he'd take other action to recover the debt.

~~~~~~

The following Tuesday came and Danny checked his bank account several times. By lunchtime, he'd waited long enough. He rang Emma, ready to give her both barrels. He felt sorry for her, working for that absolute dickhead. But she was the only one he had contact details for and enough was enough.

The first time he rang, it went straight to voicemail. He hung up, without leaving a message. Half an hour later, he got the same result. Twenty minutes further on, he was about to give it up as a bad job. Suddenly, just as he was going to end the call, Emma came on the line.

"Hi, Danny," she sounded upset.

"Hi, Emma love. Look, I know you sorted out the payment last week, but I'm still owed the completion bonus. I'm not backing down, Mitchell owes us. We did a cracking job and I expect to be paid what was agreed. I took an extra lad on and put some other jobs on hold for this."

"I know. And I know you did a great job. This is just what he's like I'm afraid. All the time. And I can't deal with it anymore. I've quit today. And I've been signed off with stress for a couple of weeks, so hopefully, I won't have to face him too much more before I leave."

"Ah, love, that's not right," he said, shocked and yet not surprised. "You've always been great to deal with. It's just that boss of yours who's an utter prick."

A resigned laugh at the other end of the phone.

"Listen, Danny, if it helps, I know Mitchell is due to be working from home this Friday. You could try and pop round, see if you can get him to pay up. I don't know what else to suggest."

Perfect, he thought. Absolutely perfect. "That's brilliant, Emma. I'll do just that. Thanks for your help. I hope you get another job soon."

~~~~~~

Friday 3rd November. It was late morning when Danny parked up in his transit van as close as he could to the townhouse on Elystan Place. He'd gone to his current jobs first thing, made sure the lads were all fine and then drove over to this wealthier part of town. It must be why they have so much money, he thought, because they don't pay their bloody bills.

He rapped the door knocker. No one answered.

He rang the doorbell.

A few moments later, the door began to open. As Mitchell's eyes met Danny's, the taller man acted quicker than the man inside. Danny's foot flew forward, just as Mitchell tried to shut the door on him. He forced the door open, barged his way into the house and slammed the door behind him.

"Morning, Mitchell," he said, a greeting that was anything but friendly.

"Get out of my house!" said Mitchell, more in indignation than with any modicum of authority.

"I will when you've paid me what you owe me."

"I don't owe you anything. I paid your bill last week, even though you took longer than you said."

"I took one day longer because you kept changing things, pal. And I did that extra day for nothing. You owe me the completion bonus."

Mitchell laughed but looked smaller, weaker, scared. He'd spotted what Danny had taken from inside his jacket. Physically, he was no match for this man, even without the wrench he was now wielding.

"So this is how you do business, is it? I've got a good mind to call the police."

"I only do business like this when arrogant weasels don't pay me what they owe me. Go ahead, call the police, you prick. Alternatively, sort out my payment. Or else."

Mitchell tried desperately to hide his fear. But truth be told, he was shitting himself. Danny was no bully, but it felt good to make a real bully feel like this.

"Fine. I'll transfer the money later on. I give you my word."

"Your word means jack-shit to me, pal. I want the cash and I want it now."

Mitchell looked torn, indecisive. He did have a solution. A quick way to get this brute out of his house.

"Okay, I've got some money in the safe. Stay here and I'll get it for you."

"Don't tell me what to do. I'm keeping an eye on you, so get a move on and get up there. Some of us have got proper work to do today."

He almost ran up the stairs and headed towards the safe. Danny followed him, waiting at the top of the landing, watching him closely.

Six numbers punched in, a beep after each one, then a double beep; it jogged a memory in Danny's head. As Mitchell turned the handle and opened the door to the safe, he had to hold his gasp in. He didn't have an unrestricted view into the safe, but he could see there was a huge amount of cash in there.

Mitchell quickly grabbed a bundle of cash and pushed the door closed behind him, attempting to conceal the contents from Danny's view. He took a few notes from the wad, counting out ten in total and keeping them to one side. He walked towards Danny and, petulantly, handed him the remainder of the bundle.

"Now get out, you thug."

"Gladly. And the only thug here is you, pal. You should be ashamed of how you treat people. I hope you get what's coming to you one day. Emma is better off without you."

"She won't be finding another job in a hurry, the silly little slag," Mitchell retorted, taking a step back as Danny swung round.

Danny looked him up and down. A pathetic excuse for a man, who only knew how to bully people to get on in life. He pitied him in a way. And equally despised him.

"What an absolute dickhead," he said, slowly and deliberately, staring him square in the eyes. Then he waltzed down the stairs, through the lounge and slammed the front door on his way out.

9

4 November 2017
Brentford vs Leeds United
Griffin Park, London
Kick-off: 5:30 pm

Two weeks on from Robbie's first game, there were three generations of the family at Griffin Park.

Brentford had won their two away games since the best day EVER of Robbie's life. They were pushing away from the bottom of the table. But Leeds were a tough team and battling for the play-offs.

The late kick-off and dark winter's night added to the air of expectation. And the Bees' biggest crowd of the season was swelled by a large West Yorkshire contingent. They had an air of menace about them; Liam knew that well enough from his younger days. But he also knew they were generally a sound group, more noise than nuisance these days. Besides, Robbie was oblivious to it and felt no threat, walking up to the ground side by side with a bunch of Leeds fans.

Liam's dad, Pete, had brought his own son to his first game back in 1992, twenty-five years ago now. The thought of going to a match with his only grandchild made him almost burst with happiness. He knew Liam was struggling money-wise, so he'd suggested it as his treat. Liam's hesitance only confirmed Pete's suspicions that his money worries were much worse than he was letting on. So he said he'd drive them there and made up a story about a small win on the pools, to pay for everything. That swung it.

Granddad, dad and son settled into their seats in the Braemar Road stand. Robbie was a little bit disappointed not to be in the standing section again. It was great fun when the crowd moved, especially when they scored. But he didn't show it. He was just so happy to be back here again. And so soon. He knew his grandpa had something called roomy Arthur eye tis. So he thought that was probably why he wanted to sit down for the match.

It had got dark during Robbie's first game, but the sky was already black before kick-off this time. It was starting to get chilly and the scarf that Pete had treated his grandson to was a necessity tonight. The scarves swapped themselves back round the generations as they came out of the shop earlier. Robbie looked down proudly as his dad fastened his scarf around him. His scarf. His very own scarf!

The floodlights being on from the start ramped up Robbie's excitement. There was something special about an evening kick-off.

GOAL! Halfway through the first half and Brentford took the lead. All three of them leapt to their feet, the youngest the sprightliest of the lot. Sat in the middle of the two men, Robbie hugged his dad first and then turned to hug his granddad. This was great. Liam thought so too. What a cracking result this would be if they could hold on for the win.

As the half wore on, it was fairly even, with both sides having chances. And then, on the stroke of half-time, Brentford were awarded a penalty. Come on Ollie, Liam thought, give us a bit of a cushion for the second half.

PENALTY MISSED! Damn, he blasted it over.

Half-time: Brentford 1 Leeds United 0

They all tucked into a sausage roll and a hot chocolate at half-time. Just what they needed on a chilly evening. Pete was happy treating his family; to see the beaming smile on Robbie's face was worth every penny. He chatted away during the break. "Granddad, do you know we'll only be one point behind Leeds if we win today?" Pete looked at his son and winked. The familiarity of a seven-year-old getting into his football team for the first time. The hopes. The expectations. The dreams.

Like most football fans, those dreams would regularly be shattered. But without them, what is the point of supporting your team? And you can't appreciate the ecstasy without having suffered the agony.

The second half ebbed and flowed, with opportunities for both sides. And then midway through the half, Brentford's keeper struggled to hold onto a cross. The equaliser rolled into the net, the away end went wild and Liam felt a sense of foreboding. He turned to Robbie beside him. He looked crestfallen and yet still completely mesmerised by the game.

"Can't win every game, kidda," Pete said to him.

"Loads of time yet, granddad," said the hopeful youngster.

And sure enough, Robbie was right.

There were some tense moments. It could have gone either way. And then, in the 85th minute, they got another free kick…

GOAL! All three of them leapt up in unison. Liam lifted Robbie up into his arms with his hug this time. And he also gave his own dad a hug. What a brilliant goal! And what a goal to win the match. Hopefully.

Still five minutes plus injury time to get through without conceding. Could they do it?

They were on the edge of their seats for the rest of the match. The board went up showing three minutes of injury time. Pure torture. Blow your whistle ref. Blow. Your. Bloody. Whistle.

And then the ball hit the net. GOAL!

They've only gone and done it. Not just one late goal this time, but two. The second making absolutely certain of the points.

Brilliant. Just bloody brilliant.

Full time: Brentford 3 Leeds United 1

10

Liam gave Pete an extra tight hug when he dropped them home after the match.

"Thanks, dad," he said, emotion cracking his voice slightly. "We both had a fantastic time today. I really appreciate it."

"I had a great time as well, son. What a match ey? And what a result. Glad we went."

"Robbie's well and truly hooked now," said Liam. With that, Pete caught a tinge of regret in his son's expression. Trapped between the pride that your son wants to follow your team and the realisation you can't afford to take them to games. Pete almost felt guilty when it dawned on him that he'd encouraged the latest jaunt. But that soon subsided when he thought about the game and how much they'd all enjoyed it. He wouldn't have missed it for the world.

"He reminds me of you when you were that age," said his dad, a pensive look on his face.

They looked each other in the eye. They were a really close family, but Pete was struggling to get through to his son. Struggling to find out how bad things were.

He'd tried to broach the subject of money on the journey home. Robbie was fast asleep on the back seat, worn out after the exhilaration of the game. But Liam had been evasive and Pete had to drop it. He'd told his dad that, yes they were struggling a bit, but he'd started to get things under control. They just needed a bit of a break that's all. And to win the lottery, he joked.

Pete had offered his son another loan if it would help, but Liam told him not to worry. He should be spending his hard-earned pension on himself and his mum, not bailing out one of his grown-up children. The reality was that any sort of loan his dad could afford wouldn't even scratch the surface. Liam was grateful beyond measure, but he didn't see the point. So he kept quiet. They spent the rest of the journey home talking about Brentford's chances of moving up the table. Then the conversation moved on to Liam's younger sister, Lucy, and her girlfriend Michelle, and Liam's older brother, Michael, who lived in Thailand.

"Right little man, let's get you out," said Liam, opening the back door and trying to stir his slumbering son.

He had to shake Robbie to wake him up. He was completely out of it. As he came to, he remembered the special evening he'd just experienced and a smile spread across his face.

"Are we home? Is granddad coming in, dad?" Liam and his dad could just about decipher what he said, as the words came out amongst a huge yawn.

Pete shook his head. "Nah, I need to get back and have my dinner with your gran mate. She'll have it all ready for me. But we'll see you again in the next few days yeah? And let's see if we can sort out another match before Christmas. If you behave yourself for your mum and dad mind."

Liam shot him a look, to begin with, but once he'd mentioned 'before Christmas' he cut his dad some slack. It was almost two months to Christmas, so treating his grandson once more during that timeframe wasn't exactly excessive. It wouldn't make Robbie expect to go to every game. He hoped. As much as he'd loved to have taken him.

With that, Robbie threw himself into Pete's arms, "thanks, granddad, you're the best."

Pete hugged him back and kissed the top of his head.

"Right, I'll be off. Say hello to your mum from me, Robbie," he shouted after the boy as he ran towards their flat.

"Thanks again, dad," said Liam, shaking Pete's hand. "Give my love to mum."

Pete jumped into his car and waved to Liam as he drove off. He'd have a chat with Jackie tonight and see what she thought. Whether she had any ideas on how to get Liam to open up. He worried about his son. Whether he was coping with everything that had happened to them over the last year or so.

Liam jogged to the flat entrance and saw Robbie waiting for the lift. Poor kid was shattered, but still on top of the world.

Callie greeted them as they walked into their flat. "Wow, I saw the result. Did you have a good time?"

Liam was about to answer in the affirmative but was beaten to it by his son.

"Mum, I think it was even better than last time. If that's possible. We scored TWO goals to win it, really late on. It was A. MA. ZING. And it was BRILLIANT being there with granddad. I'm so happy I could burst."

~~~~~~

Liam and Callie settled down on the sofa later that night, with Robbie fast asleep, tucked up in bed.

"He has a knack of summing things up perfectly doesn't he?" noted Callie.

"Yeah, bless him."

"Your dad ok?"

"Yeah, fine. Apart from quizzing me about money on the way back. Asked if we needed any."

"What did you say?"

"I told him no."

"Really?"

"We already owe them a grand, Callie. I can't take any more from them, it's not fair. And besides, it wouldn't put a dent in what we owe."

"Really?"

Shit! He hadn't meant to say that. Didn't want to cause Callie any extra stress, on top of what she was already going through.

"Don't panic, babe, we'll get through this. Just let me worry about the finances and I'll sort it out, eventually. It'll take time and we need to be really careful with our money. But we'll get there."

"God, I hope so Liam. It feels like we're fighting a losing battle at the minute."

He kissed Callie and flicked the sound back on the TV, hoping that would bring an end to that particular topic of conversation.

As she dropped off on the sofa later, Liam's guilt at keeping their true financial situation from her began to envelop him. He was doing it for all the right reasons, but even so.

He was about to switch the telly off and wake Callie to go to bed when his phone buzzed with a text message.

Probably his dad, he thought. Either saying sorry for pushing him on his money situation or reiterating that he could lend him some more money if he needed it.

It wasn't from his dad.

It was from Danny, a bloke he'd known for about six years. A bloke he'd confided in about his money worries. Because it was easier to confide in someone who wasn't a close friend, who wasn't close family. Plus, Danny had caught him at a weak moment, when he needed to get things off his chest.

Might have the answer to your prayers.

Gimme a call on Monday.

But don't tell anyone, this is big.

And delete this message ok?

Cheers.

Liam wondered what the hell it could be. If it really was the answer to his prayers, he had to find out.

11

Liam was sat in the front of Danny's Transit van, parked up outside a builder's merchant in West London.

He was still in shock at what Danny had just told him.

"You think I should burgle this guy's house?"

"It'd sort your money worries out, mate. And I reckon, pound for pound, it's one of the easiest jobs going."

He tried to take it all in. Danny was a reformed burglar. He'd given him all the inside information he would need. He'd even told him a date in a few weeks when the owner would be away for the night. Danny would make sure he had a cast-iron alibi himself so that he didn't come under suspicion. After all, he'd be the prime suspect; a fact which would be exacerbated due to his past.

"And the guy is an absolute wanker, he bloody deserves it," laughed Danny.

Liam smiled. Danny was a good sort. He trusted his judgement on people. If he didn't like you, there was generally a good reason why.

"Listen, I finished on the job a few weeks ago, but I put some things in place before I left. Just in case. I had a feeling he was gonna give me the runaround, so you could call it a bit of an insurance policy. He paid me eventually, but I had to threaten him to cough up. He's got what's coming to him."

Liam thought about it. The opportunity to possibly net two hundred grand, all in one night. A quick in and out. No one having a clue that he was involved or making the connection between him and Danny. His debts paid off and then a huge chunk towards a house for the three of them. A proper house, with a garden; somewhere he could have a kickabout with his son.

"Do I need to decide now?"

"Nah, you go away, have a look at the stuff I've given you and have a think about it. If you're gonna go ahead, let me know at least a week in advance, so I can get my movements all sorted for that night. Ok?"

He nodded.

"Cheers, Danny. I appreciate this, I do. I dunno what I'm gonna do otherwise. There's no end in sight with these interest payments."

"I know, kid, I know. If I could do anything to help I would, I just don't have a lot of cash floating around myself. Loads of what I make goes on the mortgage and my pension. But this is a great opportunity. If I was in your shoes, I'd do it, without a second thought."

"Yeah. It's… I've… I've never done anything like that before. Never. Not even done any shoplifting as a kid."

"I understand. But you'd only have to do it this one time and your problems would be sorted. Get in, take what you need and get out. Job's a good 'un."

Liam was so conflicted. Some lowlife had burgled his gran's house a few years back and he'd wanted to kill them. She felt violated, never felt safe in her own home again. If he did this, he'd be a hypocrite. Did he want to run the risk of being caught? Getting a criminal record?

On the other hand, his debts were crippling him.

He glanced at his watch. "Shit, I need to get back to pick Robbie up from school. Look, I'll let you know as soon as poss. And thanks for thinking of me. I appreciate it."

He gave Danny a homie handshake, leapt out of the Transit and into his own van. Half an hour later, he'd parked up just in time to catch Robbie heading out of school. His son was wearing his Brentford scarf and carrying his new Brentford gym bag. That kid, he smiled to himself.

When he saw Liam, Robbie said a rushed farewell to his schoolmates and ran out of the school gates towards him.

"Dad! I scored a hat-trick in PE today. I could be the next Yursifchun!"

Liam laughed at Robbie's attempted pronunciation of his favourite player.

"Wow, you could be! Should we get you signed up for the Bees now?"

The little lad nodded enthusiastically. The thought of playing for his beloved Brentford was beyond his wildest dreams.

"Can we have a McDonald's to celebrate?" the youngster looked at him with pleading eyes.

Liam's heart sank. "Ah sorry mate, we're just a bit skint this week. Another time, yeah? Besides, I bet Jozefzoon doesn't eat burgers. Not if he wants to keep scoring goals. I bet he eats loads of pasta though."

He'd tried to divert things onto another topic, to lessen the blow. But despite his son's "Okay, dad" response, he could see the disappointment in the young boy's eyes.

When they got home later, there was a pile of bills on the doormat. Final demand after final demand. He hid them from Robbie's view, but if he didn't already feel bad for letting his son down, again, he certainly did now. It was soul-destroying. No light at the end of the tunnel. Unless of course...

Later that night, with Robbie tucked up in bed and before Callie got home from her shift, Liam sent a simple text message.

It wouldn't mean much to anyone else, but the recipient would understand what it meant.

I'm in.

12

It had been almost three weeks since Liam and Robbie's last trip to Griffin Park. The two of them had only missed one home game in that time, a 1-1 midweek draw with struggling Burton Albion. And the Bees had lost their only other game since beating Leeds, to slip back into the bottom half of the table.

Nevertheless, Robbie followed his team's fortunes keenly, learning all about the players. Jozefzoon was still his favourite, although it was a close-run thing. Brentford had some promising attackers.

He also kept track of the upcoming fixtures. The next match at Griffin Park would be their first real home 'derby' of the season against Fulham. He wondered what it was like to go to a derby game. Was it really different to the other matches he'd been to?

Just over a week before the Fulham game, Robbie's excitement soared. The school announced in Friday assembly that they once again had tickets to give away. He squeezed his eyes shut and made a wish.

Robbie's primary school was given free tickets every so often, as part of the various Football in the Community schemes each club ran. He hadn't been interested when pupils were offered Chelsea or QPR tickets. And he'd shown similar disdain when Fulham home tickets were up for grabs. But Brentford at home against Fulham? He was *desperate* to win those.

The school tried to ensure every child had a fair chance of winning. They didn't base it on a perfect attendance record. It would discriminate against any child with a genuine illness or reason for absence. Nor did they base it on academic achievement. That would act as a disincentive for those kids who always tried their best. Instead, they asked all pupils who would like to go to write their names on the notice board. And, if it was over-subscribed, then they worked out the fairest way to award the tickets.

There was never a ridiculous demand for Brentford tickets. But as Robbie had won a couple of months ago – his first-ever game – he didn't think he'd stand a chance this time. Plus, the demand would be greater, as some of the Fulham kids would try and secure tickets too. Even so, at the first opportunity, he ran to the notice board and put his name on the list.

He wouldn't find out whether he'd got the tickets until Monday's assembly. But he couldn't wait to tell his parents that there was another giveaway.

"It's ok to go, dad, isn't it if I win the tickets again?" he said with hopeful eyes, as Liam picked him up from school later that day.

"Yeah, I'll just have to check my shifts." Liam had a feeling he wasn't working, but he also wanted to make sure Callie didn't mind. She might want to take him instead.

When Monday came, Callie had no problem getting Robbie out of bed and ready for school. She almost had to hold him back from leaving the house. He was so keen to get into assembly and find out whether he'd been chosen.

If winning the tickets back in October felt like winning the lottery for Robbie, finding out he wasn't one of the lucky five this time felt like losing it. He was devastated, but such was his character that he congratulated a couple of the other children. The ones he knew at least. There was Jake in his class, who was a Fulham fan. And Chloe in the year above, who didn't support anyone in particular, just loved playing and watching football. He was actually really pleased for them, not jealous. Envious, but not jealous. He asked them if they'd tell him all about it the following week. He wanted to hear what it was like, going to a derby game.

As he trundled out of school later that day, Liam could tell immediately how the ticket ballot had turned out. He was gutted for Robbie. He felt like such a shit dad, that he couldn't even afford to take his son to a football match. Tomorrow night was 'the' night. When he'd hopefully get back on track and sort out their future. He resolved there and then that, as soon as it wouldn't raise any suspicions, he'd buy a couple of season tickets. Three, if Callie wanted one too.

He was impressed by Robbie's resilience in the face of his bad fortune. He focused on the here and now, chattering away all the way home about that evening's match. It was another local derby, but an away game. Strangely, it was closer to Liam and Robbie than even Brentford's ground. Almost round the corner, in fact.

Tonight was QPR v Brentford. It was a shame Robbie would be tucked up in bed while the match was on, but it wouldn't be the only game he'd miss for that reason. And Liam had had an idea to bring a smile back to his face.

He knew the team coach would arrive at Loftus Road about an hour before kick-off. It was just over ten minutes' walk to the ground from their flat, a little longer at Robbie's normal pace. However, he had a feeling his son would walk a lot faster once he knew what they were going to do.

So, after they'd eaten and Robbie had done his reading homework, Liam told him to go and put his Brentford scarf on, get his coat and pop his trainers on. The youngster was intrigued.

"Are we going to the match?" he asked, his eyes wide with anticipation.

"We're not going to the match, but we are gonna see if we can catch the players getting off the coach and going into the ground."

His eyes grew wider. If that was even possible.

"But there's one condition." He nodded. "Once they're inside the ground, we're walking straight back home, ok? If I don't get you in bed by 7.30 on a school night your mum will kill me! Deal?"

"Deal!" He high-fived his dad, ticket lottery forgotten.

They made it to the ground in eleven minutes flat.

The atmosphere was bouncing in the throng near the players' entrance, as they waited for the coach to arrive. Once again, the night-time kick-off and the fact it was a derby match heightened the air of expectation. Liam wished they were going in, but this was a decent compromise.

Suddenly the coach pulled round the corner and headed towards them. He grabbed hold of Robbie and hoisted him up onto his shoulders, so he'd get a decent view.

As the team disembarked, there was plenty of booing and jostling, a reminder that it was a derby. Others, whether home or away fans, simply wanted to catch sight of the team, get selfies or grab a few words with a player. Robbie gave his dad a running commentary, although he didn't recognise some of the players out of their football kit. Finally, he saw him.

"Dad, dad, there's Yursifchun. Look!"

All too soon, the players, coaching and backroom staff were off the coach and inside the ground. Time to head home.

Liam lifted Robbie down and was heartened to see his beaming smile.

"Dad, that was brilliant!"

He'll make a cheap date when he's older, Liam thought.

Robbie was in bed by his normal bedtime that night but didn't get straight to sleep, after all the excitement. When Liam checked in on him around 9.30pm, a sleepy voice asked "Did we win, dad?"

"There's a couple of minutes to go, but we're winning 2-0. Now get back to sleep or you'll be shattered tomorrow."

The next morning, Liam had to break it to Robbie that QPR had scored two goals in injury time to snatch a draw. He looked devastated. But when he got to school he'd find out that being a football fan was a rollercoaster of a journey. Because Jake was off sick. With chickenpox. He wouldn't be able to go to the match on Saturday after all. So Robbie was offered his tickets instead.

When Liam found out, he was almost as pleased as his son. Though he began to wonder whether Robbie had some voodoo powers.

-13-

In the early hours of 29th November, a man dressed from head to toe in dark clothing crept out of the shadows. He moved like a lizard towards his target. The house on Elystan Place was now in clear sight, but he diverted to the right before he got there. He wouldn't be going in through the front entrance.

Liam had arrived a few hours ago, knowing that parking round here was a complete nightmare. He'd finally managed to find a space a few streets away from the house he was intending to break into. At least he wouldn't be seen loading his booty right outside the address. But his illegal haul could be heavy. He'd have to pray he didn't encounter anyone in the few hundred metres between the house and his van.

He'd waited until after 10:00pm to get here, so the residents' parking restrictions were no longer in place. However, most spaces had been taken up by then anyway. He imagined a parking spot in these parts was worth as much as these very expensive townhouses. Okay, that was stretching it a bit, but easily as valuable as his flat.

After sitting in his van for a couple of hours, Liam was as stiff as a board. He'd had a brief kip in the front seat, as he waited for the minutes to tick by. But he was wary of going to sleep for too long. He didn't want any of the locals to query what he was doing, whether he was up to no good. Luckily his work van was unbranded and relatively anonymous. It was a silver VW Caddy, almost car-size, based as it was on their popular Golf model. So it didn't stick out like a sore thumb, although it still didn't match up to some of the decent motors parked up around here.

He'd intended to drive round the area numerous times over the last few weeks so that he knew it like the back of his hand. But the reality was that work and home life had got in the way; he'd only managed it twice. He felt like such an amateur in all this. Not only did he lack knowledge about the surrounding area, but his burglar's disguise was a cobbled-together mish-mash of clothing. Dark blue jeans, green trainers, a burgundy sweatshirt, dark green bomber jacket and Callie's purple woolly hat were the best he could muster. More likely to get nabbed by the fashion police than the Met, if he was honest with himself.

It was a cold night, barely above freezing, which worked in his favour. Callie's hat, while looking ridiculous under the glare of the streetlights, helped to conceal his identity as much as possible. Despite the cold, Liam was beginning to sweat, no doubt brought on by the thought of what he was about to do.

On a chilly, midweek night, it was relatively deserted at this hour, but he couldn't afford to be complacent. He needed to be on his guard until he was safely back in his van and driving home. Every step he took, he looked around, watching for any movement or anyone watching him.

He was lucky that this was a quiet part of the street, with mainly residential buildings. Further back, near where he'd parked, the road branched out into a square. The properties diversified to include upmarket bars, restaurants and shops. People were more likely to be walking around at that end of the street than here. Even so, at this time of night, they were few and far between.

Liam had turned off to the right before reaching his target because this was the easiest point of entry. A private road, for residents only. Sneaking round here to the rear of the properties would provide him with the best route into the house. If he could stay undetected.

Although he was now off the main road, he still couldn't take anything for granted. If he was discovered back here, by one of the other residents, he'd have to come up with a plausible excuse. If not, they'd call the police without a moment's hesitation. And if they found out what he was carrying, he wouldn't have a leg to stand on. He had to be silent, yet swift. Get the job done, get out and get away.

He looked up at the neighbouring properties as he snaked around the back of the houses. The only light emanating came from a window on the first floor of a house two doors along from his target. Not ideal, as he'd be entering from the first floor, but it was better than he'd hoped for. He switched his glance to the apartment block that backed on to these houses and his heart sank. There were four windows lit up. Three of them had curtains pulled across, but the fourth was open for everyone to see in. Worse than that, for the occupants to see out.

He hid in the shadows below his intended target, considering his next move. Waiting to see if the night owls would retire for the evening. In the stillness of the night, the doubts began to creep into his head. He'd been an idiot to think that this could be straightforward; you didn't get to steal a shitload of money that easily. He had to decide here and now, was he going to go ahead with it, or was he going to make a run for it and write it off as a bad job? He agonised for the next few minutes. Finally, he made his choice.

He might not look like a pro, feel like a pro or have done all the groundwork like a pro. But he had to act like one. Tonight was the night. His one and only chance to make their financial worries a thing of the past.

By now, one of the windows opposite had reverted to darkness, though it wasn't the one that was open to the world. He began his cautious and quiet ascent up to the first-floor roof terrace. He glanced behind from time to time to make sure he wasn't being watched. With his holdall slung across his back, he made light work of shimmying up the drainpipe. Its cast-iron construction made it a sturdy climbing tool. So far, so good.

Clinging on to one of the railings that surrounded the roof terrace, Liam removed the flattened holdall from his back and slotted it through the gap. It would've been quicker to throw it over the top, but he couldn't risk it landing with a thud and disturbing anyone. The tools inside would amplify any noise. He glanced around, checking all angles and ensuring the coast was completely clear. Then he hoisted himself up and over the railings, landing stealthily onto an attractive roof terrace.

The terrace was completely decked out for a variety of uses. A table and chairs for outdoor eating, plus a seated area with rattan furniture and a few potted plants. It was bigger than their lounge. As he crouched down, out of sight of the world around him, he spent a few moments daydreaming. How good would it be to be sat here with his mates, drinking cold beer, enjoying the outside space of his multi-million-pound home? Christ, get real, he told himself. And get a grip on the here and now.

The next bit was the most challenging part. If this went wrong, the game was up.

He felt around for the tool in his holdall. A lock picker that Danny had 'obtained' for him. He'd need to make it look like a proper break-in on his way out, but he'd be ready by then for a quick exit.

Liam's nerves were jangling. From the moment the lock clicked and he opened the door, he had forty-five seconds. Less than a minute to get into the house, through the study and downstairs, into the lounge where the alarm box was located. And, still within that timeframe, to enter the code that Danny had given him. And then to hold his breath. Because he didn't know for sure if the house-owner had changed their alarm code since Danny finished working there six weeks ago. Or whether they'd cottoned on to the fact that Danny had manipulated a time delay for the balcony doors.

Failing on any aspect would send the alarm blaring and leave him with no chance of escape.

He took a deep breath and got everything ready. He set the countdown timer on his phone for forty-five seconds and positioned the torchlight around his head. Then he began to pick the lock, exactly how Danny had shown him.

In the distance, he could hear emergency sirens. He was unconcerned. These were the noises of London at any time of day and night, but even so, they broke the stillness of the evening. Then, seconds before he was about to click the lock, he became aware of another light going on around him. This one was closer than two doors along. This one was next door and it was coming from the floor above him.

Shit, shit, shit!

Liam grabbed at the switch on his head-torch. If anyone looked out now, they might be able to see his form in the half-light of the roof terrace. They may have already spotted his head-torch before he'd switched it off. He pressed himself up against the door. Waited for a minute. Counting the seconds in his head, not daring to move an inch. Another minute passed, though it felt like an hour. Nervously, he looked up at the window. And breathed. It was a bathroom window. With opaque glass. Thank Christ!

He swore in his head at the unwelcome distraction that had delayed his progress. Seeing the bathroom light go out from the corner of his eye, he focused back on what he needed to do. A few seconds later, he heard the lock click, pressed start on his timer, pushed down the handle and opened the door.

Liam burst through the door, thankful for the street lighting that allowed him some sight of the inside of the house. He'd gone over the floor-plan Danny had given him so many times, he knew the layout off by heart. But now, in the dim light, with just his head-torch to guide him, it was difficult to make everything out.

He was caught between having to move like lightning while taking care not to barge into or stumble over anything. There was no margin for error here. Even so, it was nearly over before it began, as he almost tripped over an animal rug on the floor.

The clock was ticking down. He could hear the alarm beeping. It was an ominous noise amidst the silence of the house.

He ran through the study, not even glancing at where the safe was. He found the opening for the staircase, almost shot past it in his haste. He sprinted down the stairs, turning back on himself halfway down as he manoeuvred around the dogleg.

And still the clock was ticking. No time to check how long was left. Just get to the alarm. Get there in time.

As Liam hurtled to the bottom of the staircase, he turned left into the opening to the lounge. He almost collided with one of the chairs. Finally, he could see the alarm box in the dusky light.

Still, the clock was ticking.

He flipped the cover down. The code was imprinted on his brain. Do it carefully. Don't fuck it up now, he told himself.

His gloves were thin enough not to mess up the numbers. Just. It wasn't a huge keypad.

Here goes nothing…

Four. Two. Nine. One. Enter.

He held his breath. The beeping ceased.

Two seconds later, an alarm went off. His heart stopped.

"Shit!" he thought to himself, almost dropping his phone with shock, as he knocked off the timer alarm. He allowed himself to breathe again and smiled at how shot his nerves were. All was going to plan so far, but he was still shaking uncontrollably.

Focus, Liam! Let's do this.

He ran back upstairs. Back to the study area he'd sprinted through a minute ago. He hadn't looked over at it earlier. Now he could. The large free-standing vault. The reason he was here.

It was a Burton Euro Vault, one of the largest in the range. Free-standing, although no doubt bolted to the floor, it was almost one and a half metres high. It was a significant piece of kit; whoever lived here must have some serious valuables. Quite why the rest of their security was so lax was beyond him. But with any luck, he would be the beneficiary of such carelessness.

He knew everything he needed to know about this safe, having studied it forensically for the last few weeks. Once again the keypad was on the small side for someone wearing gloves. He'd need to take extra care. He knew there could be a time delay if he accidentally entered the wrong code. And he didn't have time to hang around. He had to get it right first time.

He took out his phone and double-checked the six-digit code that he'd stored in his notes app.

Here we go.

As he entered each digit, it lit up on the keypad and was accompanied by a single beep. If the code was still correct, there'd be a double beep once he'd entered all six digits.

Two. Beep.

Zero. Beep.

Two. Beep.

Nine. Beep.

Nine. Beep.

Two. Beep.

The moment of truth. The nanosecond of anticipation was agonising.

Beep beep. It had worked!

He now had 3 seconds to open it. Quickly, he twisted the lever and swung open the door.

"Jeeeeeeeesus!"

The shocked whisper shattered the silence and Liam cursed himself in his head for making even the slightest of noises. Now was not the time to mess this up. Not now he'd seen what was in the safe.

"My God, there must be millions in there," he thought, "and who the hell has this many watches? Are they real?"

Breguet. Breitling. Rolex. And plenty of brands he'd never heard of, but wow, they looked expensive. His heart was beating like mad. His mind was racing. And his gloved hands were now visibly shaking, as he reached into the safe.

"Pull yourself together," he told himself, "this is gonna set you up for life."

No time to be choosy, he stashed as much as possible in his holdall, grabbing almost half the cash and about fifty watches. The bag was rammed.

And then he saw it.

At the back of the top shelf. The small, black book. Almost hidden against the lining of the safe.

Almost, but not quite.

He snatched it, thinking it might contain details about the watches or shine some light on who lived here. But he didn't have time to even open it right now, never mind take a look at its contents. So he shoved it into the holdall and gathered his wits once again. The clock was ticking; he needed to get out.

Now for the really hard part. He'd need lady luck to shine on him now more than ever.

Without zipping the holdall up, Liam did a quick recce, making sure he hadn't left his tools or anything else behind. He took a sturdy length of rope from the front of the bag and looped it through the handles. Quietly, he closed the door of the safe. No need to re-enter the code; the owner would know they'd been robbed. Simply walking through the front door would flag up the fact that their house alarm was no longer set. And once they came up here, they'd see the destruction he was about to cause.

Before creating the only noise of the evening though, he picked up the holdall by its handles and gently opened the door out onto the terrace. He glanced around to see if he was being watched. A couple of the lights opposite had now gone out; the light two doors along remained on. His chances weren't likely to be any better than this, so it was now or never.

The holdall was a tonne weight, but he didn't have time to moan about it. Moving over towards the railings, he hauled the bag onto the top of the iron bars. He grasped hold of the rope attached to it and began to lower it down, straining under the weight. The holdall almost crashed into the downstairs window as it gained momentum further down. Finally, it touched down safely on the ground. He released his grip on the rope and let it slither to the floor.

Next, he grabbed the wrench he'd left on the terrace earlier. Ensuring that his own route across to the railings and down to the street below was unhindered, he said a quick prayer in his head. He needed to make it look like a forced entry, rather than someone picking the lock. A chancer, rather than a professional. So he closed the door, wedged the wrench into the small gap between door and door frame and then let rip.

The noise was much louder than Liam had anticipated. The sound of splintering wood echoed through the stillness of the night. Somewhere nearby, a dog barked.

Time to go.

Slotting the wrench inside his jacket, he ran towards the railings, hoisting himself up and over in one swift movement. Now, more than ever, his actions were urgent. He shimmied down the drainpipe, like a firefighter down a pole, hitting the ground with a thud. Quickly, he removed the rope from the holdall, putting it and the wrench into the bag and zipping it up.

Despite his impressive speed, the noise from forcing the door open had woken someone. A light came on in the house next door. This time it wasn't the bathroom window. Next, they put an outside light on, which shone across a similar roof terrace to their neighbour's. He could hear them opening the door onto their terrace.

Time to run.

Liam hurled the holdall onto his back, ignoring the weight, putting all his focus on moving as swiftly as he could. He darted away from the house, moving stealthily, staying in the shadows, praying he couldn't be seen.

Turning the corner, he was now close to the main road. He'd need to slow down to a quick walk here, so he didn't raise suspicions with anyone he might come across.

And then he heard the sirens, saw the flashing blue lights up ahead.

Shit!

It can't be, he thought. It was too quick. Even if that neighbour had called 999 straight after getting outside. There's no way on earth the police would be anywhere close yet. Even if they'd been passing. Even for these rich bastards. Hold your nerve, Liam. It's not you they're after.

He ducked back into the driveway and moulded himself into the wall.

Drive past, he begged. Drive past.

His prayers were answered. The speeding squad car flew straight past. Straight past the house he'd just broken into. Up to the junction at the top of the road. And then disappeared out of sight.

Time to move. Again.

He turned left out of the driveway and walked as quickly as he could without arousing suspicion. He crossed over the first side road, noticing someone on the opposite side of the street. One more block to go. Past a restaurant and a couple of shops. Almost there.

He turned into the side street and quickened his pace further. It would be beyond tragic for him to be apprehended now.

Another fifty yards.

Finally. He'd made it to the safety of his van. He opened the back door, almost threw the holdall in. Immediately he felt both relief and agony from having the immense weight removed from his shoulders. He took off his gloves and hat and popped them into the side pocket.

Jumping into the driver's seat, he put on his seatbelt and started up the van. Thank God, it started first time. It had occurred to Liam that some things might have been beyond his control tonight. That even with all the planning in the world, something unexpected could scupper everything. Even if he'd made it out of the house, what would he do if he'd been stopped by a passer-by? If he'd been clamped? Or his van didn't start? He was now, quite literally, on the home straight.

Then he saw the blue lights, caught sight of the police car speeding along the road ahead of him, heading in the direction of Elystan Place. He pulled out of his parking space and up to the junction. Casting a glance to the right, he saw the squad car's brake lights illuminate right outside where he'd just been.

The car parked up.

The neighbours had seen something.

-15-

Liam crept through the front door of the flat. The second property tonight he was trying to enter without being disturbed.

His breathing had calmed immeasurably since leaving the house on Elystan Place, but it was still palpable in the stillness of the night. Never mind the adrenaline that was still coursing through his veins. Lugging this tonne weight of a holdall brought back unwelcome memories of his army days.

In an attempt to take deeper, quieter breaths, he put the flashbacks out of his mind and focused on the job in hand. If he'd been rumbled during the robbery, he'd end up with a spell inside. If he woke up the inhabitants of this property, he probably wouldn't live to tell the tale. Callie would kill him if she found out what he'd done.

Living on the fifth, and top, floor of their apartment block could be a pain at times. When the lift broke down, it was a nightmare having to climb those stairs. Although it did mean they had the benefit of a small attic. Amongst all the junk, it'd be the perfect hiding space for the holdall, while he worked out what to do next. Callie rarely ventured up there.

What was he supposed to do with it right now though? He couldn't chance it in the dead of night. Unclicking the hatch, the creaking of the loft ladder, it was bound to wake someone. But in their small flat, there weren't a lot of other options. Hiding it in their wardrobe would be even more likely to wake Callie. And Robbie only had a chest of drawers in his room opposite his single bed.

Shit! Why hadn't he thought about this before carrying out the job? Everything else had been planned to the last detail. For some reason, he hadn't thought about an alternative to leaving his stash in the van overnight. The sheer amount of cash and valuables he'd stumbled across had taken him by surprise. He could no longer risk his van being broken into. The irony wasn't lost on him, as he racked his brains for an alternative.

Jolted from his thoughts by the sound of Callie stirring from the bedroom, he had to act quickly. Heaving the bag, he made a dash for the bathroom, locking the door just as the bedroom door opened.

"Liam, is that you?" a voice called on the other side, loud enough for him to hear but quiet enough not to wake Robbie a couple of doors away.

"Yeah, babe. Just got back. Sorry I was trying not to wake you. Gonna freshen up and then I'll come to bed."

"Okay, I'm getting a glass of water. Don't be too long. I'm knackered, need to get back to sleep." He could hear the sound of her yawning at the other side of the door, emphasising the point.

"Don't worry, I'll be quick, babe," he said, sitting on the downturned lid of the loo, rubbing his temples. Desperately thinking of options.

He turned on the shower over the bath. Might as well sound like he was freshening up. Now that he'd stopped still for a few minutes, he realised he was dripping with sweat from this evening's exertions. Peeling off his clothes and dumping them in the washing basket, he stepped into the bath, allowing the water to wash over him.

The relief it brought was momentary.

"Fuck, Liam, what the fuck have you done?" It was meant to be a straightforward burglary. An easy target, helped by an inside job. Take enough to pay off his debts, set his family up in a proper house. In a better area, where Robbie wouldn't get dragged into any gang culture as he got older. Maybe even have more kids.

He was ashamed to admit when he saw inside the safe, his greed had gotten the better of him. He was jealous of the riches on display. Why shouldn't he and his family have a taste of this life? He'd worked so hard to get on in life, but something always seemed to scupper his dreams. This felt like a once-in-a-lifetime opportunity to sort out their future. So, why was he now feeling like he'd made a mistake? A big mistake.

For one thing, he *had* been too greedy. He reckoned he'd taken nigh on a million in cash and fifty designer watches. How the hell was he going to get rid of the watches alone, without coming under scrutiny? And the money. He couldn't go on a spending spree without raising alarm bells somewhere. Money laundering was a skill, a dishonourable profession. Christ, he'd be lucky to spend one £50 note round here, without raising suspicions!

Splashing his face one last time, he stepped out of the bath and towelled himself down. And then it struck him. A hiding place. A temporary hiding place at least.

He grabbed the tools from the front pocket of his holdall. Flat-headed screwdriver. Perfect. Working as quietly as he could, Liam removed the front panel from the bath surround. He tried to shove the holdall in, but there wasn't enough room. Cursing, he put his gloves back on, unpacked the wads of cash and stacked them roughly around the bath. Finally, there was room to squash the remaining contents and the bag itself into the space at the very front. Silently, he eased the panel back into position.

Praying Callie had fallen asleep, to avoid any awkward questions, he breathed a sigh of relief. Things might work out, after all.

As he slipped into bed beside her, Callie stirred.

"I thought you weren't going to be long?" she asked sleepily.

"Sorry, I must have had something ropey to eat," he lied, "stomach's doing somersaults."

"Okay, I don't need any more details, thanks. How was the job?"

"Complicated, but it's all sorted now." That wasn't really a lie, he told himself. She didn't need to know he was referring to the burglary, rather than the cover story of an emergency call-out.

She yawned again and leant over to give him a kiss. "Oh, God, I need to get back to sleep. I'm soooooo tired. Night, love."

"Night, babe." Liam kissed and hugged her before Callie rolled onto her other side and fell straight back to sleep.

Liam was left alone with his thoughts.

Whose house had he burgled? Why did they have all those watches in their safe, never mind all that cash? And how the hell was he going to make use of his ill-gotten gains, without being rumbled?

He'd forgotten all about the little black book.

He'd shoved it in the bag in a rush, not even knowing why he'd taken it. Clueless about its contents. It looked so innocuous. But if he thought *he'd* been too greedy in taking too much cash and too many watches, he was about to discover a whole new level of avarice.

16

It was the morning after the night before.

Liam felt hungover, despite not having had a drink. His head was pounding from all the over-thinking and his mouth was as dry as a desert from the stress of what he'd done last night.

He looked at his phone and groaned. At least it was Callie's turn to take Robbie to school. But he had to take full advantage of having the flat to himself for that half-hour. Hauling himself out of bed, he threw on his boxers and t-shirt and crept out of the bedroom.

He sighed as he went into the bathroom. The memory of what he'd stashed next to the bath almost broke him out into a cold sweat. He shuddered at the thought of what lay ahead and had to force himself to get on with his morning ritual. Flushing the loo, he brushed his teeth and was shocked at how rough he looked in the mirror. "Christ, get a bloody grip," he whispered to himself. He splashed cold water on his face, slapped his cheeks a few times and grabbed a towel. Running a comb through his hair and styling it with a bit of gel, he began to look vaguely human again.

Callie would be getting up in a few minutes, so he went into the kitchen and started getting breakfast ready. Lost in his thoughts, he jumped as he saw a figure appear in the doorway.

"Morning, love," Callie chimed. "Wow, there's a guilty conscience! What have you done to be so jumpy? You leapt out of your skin there," she laughed. If only she knew.

"*Robbie! Time to get up!*" Callie's voice carried through from his son's room as she sought to stir a sleepy seven-year-old.

Liam glanced at his young son as the three of them sat eating their cereal. He was the main reason he'd done what he did last night. Robbie and Callie were the most important people in his world. He'd do anything for them.

"Dad, can you take me to school today?" asked Robbie out of the blue.

No! No no no! Not today, Robbie. Not today!

"Ah, mate, I'd love to, but I need to get my head down for an hour or so before I get back to work." Plausible enough, he thought.

"But I wanted to talk to you about the game on Saturday," Robbie whined.

"You can talk to him about that when you get home from school," Callie interrupted. "Your dad was working late last night, so he needs a kip, or else you won't be going to the game at all."

He shot her a thankful look, as she cleared the dishes away into the kitchen. God, she got him out of some scrapes at times, but she had no idea how important that moment was to their future.

Kissing Robbie on the head as he and Callie left the flat twenty minutes later, Liam's mind was racing as to what he needed to do. The second the door closed, he sprinted into the bathroom and got his tools from their hiding place.

Taking off the bath panel was a noisy but quicker task than it had been in the middle of the night. He gasped as he saw again how big the haul was. But this was no time to linger. The clock was ticking.

He put his gloves back on, grabbed the holdall and began to refill it with the wads of cash.

It occurred to him that he'd barely felt any feelings of happiness since the burglary. Despite the life-changing sums of money and other valuables, all he'd felt was fear and anxiety. Had he made the wrong decision in breaking into that house? Would it change his life for the worse rather than the better?

Pushing those thoughts to one side, he practically had a heart attack when he heard the front door.

"Christ almighty!" he cursed. Then breathed again as he realised it was only the post dropping through the letterbox.

Glancing at his watch, he saw he only had another twenty minutes at most.

He heaved the holdall into the hall and grabbed the stick to open the loft hatch. Pulling down the ladders, he groaned at the thought of trying to get the huge, heavy stash up the flimsy steps. Never mind through such a small opening. All the while the clock was ticking.

No time to dither, he told himself. Get it done.

Fuck, this bag weighs more than Robbie, he thought. He manoeuvred it onto the rickety steps so he could drag it up as he climbed. Slowly, but surely, he made his way towards the hatch. He was sweating through both fear and exertion. All the while, the clock was ticking. There could only be another few minutes or so now before Callie would walk through that door and catch him.

As he reached the opening, he had to squeeze the holdall to get it into the loft. It was a tight fit but, after a few hefty pushes, thankfully, it went through. He'd intended to go up after it and conceal it somewhere. But he was so conscious of time. He just shoved the bag into the attic, shunted it across and then almost fell as he rushed back down the steps.

The minutes were running away from him. He suddenly remembered he still had the bath panel to put back on. Goddammit, he was going to run out of time. Callie would find him. She'd find out what he'd done and she'd go mental. She'd probably call the police herself. Or worse, she'd walk out and take Robbie with her.

He hurled the ladders back up into the loft and clicked the hatch door shut. Heart pounding, he ran into the bathroom and closed the door behind him, just as he heard the front door open.

This time it wasn't the postman. This time it was Callie.

17

Callie quietly shut the front door and looked in on him in their bedroom. Discovering he wasn't there, he heard her calling his name.

"Hey, babe, won't be a minute."

"Good, I'm desperate to dive in the bath before work."

Shit! Liam had to do something about the bath panel and quickly.

Thinking on his feet, he replied, "Hey, I thought the bath was leaking, but it seems fine. Just been having a look to check."

He moved to put the panel back on, no longer having to be silent.

"Oh, God, why was that? That's the last thing we need right now," Callie said from the other side of the door. He could hear the worry in her voice and immediately felt bad for giving her something else to worry about.

"Ah, I think it was me splashing about half asleep in the shower last night," he said. "Sorry!"

"What's that?" Liam thought to himself, as he was lining up the bath panel to fix it back into place. He reached into the bath surround and grabbed the thing that caught his eye. Of course! The little black book. He flicked through the pages, a mix of random numbers, initials and what looked like dates. Baffled, he thought about chucking it straight in the bin. But he'd need to be careful how he disposed of it, in case it was a vital piece of evidence and came back to haunt him. Why was it in a safe anyway, if it was so worthless?

He decided to hold onto it for the time being. See if he could use his army skills to decipher what the scribbles meant. Resting the book on the end of the bath, he banged the panel back into place and dragged himself off the floor. God, he was aching after his recent exertions; he was starting to feel all of his thirty-two years.

As he opened the door, he poked his head out to see where Callie was. Coast clear, it looked like she was in the kitchen. Grabbing the book, he made a dash for the bedroom and hid it in his bedside table. Finally, he could relax for the first time in a while.

"Robbie ok?" he asked, grabbing his wife from behind and giving her a playful squeeze.

"Yeah, bless him. He's never shut up about the match on Saturday and how much he's looking forward to going again. He reckons one of his teachers is a Brentford fan. God help them, you know what he's like when he's got a new favourite thing!"

They both laughed at the thought of their excitable son. Robbie could develop an encyclopaedic knowledge of his latest craze. He'd chat for hours about it to anyone who showed the slightest bit of interest.

Liam couldn't help feeling proud of his young son. Although he'd been a Bees fan for many a year, he'd worried that Robbie would grow up to follow one of the glory teams in the area. Lots of his schoolmates followed Chelsea, Spurs or Arsenal, even though none of them could ever afford to go to a game. Even when QPR got promoted to the Premier League, most of the kids at his school showed no interest. It was insane! They were only a ten-minute walk away from Loftus Road.

Kids these days were so desperate to follow one of the winning teams. They didn't seem to appreciate what football could be about. The belonging, the afternoon out, the banter, even the bad times that made the good times so much better. And once in a while, those precious moments, when your club did something extra special. Relatively speaking, but still, he wouldn't trade that for the world. Those glory-hunting kids might think they were part of the trophy wins. In reality, they were missing out on so much.

Of course, other priorities often took precedence. Liam had stopped going to the games regularly a few years ago when Robbie was a toddler. Their recent money troubles had brought match-days to a complete halt. He missed meeting up with his mates and the enjoyment of watching a game live. The last couple of games had re-ignited his passion.

"Hey, are you having a kip before you start your shift or what?" asked Callie. "Cos I *really* need a long hot soak before facing the world this afternoon. Work's pretty manic at the minute."

"Yeah, just another hour or so, last night was pretty knackering," he replied, giving her a peck on the cheek.

Jumping back into bed, his thoughts meandered back to his beloved Bees. His final full season had been the year they'd been promoted back to the Championship; what a season that was! They went on an unbelievable run from October through to March. A single defeat in all that time pretty much sealed their promotion. He wished Robbie had been old enough to take to the matches then, but at least now he was starting to get the bug. Happy days…

As sleep caught up with Liam, Callie was getting into a lovely warm bath. Ah, the bliss of hot water and bubbles. Usually, she'd save this treat for the end of her shift, but she was dreading going into work. She didn't need to leave for another couple of hours, so what the hell? Therapy in itself.

Speaking of therapy, she had another couple of shifts to get through, then another session with her psychologist.

She wasn't sure how much the counselling was helping. She knew it was the right thing to do. She needed something to try and rid her of the nightmares, but she couldn't see how anything would take away the impact of that night. Would the guilt ever go away? Could she banish those images from her memory? Or the final words she heard from that poor woman?

Drying herself off twenty minutes later, she wrapped the towel around her and headed towards the bedroom. Hearing Liam snoring his head off, she smiled and headed into the kitchen instead. Coffee and a biscuit while watching Homes under the Hammer. Perfect. Getting dressed could wait a little longer.

Liam woke from his nap with a start as the alarm rang out on his phone. Callie was in the bedroom getting ready for work, but he'd slept through the intrusion. He must've been well out of it.

"Hey, sleepy, I've gotta head out in a few minutes. Rach is picking Robbie up later. Are you ok to go and get him when you finish work?"

"Yeah, that's fine. I'll give Rach a bell when I'm on my way. Be good to catch up with Matt."

"Great. Don't stay too long, though. Robbie needs to get to bed at a decent time, or he's a nightmare the next morning."

"Don't we know it!" he groaned, as he stretched and got out of bed.

These split shifts, coupled with being on call, were draining. At least it meant they could juggle the childcare between them and still work full-time. Although they did have to count on Callie's sister, Rachel, helping them out every now and again.

He'd give anything for Callie not to have to work full-time, especially after what she'd gone through a few months ago. The repercussions of that awful night were still heavy in the air. He knew she was trying to be brave and make out she was coping. But he had a feeling she wasn't. Nobody should have to see those things. To go through that.

A short while later, Liam jumped in the shower as Callie headed out of the flat. He still had another hour or so before he had to leave for work, so he settled down in front of the TV to dry off. Another downside to shift-working, as far as Liam was concerned. Daytime telly was generally shit. Although he quite liked the programme Wanted Down Under. He caught the last twenty minutes, when they decided whether it was the right decision to emigrate. He'd often wondered whether they should consider moving to Australia. Maybe now it was a realistic possibility if he could find a way to launder the money he'd stolen?

Still visualising a better life down under, Liam was rocked from his daydreams when the next programme came on. Caught Red Handed. Christ! Grabbing the remote, he went to switch over to another channel. A bit too close to home there, he thought, almost with a wry smile.

He jumped out of his skin when his mobile rang. "Jesus, chill out, or you'll give the game away," he said out loud.

He began to breathe normally again when he realised it was Danny calling. They'd agreed to do a quick catch-up, to check all was fine after the night before. Everything had gone smoothly of course, but he was grateful for the opportunity to speak to someone about it. To get off his chest how much there was and see if Danny had contacts to get rid of the goods. He picked up the phone and was about to speak when something on TV stopped him in his tracks.

"I'll call you straight back. Don't go anywhere, ok?"

"Wha…" The urgency in Liam's voice panicked Danny. But before he could say anything, the call had been ended.

Switching over from Caught Red Handed hadn't brought any respite for Liam. Far from it. The news was on BBC2. And just after he turned over, a story came on about a burglary. Last night. In West London. He watched open-mouthed as the property he'd burgled came onto the screen. And then his heart almost stopped when he found out whose house it was.

18

"Bloody hell!"

Liam stood bolt upright when he realised whose house he'd broken into last night.

"*…investigating an attempted burglary last night at the London home of Premier League Chief Executive Mitchell Roberts. The burglary took place while Roberts was in Liverpool for a meeting of the Premier League Executive Committee. The Metropolitan Police say that, whilst a few items of jewellery were stolen, it appears the intruder was disturbed before they could make off with anything of significant value. Mitchell Roberts has so far declined to comment.*"

As the news hit home, so many thoughts raced through Liam's head. Why were they saying an attempted burglary? Why were they downplaying how much was taken? How come he had all that cash? And those watches? But most importantly, would the police be hot on his heels when it was someone so high profile?

He redialled the most recent number on his phone.

Beep beep. Beep beep. Beep beep. Beep beep. Beep beep.

He paced around the room. He realised he was sweating, even though it was the middle of winter.

Finally, the person at the other end of the phone answered.

"What's up, mate? You got me worried," came the perplexed, but unaware, greeting.

"Shit, Danny. That house last night. It's just been on the news. I thought you said the guy was no one famous? It's owned by the boss of the Premier League. Did you know that? I mean, Christ, he's really high profile."

"What? I didn't know, Liam. I swear! I thought he'd inherited his money or got rich by chance. You know me, I'm no footy fan. I had no idea," replied Danny, an apologetic air to his tone.

"Ah, Jesus, the cops are gonna be all over this aren't they?" The rising panic in Liam's voice was now evident to both men. "And I went over the top with my stash as well. I'm gonna go down for it."

"Calm down, mate. Listen, there's no way they can trace any of this back to you. I've got a rock-solid alibi, so they'll make it look like they're investigating and then they'll give up after a few weeks."

He wished he had Danny's confidence – or lack of it – in the Metropolitan Police, but the story on the news was the last thing he needed to hear right now. He knew there'd been huge cuts to police forces in recent years, but this was exactly the sort of high-profile case they'd want to be seen to solve. Suddenly, his ill-gotten gains felt hotter than the hinges on the gates of hell.

"But, Danny, I reckon I must have about a million quid in cash and a shedload of designer watches."

A long whistle came down the earpiece.

"Fuckin hell mate, you *did* go over the top didn't you? I knew he had a fair old pile in that safe, but I didn't realise it was that much."

"There was more. I left half the cash and loads more watches. Christ knows what that's all about. I mean, what's the boss of the Premier League doing with all that stuff? The news said an attempted robbery too. And not a lot was taken."

"All sounds a bit suss if you ask me," replied Danny.

Exactly, Liam thought. Why would they say that? To make sure he wasn't burgled in the future? Or were the police, or more likely Roberts, covering something up?

The calmer voice in the conversation interrupted his thoughts again. "Listen, we should keep our distance for a few weeks. I'll get rid of this burner once we hang up, but if you're desperate, ring my work phone. Pretend you're looking for work or something, don't mention anything about the job. We can arrange to meet up and talk where no one's listening. Alright?"

"Ok. Before you go, do you know any decent fences? Or laundrymen?"

"Yeah, I'll dig some details out. But mate, lay low with your stash for a few weeks yeah? I'll get in touch with you once the heat's died down and give you some contacts. In the meantime, don't do anything with it. And for Christ's sake, make sure it's well hidden."

The two men hung up, leaving Liam alone with his thoughts again.

What had he done? Why had he been so fucking greedy? The burglary was supposed to be about setting them up for a better life, not living a millionaire's lifestyle. Although, he'd probably be in the same predicament even if he'd taken much less. The house belonged to someone in the public eye so, either way, he was in the shit. He had to deal with the situation, make sure he didn't get rumbled and hope his family didn't suffer because of his stupidity.

First of all, he needed to calm down and not arouse any suspicion. That meant with Callie as well as the Met. He'd been on edge even before last night, with all the planning. His anxiety had gone into overdrive since he'd got home from the burglary.

At least he knew he could trust Danny. He was old school. Honour amongst thieves and all that. Back in the day, he did a bit of house-breaking. He hadn't known much else with the upbringing he'd had. He got caught every now and then and served his time. But since he got out in the early 2000s, Danny had gone on the straight and narrow. Well, mostly.

He'd met Tina before his last stretch and they'd kept in touch during his time inside. She could see he was a decent enough bloke deep down. He just hadn't had the best start in life. So, when he came out of prison the last time, she encouraged him to put his other skills to good use. He could turn his hand to anything around the house – making stuff, fixing stuff, painting stuff. Over time, he built a reputation for quality work. His past had been almost wiped out.

He was also a bit of a character was Danny. One of those blokes who knew anyone and everyone. A charmer, but a genuine one. The result was that his thriving business brought him and Tina a happy and stable life, as word spread around London. And, though he could've taken on extra workers and built up a booming business with this new reputation, he preferred to keep life simple.

Liam was almost envious of Danny. Not in a jealous way. It was just that he'd found his way in life, despite the challenges of his younger days. And, unless it all went drastically wrong, he and Tina were set for the rest of their lives together.

Liam on the other hand had always tried to do things the right way but never seemed to get a break. After nearly eight years in the army, he had little to show for his service to queen and country. Apart from his PTSD. And Callie used to love her job as an emergency call operator until that night took its toll. Now, the cost of living in London had become so extortionate versus what they both earned. Living week to week on their salaries, it only took one thing to have a major effect on their finances.

Of course, the last eighteen months had brought more than one unplanned expense. The impact had been devastating, both financially and mentally. So when the opportunity to break into Elystan Place arose, how could he turn down the chance to get back on his feet?

In the cold light of day, he was starting to wish he had.

Had he really been so naïve to think he could get away with it all?

19

2 December 2017
Brentford vs Fulham
Griffin Park, London
Kick-off: 3:00 pm

No matter what happened over the next few weeks, Liam had a feeling that today would be the last match they'd attend for a while. He couldn't get away with buying some tickets before Christmas, despite all the cash in the loft. And Brentford's match on Boxing Day was a night-time game. It was also constantly on his mind that the police could knock on the door one day, bringing his family life to a shuddering halt. So, he hoped the Bees would give Robbie a match to remember.

They'd done a pretty good job so far. Lucky little bugger!

Liam still wasn't splashing the cash; he didn't want to raise any red flags with Callie. But at least he had the luxury of not having to watch every last penny, knowing there was light at the end of the tunnel. So, although they caught the bus across once more, he'd arranged to meet up with his mates before the game. And he was going to treat Robbie to a burger from the match-day van.

He hadn't seen his mates for quite a few weeks, money had been so tight. He'd been too ashamed to open up to them and admit he was going through a torrid time financially. It was embarrassing, not being able to afford a round. So the easiest thing of all was to avoid them, invent an excuse why he couldn't meet up and hope it sounded genuine enough. One day he'd tell them the truth; one day when he found the strength. In the meantime, he'd been left hoping he didn't lose touch. He'd known half of them since his schooldays.

When he messaged one of the lads on Wednesday night, he was heartened to get an almost immediate response.

Great to hear from you mate.

Yeah, there's a few of us there on Saturday.

See you in the Newie any time after 12?

Steve was a good lad. He loved his drink and he could get into a few scrapes every now and then, but he was great with kids. A natural uncle-type figure. He didn't have any of his own kids yet, hadn't found the right woman to put up with him. But he'd met Robbie a few times over the last couple of years. This would be the youngster's first game as 'one of the lads' and Liam was relaxed, knowing a couple of his mates would watch out for him.

They got there around 12.30pm. Robbie was eager to have another new experience at the game. He loved that some things were the same each match and other things differed. He had his Brentford scarf on, of course. And they'd be back on the terraces of the Ealing Road end, where he'd watched his first-ever match. So he couldn't wait for that. But this time, he'd be going to the pub beforehand and going in the ground with his dad's mates. With each match he attended, Robbie was becoming more and more a 'proper' football fan.

As they walked into the New Inn, Liam spotted Steve and the others over in their usual corner. They greeted him warmly, taking the piss, but clearly pleased to see him.

"Where the fuck have you been hiding out?" asked Andy, the loudest of the group. "I thought you must've started going down the Bridge or summat, it's been that long."

"As if I'd support those dickheads," said Liam. "Nah, just been a bit brassic that's all."

"Here, mate, what do you want to drink? Your usual?" asked Steve.

"Yeah, I'll get them."

"Nah, it's my round. You can get them in next time. In fact, you can get them in after Si puts his hand in his pocket, the tight bastard. He never buys a friggin drink," winking over at Si. "What do you want, little man?"

Robbie looked up at his dad, not knowing what he should ask for. This was a rare experience for him. Did they do cartons of orange juice in pubs?

"Cheers, mate. Get him an orange squash. He'll be fine with that."

Robbie spent the next hour and a half entranced by the group of men. They talked about their football team. They moaned or bragged about their girlfriends. Ribbed each other about being under the thumb or 'Billy no-bird'. Then reverted back to the football. They were generally quite positive until they got onto their previous game.

"We were fuckin robbed on Monday night," said Andy.

"Did you go?" asked Liam.

"Yeah, me and Si went," he said, acknowledging one of the others.

"That ref was shit," chipped in Si. "Didn't give a blatant foul against Ollie before their first goal. Then gave them a free kick that never was for the second."

"Yeah, we've only got ourselves to blame though, we keep throwing points away. We'd have been 10th if we'd managed the game out."

Andy and Si both looked incredulously at the bloke who'd just spoken.

"Fuck off, Rich! You can't do a lot when the ref makes such shit decisions," replied Andy, playfully punching him in the arm, spilling his pint.

"Exactly. Dick by name, Dick by nature, ey lad?" added Si and the rest of the men roared with laughter at Rich's expense.

Robbie joined in, not having a clue what they were laughing about. Their hilarity was infectious. Although he knew Rich was right. Brentford had dropped eighteen points from winning positions so far this season. He had everything crossed that today wouldn't be one of those days. He'd yet to see them lose when he was actually at the match. He couldn't imagine how that felt, how the crowd would react. Whether it would be the ref's fault or one of their own players. Or the manager. Or just through the pure brilliance of one of the opposition players?

Today was a big game though. Brentford fans classed Fulham as their biggest local rivals, even if the feeling wasn't reciprocated. QPR were second on that list, so today's match had even more resting on it than the other night. Three points for Brentford this afternoon would see them leapfrog Fulham, almost a double win as far as Liam and his mates were concerned. It was always twice as sweet getting one over your local rivals.

Liam had managed to sink four pints during his time in the pub. He'd only had to buy a round for five, including Robbie, rather than the full group of lads. It felt good to be back amongst his mates and not be paranoid about every single penny he spent.

Most of the lads from the pub would be going in the Ealing Road end with Liam and Robbie. Another new experience. Callie would no doubt be horrified by the language he'd been listening to so far. Chances were, it'd get a lot more colourful during the game. But as far as Liam was concerned, this was part of growing up and going to football. He'd pull Robbie up if he started repeating some of the language. But as long as there wasn't any racist or homophobic stuff being said, he wouldn't be precious about what the crowd was shouting.

As they spilled out of the pub towards the ground, Liam's hunger pangs hit him. Time for that burger. He was starving, so no doubt Robbie was too, despite the packet of crisps Andy had treated him to.

There was a burger van on Braemar Road that would always remind Liam of match-days. The aroma of the sizzling meat and onions, ah the onions, pervaded the whole street along the side of the ground. It was divine. The burgers didn't always match up to the expectation created by the smell, but at least they filled a hole.

"Gonna grab a burger, lads. See you in there," he shouted, as the others headed over to the turnstiles.

"Fat bastard," one of them yelled. Liam laughed, the insult ironically came from the largest bloke in the group.

The burgers were a lot less messy than the pies had been that first time. Liam still had to wipe ketchup from around Robbie's mouth and dust the breadcrumbs from his scarf. Apart from that though, the flat, lukewarm patty was a far cleaner option. Burgers devoured, Liam guided Robbie through the turnstiles. There was time for another pint, but he didn't want to get pissed in charge of his son. So he grabbed them both a bottle of water, before spotting his mates further up.

"Lightweight," Si greeted, spotting Liam rock up, water in hand.

"Some of us have got responsibilities," Liam said, glancing down at Robbie.

"Lucky bastard. I only see Freddy once in a blue moon these days. And he's not really arsed about coming to the match with his dad. Much more interested in going to Spurs with his flashy stepdad. Spurs, I mean fuck me!"

Liam felt sorry for Si. He gathered the break up with his ex-girlfriend had been messy and now his son had had his head turned by her new bloke. He knew he had his own troubles, but at least he had Callie and Robbie. Or he did for now, anyway. If Callie found out what he'd done the other night, who knows what her reaction would be? Or, even worse, if he got put away? He felt a shiver down his spine as his mind wandered briefly.

He snapped back to the present as Robbie grabbed his sleeve.

"Dad, can we go on the terraces yet?"

There was still a good half hour or so until kick-off, but he could tell by the look in Robbie's eyes he was desperate to get outside.

"Lads, I'll see you out there, ok? He likes to watch the players warming up."

They found a good spot on the terraces and he lifted Robbie up to sit on the crush barrier. The memories of his very first match a mere six weeks ago came flooding back for both of them. It felt like a lifetime ago to Liam.

"I heard your favourite isn't playing today, mate," he said to Robbie.

A shocked look from the little boy.

"Why not, dad?"

"He's injured."

Robbie looked downcast, but bounced back with, "We'll just have to hope Ollie scores then, won't we?"

He had to hand it to his son. His optimism for his team was never-ending. He was trying to remember whether he was that positive when he was his age. He didn't think he was, but he definitely wasn't as cynical as he was now. He loved the hopefulness of youth. Though he knew it wouldn't last forever. Over time Robbie would learn about heartache as a football fan. Brentford would go on a bad run, sell their best players, his favourite players, get relegated. But he'd also experience more of the joyful moments. Exciting games, last-minute winners, beating your local rivals, a cup run, a promotion or two. Hopefully.

The entertaining game that followed captured perfectly the highs and lows of a football fan.

GOAL! Halfway through the first half, Fulham took the lead; deserved reward for the better team. Steve, Andy and Si weren't alone in their cursing when Fulham bundled the ball into the net. Liam noticed a smirk across Robbie's face as he turned round to face him. He was gutted Brentford had conceded a goal, but he was finding his dad's mates hilarious. Especially the language they used when they were expressing themselves.

GOAL! Not long afterwards, the swearing was celebratory as Brentford equalised.

"Fuckin get in!"

He clung to Robbie amidst the celebrations on the terraces. His mates were pretty boisterous and didn't hold back, although it was just as much Robbie's excitement as theirs.

Half-time: Brentford 1 Fulham 1

Liam had to admit they were lucky to go in level at half-time. Fulham had definitely been on top in the first half. He wondered if this would be Robbie's first defeat. It had to come sometime, but he didn't want it to be in a derby game.

He needn't have worried.

GOAL! With lucky charm Robbie on their side, Brentford rose to the challenge, taking the lead shortly after the break. A few minutes later Fulham had a player sent off, allowing Brentford to press home their advantage. GOAL! Late on in the game and Ollie scored to secure the three points. Yet again, Robbie's prediction had come true.

The atmosphere throughout Griffin Park was bouncing, but especially on the terraces. Robbie was in his element. He joined in with the chanting, clapping and raising his hands in unison with the rest of the crowd.

Liam decided there and then that season tickets were way up on the list of priorities. He had to work out what he was doing with the money first, not get rumbled and create a better life for his family. But as soon as he was able to sort tickets, that's what he'd be doing.

Coming from behind to win a game? Fantastic. Beating your closest rivals? Brilliant. Celebrating with your son and your mates? Absolutely fucking priceless.

Full time: Brentford 3 Fulham 1

-20-

It was just over a week after the burglary and Liam had started to calm down a little. He was no longer jumping out of his skin every time he heard a police siren, the phone rang, or anyone knocked at their door.

His focus was turning to how he could start paying off his loan, without raising suspicions.

He had to sit tight on his haul, but there was nothing to stop him planning his finances in the meantime. Even if Danny gave him some contacts, it may not be the magic wand to wipe out his debts. And he had no idea how he'd ever explain things to Callie, without causing an almighty row and the possibility of her storming out.

It was so frustrating that he could clear his debt in one fell swoop. But he'd be mad to do so. It would set alarm bells ringing straight away. Instead, he needed a clever way to whittle down the arrears, in the minimum amount of time.

With Callie and Robbie at work and school respectively, he had a few spare hours before starting his shift.

First things first. Counting his haul.

He needed to know exactly what he had in the attic. He'd not touched the holdall since the day after the burglary. Had he actually taken a million, or was it more or less than that? What sort of watches were they and how many of each did he have? Were there any identifying marks on any of them, which would make them impossible to sell on? Was the money marked in any way? Christ, imagine that, stealing a million quid and not being able to do a damn thing with it. That would be just his luck.

Lugging the holdall down from the loft was no small feat, thanks to its weight and the shakiness of the pull-down ladder. Liam was also shaking, but he couldn't afford to topple over. If he knocked himself out and was rumbled by Callie, the evidence around him would've been damning.

It was the biggest holdall they owned. Large enough for both of them to use for a weekend away, or even longer. Though chance would be a fine thing. It also reminded him of the army issue holdalls. Those memories crept back into his brain, stirring recollections of more unpleasant things. The body bags. That feeling the first time he had to scoop up one of his mates after their convoy had been attacked. The back-breaking weight of that body bag would stay with him forever. Back-breaking and heart-breaking in equal measure. Was that an excuse for what he was doing now? No, but it did explain his sometimes irrational behaviour.

He forced himself to snap back to the present, pushing those dark feelings to the recesses of his mind.

Christ this was heavy! The holdall was rammed, which made him think again, why the fuck had he been so greedy? He could've taken half as much, ignored the watches and still been clear of his debts. Still set up for the future.

Idiot. Bloody, stupid, fuckin' idiot!

It was too late for regrets now, he had to deal with the situation. He heaved the holdall into the lounge and hurled it onto the sofa.

As he searched around for a pen, he grabbed the nearest scrap of paper to scribble on. An envelope with a red 'Final Demand' stamped on it. Christ, rub it in some more, he thought.

He made a start on counting the wads of cash. He was conscious he could be rumbled at any point, so took care to avoid having his prints all over the valuables. Only this time, he put on latex gloves, to make it easier to flick through the notes.

Luckily for Liam, a lot of the cash was bundled and wrapped in lots of £2,500. So he began by counting the loose notes, figuring the bundles would be a lot quicker to tally up. They were all £50 notes, not a single lower value amongst them. Jesus, who had purely £50 notes in their possession? Different world!

Ten minutes later, he'd finished counting out the loose £50s into piles and adding them up. Four hundred and three in total; a quick calculation on his phone and he saw that amounted to £20,150. He whistled. He'd have been well on track with that, never mind the almighty pile of bundles still to be totted up.

Another ten minutes later, maybe more, he was only halfway through counting out the cash bundles. His envelope was nigh on full of scribbles and he still had the other half to add up, as well as all the watches. He needed more paper. A book would be handy, keep the details all together and out of sight.

Liam rooted around in Robbie's room for some sort of notebook, but could only find his schoolbooks. He couldn't pinch one of those. Then he remembered. That little black book! He retrieved it from the bedside drawer. He had no idea what was written in there; it made no sense at all. But he needed something to write down the details of his stash in. He might as well keep the two things together.

Quickly, he transferred the information he'd already written down into the back of the book, where there were numerous blank pages. He'd destroy the envelope later.

Another ten minutes passed and he'd completed his first task. He was aware there was a shitload of money. It was only when he entered the number of batches into his phone that the full reality dawned. Three hundred and eighteen bundles. He saw the figure in cash terms. Wow. Add that amount to the loose notes and the total in cash was a cool £815,150. Eight. Hundred. And. Fifteen. Thousand. Fuck me, he thought, not quite the million I'd estimated, but not far off. He took a sharp intake of breath and refocused.

On to the watches.

Another half-hour went by, while Liam laid the watches out on the coffee table, sorting through the various brands. Some of them he knew, others were a complete mystery, but they all looked very, very expensive. He recalled seeing Breguet, Breitling and Rolex on the night of the break-in. He'd also heard of Cartier and Hublot. But Patek Philippe, Audemars Piguet, Chopard and Vacheron Constantin were new ones on him. He came across a USB stick randomly mixed up with the watches. He must have inadvertently grabbed that at the same time. He kept it to one side. He didn't have a laptop, so there wasn't much he could do with it, for now.

There were forty-three watches in total, spread across those nine brands. Even at a conservative estimate of four grand a watch, that would make them worth £172,000. Having done a quick search on one of the Patek Philippe watches, its £21,000 price tag blew Liam's mind. Realistically, he could have half a million quid from the watches alone. Mental!

Conscious of time, he focused back on the task at hand. He wrote down a code for each brand and the quantities of each one.

PaP 3 (code for Patek Philippe)

AuP 4 (code for Audemars Piguet)

Chop 3 (the abbreviation for Chopard)

VaC 4 (code for Vacheron Constantin)

Hub 5 (short for Hublot)
Car 2 (the abbreviation for Cartier)
Rox 9 (code for Rolex)
Brg 6 (code for Breguet)
Brt 7 (code for Breitling)

Not exactly the most sophisticated piece of coding he'd ever done, but it would do for now. Maybe it was what criminals did, he thought, wondering what the front section of the book was all about. Now that he'd counted his stash, he was convinced the contents of the book were dodgy. Something didn't add up.

He'd love to have gone through each watch in turn and search on the internet for how much it was worth. His paranoia wouldn't let him. He couldn't run the risk of anyone catching him, as unlikely as it was right now. And it would be idiotic to raise any red flags with his online activity. Time to get everything back in the bag and face hauling it up to the attic once more.

Having packed everything in a more organised manner, Liam zipped up the bag and took a breath. He braced himself to lift the weight of a small child again. A few minutes and much swearing later, he'd hauled the bag back up the shaky ladder. After a brief rest at the top, he shoved it into the loft, hoisting himself in after it this time.

Liam touched on a dead spider as he fumbled around in the darkness for the light switch. Once his eyes adjusted to the light, he remembered how much crap they had stored up here. They'd only lived in this flat for eight years, yet the stuff they'd accumulated in that time was ridiculous. One day he'd have a good clear out. Not today.

Liam coughed as he inhaled some of the dust. He grabbed the holdall and began to heave it into a good hiding place. He wanted to make sure that, even if Callie came up here, which was rare, she wouldn't see it. About the only time either of them ventured up there was Christmas…

Christmas. Ah, bugger. It was the 8th of December. They didn't normally put their tree up for another week or so. He couldn't run the risk of Callie deciding to do it when he was at work one day. He'd have to get all the Christmas stuff down before then. He'd have to do it now.

Shit! He only had another hour before he had to leave for work. He still had to grab a bite to eat, get showered and changed. But this was more important. He located the tree first and lugged it down the steps. At least it was a four-footer, not heavy, just difficult to manoeuvre through the hatch. Then he went back up to get all the decorations. Baubles, streamers and Christmas card holders. A wreath, candelabra and a few other bits and bobs they'd collected over the years.

Once he'd got everything down, Liam was relieved he still had time for a shower. He was desperate to get the cobwebs and dust out of his hair, freshen up from his exertions. He'd have to grab a burger or something on the way to work, otherwise he wouldn't last through his shift. But at least he'd cleared another potential obstacle. He'd leave a note for Callie, see if she wanted to put everything up with Robbie over the weekend.

As he was about to leave, he remembered the little black book and the envelope. Jesus, that would've taken some explaining, he thought. He hid them swiftly in his bedside drawer and then finally grabbed the USB stick. All clear. He tucked the gadget into the change compartment of his wallet. That would have to wait for another day.

He set off for work, happy in the knowledge that he'd quantified his stash and made a pre-emptive move on the

Christmas decorations. He still had no idea how they'd pay back their debts, but this was a step in the right direction.

He hadn't realised he'd missed one of the decorations. It had been pushed back when he'd moved the stash into the loft. And was now hidden behind the holdall. Waiting to be discovered.

"Thanks for coming, everyone. We'll keep this brief. We've had a breach."

Gasps went around the room.

The chairman continued. "Ok, Mitchell, would you like to explain everything?"

Mitchell cleared his throat.

"Thanks, chairman. As you're aware, I was burgled last month and the safe was broken into. The thief took a substantial amount of money and watches."

"Yes, we know that. Not ideal, but we can live with it. I assume you've increased your security since this happened?" enquired the man directly opposite Mitchell.

"Yes, yes I have," he responded.

"So what's the problem?" one of the others asked.

He shifted uncomfortably in his seat. He was loathe to say the next bit.

"Well, it now transpires that they also took the black book."

One or two of the attendees were open-mouthed in disbelief, another put his head in his hands.

"For fuck's sake!"

"How could you be so stupid?"

"Idiot!"

"Ok, everyone. Mitchell hasn't done this on purpose. It's naïve of him we know, but let's face it, the contents won't necessarily mean anything to anyone. All being well, this will just blow over, if we sit tight."

"You'd better hope so," commented the man to Mitchell's right, in a lower volume, but with a much more menacing tone.

"Well, we're taking steps to minimise the damage," cut in the chairman again. "There's a possibility it was an inside job, by a builder Mitchell employed. We're looking to track him down and see if he was involved. If he was, we'll make sure we get our property back."

"Whatever it takes." It was the man to Mitchell's right again. Pronounced. And ominous.

Mitchell had a growing unease. He'd had to come clean about the black book going missing. He'd put it off for a while. When he realised he'd need to produce it at some point, he knew he'd have to confess and face the consequences. Better to get it over and done with. He almost wanted them to fire him, he felt so out of his depth. This wasn't the dream job he thought it was going to be.

Unfortunately, they didn't get shot of him there and then.

But the tone of the summit and the threats that hung in the air ensured Mitchell stayed silent for the rest of the meeting. He'd spent hours beforehand mulling it over. Whether he should tell them. About the other thing that was missing. Seeing their reaction over the book, he decided to keep it to himself.

After all, they didn't even know it existed.

-22-

Liam got home from his twilight shift one Friday night and was surprised to see Callie waiting for him when he walked into the flat.

Robbie was staying over with her sister, Rachel, as she was meant to be going to her friend's house for drinks. She hadn't been out with any of her friends much recently, due to their money worries. But they could get away with a bottle of wine once in a blue moon to try and keep up appearances.

Callie's face was like thunder. Liam froze.

"What the hell is going on?"

"What are you on about?" He was baffled, yet still terrified at the thought that she'd discovered his secret.

"What am I on about? You know what I'm on about. Unless Robbie has taken to robbing banks!"

She spat that last sentence out.

Shit, shit, shit. What did she know?

"Please Cal, tell me what's up and we'll talk about it. Ok?"

She stormed into the kitchen, closely followed by Liam. What he saw on the worktop stopped him in his tracks.

A wad of notes and one of those designer watches.

"I can explain," he began. And then thought to himself, hell no, I can't. You'll kill me.

"I'm all ears. And it'd better be good."

He racked his brains. What was he going to say? How was he going to explain it away?

"Well then?" Callie was becoming impatient.

It dawned on him that he couldn't make up a story. If she found out further down the line that he'd lied, she'd never ever forgive him. That's if she was even still around by then.

"Babe, I…"

"Don't 'babe' me. I want answers!"

How the hell was he going to explain this? Where did he even start?

He felt bile rise from his stomach. His legs felt like jelly. His head was pounding. His hand shot out to the worktop to steady himself.

Callie put aside her anger momentarily to show some concern for her husband. He'd turned a ghostly white before grabbing the worktop. He had some explaining to do, some *serious* explaining, but for now, she needed to make sure he didn't collapse. Or worse.

She touched his hand.

"Christ, Liam, what have you got yourself into? Come on, get yourself sat down and you can tell me about it."

"I think I need a stiff drink," he said, his voice trembling.

"Well, we haven't got any beer or spirits, so you'll have to make do with some wine."

She grabbed the wine out of the fridge and followed him into the lounge with a couple of glasses. She figured she'd be needing some alcohol too. So much for a chilled night, catching up with her friend. At least she'd already bought the bottle.

Liam's heart had calmed slightly by the time Callie joined him on the sofa. But he was still a nervous wreck. He still had no idea what he was going to say, or how he was going to explain what he'd done.

As she poured them a glass each, he could see she was still angry. At least she'd lost the murderous look that greeted him a few minutes earlier.

"What made you go up in the loft?" he asked.

"I was looking for that sparkly little tree."

Brilliant, he thought. Our whole lives are gonna be turned upside down because of a sodding sparkly little tree. He'd forgotten that mini LED tree, with the twinkly lights. They'd had it since Robbie was a baby. It must have been hidden away somewhere. Jesus, why hadn't he realised? Why hadn't she said anything at the time? He could've gone straight back up and found it, prevented all of this from happening.

He took a gulp of his wine. Here goes nothing, he thought.

"So, you know Danny, the old guy who gives me some casual work from time to time?"

She nodded, taking a sip of her own, bracing herself for what she was about to hear.

"He got in touch a few weeks back. Told me about a house he'd been working on, where the owner was an arrogant prick. But where there was a large safe and low-level security. He managed to find out the passcode and gave me some other inside details. He knew we needed the money."

"Needed the money? I know we're strapped for cash at the moment, but we're not so broke that you needed to rob someone!"

The guilty look on his face confirmed her growing fears.

"Oh, God," Callie sobbed the words, hugging herself at the prospect of what else he was going to tell her.

"Babe, I didn't want to worry you. Honestly, I kept it from you for all the right reasons. You were going through enough as it was. Then, that night, of course. And then obviously things just got worse and worse from then on. The loan, the credit card, me losing my job. It just all spiralled out of control."

"So, how much do we owe?"

Liam winced as he said, "Over thirty grand."

She gasped. "Oh my God! How the hell are we ever gonna be able to pay that back?"

"Well, I guess if it was like a mortgage or something, we might have had some hope. But not when it's a payday loan, on top of all the other stuff. It just goes up and up."

He put his head in his hands. She took another drink from her glass, cursing him for being so damn stupid.

"So, instead of asking for help or coming clean about the size of our debts, you decided to rob a bloody house?" Her voice was rising again now, the anger coming back in waves.

"Callie, I couldn't see any other way out. I was desperate." You don't know how desperate, he thought to himself. "The job was straightforward enough. I just got a bit greedy when I saw how much was in the safe. But I still left a shedload of stuff behind. It was mental how much there was."

"Liam, that's a *serious* amount of money in the loft. And all those watches! Whoever you robbed isn't gonna take this lying down. And the police are gonna be all over it."

He felt the bile in his stomach rising again. "Er yeah, that's another thing," he said, dreading what he was about to say next. Whose house it was.

They argued for most of the evening while finishing off the rest of the bottle. They didn't go out for another one. Despite Callie now knowing about the money and the fact they could afford the best Champagne on the planet. Liam didn't dare suggest it, even though he could've sunk a vat of the stuff right now. He was desperate to drown his worries in alcohol, but it

121

wasn't really the answer. Besides, spending a fifty-note in the Premier downstairs would set off alarm bells that weren't worth ringing.

They talked, argued. Argued, talked. Cried at one point. And then, finally, fell silent when there was nothing more to be said.

"Right, I'm off to bed," said Callie. "You can sleep in Robbie's room."

"Cal, I'm sorry. I'm really, really sorry. I did it for us. You and Robbie are my world. Can you forgive me?" The pleading tone of his voice sounded desperate. But he was desperate.

"I don't know, Liam. I honestly don't know."

He didn't stay in Robbie's bed that night. He slept on the sofa, having tortured himself with the various scenarios that could play out. It must have been after 4am when he eventually drifted off. By the time he woke up around 9am, Callie was gone.

-23-

Liam frantically called Callie's number.

No answer. He rang again. No answer. One more attempt. This time she picked up.

"Leave me alone! I don't want to talk to you, ok?"

"Ca…….." She hung up abruptly, without giving him a chance to say anything.

Realising he wasn't going to get any joy with Callie, his mind focused on practicalities. Had she gone to Rachel's or did he need to go and collect Robbie? He rang his sister-in-law. Thankfully, she picked up after a few rings.

"Rach, is Callie with you?" he asked.

"Yes, but she doesn't want to speak to you. What's happened between you two? She's in absolute bits."

"I know, I can't talk about it right now. I just wanted to check and see if Robbie needed picking up."

"No, he's fine here, thanks. But please don't come round. Give her some space for a while."

Rachel hung up the phone without waiting for a response and Liam was left with his own thoughts again. His own torturous thoughts.

He spent the next half-hour wallowing in his misery.

Finally, he decided to shower and get dressed. Twenty minutes later, his coffee was almost doing the trick in waking him up fully. Time to do something constructive.

He scrolled through the contacts on his phone until he got to DW Property Services. Dialled and waited for an answer.

Eventually, he picked up.

"Hi, Danny, it's Liam. I was wondering whether you've got any jobs that need a sparky? I could do with some extra cash right now."

"Hi, mate. Erm, I haven't got anything at the moment. But I can put the word out for you. Fancy meeting up for a pint and see if there's anything I can help with?"

"Yeah, that would be good. Anytime over the weekend would suit me. The missus is staying with her sister for a couple of days."

A slight pause on the other end of the line. Danny was unsure what that meant. Was it bad news? Had she rumbled him or was this a normal occurrence?

"Yeah, ok. How about this afternoon? I could meet you in The Crown about 3ish."

"Perfect. I'll see you then. Cheers, mate."

Right, time to kill until he met up with Danny. What was next on his mental list?

The little black book. Again. He'd only flicked through it a few times over the last couple of weeks. With such cursory glances, he was none the wiser. He had no idea what the 'code' meant. If it even was a code.

He took the book from its hiding place and grabbed another coffee, hoping to give his mind some clarity.

He gazed at the offending article. It was so innocuous. Just an A5-sized black leather-bound book, with lined paper inside it. Similar to a diary in terms of the number of pages, one of those week-to-view ones. Totally unassuming. Who knows, maybe it was? Maybe it'd just been thrown in that safe in a hurry and meant nothing, was worth nothing.

But Liam had this nagging doubt that it was something.

He turned to the first page.

17th

MD3

CS 2 Scarabs, 1 Lucifer

There were various other entries, with different MDs. And some had CR rather than CS beside them, without any numbers. There was always an 'O', or was it a zero, and 2 initials after it, at the end of each entry.

On the next page, he spotted another entry:

MD28

CS 1 Lucifer, 4 Scarabs

There were those two terms again, Scarabs and Lucifer. What could they mean?

He flicked on further through the book and was similarly baffled. At the top of the page was this scribble, followed by a whole raft of MD entries, like before:

End of 18th

OAP £20

Several pages later and he reached what appeared to be the start of the next section.

End of 19th

NE Lucifer & Citizens

Lucifer £23.1, OAP £22.6, Citizens £21.1

Again, it was followed by lots of MD codes. He guessed around twenty, more or less. He skimmed through the rest of the book until the blank pages began. Then he thumbed back and looked at the last few written pages. The MD parts were a recurring feature, but what piqued his interest was at the top of the page. Not every page, maybe every fourth or fifth one, he'd find the following:

End of 23rd

OAP £84.1, Citizens £81.6, Cannon £25.6, Lucifer £21.8

And so it went on:

End of 24th

VOID

End of 25th

OAP £100, Cowboys £88.1, Citizens £86.6, Scarabs £36.6

End of 26th

Citizens £93.3, Lucifer £54.2, Cowboys £41.7, Scarabs £39.8

Again, each one was followed by numerous MD entries. Towards the end, another 4 and 1 entry caught his eye.

MD18

CS 4 Citizens, 1 Cowboy

Liam's head hurt trying to crack the code. He was powerless to stifle a huge yawn as his eyelids began to drag themselves down. It was no wonder; he'd had such little sleep the night before.

Giving it up as a bad job once more, he decided to get his head down properly for a couple of hours. He set the alarm on his phone and jumped into the bed he hadn't made it into last night.

He slept so soundly that the code he'd just been looking at became subconsciously imprinted in his brain.

He was early for his pint with Danny, so Liam grabbed a table towards the back of the pub. It was busy, which was good; the background noise would cover up their conversation.

He watched Soccer Saturday while he waited for Danny to turn up, sipping his pint slowly. He had to make it last as long as possible, he'd only come out with a tenner.

Brentford were playing at home to Barnsley today, but up until last night, he'd had to maintain the pretence of having no money. So, even if Callie hadn't walked out, they wouldn't have been going to the match. Robbie had asked the question earlier in the week but hadn't kicked off when the answer was no. Going to the game at the moment was still a huge treat for him.

Maybe, one day, they'd have season tickets and go to every game. Maybe. If Callie came back to him. The alternative didn't bear thinking about.

He put those thoughts to the back of his mind as he spotted Danny making his way through the crowded pub. He waved to grab his attention.

"Alright, Liam, mate?" the older man greeted him warmly, as he set a couple of pints on the table.

"I've been better, to be honest. But good to see you. How are you doing?"

"Can't complain, pal. Work's good, Tina's happy and keeping me out of mischief. Mostly." Danny winked. "Here, get that down you, you look like you need it," he said, offering him the second pint.

Liam didn't stand on ceremony and took a huge swig from his first glass.

As he put his pint back on the table, he blurted out, "Callie found the holdall." He looked like his whole world had caved in around him. Which of course it had.

"Shit. How?"

"I'd hidden it away in the loft. She hardly ever goes up there. She went looking for some extra Christmas decorations and came across it."

"So, have you told her?"

"I had to, she was ready to kill me. And, if I'd spun her a line and she found out the truth, later on, I'd be in even deeper shit than I am now."

"Aw, Jesus. How did she take it?"

"Badly. We had a massive row last night and she's gone to stay with her sister. Just upped and left this morning, before I woke up."

Danny rubbed his beard, thinking about options.

"Will she go to the cops?"

"Nah, I don't think so. Even if she hates me forever, I don't think she'll dob us in."

"Well, that's one thing anyway." Danny looked at Liam and felt sympathy for the bloke. He was a decent fella, who'd fallen on hard times through no fault of his own. Having given him the opportunity to sort himself out, the last thing he wanted was for him to end up even worse off.

"I need to start sorting our debts while she's gone. They're crippling us. At least if I can try to get things on a better footing, she might come back. You said you had some contacts?"

Danny nodded and dug out a piece of paper from his back pocket.

"The first one's the laundry guy. He'll take a 20% cut, but it's worth it. He'll be able to make things look legit and set you up for life. The second one's the fence. He's a bit of a wide boy, but he's the best around when it comes to designer stuff, especially watches. I reckon he'll try and double his money, but if it gets that hot shit away from you it'll be worth it. You can then get the first guy to feed that cash through as well."

"What about timing?" Liam asked, hopefully.

"I'd give it until after Christmas, to be honest, mate. Start of next year? Maybe longer. It's still early days."

Liam looked disappointed, even though he knew the guy spoke sense.

"Look, mate, there's something I haven't told you," Danny continued. "I had a visit from the cops this week. Luckily I've got a rock-solid alibi, but they're still on the case. I didn't say anything to you, I thought it was best to keep our distance. They don't have any connection between us, other than a bit of work here and there. But they gave me a right good grilling."

Danny's revelation made Liam's heart beat faster. He was worried.

"Listen, you should be fine if you sit tight and don't do anything that raises suspicions ok? Just be patient. I know it's tough at the moment, but it'll be worth it in the end."

Liam nodded, but still looked shattered. Danny imagined he was more concerned about Callie leaving than any other consequences.

"Mate, she'll come back eventually. Once she gets over the shock of it, she'll understand you were only trying to sort things out. Just be prepared to eat humble pie when she starts to come round."

Liam laughed. "Cheers, I hope you're right. And thanks for this," he gestured with the piece of paper, then tucked it safely into his wallet.

"Right, I best be off," said Danny, sinking the rest of his pint. "Try not to get in touch for the next few weeks, unless you're desperate. It'll help to keep the cops off the scent at least."

Liam nodded and waved his pint at Danny in a friendly gesture. "Understood. You take care."

Danny walked out of the pub, leaving Liam to finish the pint he'd bought him. He laughed inwardly at the thought of giving someone else relationship advice. Tina would find that hilarious.

As he headed towards his van, he was oblivious to the person watching him. They hadn't got there in time to see him go into the pub or discover who he'd met with. But now they'd located him, they were on his tail.

-25-

Once Danny had left the pub, Liam's attention returned to Soccer Saturday. Or at least he was half-watching it.

There were so many thoughts racing through his mind. Callie, Robbie, the money, Danny, the police, the watches, the little black book.

He took a swig of his pint and tried to clear his head.

Focus on one thing, he told himself, or you'll go crazy.

He looked at the big screen. Scanned through the scores. A few of the so-called 'Big 6' were playing this afternoon, which felt unusual these days. It seemed as though broadcasters had an aversion to their games kicking off at 3pm on a Saturday.

So many games were on TV now. As a football fan, he liked to watch a few games on the telly. More than anything he loved watching games in person. There was no substitute for being there. But the way football was heading, there didn't seem to be any appetite to cater for the match-going fan. Kick-off times were all over the place, with no consideration given to away fans in particular. And the way this skewed the schedule had to have a bearing on the outcome of certain games.

At least being a Brentford fan meant the impact of all this so far had been minimal. The Bees had spent all but four seasons of their existence outside the top tier. But Liam cared about the game as a whole. He cared about his son's love for the game and what it would look like in *his* future. As a fan, he didn't like the way football was headed. Money was at the root of it all. Obviously.

That subject again.

Just like that, the diversion of football led him back to the topic that was causing him so much grief.

He sank the rest of his pint. At least he'd enjoyed a couple of beers this afternoon. They'd been in short supply over the last few months. He puffed out his cheeks and looked up at the big screen again. It was approaching half-time. Brentford were drawing nil-nil. The Premier League's 'big' teams were mostly ahead in their games. Arsenal and Man City were both winning, while Chelsea had a free-kick on the stroke of half-time. Ah, they've just scored. A handful of people dotted around the pub cheered, with a few shouts of 'get in!'

That was his cue to leave. Liam had a few mates who were Chelsea fans, but he couldn't abide the club. Another example of how money had ruined football.

It was less than ten minutes' walk home from the Crown, but he was in no hurry, despite the wintry chill outside. He didn't have anything, or anyone, to rush home to.

As he ambled back up to Uxbridge Road, he realised he'd barely eaten all day. With everything that had gone on, food hadn't been top of his list. Suddenly he was ravenous. There was a KFC on the corner and it always smelt amazing. He didn't think he could walk past without going in. And he still had a fiver in his wallet.

Ten minutes later, he'd jogged home, brown paper bag in hand. There was no sign of Callie and Robbie in the flat, so he grabbed his meal out of the bag and flopped onto the sofa. He tucked into his fillet burger and chips and took a gulp of the Pepsi. The latter tasted strange after his beers, but the food was divine. Just what the doctor ordered.

The little black book was still lying on the coffee table. He picked it up and ruffled the pages, sighing as he did so. It was still a mystery. As he threw it back on the table, he grabbed the remote.

They didn't have Sky, too much of a luxury. So he flicked on Final Score on BBC1. He could've scrolled through his phone, but he liked to watch the videprinter. It added to the excitement to see them switching to matches as things happened.

He knew the Brentford game was still goalless though. He had goal alerts on his phone and it hadn't buzzed at all. A good one for them to miss, after all, he thought, sadly. He'd convinced himself Robbie was a lucky charm. He'd been to three great games so far and since he'd started taking him, Brentford had climbed five places up the table. Liam felt bereft thinking about his son but told himself this was just temporary. Callie would come round and forgive him. And they'd work out what to do with the money. Everything would be ok. Wouldn't it?

The matches were reaching their climax, so he put the current situation out of his head. Focused back on the football.

"…*Huddersfield have made absolutely certain of the points here, with a well-taken penalty from Aaron Mooy in the 89th minute. They're now 4-1 up at Watford, with both sides down to ten men. This will be their first away win since they won on the opening day of the season, at Palace. And their first away goals since then as well. A crucial three points for Wagner's team today.*"

Back to Jason Mohammad in the studio. But not for long.

"…*Manchester City also have a fourth goal. And it's a second goal of the game for Raheem Sterling, who capitalised on Eric Dier's mistake to virtually walk the ball into the net. It's been a wretched day for Spurs, who've been given a masterclass by Guardiola's team.*"

The late goals were raining in. Mohammad switched to a game in the Championship. Derby had scored their second goal in the 91st minute, to wrap up a win against Aston Villa. The final scores were now coming in thick and fast on the videprinter. Then suddenly, they cut back to the match summariser at the Etihad.

"…*another late goal here, Jason! Purely a consolation for Pochettino's side against the Citizens, but what an absolute cracker. Christian Eriksen, in the 93rd minute…*"

A light bulb lit up in Liam's head. Something jogged a memory. What was it?

Oh God, it was the little black book!

He grabbed it off the table and flicked through the pages, trying to find the one he'd been looking at earlier that day.

There it was.

MD18

CS 4 Citizens, 1 Cowboy

So, Man City were the Citizens. He'd totally forgotten about that nickname. Spurs, Hotspurs, they were linked to cowboys. MD18 seemed so obvious now. It probably stood for Match Day 18 (a quick check on his Sky Sports App confirmed that it was). The Premier League had taken to using that term in recent years. CS? Not sure.

Finally, he felt he'd made some headway. He skipped back to an earlier page and deciphered another group of codes in the same way. Yes! He'd cracked it. Or at least he'd cracked a big part of it. There were still some elements he didn't understand, but he'd made the initial breakthrough. For the first time that day, he felt a little shred of happiness inside.

And then it hit him.

This was written in a book that Liam had stolen almost three weeks ago. And yet, this was the correct score for today's game. CS correct score, you bloody fool, not seeing what's straight in front of you.

Jesus Christ! What the hell was going on?

Danny drove straight home from the pub.

Tina had asked him to be back in plenty of time so they could go to the cinema for an early evening showing. As long as the traffic didn't build up too much on the way home, he should make it nice and early.

She wanted to see *The Shape of Water*. He wasn't that fussed, it sounded a bit boring. Despite the fact it was being touted for an Oscar in the States, it wasn't really his sort of film. The sci-fi genre didn't do it for him, but he'd chosen the last film they went to see, so tonight was her turn. If he didn't like it, he could always drift off to sleep. She wouldn't mind, as long as he didn't moan about watching something he didn't like. Or snore.

Danny liked suspense, crime or thriller-type movies. Even comedies, as long as it wasn't clichéd. He preferred British movies for the latter. The American sense of humour could be questionable at times. His favourite film of all time was American though. Pulp Fiction. An absolute masterpiece in his opinion. All the different storylines, intertwining and impacting on all the characters as a result. Brilliant. He could watch it over and over again. And he had. Many times. Much to Tina's annoyance.

He smiled as he thought of his partner. She'd been his absolute rock for the best part of fifteen years. He shuddered to think where he'd be now if he hadn't met her and if she hadn't seen the good in him. It was obvious actually; he'd either be dead or back in prison, again. Danny was stuck in a vicious cycle when they met. It was Tina's intervention that made him break the sequence.

She gave him a reason to go straight, as well as the encouragement to use his skills more productively. They'd lived together since 2005, buying a decrepit but large terrace on a nice road in South Ealing. Danny had soon turned it into a beautiful home, even with the amount of work he had on. He was a grafter after all. They loved living there.

They were both in their forties back then, so they didn't have any children together, but Tina had a son from her first marriage. Tom was thirty-five now and had given them three cherished grandchildren.

Tina had never spoken to Danny about getting married. They were happy as they were, so why change things? But, he'd noticed the look on her face when she was at other people's weddings. The little tears in the corners of her eyes. And if God forbid, anything happened to one of them, it just seemed, you know... Jesus! He could tell he was getting on a bit when he started thinking like that. But providing for your loved ones was important to Danny. So a few weeks ago he'd made a momentous decision.

He'd decided to propose on Christmas Day. They were due to go to Tom and Nat's for Christmas, so it was the perfect opportunity to involve them in the proposal. Normally he wouldn't dream of doing something like that in front of an audience. But he felt sure the answer would be 'yes'. And he wanted the others to be a part of it.

Christmas had been pretty shit for most of Danny's life. Since he'd met Tina though, it had become a special time for him. He felt lucky to have inherited this family and he wanted to make this Christmas the best one yet. One they'd treasure forever.

You soppy old git, he thought to himself. What has that woman turned you into? He smiled, secretly content to be a soppy old git. He wouldn't tell Tina that. Well, not yet anyway. Nine more days until he'd open his heart, lay it bare in front of their family. And pray that the response was 'yes'.

As he turned off Uxbridge Road onto Gunnersbury Lane, he didn't spot the dark-coloured saloon a couple of cars behind. Left indicator blinking.

Having given a cast-iron alibi to the police a few days earlier, Danny had put the burglary to the back of his mind. He was no longer a suspect. He would've preferred to keep his distance from Liam a little longer, not meet up today. But he knew the lad was struggling. Hopefully, he'd set his mind at rest.

He'd warmed to Liam from the outset. They'd met on a job together shortly after he'd left the army. He was confident and professional in a lot of ways and yet like a fish out of water in some respects. Danny guessed it was like that for a lot of servicemen and women moving into 'civvy street' for the first time.

He'd done a good job, so Danny kept his details for whenever he needed a sparky in the future. Good tradesmen were worth their weight in gold these days. He didn't have anything full-time, so Liam did a few casual jobs here and there when he was able to. A bit of unofficial overtime that worked for both of them. The younger man was newly married with a big mortgage and a kid on the way. A bit of extra cash in those early days helped keep their heads above water.

Liam was close in age to Tom, so Danny liked to think, in similar circumstances, someone would do the same for him. The run of bad luck that lad had endured over the last eighteen months had been unreal. He wished he'd been able to do more, but the burglary seemed like a helpful solution. Easy enough to get in and out, plenty to steal and the guy who lived there was a dick anyway; he deserved it.

He pulled into their street and looked for a spot. The Transit van meant he often struggled to get parked, but he spied one big enough not too far away.

As he locked up, he felt his phone vibrate with an incoming call. Blocked number. He answered it anyway. In his line of work, plenty of people rang from private numbers, so he couldn't afford to ignore any calls. The number of cold calls could be a pain, but he'd have missed out on some lucrative work otherwise.

He put the phone to his ear as he started to cross the road. "Hello?"

Silence.

"Hello?" he said again, with a slight air of impatience this time.

Distracted by the call, Danny suddenly realised a black BMW was heading towards him at speed. The driver must have seen him by now. But the car wasn't slowing down.

In the nick of time, he leapt out of the way. The car clipped the bottom of his leg, as he tumbled to the ground on the opposite side of the road.

"Argh!" he cried out in pain, as his body hit the tarmac.

The car had stopped about fifty yards away, in front of him, but on the other side of the road. The driver's door opened, but no one got out. An obscured face poked out and looked back at Danny.

"You stupid bastard! Why didn't you slow down?" He was furious with the driver. Fair enough, he hadn't been paying attention, but he was sure the car had been driven at him deliberately. If not, then it was sheer recklessness. This was a residential street. What if that had been a child? One of their grandchildren even?

Silence from the driver.

Gingerly, he got to his feet. His leg hurt like hell from the impact and he'd jarred his elbow crashing onto the ground.

As he did so, the car door slammed shut. The brake lights went off. The car pulled away, at speed. Disappeared out of sight.

In his shock, Danny hadn't thought about taking down the number plate. He didn't even clock the car model. He would live to regret that oversight.

-27-

Liam was still in shock. His mind was trying to make sense of what he'd discovered.

Was it a gambler, trying to predict the right results? They must be shit hot, he thought. That was a damn good prediction for today.

No, that was impossible. He'd found that book in the possession of the guy who was in charge of the Premier League. There was a ban on football betting within the game itself. Footballers could be suspended for a long time if they placed bets on teams they had no connection with whatsoever, never mind a game they could influence. That surely had to apply to those working for the football authorities as well? Especially the bloke at the top!

So if it wasn't related to gambling or betting, then what other logical reasons were there?

Liam had a nagging thought at the back of his mind. But it was so improbable that he let it stay there for now.

Instead, he started to go through the pages more methodically.

He went back over the codes that were immediately before today's 'result'. Realising MD was Match Day was a big help. His starting point was working out which date related to which Match Day. Or at least, which weekend, as the matches could be played any time from Friday through to Monday.

He then searched for which games were played that weekend and whether the code names matched up. He'd worked most of them out by now. Arsenal, their well-known nickname the Gunners, their 'codename' was Cannon. Chelsea, known as the Pensioners, they were OAP/s. Man City were simply their lesser-used nickname, Citizens. Man United, known as the Red Devils, were Lucifer. Spurs, as he'd already worked out were Cowboy/s. That left Scarabs, as far as he could see. As well as some initials scattered here and there.

Scarab, another name for a beetle. Surely not? He checked, it was. Beetle, beetles, Beatles. It must be Liverpool. Liam almost groaned at the clichés and wondered how it hadn't all jumped out at him earlier.

The next step was whether the results matched up. To his amazement, they did.

So, that left a couple of things. He still didn't know what 'O' and the two initials meant. And the 'End of 24th, 25th' and so on.

He skimmed through today's online match report, to see if he could shed any light on the missing pieces.

"Oh my God!"

He'd spotted something. He flicked back through a few of the matches immediately before today. Sure enough, his latest bit of code-cracking rang true. The two initials after the 'O' each time tallied with the initials of the match referee. Could that be significant?

Feeling pleased with himself, he tossed the book back on the table.

His mind reverted to Callie and Robbie and his mood immediately took a downward turn. How was he going to get them back? And what must poor Robbie be thinking about what was going on? He was confident Callie wouldn't have said anything to him about the burglary. It sounded like she hadn't even spilled the beans to Rachel. But if she stayed away for a while, at some point the truth might come out.

Liam thought about practicalities again. Robbie was due back at school on Monday morning; it was an hour's round trip from Rachel's house. Awkward enough for Callie to do it twice a day, but when it clashed with her shifts, would she expect Rachel to do that? His sister-in-law was a brilliant help when they needed her, but that was asking a lot. Surely that would mean Callie wouldn't be away for any length of time? Christ, would she want *him* to move out if she came back?

The prospect of being kicked out of his home made him briefly consider grabbing a fifty from the loft. Get some beer and vodka from the shop downstairs. Forget all his worries. Just for one night.

Something stopped him.

What if she came home tomorrow? If she just needed a night away to clear her head and get the anger out of her system? It was possible. What if she came back to find him hungover, the flat in a mess and evidence that he'd used some of his stash? That could be the final nail in his coffin.

Binning the idea of getting smashed, he jumped off the sofa, switched off the TV and made a start on some housework. He spent the next couple of hours sorting out the washing and giving the flat a quick once-over. His army days had instilled good standards in his cleaning and discipline. The place was gleaming. In the morning, he'd iron Robbie's school uniform and Callie's work clothes. Freshly laundered, ready and waiting in case their occupants returned.

His work done, Liam began to feel the hunger pangs again. He'd kill for a beer right now as well, but he knew they didn't have any after Callie's comments last night.

143

He stared into the sparsely-stocked fridge and searched through the cupboards seeking inspiration. Not a lot of choice. Some sort of pasta dish seemed the best option. Heating some oil in the frying pan, he chucked in a tin of tomatoes, chilli flakes and garlic powder. Pasta twirls boiled away in another pan. There was no garlic bread sadly, but he grated a bit of cheese over the top instead. Pleased with his concoction, he settled down in front of the telly.

Two hours later, he was still there, bursting at the seams. He'd eaten far too much, so he'd actually sat through the Saturday night dross, unable or unwilling to move. He repositioned himself now, but only to lay out across the sofa for Match of the Day. The iconic music began. The titles came up on screen. The running order mentioned the Man City v Spurs game. It jarred his brain once again.

He remembered something.

His dad had taken him to his first match just over 25 years ago. Brentford were in Division 3. As in, the division that was two below the top division. However, when they got promoted at the end of that season, they went into Division 1. The reason? The brand new Premier League. Launched amidst a fanfare of hype, it was the first season of this shiny new competition.

Liam was too young to comprehend that at the time of course. But as he'd grown up and looked back on those early days, he understood the restructuring. Brentford got promoted and suddenly, albeit in name only, went up two divisions. He'd always found it quite amusing, once he was old enough to fully grasp the concept of leagues.

So, the Premier League began in season 1992/93. He counted on his fingers. Twenty-five, twenty-six. This season was the twenty-sixth season of the Premier League.

144

His mind whirred.

The book was still on the coffee table, despite his earlier clear-up. He was going to take it with him when he went to bed. Hide it in his bedside drawer again. Just in case Callie came back early in the morning. He didn't want it to be the cause of reigniting their fallout, even if she knew nothing about it yet. He'd vowed to put it out of his mind until they got their lives back on track.

The highlights of the Man City v Spurs game came on. He couldn't switch off.

He grabbed the book and flicked back to the page where it read:

End of 26th

Citizens £93.3, Lucifer £54.2, Cowboys £41.7, Scarabs £39.8

He knew now what the codenames meant. So that was Man City, Man United, Spurs and Liverpool. What were the numbers all about though? He looked at the current league table after today's matches. Man City and Man United were first and second, but Liverpool and Spurs were lying in sixth and seventh place. He was baffled. Besides, the season was only halfway through.

Turning a few more pages, he looked at the previous one:

End of 25th

OAP £100, Cowboys £88.1, Citizens £86.6, Scarabs £36.6

He brought last season's final table up on his phone. Chelsea, Spurs, Man City, Liverpool.

It matched! Another part of the code he seemed to have cracked. It must be prize money or something, he thought.

Fuck, his head hurt. Trying to break this bloody code was a nightmare. What was he doing? And what did it matter anyway? His priority was his family. Not some stupid book! For all he knew, there could be a perfectly reasonable explanation for those

145

notes. He had to focus on what was important. Starting now. He tossed the book on the sofa, flicked the switch on the remote and took himself off to his cold, empty bed.

Unearthing the full magnitude of those particular scribbles was now some way off for Liam. But he would find out. Eventually.

-28-

Danny and Tina still went to the cinema that Saturday night, despite Danny being in a lot of pain.

He played down the incident as he didn't want to worry her. Told her that some boy racer had clipped him as he was crossing the road and he banged his elbow when he fell.

She wanted him to go to casualty and get checked out, but he didn't want any fuss. Sitting in A&E on a Saturday night was something he would've only entertained if it was a matter of life and death. The sights you saw in there, especially on a weekend. Kill me now, he thought. They'd have missed the film by going to hospital, never mind actually waiting there to be seen for hours on end.

So Danny put a brave face on things and limped his way through the evening, in more ways than one. The film was pretty much as he'd expected, although Tina enjoyed it. She was engrossed by the storyline, but it wasn't his sort of movie. He pretended to drift off halfway through, so he could have his thoughts to himself for a while.

He mulled over the events from earlier in the day. What the hell had happened? Did that guy deliberately drive towards him? Was it anything to do with the burglary? He suddenly remembered about the phone call. Was that connected in any way?

"Nah, you're being paranoid," he thought. It'll be some arsehole who hadn't been paying attention and then scarpered when they saw he wasn't badly hurt.

It'd been a few weeks since the burglary, so surely anything like that would've happened before now? He appreciated why he was the prime suspect. He'd had access to keys and the alarm code during the Elystan Place job. Even though there'd been a six-week gap between that and the burglary, he was bound to come under suspicion. He knew it would happen, which was why he put in place the strongest possible alibi.

Despite his past, the police seemed more than satisfied that the burglary was nothing to do with him. He'd been, pretty much, straight for the last fifteen years. They had nothing else to link him to the break-in. Besides, as far as they were concerned, hardly anything was taken.

He'd have to box clever for the next few weeks and months; make sure he didn't do anything dodgy. But he reckoned he was in the clear.

Still, after today's episode, he had a nagging doubt.

After the film had finished, Danny and Tina headed back, stopping off for a curry on the way home. It was great to have a nice Indian restaurant round the corner. They were regulars, so they always ended up with free poppadoms and the best table available.

"You okay, love?" Tina asked as they both tucked into their starters.

"Yeah, I'm fine. Bit sore that's all."

"Well, if you're still not right tomorrow, we should go to casualty."

"Honestly, I don't need to, there's nothing broken."

"How do you know? You might need an x-ray. You could have internal injuries or something."

He smiled at her concern.

"I'll be as right as rain by Monday, love," he said, hoping that would be the case, but doubting it. The pain in his leg still hadn't subsided and he was worried it was getting worse. Maybe he'd have to listen to Tina after all; she was normally the voice of reason.

The conversation had moved on by the time their main courses arrived. Tina was having chicken jalfrezi tonight. She generally flitted between that and a chicken bhuna. Whereas Danny was a lamb madras person. Every single time. Mushroom pilau, chilli naan bread. Job. Done.

"I can't believe it's nearly Christmas," said Tina. "You're happy we're going to Tom and Nat's aren't you?"

"Gawd, yeah. It'll be lovely to see them," Danny replied. I need them for moral support too, he thought. He suddenly felt nervous about what he was intending to do on Christmas Day

"I know it can be a bit manic in their house at times, with the three kids, but it's going to be so special. Libby's first Christmas." A little twinkle appeared in Tina's eye, at the mention of her only granddaughter. She was eight months old now, a little surprise package, unplanned but very much doted on. She'd completed their family in lots of ways. Even her two older brothers, Harry and Josh, were a little less boisterous around her. Danny chuckled at the thought of Libby developing her own character. She'd have her brothers wrapped around her little finger before too long.

"Well, it's not exactly a rest from work, darlin', but I love spending time with them. You know I do." Tina smiled, not fully appreciating what life with her meant to Danny.

A couple of pints later and they both walked, or limped, the short distance home.

An ordinary, middle-aged couple. Arms linked. Smiling. Content with life. Enjoying each other's company.

As they closed their front door, someone pulled out from the opposite kerb and drove away.

-29-

Liam lay in bed, gazing at the ceiling, thinking of everything that was going on.

He'd woken from his slumber a few minutes ago, but his alarm wasn't due to go off for another half-hour. He considered getting up and then remembered, there wasn't a lot for him to get up for.

He'd had a restless night. His mind was turning over and over, thinking about Callie and when – if – she'd be coming home. The house was so quiet without Robbie.

And then he remembered what he'd discovered last night.

What the hell was that book all about?

He groaned. He needed to stop thinking about that flaming book and get his mind back on what was important. He had to try and get his family home as soon as possible. He'd have to build some serious bridges with Callie, beg her to forgive him.

Despite the lack of quality sleep, he grabbed his phone, cancelled the alarm and dragged himself out of bed. Half an hour later, showered and dressed, he was feeling vaguely human again.

After a quick breakfast, he tackled the ironing from yesterday's laundry. Everything was ready for Callie and Robbie, should they return.

The separation was killing Liam. He and Callie had spent the majority of his army stint living apart, but this was different. This was the biggest argument they'd ever had and he'd never seen her that angry. She'd never walked out on him before either. They'd had rows, fallen out in the past, but this was a biggie.

Trying to keep busy, he remembered there was no proper food in the house. Callie kept an ongoing list on the fridge door, so he took that as his starting point. A quick scout around the cupboards gave him other ideas. Then he added a few essentials – beer, whisky, wine. Finally, he nipped up into the loft to grab a few hundred quid from the holdall.

"Fuck it," he'd thought. "I'm gonna spend some of it on things we need." After all, what was the worst thing that could happen now?

Liam left Callie a note, telling her he'd gone shopping and mentioning the clean clothes. He knew there was only a small chance she'd be home today. Even so, he didn't want her coming back to an empty flat, thinking she wasn't the most important thing on his mind.

When he got back an hour or so later, lugging a few heavy bags and a heavy heart, the flat was still empty. No sign of anyone having been there. Everything still in the same place.

Shit!

Everything *was* still in the same place. Including the little black book. Still on the sofa. He'd been so knackered last night that he'd left it there and gone straight to bed.

He dumped the bags in the kitchen and ran into the lounge. Phew, it was still there. He was annoyed at himself for leaving it lying around, yet relieved it hadn't disappeared. He wasn't sure why he thought it would disappear, but his mind was full of so many conspiracy theories right now. He felt as though anything could happen.

As Liam picked up the book, he thought about yesterday's result. He wondered what sort of odds you'd get on that. Individual match odds weren't particularly generous. But if you put a high enough stake on and you knew what the result would be… There was still potential to make a lot of money.

And then he remembered. It was far from the last entry in the book. As he made his way into the bedroom, to put it back into its hiding place, he flicked to the right page. Sure enough, there was an entry for the following matchday.

MD19

CS 3 Cannon, 3 Scarabs

A quick search on his phone confirmed Arsenal were due to play Liverpool next weekend. On the Friday night in fact. He checked out the current odds. A 3-3 draw was currently 40-1. Hmmm. He'd be watching out for that result with more interest than usual.

Cursing himself for getting drawn in again, Liam put the book away and focused back on the most important issue. Callie.

He'd been thinking about stuff as he wandered around Aldi earlier. He'd decided to send her a quick text and see if she responded. Just a simple message, so she knew he was thinking about her. Without any pressure to reply.

Despite pondering what to say while he put the shopping away, it still took him a good half-hour to compose the text. Liam agonised over the wording. And the length of the message. And then, once he'd finally decided on the content, he hesitated for a long time over whether to press send or not. He was in two minds. Was it the right thing to do or would it make things worse?

It was about midday by the time he eventually found the courage to send it.

Missing you.
Please forgive me, Cal.
I did it for us.
Love you, Liam xx

He held his breath as the message left the screen and confirmed it had been delivered. He waited, staring at his phone, willing it to spring into life. Letting his breathing return to normal again, he gave himself a reality check. If Callie was going to respond, it wouldn't be immediate. He had to be patient or he'd drive himself round the bend.

Callie never responded to the text.

She was already driving back to the flat when it came through.

-30-

Liam was making his lunch when he heard the front door open.

As he dashed into the hallway, he saw Callie, closing the door behind her. She was alone. His heart leapt and sank in the same moment.

An awkward greeting passed between them.

"How are you?"

"I've been better." Her response didn't sound like she was in the mood for conciliation.

"Are... are you staying?" Liam hadn't meant to say those exact words. They didn't sound particularly welcoming, but he was keen to know where things stood.

"I've no idea. We need to talk."

Or argue, he thought. He couldn't see them talking things through rationally. Not without her getting angry and upset again. It felt as if she'd been away forever, but she'd only been gone for just over a day. He didn't see what could have changed so drastically in that time to make her forgive him.

However, he was desperate to give it a chance.

"Where's Robbie? Is he ok?"

"He's fine. Rach is taking him out for the afternoon, while we talk."

Callie was quiet. Distant. Not her normal self.

"What does he think is going on? You haven't said anything about the burglary have you?"

"Of course not. He's seven, for God's sake!"

Good point, but still, said like the biggest put-down ever.

"Have you told Rachel?"

"No, she knows we've had a massive row obviously, but she doesn't know what it's about. And as for Robbie, I've tried to play it down. Told him we've just had a bit of a falling out like he sometimes does with his school friends. That there's nothing to worry about…"

Liam took a sharp intake of breath. Thank God! It was going to be alright after all, he thought.

"…because he's a kid and he doesn't need to be anxious about all this. But that doesn't mean we are fine. Far from it."

With that crushing blow, Callie made her way into the lounge and flopped onto the sofa.

Holding his emotions in check, he spoke. "I'm making a sarnie for lunch, d'you want one? And a brew?"

She nodded, a small tear forming at the corner of her eye. He made a hasty exit, to save her from breaking down in front of him.

As they sat and ate lunch together, Liam was surprised how calm the conversation was in comparison to Friday night. It was stilted at times, but Callie had obviously had time to think about things and compose herself. He was a little unnerved by it. He couldn't help thinking there was some bad news to come at the end of it all.

He couldn't dwell on the negatives though. He had to rescue this desperate situation, somehow.

By mid-afternoon, he was feeling a bit more positive. They hadn't snapped at each other in the last hour, so that was progress. And Callie appeared to be more understanding about the financial mess he'd gotten into, without blaming him for everything. After all, the events that had led to their misfortune

156

were beyond their control. Yes, Liam had made bad choices. But as his dad always said, good people sometimes make bad decisions; that doesn't make them bad people.

And then there was the burglary.

"I still can't believe you've done what you've done," said Callie now, so quietly, it was almost a whisper.

"I'm so sorry, Cal. Believe me, I am. It's not who I am. You know that."

"Maybe it wasn't you. Not before. But it is now."

"It was a one-off. It's not something I'm EVER gonna do again. And I know I got too greedy when I saw how much there was. But this is someone who can afford it."

"But it's someone famous, Liam! Or at least in the public eye. Surely the police are gonna be all over this case and want to solve it for that reason alone? Never mind the sheer amount of money that's involved?"

Despite his own doubts, he tried to address Callie's concerns.

"They're playing it down on the news. They've even lied about what was taken. Honestly, Cal, I'm starting to think he shouldn't have had all that stuff in his safe. He must be worried about the cops looking into it too closely. Another few weeks and we could be totally in the clear."

He could see her wrestling with her conscience at what he was saying.

"And then, what?" she asked.

"Then I need to work with a money launderer, so we can make it look legit. And a fence, to get rid of the watches."

Callie put her head in her hands.

"Look, Danny knows people who've done this before. Not with as much money, granted, but still with a decent haul. And they've gotten away with it. It is possible."

157

"It sounds like an absolute nightmare to me. I mean, it'll be a relief if we can pay off our debts, but why did you have to take such a stupid amount of cash? What the hell were you thinking?"

"I dunno. My head was all over the place. I was wondering "Why not? Why shouldn't we have a bit of the good life?" We've both worked our arses off all our lives and what have we got to show for it? A tiny flat and a mountain of debt we'd never be able to pay off. Let's face it, the only way we could deal with the debt would mean us losing the flat. So yeah, why not?"

Callie sighed loudly, frustrated that Liam thought he was owed this. "That doesn't mean it's okay for you to rob someone."

"I know. I know. I was desperate and this seemed straightforward. It *was* straightforward."

"Stealing it, maybe," she replied. "But that's only half of the job."

He nodded in agreement. If only he'd thought more about the other half when he was piling so much cash into his holdall.

She glanced at her phone to see what time it was. Nearly 4pm. She needed to make a decision.

Liam looked worried. Callie put him out of his misery, at least for the time being.

"I'm gonna ask Rach to bring Robbie home," she said. "She said we can stay with her as long as we need to, but it's not fair on her or Robbie trying to get him to school from her place."

He breathed again.

"But this doesn't mean everything's fine. We're all gonna be on hot bricks for God knows how long, thanks to your idiotic actions."

"I know. I can only say sorry so many times. I'll try and make everything right again. I promise." He was struggling to convince himself. But he had to do this. There wasn't an alternative.

158

He looked at Callie and thought he could see her face softening just a little. He wanted to hug her and tell her it would be alright, as long as they stuck together. However, he didn't dare get too close, for fear of rejection. It had to be her making the first move, or he could blow this altogether.

At that moment, a thought occurred to Callie.

"By the way, isn't Danny the main suspect in all this?"

"Nah. He's got a rock-solid alibi, so he should be in the clear. The police have given him a good grilling, but they've got nothing on him. That means we should be fine too."

That seemed to give her some reassurance.

Liam cleared the plates away while Callie rang Rachel. He'd get further into her good books when she got off the phone. Tell her about the washing and ironing he'd done, the shopping, the cleaning. Brownie points were about to be earnt.

She hung up on Rachel and turned to Liam, shattering his plan in one fell swoop.

"You'd better get the sleeping bag out of the loft. You're on the sofa."

"Dad! Why are you sleeping in here?"

Liam woke with a start, rubbed his eyes and remembered where he was. The sofa. His back ached as he sat up.

"Alright mate?" Thinking on his feet, he continued, "I was snoring and your mum couldn't sleep, so I came in here to give her some peace."

Apparently satisfied, Robbie ran out of the room and went to wake his other parent.

Not like him to be up with the larks, Liam thought, glancing at his phone and seeing it was only 7am. Robbie normally had to be yelled at to get out of bed.

He'd soon find out why he'd woken so early.

He heard muffled voices coming from the bedroom next door and then the sound of the door opening.

"Don't worry, we'll get it sorted," came the reassuring words from Callie. "But first, let's get you freshened up, ey? Pop your pyjamas on the bedroom floor, love, while I run the bath."

Liam wondered. Had Robbie wet the bed?

It had been a couple of years since the last time. When he first started school he struggled to fit in straight away. A lot of the kids he'd gone to nursery with had gone to other local schools, so he had to make new friends. That was hard when most of them already knew each other. The anxiety caused him to wet the bed regularly for a few weeks. They even saw their GP about it but were told it would rectify itself in time. And sure enough, once Robbie had settled in and got some new pals, the bed-wetting ended as quickly as it had begun.

If it had returned, that could only mean one thing. Their seven-year-old was worried.

Liam immediately felt guilty. This was all on him. If he hadn't got them into such horrendous debt. If he hadn't carried out that stupid burglary. Callie was justified walking out on him, but the upshot now was that their child was suffering. Poor thing, what must he be thinking, to be so anxious?

He dragged his aching body off the sofa and went to find Callie. His fears were realised, when he saw her in Robbie's room, stripping the bed.

Anticipating she'd blame him, he asked nervously, "Is it what I think it is?"

He braced himself. Waited for her to bite his head off.

Surprisingly, Callie just sighed and replied "Yeah, poor thing. He's mortified. He's that bit older now, that he understands things a bit more, so he's really embarrassed."

"I'll have to tell him about when I was in my twenties and pissed the bed on a regular basis."

"Er, that might have had more to do with drink than any emotional hang-ups," Callie replied. "The last thing I want is for him to turn to booze." Liam thought he'd almost detected a smile there. Instead of this tearing them even further apart, maybe the joint responsibility would work in their favour?

"Here, let me do that. You go and see to Robbie. I'll sort this and get breakfast ready."

"Thanks, love."

Love? Bloody hell, he'd have to get Robbie to wet the bed more often.

The three of them had a more leisurely breakfast than usual, due to the early wake-up. They chatted happily, asking Robbie what he had on at school and talking about their own days ahead. Neither of them were at work until later, so they decided to take him to school together. It was such a rare occurrence, Robbie was overjoyed.

It was about a ten-minute walk to school, though it was often double that with Robbie in tow. He'd get distracted by his surroundings and, as a curious kid, he always had lots of questions.

Robbie's excitement wasn't purely about both of his parents taking him to school though. Today marked the start of his final week at school before Christmas. School was much more fun just before the holidays. It was almost as if the teachers were looking forward to being off as well!

By the time he broke up on Friday, there'd only be two more days until Christmas Eve. Robbie still believed in Santa, although he'd become a little sceptical. How could he possibly get all around the world in one night? So he'd decided to try and stay awake as long as possible on Christmas Eve, to see whether he could spot him. One of his friends, Alfie, reckoned he saw him last year, putting something in his stocking at the end of his bed. Robbie was going to ask his mum and dad if he could have his stocking there this year; it might just work.

"You alright, mate?" his dad interrupted his thoughts.

Robbie answered with an enthusiastic nod and a huge smile.

"I was thinking about Christmas Eve. Can I have my stocking at the end of my bed this year?"

Robbie and Callie exchanged a glance. Relieved that, for now at least, they were returning to some sort of normality.

"Erm, yeah, any reason why?"

"All my other friends do that's all," he replied.

"As long as you promise to stay asleep all night. Otherwise, Santa won't come." Callie wondered whether this would be the last year they'd be able to keep this pretence going. Whether this was the final Christmas of innocence. Of believing.

Robbie nodded again.

They'd reached the school gates and Robbie spotted one of his pals in the schoolyard. He was itching to get away. Liam and Callie knew the drill by now. No goodbye kisses for their little one anymore. Not in front of his schoolmates anyway. A simple "see you later, have a good day," and he was off, not even looking back to wave to his parents.

Now they were on their way home, Liam's apprehension was growing. They walked along slowly, but with purpose, silence hanging between them. Alone again for the first time since yesterday. Would Callie revert back to angry mode? He wouldn't blame her. He couldn't blame her. But he was determined to get back on track. What he'd done was wrong, he knew that. But it was all for them. He couldn't bear the thought that by trying to save his family, he may have lost them.

It was Callie who broke the silence.

"Liam, I'm still mad as hell at you for what you've done. But we can't let this affect Robbie."

He muttered his agreement.

"We need to get back to normal. However you sort the money out, we'll cross that bridge when we come to it. If you go down for it, God knows what'll happen. But in the meantime, I want us to try and put it to the back of our minds. I want us to enjoy Christmas and I want Robbie not to worry about us, ok?"

"I'll do anything. As long as we're ok."

"I understand why you did it, I know you must have been desperate. But I'm still struggling with why you took so much. What was going through your mind?"

Liam shook his head. "All sorts to be honest. I wasn't thinking straight. And I knew it was a one-off. But I promise you I'll make it work. And if the worst does happen, and I end up inside, then I don't blame you if you want us to split up. It would kill me, but I understand."

"I don't want to split up with you. I want to bloody murder you for what you've done, but I don't want to split up."

And that was that. They walked the rest of the way hand-in-hand. Liam felt an unbelievable sense of relief. Callie had forgiven him.

Forgiven, but not forgotten.

-32-

"Thank God for that," Callie whispered, as she nipped into their bedroom.

"What's that, babe?" asked Liam.

"Sheets are dry again. That's three days on the trot."

Relief swept across both of their faces. The bed-wetting appeared to have stopped. Hopefully, it was a sign that Robbie's anxiety had also subsided.

Liam had moved back into their bedroom and while they weren't having sex yet, they were in a much better place. They made sure Robbie saw them being loving at every opportunity. Without going overboard. It looked like it had worked.

Christmas was just days away and Callie had sorted what she could for Robbie. The bigger stuff was from a charity shop. It looked almost new, so she hoped he didn't notice a couple of giveaway signs. Padded out with a few cheap things like chocolate, sweets and the obligatory satsumas, it would create a decent pile under the tree.

Callie and Liam had stopped buying gifts for each other last Christmas. They'd made a pact that, once they had things on a more even keel, they'd go back to treating each other again. But in the short term, it was no big deal. They had more important stuff to worry about than a nice new handbag or some aftershave.

Liam had the luxury of a day off today. He had a couple of shifts over the weekend and was on call on Boxing Day. Luckily, someone else had drawn the short straw for Christmas Day itself. They'd dropped Robbie off at school, together again, and Callie

165

was getting ready for her latest mid-shift when she shocked Liam with her idea.

"Are the Bees playing at home over Christmas?"

"Er, yeah. I mean the Villa game's on Boxing Day night, but we've got a 3 o'clock kick-off against Sheff Wed a week tomorrow. Why?"

"You don't fancy taking Robbie to it for his Christmas present, do you? I feel like Christmas is gonna be a bit of a letdown for him. I know we've tried hard not to focus on material stuff. But every time we've been in the shops the last few months, he's been besotted with that new Transformer thing. I reckon if we can give him some tickets for the match, he wouldn't be bothered about anything else. He's really getting into it."

"Not surprised, he's been to some cracking games! I reckon he's a good luck charm."

The penny suddenly dropped.

"Are you saying you want me to use some of the money in the loft?"

Callie looked guilty. "It's not gonna raise any suspicions if you just use one or two notes is it?"

It occurred to Liam she hadn't queried where he'd got the money from to do the shopping last weekend, but he let that go.

"Yeah, it should be fine. I wouldn't want to spend any more than a few at a time, but you're right, it shouldn't raise any flags or anything."

Callie smiled, happy at the prospect.

"Do you want to come too?" He was hoping she did. Callie used to go occasionally back in the day and always enjoyed it. She fitted in easily with his mates too. Only circumstances had prevented it over the last few years. It would be great to go as a family.

"Yeah, as long as I don't have to work. That would be nice."

"Do you mind if I ask my dad if he wants to come along? He really enjoyed it the other week."

"If you can come up with a plausible reason why you can afford it, the more the merrier." At that, Callie grabbed her bag, her phone and her keys, gave him a quick kiss and said, "Right I'm off, see you tonight."

Liam was starting to feel much more positive about things. He'd tell his dad he'd won £100 on a scratchcard and he wanted to repay his generosity for the other week. Spending a quid on that wouldn't worry his dad, it was hardly rash behaviour.

First things first. Make sure he could go.

"Hey, how're things?"

"Pretty good, son, can't complain. How's everything with you?"

"They're ok. In fact, a bit better than that, I've just had a little windfall. Won £100 on a scratchcard, can you believe it?"

"That's brilliant. In time for Christmas as well. You'll be able to treat that little lad of yours."

"Well, I was thinking of getting tickets for the Sheff Wed game, dad, and we were wondering if you wanted to join us? Callie's gonna come along as well, she hasn't been for a few seasons. I've got enough to treat you to a ticket. Just a little thank you for the other week."

"Ah."

Hmmm. Not the response Liam was expecting. He heard muffled voices. As though his dad had his hand over the phone and was having a conversation in the background.

Pete laughed on the other end of the line.

"We've already got you tickets for the game, son. It's Robbie's Christmas present, but we thought the three of you would enjoy going. So I've got us five tickets altogether. Sorry to spoil the surprise."

Liam was genuinely choked at his dad's thoughtfulness.

"Ah, dad, that's brilliant. Far too generous of you mind. Again."

"Well, if we can't spoil our only grandchild, who can we spoil? You keep that money for yourself. Give yourselves a treat. I'm sure you're overdue one."

Following a quick catch-up with both of his parents, Liam hung up. He suddenly had a thought. Why not buy Robbie the Transformer toy he'd set his heart on? Callie was happy for him to spend a bit of the stash after all.

Decision made. Later that day, he swiped a few more notes from the loft, just in case, and then jumped in his van.

The traffic was horrendous. Parking was an even bigger challenge. Friday afternoon, the last one before Christmas. Where had all these people come from? God, he hated shopping at the best of times, but Christmas shopping was a total nightmare. At least that was one benefit of being skint!

He was a man on a mission, but the hordes of shoppers meant it still took him over an hour to get sorted. The crowds, the queues, the general hubbub inside the shopping centre, it was enough to drive you insane. He was chuffed he'd got the present Robbie had set his heart on. Other than his satisfaction about that, the whole experience left him cold. Was he a scrooge? Maybe. He'd rather be that than actually enjoy this shit.

Battling through the heaving traffic again on the journey back, he switched the radio on to chill out. He was relieved he didn't have to pick Robbie up until later today. It was one of his pal's birthdays and his parents were taking him and a few friends for a burger straight after school. Poor kid, having a birthday so close to Christmas. At least Liam was under no time pressure as he inched his way home.

"What a fuckin' tune," he said, turning up the volume, as Rag 'n' Bone Man's Human came on. He joined in with the chorus, not a care in the world. As he drummed away at the steering wheel, the lyrics began to resonate. This could be his song. Pangs of guilt began to eat away at his good mood. Then suddenly, he caught sight of one of the posters in the window of Ladbrokes.

SCORE!

ARSENAL

TO BEAT

LIVERPOOL

2-1

£10

WINS YOU

£60

The Friday night game. It was tonight.

He still had £300 burning a hole in his pocket.

Should he?

His curiosity got the better of him. He flicked on his indicator and pulled over. Without realising it, he was about to set in motion a sequence of events. With tragic consequences.

-33-

Robbie was tucked up in bed, caught between excitement and exhaustion after the final day of term. He'd enjoyed his burger but was struggling to suppress the yawns when his dad picked him up. He'd gone out like a light earlier, so Liam was chilling, waiting for Callie to get home from work.

He relaxed on the sofa, watching TV, but keeping half an eye on the score on his phone. At half-time, Liverpool were winning 1-0. Not quite the predicted goal-fest yet. In fact, it was reported that Arsenal had only had one shot at goal all half, and that was off-target. Liam was beginning to doubt the little black book. Was it a record kept by someone? The future results, were they predictions, but then altered afterwards? Ugh, who knew? His head hurt trying to make sense of it all.

Seven minutes into the second half and Liverpool doubled their lead. Now he didn't know what to think. But a 3-3 draw still seemed unlikely. Liverpool appeared to be in control of the game. He was glad it hadn't been 'his' money that he'd gambled. He'd have been beyond devastated to have lost that amount of cash on a stupid bet.

He left his phone on the sofa and went to grab a beer from the kitchen. Callie would be home in a couple of hours, but shift working played havoc with her appetite. She'd have had a ready meal or something similar during her shift. She'd still want a quick bite to eat when she returned though, to stave off the hunger pangs during the night. It was difficult for her to switch off when she got back late at night. Any sort of emergency during her shift would play on her mind. It took a while for her to relax and drift off to sleep.

Liam had a quick look to see what he could rustle up for her coming home. Cheese on toast seemed the best option, so he sliced some cheese ready for later. Grabbing a can out of the fridge, he popped his head into Robbie's room. He smiled as he saw the almost star shape in bed. One leg was sticking out of the duvet and his beloved Spiderman figure was clutched to his chest. Robbie was fast asleep, so Liam gently closed the door and took his can into the lounge.

He picked up his phone to see if there'd been any more action in the match.

"Fuck. Ing. Hell."

He almost dropped his phone and his beer in shock.

Arsenal had literally just scored. Their third goal. They were winning 3-2. They'd scored within a minute of Liverpool's second, then netted another two quick-fire goals. In the six minutes since he'd been away from the sofa, Arsenal had scored THREE times. The 3-3 result was now more than a possibility. He felt like pinching himself.

Calm down, he thought. There's still a long way to go. Over half an hour in fact.

And then it happened.

Thirteen minutes after his return to the lounge, Liam's heart almost stopped beating. Liverpool scored again. 3-3. The bet was now on. Twelve. Thousand. Fucking. Pounds.

Still, nineteen minutes to endure, plus injury time. More than enough time for another goal.

He almost couldn't bear to look at his phone. And yet, at the same time, he couldn't bear not to. So for the next twenty-four minutes – including an excruciating five minutes of added time –

he remained almost motionless on the sofa. Occasionally his thumb would drag the page down to refresh it. He'd hold his breath, hoping, praying. And the minutes ticked away, agonisingly slowly.

Finally, the full-time confirmation flashed up on his screen.

FT 3-3.

Liam jumped up and punched the air with delight. He almost yelled "Get in!" before remembering Robbie was fast asleep nearby. Part of him wanted to rush into the little lad's room, wake him up and throw him up into the air in wild celebration. Luckily for Robbie, the adult in Liam took over. He tried to calm down. Breathe. Think.

The first thing that occurred to him was that it was, effectively, legitimate money. If he got paid by cheque, he could prove where his winnings came from, so he could pay off a huge chunk of his debts. He couldn't wait to tell Callie. After the upheaval of the last seven days, this would be a welcome relief. Some good news at last.

Ah. Hang on, what would she say? He hadn't mentioned the book to her yet. She thought she knew everything about the burglary. He'd forgotten to mention he'd also stolen an innocent-looking black book. That had just won them an utter fortune.

It dawned on him how lucrative the book could be. There were still lots of 'predicted' scores for future games, to the end of the season. It was alarming but, for now, he was prepared to use it for his own benefit. Morality could wait until they were back in the black.

He decided to tell Callie about the book. They'd agreed to be upfront about their financial problems from now on. No more secrets. He prayed she'd take the news positively.

He only had another hour to wait.

As soon as he gave Callie her cheese on toast, Liam decided he couldn't keep his news to himself a moment longer. With trepidation, he told her there was something he hadn't mentioned about the burglary.

"You've got to be kidding me! I thought you'd told me everything?"

He explained about the contents of the book. About the code and the future score 'predictions'. How his curiosity had got the better of him, driving back from getting the Transformer toy for Robbie.

"The Transformer toy?" Callie asked, puzzled.

"I'll come back to that," said Liam, realising there were even more explanations to come. "I need to tell you about this first. I had to find out whether the score tonight was going to be right. So when I ended up outside a bookies on my way home, I nipped in and put a bet on. I had some extra notes on me from last weekend and today, so I put £300 on."

"Three hundred quid! Christ, Liam, we don't have that sort of money to risk on a bet," Callie exclaimed.

"That's just it, we do. We wouldn't miss it if we lost. And that sort of stake isn't gonna raise any alarm bells anywhere, so it was safe to do it."

"Okay, I'll let you off. I'm presuming you lost?"

"No. The bet came in."

"Really?"

"Yeah. And best of all, the winnings are kind of legit. We can use them to pay off our debts."

"That's great, love," Callie said as she savoured the last bit of cheese on toast. She was yawning, eager to get into her warm, cosy bed. "How much did you win?"

They'd been talking in hushed tones ever since she got back, mindful of Robbie being asleep nearby.

But there was nothing hushed about Callie's response when he mentioned the twelve thousand pounds.

~~~~~~

Liam was knackered by the end of his shift the following day. He'd been up since the crack of dawn, despite not getting to bed until after midnight. Callie had recovered from her shock at hearing the winning amount, but it still led to a long discussion about 'the book'.

Initially, she voiced her concerns about whether the bet could lead the police to them. Or worse, if there was something dodgy going on, could it actually put them in danger? He'd managed to put her mind at rest, telling her that loads of people gambled the same and more every day of the week. It wasn't unusual and it was unlikely to raise any flags with anyone. Even so, he decided he needed to be on his guard, both now and in the future.

They'd both agreed he would pick out one or two results over the next couple of months and put a similar amount on those scores. He'd choose different bookies so he could stay anonymous. And drive a bit further away each time, to put some distance between home and the dodgy activity. But the thought of being able to pay off their debts in the near future, kind of legitimately, appealed to them both. The stash in the loft felt unreal, it was such a big amount. It might never be spent. But using a tiny fraction of it here and there. That could work.

Just one more shift tomorrow to get through, then he could start to enjoy the festivities. He'd been surprised by Callie's positive reaction when he told her about the Transformer toy. It seemed, like him, she wanted Robbie to have something special

174

at Christmas. He didn't get much the rest of the year, especially these last twelve months. And Liam hadn't gone against her wishes; they just didn't need to buy the footy tickets anymore. This was shaping up to be the best Christmas ever for Robbie. His dream toy, tickets to see his favourite team again and his parents getting back on their feet.

Despite his tiredness, Liam was making a small detour to the bookies after the end of his shift. He couldn't quite believe how much he'd won last night. It felt surreal. Though it still seemed more tangible than what was gathering dust in the attic.

The traffic was a bind, albeit a slight improvement on yesterday's jams. Today though, he couldn't care less. Today, he felt like the weight of the world had been lifted off his shoulders. He could've waited until after Christmas, avoided these queues. But he was desperate to get his hands on his winnings. To start getting his life back.

His haste would help to keep him safe. For now. Because right now, they hadn't found out about his first bet. Not yet.

-34-

Christmas Day 2017
Hanover Court, Uxbridge Road
Kick-off: 3:00 am

Robbie woke briefly as a shadowy figure left his room, gently pulling the door shut. He thought it might have been Santa who'd crept in to fill his stocking at the end of the bed. But it was dark and he was still half asleep, so it was difficult to make out who it was. He couldn't see whether he had his famous red suit on, which would've given the game away.

Robbie had been determined to stay awake to find out for sure if Santa existed. He'd managed to keep his eyes open for what seemed like hours. But as his tired lids gave up the ghost and closed, he drifted off, dreaming about the following day.

At 3am he attempted to wake his sleeping parents, to see whether it was time to get up and open his presents. Having only got to bed a couple of hours before, the answer from a drowsy Callie was a very definite "no, go back to bed." Liam slept through, snoring his head off.

At 5am he tried again. This time, Liam woke up and dragged himself out of bed, leading the excited boy back to his room. "Not before 7 o'clock, ok kidda?" he instructed, kissing his forehead and praying that he'd drift off until at least 9am.

At 7am on the dot, Liam heard a knock at the bedroom door.

"Daaaaaaaaad! Is it time now? Pleeeeeeeeaaaaase?"

Woken from her sleep, Callie looked at Liam, then at the clock and sighed. They were both knackered. But they were also

176

looking forward to seeing Robbie's face when he opened his presents. She threw the duvet off herself and into the middle of the bed. Opening the door to an expectant seven-year-old in the hallway, she smiled, "I guess this is where we have to get up is it?" Robbie nodded, clinging on to his Spiderman toy and jumping up and down with excitement.

"Tell you what, come and give me a hand in the kitchen first. I need to get the breakfast stuff ready, while your dad gets sorted. And then we can go into the lounge." Callie shot Liam a look. He knew what that meant, they'd planned this in advance.

Liam leapt out of bed, grabbed his phone and made his way into the lounge. He turned the Christmas tree lights on, dimmed the normal lights and stood back to admire. He had to admit, it looked great. It wasn't a huge pile of presents. They didn't believe in spoiling children, even if they could spend what was in the loft without a care in the world. But there was enough to create a sense of wonder and joy. And best of all, there was the one thing that Robbie had really set his heart on.

Liam heard Callie on the other side of the door now, saying loudly, "well, should we see if he's been?" That was his cue. He started recording the video on his phone, as Callie slowly opened the door into the lounge. He watched Robbie closely as the tree and its surroundings were revealed to him. Liam almost had a lump in his throat, seeing the look of awe on his son's face.

"He's been, mum! He's been! Wow!"

It was nothing short of magical and he'd caught it all on film for posterity. Liam and Callie looked at each other and smiled.

"Go on then, are you going to open your presents?" asked Callie, pushing her son forward towards the tree. She turned the lights up a little as she came into the room, now that he'd experienced the full effect.

Robbie darted to the pile of presents and sat cross-legged in front of it. He looked bewildered and turned to his parents.

"Which ones are for me?" he asked.

"They're all yours, son," Liam replied, regretting he hadn't bought Callie anything with some of his newly acquired riches. At least it was the same for both of them though and he wasn't sure she'd have appreciated the gesture. They were back on good terms, but he didn't want to jeopardise anything.

Robbie's mouth was agape at the prospect of all these presents. He didn't know where to start.

Callie read his confusion and plonked herself on the floor beside him.

"Why don't you start off with this one, love?" she said, passing him one of the smaller presents. They'd keep the Transformers toy until last; he'd appreciate it even more that way.

Twenty minutes later, having ripped open all but one of his presents and exclaimed "I love it!" for virtually everything, it was time for his final gift. Callie picked it up and surprised Liam by saying "And this one isn't from Santa, it's from me and your dad."

A wide-eyed Robbie looked shocked. He didn't realise you got presents from your mum and dad, as well as from Santa. Unbelievable, how lucky was he?

Excitedly, he tore open the largest present of all. Liam had begun filming again and caught the exact moment Robbie saw what was inside.

The little boy was so overcome with joy, he almost couldn't breathe.

"I...don't...believe...it. It's... it's... the exact one I REALLY wanted. This is the best present EVER! Mum, dad, thank you, it's brilliant. I absolutely LOVE it."

He hugged Callie beside him on the floor and then leapt up to hug his dad on the sofa. Liam's phone was discarded as he squeezed Robbie tightly. They'd treasure the video for years to come, but nothing beat the here and now. Why would you turn down a hug from your son, just to keep filming?

Liam and Callie looked at each other once more. She was beaming and he was sure he caught her with a little tear in her eye. He imagined he looked the same, although he'd deny it if she asked.

This was already the best Christmas ever. He couldn't have imagined this a little over a week ago when it felt like his world had collapsed. His parents would be surprising Robbie with tickets for the Sheff Wed match later. At this rate, he'd combust with excitement before they made it to the game!

They left Robbie playing with his new Transformer as they went to sort out breakfast.

"Hey, Happy Christmas, babe," said Liam. He pulled Callie towards him and gave her a passionate kiss. To his surprise, it was reciprocated.

"Happy Christmas, love. How special was that? Did you get it all on your phone?"

"Amazing, wasn't it? Yeah, I got everything up until the bear hug he gave me," Liam laughed. "What made you say the Transformer thing was from us?"

"I figured Santa gets far too much credit, to be honest. With the luck we've had this past year, I'm struggling not to be cynical about things like Santa. I know I need to keep the pretence going for Robbie's sake. But I reckon you and I deserve a little bit of appreciation from our boy too. You did the right thing getting that toy. Thank you."

Callie gave him another quick kiss on the lips and peeled herself away from him to dish out the cereal.

A few hours later, they arrived at Pete and Jackie's house in Gunnersbury. Robbie was clinging to his new favourite toy, while his parents were teasing each other about who was driving home later on. Lucy and Michelle commandeered their young nephew straight away. They were keen to see what this Transformers thing was all about. They both loved kids, hoped to have one of their own someday.

As Pete asked what everyone wanted to drink, Liam was taken aback when Callie said she was the designated driver. She winked at him, acknowledging she was in a good mood and didn't mind. No doubt he'd have to make the same sacrifice before too long, but he couldn't wait to chill out and have a few beers today.

He grabbed her as they went into the kitchen, squeezing her backside in appreciation. Callie turned and gave him a lingering kiss.

"Oi, get a room you two!" An apron-clad Jackie peered out from under the turkey foil, having checked her husband's culinary skills.

They both laughed. Liam's mum didn't seem the least bit frazzled, rising to the challenge of cooking the best roast dinner of the year. She'd had loads of help already from Lucy and Michelle, while Pete was in charge of the turkey itself.

"Happy Christmas, mum," Liam said, with a hug and a kiss.

"Happy Christmas, love. Where's my favourite little grandson? I've not seen him yet."

"He's in the front room. He's been kidnapped by his aunties," he said, chuckling. "I'll go and grab him in a sec, he'll want to see his granny."

"Granny? I'll give you granny, young man, I'm his grandma. It has a much nicer ring to it."

Liam surreptitiously swiped a chipolata off the turkey plate and popped it in his mouth as he stepped aside. Callie moved towards her mother-in-law, offering a warm hug as she too wished her a Happy Christmas.

"How are you, love? It's been a while since we've seen you."

"I'm good, thanks," Callie replied. "We've had the best morning with Robbie. Is there anything I can do to help?"

"It's pretty much under control, amazingly. I'm almost ready for my first glass of wine. Been looking forward to today, having everyone together. Are your mum and dad keeping well, Cal?"

Liam's dad tossed him a can from the fridge, sorted out the other drinks and then left the two women to catch up. The men went to see if Robbie had bored his aunties to tears yet, showing them everything the Transformer could do.

A couple of hours later and they were all well fed and in most cases a bit tipsy. Everyone still had their party hats on, though the gifts and naff jokes from the crackers had long since been discarded.

Jackie made a grand entrance to the dining room with her Christmas pudding. The flames licked around the top of the dessert from the brandy she'd poured over. The adults applauded the sight, while Robbie said "Wow", for easily the hundredth time that day.

As they cleared the pudding bowls away later, Jackie stood up and declared, "I think it's about time we did presents, don't you?"

Liam and Callie both squirmed in their seats.

They needn't have worried.

It turned out the present giving was aimed entirely at Robbie. Pete and Jackie were first up, passing him an envelope, as they all still sat around the dining table.

Robbie was unsure what it could be. He'd never had an envelope for a present before. He unsealed it and pulled out a Christmas card. That was strange. Grandma and granddad didn't normally get him a Christmas card.

As he opened it, three tickets fell out onto the table. He caught sight of the logo on them straightaway.

"Wow! Are we going to the match again?"

"Yes, lad, the five of us are going on Saturday. Even your grandma's coming," Pete advised his grandson.

"Wow, that's brilliant. Thank you!" He jumped down from his chair and went to hug them both. Their gift had had the desired effect. He was over the moon.

He showed Callie and Liam the tickets as he went back to his place at the table. He was beaming from ear to ear. He had barely taken his eyes off the tickets since they'd fallen out of the card.

"Sheffield Wednesday," he said to his dad.

"Yeah," said Liam, "hopefully it'll be another cracking game. You're a good luck charm, my boy."

Lucy did a subtle cough. A wrapped present had appeared on the table between her and Michelle.

"I think this one's for you as well, mate," she said, passing it across to Robbie.

His eyes lit up again. He couldn't believe how many presents he was getting today.

He tore open the paper and almost cried with happiness at what he saw before him.

"It's a Brentford shirt," he said. "It's my very own Brentford shirt." His voice was almost a whisper; he was overwhelmed.

"It certainly is," said Michelle. "Turn it over."

Robbie turned the shirt around and saw his name on the back, together with the number 7.

He leapt from his seat once more and squeezed his two aunties so tightly, they thought he'd cause them some damage.

"I absolutely love it. Thank you so much."

"You two, that's so generous of you, thank you," Callie said, as Liam nodded his agreement.

"Well, if we can't spoil our favourite nephew, who can we spoil?"

By the time they'd all finished the cheese board, Robbie was beginning to flag. It had been a long day for him, with so much excitement and elation. Though he may have been the master of his own downfall, with the aborted early wake-ups.

As the family members said their goodbyes, Liam scooped up his shattered son and popped him in the back of the car.

Pulling onto Chiswick High Road, Callie could see Robbie in her rear-view mirror. Damn, he was starting to fall asleep. It was only another ten minutes until they got home, so she desperately wanted to keep him awake.

"Hey, Robbie, have you had a good day?" she asked.

"I had the best day, mum. It was beyond my wildest dreams," he said, yawning the last few words, but still being understood.

"That's brilliant, son," Liam chipped in. "So, what was your favourite present?"

Robbie thought for a while. His parents waited in eager anticipation.

A long pause and then…

"The chocolate reindeer."

At that, he closed his eyes again, without falling asleep. He was thinking to himself, "How am I supposed to decide which present was the best? They were *all* fantastic." His three favourites were the Transformer, the football tickets and the Brentford shirt. But he got those from three different people. The last thing he wanted to do was upset any of them, by choosing someone else's present as his favourite. He loved them all equally.

So he chose the first thing that came into his head from Santa. After all, he wanted Santa to know he was grateful or he might not come back next year. And that chocolate was pretty yummy. Mum and dad would understand, he was sure.

In the front of the car, meanwhile, his flabbergasted parents drove the rest of the way home. In stunned silence.

Christmas Day 2017
Salisbury Road, South Ealing
Kick-off: 7:00 am

Danny woke early on Christmas morning. He was an early riser anyway, but today was one of the most important days of his life. The day of the proposal.

It hadn't really occurred to him what would happen if Tina said no to him. Maybe that was what had woken him from his slumber. The horror of that thought. Hopefully, it wouldn't mean the end of their relationship. Danny felt sick at the prospect.

He rolled over and looked at Tina, still fast asleep beside him, unaware of the torture he was going through. No need to wake her up though. He crept out of bed and went downstairs to make a start on breakfast. Bacon and egg baps. A bit of a treat, seeing as they wouldn't be eating their Christmas meal until mid-afternoon.

He checked his watch and saw it was just after 7am. Tina would happily sleep for another hour if she wasn't awakened, so he made a brew and tried to relax. He could use this quiet time to rehearse what he was going to say and do later that day. He wanted it to be perfect but worried his nerves would get the better of him.

Danny had considered popping the question on Christmas morning when it was just the two of them, at home. Breakfast in bed, followed by the proposal, producing the ring from his bedside. Tina would say yes and then the loved-up couple would head off to Tom and Nat's for the afternoon. They'd celebrate with endless Champagne and have the most wonderful Christmas Day ever.

Unless she said no.

By involving Tom and Nat, he'd have some moral support when he needed it most. They were ecstatic when he told them his plan, convinced she would say yes. The kids weren't in on it, of course, they couldn't keep a secret to save their lives. They would have asked Tina about it on the phone in advance or blurted it out as soon as they turned up on the doorstep.

If you want to keep something secret, never, ever tell the kids.

Danny was overthinking things, his confidence was faltering again. What if she did say no? No, it would be fine. Surely she wouldn't want to ruin Christmas Day? Especially for the kids? Not the reason he'd want her to say yes, but at least it made him bold enough to go through with it.

He spotted himself in the hall mirror as he carried his tea into the lounge.

How the hell could she turn down this fine figure of a man?

He was tall, six foot three; not so dark, more of a silver fox these days; and handsome in a rugged sort of way. Although his rugged looks would be more at home on a building site than a film set. Admittedly his middle had spread out as he'd got older. The last fifteen years had been much kinder to him than the previous forty-three, but even so.

As he looked closer, the doubts returned. Maybe he shouldn't have asked that question.

Danny moved away from his reflection and spent the next half hour going over and over the proposal. Finally, he began to feel more self-assured. She would say yes.

Right, let's crack on and get this show on the road, he thought.

No noise coming from upstairs, so he took a chance on Tina still being asleep. He unpeeled a few slices of bacon into one frying pan and toasted the muffins while it sizzled away. In a smaller pan, he started frying the eggs. Danny wasn't much of a cook but he could make a mean breakfast bap.

While everything was cooking, he made them each a mug of tea and then set out the tray. Once the baps were assembled, he tore off a couple of sheets of kitchen roll and checked he had everything. Ketchup! He grabbed the plastic bottle out of the cupboard and made his way carefully up the stairs.

He'd timed it to perfection. As he entered their bedroom, Tina was just beginning to stir. She rubbed her eyes as he appeared in her view. The smell of bacon cooking had begun to waft its way up the stairs and into her psyche.

"Happy Christmas darlin'."

"What a gem. I thought I was dreaming, it smells divine," Tina said, genuinely touched. "We were gonna make this together."

"Ah, I woke up early and couldn't get back to sleep. And you looked so peaceful."

"You must be excited about Santa," joked Tina.

If only you knew, Danny thought.

They devoured their breakfast in bed, in more ways than one. Afterwards, still flushed, they went downstairs to unwrap their presents. They didn't go overboard, a few little treats they were each expecting and one surprise. Nothing extravagant. Christmas these days was all about the grandchildren. At least that's what Tina thought for now.

A couple of hours later and with the ring box safely concealed, Danny and Tina set off on the hour-long journey. Tom and Nat had moved out to Hertfordshire when Harry was a baby. They wanted to raise their family in a more rural setting, but still have easy access to the city. Hitchin was the perfect solution. Tom had qualified as a solicitor and relocated with his practice. Meanwhile, Nat had secured the head of engineering position at the local college.

The success Tom and Nat enjoyed in their careers was reflected in the beautiful house they now lived in. With five bedrooms, Danny and Tina would be able to stay over and enjoy a good drink. They'd even have their own guest suite. A perfect end to a perfect day, Danny hoped.

Halfway into the journey, he pulled onto the A1 after Edgware. Tina began going through her mental checklist.

"We did pack the wine didn't we?"

"Yes, love, we packed the wine."

"And the Champagne?"

"Yes." As if I'd forget that, he thought.

"And we've definitely got all the kids' presents?"

"Will you stop worrying? We've got everything. I checked and double-checked, cos I know how much you fret about things."

Tina breathed a sigh of relief.

"Did you text Nat to tell her we're on the way?" he asked.

"I did. I thought about ringing them, but then I'd want to speak to everyone, so I thought it best to leave all that until we get there."

Danny smiled at Tina. As Tom and Nat's family grew, their house became more boisterous and chaotic. He knew she missed them terribly. Although they were only an hour away, she didn't

188

see as much of them since they'd moved out of London. Spending Christmas together, thankfully, was generally a given these days.

The A1 was quiet up to Hitchin, so even in Danny's transit van, it would be a quicker journey today. Although Tom and Nat lived on the west side of Hitchin, Danny still preferred to take the A1 and cut across. Their house was about half a mile out from the centre, but you didn't have to drive right through Hitchin to get there. So even when the traffic was busy, it was only a few minutes off the main trunk road.

Before too long, they pulled up outside Tina's son's house. Danny took a moment to admire it, not for the first time. It really was a stunning property. Tom and Nat had bought it about four years ago for less than £400,000. They'd turned it into the most fabulous, contemporary home.

A whitewashed exterior, with clean lines everywhere and modern, dark grey window frames. It had been extended significantly, turning it into a large five-bedroomed house. But the most inspired decision had been to create a beautiful open-plan living, dining and kitchen area at the rear. Bi-fold doors stretched across a huge expanse, opening onto a composite decking area. Beyond that, down grand steps, there was a lawned area for the kids to play in. All framed by mature trees at the bottom of the garden.

When the bi-folds were opened all the way across, it was the epitome of bringing the outside in. The dining table inside became an outdoor eating area, basking in the summer sun.

Obviously, it was winter now, but the house still retained its magic. Danny knew he was biased. He'd been involved in a lot of the building work. But he couldn't take the credit for the interior design or the architect's vision. He knew the house was worth around a million quid now and, in his opinion, it was worth every penny.

Before they could even get out of the van, the front door was flung open and two young boys ran up the steps to greet them. Harry was first to throw himself at Tina, closely followed by Josh.

"Happy Christmas, grandma!" they both chimed.

"Happy Christmas, you two. Blimey, how much have you both grown since I last saw you?"

Danny was next to get the wild hug treatment and a similar greeting. In the meantime, Tom had appeared at the kerbside, hugging his mum and warmly shaking Danny's hand. He was wearing the novelty apron the boys had bought him last year. 'King of Christmas Dinner' it said. Despite being a bit naff, Tina and Danny knew Tom loved it. He was the main cook in their house, not just at Christmas but all year round. Over the years he'd become quite accomplished.

"Right, it's bloody freezing, do you need a hand to get stuff in?" asked Tom.

"Of course," replied Danny. "Your mother's packed enough stuff for a week, never mind all the presents and the booze. Lucky I've got a bleedin' van son!"

Tina gave Danny a friendly punch in the arm. She grabbed a wine carrier and made her way down the steps with the two youngsters.

"For that, I'll leave you strong men to carry it all in then," she said. She had ulterior motives. She was dying to see little Libby and gasping for a drink. They'd be fine. It would only take them a couple of trips if they lugged in a load at a time.

The two men groaned but set about their task with good grace.

A couple of hours later and the whole family sat down for their Christmas dinner. The dining table looked like something out of a glossy magazine. This was Nat's domain. Despite her engineering background, she still had a creative streak.

There was a white and silver sparkling tablecloth, silky aubergine table runner and a silver stag candelabra at each end of the table. Chunky aubergine candles sat within a beautiful Christmas wreath centrepiece. Alternating chargers in silver and aubergine maintained the colour scheme. The candlelight bounced off gleaming wine glasses and cutlery. And aubergine napkins with ornate silver napkin rings completed the magical setting. Topped off with a silver ice bucket and very expensive crackers, it was simply perfect for what was to follow.

Nat beamed with pride as her guests remarked how stunning the table looked. She adored entertaining and Christmas in particular. She'd been back at work for a couple of months since her maternity leave ended. So she was more than ready to switch off for a few days and enjoy time with her family.

Still breastfeeding, Nat was taking it easy with the alcohol. But Tina had already downed a few glasses of Chablis before they'd even sat down. She could handle her drink. Even so, Nat subtly poured her a smaller glass of wine to go with her meal and placed a large glass of sparkling water beside it.

They were all about to tuck into their dinner when Danny tapped his glass gently with his knife. "A toast," he said, "to the chef of this amazing feast. And to family."

The food tasted as good as it looked and the happy family devoured their feast. Danny and Tina joined Tom in having seconds. Even young Harry had a few extra roast potatoes, chipolatas and turkey, it was so delicious.

Nat did the whole setting-alight thing to the Christmas pud but then took it back into the kitchen area to dish it up. Tom and Danny didn't question why. Although when Tina offered to help, Tom leapt to his feet and insisted she stay seated.

They served the children their desserts first. Only Harry liked Christmas pudding, so he got a small portion with some cream. Josh had profiteroles and drowned the cream-filled rolls with yet more cream. Libby was happy with her Petits Filous strawberry and banana fromage frais. She didn't know any better at her age.

As they brought the other four bowls to the table, Tom handed his mother her Christmas pud. Nat handed Danny his, together with a sly wink that was missed by Tina.

"Enjoy everyone!" said Tom, avoiding eye contact with Danny. He was nervous about what was coming up and he didn't want to put Danny off.

Having poured their brandy-laced accompaniments over the pudding, they all tucked in. Tina didn't notice the other three adults casting nervous glances in her direction. She was too busy enjoying her dessert. She loved a good Christmas pud. Wherever Nat and Tom had got this one from, it had done them proud.

"Ow! What's that?" she exclaimed. She'd bitten into something hard. She knew the old tradition of putting a sixpence in your Christmas pudding. She'd never known Tom and Nat do such a thing. As she removed the offending article from her mouth, she hoped she hadn't chipped a tooth.

"What is it, mum?" asked Tom.

"Not sure. Is it a sixpence?" Tina asked. "Have you done the sixpence thing, Nat, and not told us?"

Nat feigned surprise and shook her head. "Erm, no, I haven't. You didn't did you, Tom?"

192

"Nope. It's not a foreign object is it, mum? I know a good solicitor if it is," he laughed and the others laughed with him. Apart from Tina, who was now getting concerned at what had been in the pudding.

"It looks like a sixpence, just a bit bigger. But it's too shiny for that. Hang on, let me rub it and see… It's got some words on it."

As Tina rubbed away the pudding remnants from the shiny silver disc, she didn't realise that Danny had got out of his seat. She noticed him, now that the message on the disc was becoming clearer. Thinking he'd dropped his napkin, or was getting another beer, she saw him now, next to her. Down on one knee. That'll be painful, she thought, he had dodgy knees.

Then she looked back at the disc and saw what it said.

"It says… Oh my God! It says, 'Will you marry me?'" Tina said in shocked tones. She returned her gaze to Danny. He now had a ring box open, with the most beautiful sapphire and diamond ring on show.

Danny took a deep breath and said his rehearsed words. "Tina, my darlin', you make me so happy and I want to spend the rest of my life with you. Will you do me the honour of being my wife?"

Stunned silence, shock and uncertainty hung in the air. Tom and Nat held their collective breath. Harry and Josh looked on in wide-eyed amazement, completely silent for once. And little Libby gurgled, blew a raspberry and then laughed. Meanwhile, Danny's knee was now killing him, as was the wait for a response.

Tearing up, Tina finally blurted out her answer.

"Of course I will, you romantic old bugger! I can't think of anyone else I'd rather spend the rest of my life with. Now get up off your knees before we need to call an ambulance."

193

Danny got slowly to his feet, his knee cracking back into place. He embraced Tina, as much in relief as with love. Finally, he'd done it and she'd said yes. He was elated.

As they hugged, Tom popped the cork on a bottle of Champagne that had been waiting for this moment. Like Danny, he was relieved his mum had said yes, although he'd have been shocked if she hadn't. She and Danny were one of life's great couples, even better than the sum of the parts.

Tom had been nervous when he'd first met Danny. He was only five when he'd lost his dad and it'd just been him and his mum for the next fifteen years. So it was strange having another man around and even more so when Tina told him about Danny's past. But he came to realise his mum had helped Danny turn a corner and everyone deserves a second chance. He grew to love him over the following fifteen years; he couldn't think of a better man to marry his mother.

He looked over at Nat as he poured the fizz into glasses. She too had a huge grin on her face. She too loved Danny and was delighted at this outcome. The kids were back to being their noisy selves again. They hugged their grandparents, without really understanding what all the fuss was about. Libby threw her yogurt pot up in the air and cheered as it landed perilously close to the candles.

"To the happy couple," Tom declared, overjoyed that he got to make a toast as well.

As they snuggled up in bed later that night, Tina had to admit she was a little sozzled. She'd sunk a fair bit of Champagne after the shock proposal. Danny had gone onto red wine after the second toast of the day, so he wasn't fit to consummate their engagement either. But the two of them were blissfully happy. It had been the most perfect day. Tomorrow, they'd blow their hangovers away with a Boxing Day walk. And then reluctantly head back late in the afternoon.

Blissfully happy.

-36-

Danny and Tina stepped through the door and immediately knew something was wrong.

Tina gasped as she saw the hall mirror on the floor, smashed to pieces. The drawers in their console table were open, with keys, papers and other items strewn all over the floor.

"Oh my God! Wha……," the words stuck in her throat. The realisation swept over her. Someone had been in their home while they'd been away.

Danny immediately dumped the bags they'd been carrying and stepped in front of her.

"Wait here, love. I'll have a scoot around. Need to make sure they're not still here."

He hoped they were. Danny was fuming inside. He wanted to throttle them.

Like a sniffer dog at work, he dashed into all the downstairs rooms, glancing around to check for any signs of life. He was about to head upstairs to do the same when he saw Tina reaching down to pick up the contents of the console drawers.

"Don't touch anything. We'll call the police once I've checked upstairs, so we need to leave everything as it is. Okay, love? Why don't you nip out to the van and get the rest of the stuff?"

"What if someone's up there?" she said, almost whispering with fear.

"Well then, I'll be having a little word with them by the time you come back in," he said. His body grew in stature alongside his anger as he made for the stairs.

Tina knew Danny could look after himself. He was a giant of a man and his time in the nick meant he was no shrinking violet. But the intruder or intruders could have a knife or even worse. If they were cornered, who knew what they might do to try and escape?

Against her better judgement, she trusted Danny to handle things and dashed back out to the van. Luckily it was just one more trip. The majority of what they'd taken up to Tom and Nat's had been for the day itself or presents for them all.

As she made her way through the front door, Danny came bounding down the stairs.

"Right, love, you can relax, there's no one in the house."

Tina breathed a sigh of relief, but her mind moved on to the next issue. She could see Danny was perplexed.

"What have they taken?"

He shrugged, replying, "Buggered if I know. There's nothing that jumps out yet, but I've only had a quick look in every room. Do you want to walk round with me and see if we spot anything?"

She nodded, grateful for a reassuring hug from Danny. She hadn't realised she was shaking.

"Don't worry, love, we'll get some extra security sorted. I'll never let anything happen to you."

Tina nodded again and brushed away tears. She gave herself a mental shake, trying to pull herself together. She'd never been burgled in her life. She felt violated at the thought of someone being in their house when they weren't there. Going through their personal things and smashing stuff to pieces. Quite a lot of stuff by the looks of it, now that she'd ventured into the lounge.

It was the ultimate irony, of course, bearing in mind what her future husband used to do for a living. She knew Danny felt remorse for what he'd done in the past. It had been done out of desperation and he hadn't been helped by the system, but he still felt guilty. He realised he'd caused the fear and upset to other people that Tina was feeling now. Even if he hadn't caused this sort of mindless mess.

"Oh, God, Danny, look what they've done," Tina said, seeing the carnage in their living room. She felt the tears well in her eyes again. "Bastards," thought Danny, "was there any need for this?"

The sofa had been pulled to pieces, both seat and scatter cushions removed and thrown around the room. The TV had been tipped over, the screen smashed all over the carpet. The doors of the wood and glass dresser were open, all the display items cleared out. Recklessly discarded on the floor. Scores of framed photos, treasured family memories, glass shattered everywhere. Thankfully, the photos themselves appeared to be undamaged. The drawers at the bottom of the dresser had been treated in the same way. Papers, cards, CDs, DVDs and games everywhere. The bigger items seemed to have been opened up, the smaller items simply tossed onto the floor.

They went into the kitchen diner and saw a similar scene of devastation. It was heartbreaking. It was clear this was where the burglars had entered their property. The French windows had been jemmied open.

Despondent, Danny and Tina trudged upstairs and went through the three bedrooms and bathroom. The picture up here was the same as below; nothing had been left untouched. Tina felt sick at the thought of them going through her drawers, rifling through her underwear. It was now scattered across the bed, the floor and the top of the drawers.

Having completed the recce of their desecrated home, they made their way back downstairs.

"I need a brew darlin', my nerves are shot," said Tina, as they walked back into the kitchen.

"Ok, try and touch as little as possible and I'll get on to the police."

Danny didn't expect the police to show much interest. He knew burglaries were low on their list of priorities; successful detection was minimal. So he was prepared for them to fob him off. At the most, he knew they'd probably show up, take some fingerprints if there were any and details of what was missing. Then they'd give them a crime number so they could claim on the insurance. And they'd never hear from them again. Probably what happened to Mitchell, he thought, grimacing.

But something was bugging Danny. Someone had known they weren't there over Christmas. They'd gone through every room in their house, not caring what they smashed along the way. And they'd had every opportunity to take the more expensive items they owned. But that was just it. There didn't appear to be anything missing. Nothing. Nothing had been stolen.

30 December 2017
Brentford vs Sheffield Wednesday
Griffin Park, London
Kick-off: 3:00 pm

Robbie's fourth Brentford game involved three generations of the family once again. This time there were five of them, as his mum and his grandma came along for the Christmas treat. He knew his mum used to go when he was little and even before he was born. Apparently, it was a long, long time since his grandma had stepped foot in Griffin Park.

So far, the festive period had been a good one for the Bees. They'd won away at Norwich, the day before Christmas Eve. Then beaten promotion-chasing Aston Villa on Boxing Day. Today's game was against one of the bigger teams in the Championship, Sheffield Wednesday. That didn't mean Brentford had anything to fear. They were already four points ahead of the Owls and pushing towards the play-off places. A win today would set them up nicely for their first game of 2018. That was arguably their toughest of the season, away at high-flying Wolves.

It occurred to Liam that Brentford had been in a rich vein of form ever since he'd started taking Robbie to the matches. They'd only lost twice in twelve league games and Robbie had seen some cracking matches. There'd been loads of goals and he'd yet to see them get beaten. He knew that wouldn't last forever, but prayed it wasn't today. He wanted today to be perfect. With his mum, dad and Callie along for the ride, it would be fantastic for the whole family to celebrate a win.

It was an unseasonably mild day after the colder temperatures of the last few days. The sun was even trying to burst through the clouds. But it was winter nevertheless and it would still be dark halfway through the match.

Liam, Callie and Robbie had caught the train today. It was another new experience for Robbie, especially travelling with some of the away fans. The train wasn't rammed, as they were heading across earlier than usual. But even so, it was good-natured banter between the two sets of fans, no doubt helped by the enduring Christmas spirit.

As a special treat, they were going to have a pub lunch. They were meeting up with Pete and Jackie in The Griffin, another one of the 'four corner' pubs. Brentford laid claim to being the only football club in the entire league to have a pub at each corner of its ground.

The New Inn, Liam's usual match-day pub, was diagonally opposite. But The Griffin had been his dad's favourite for as long as he could remember. It was a decent pub for a pint for sure. And the food was good. Their burgers in particular had become legendary since the new owners took over a few years back.

Liam had told his parents he'd had a decent win at the bookies and wanted to treat them both to lunch. A thank you for the match as well as having them over for Christmas Day. Pete had been a little surprised, even worried, at the thought of his son gambling. Liam soon put his mind at rest, by telling him he didn't bet much, but this was a hot tip and he'd be using the majority of the money to help pay off their debts. He felt guilty telling his parents he'd used some of his scratchcard winnings to place the bet. But his dad wouldn't have bought him risking any of 'his' cash on gambling; not in his current financial situation anyway.

The family of three walked into The Griffin, a pub that was as familiar to Brentford fans as it was to film buffs. Liam held a slight grudge against its most famous screen appearance, in the film Green Street. It was a movie about football hooligans, focused on West Ham's fans. Didn't they have their own pubs in East London?

They saw Pete and Jackie already sat down and grabbed some drinks, while Robbie sprinted over to see his grandparents. He was desperately trying to wrestle out of his coat to show them he was wearing his new Brentford top. This would be its first proper outing, although he'd worn it around the flat at every opportunity since Christmas. Today brought a whole new meaning to the phrase 'match-worn shirt'.

Robbie had been chatting away incessantly from the moment he sat down, but once they got their food he began to people-watch as he ate. He was fascinated by the characters in there. The buzzing noise levels, the occasional songs that would break out. But best of all, the familiarity with which everyone greeted each other. He felt like one of them now. A real football supporter. This was his fourth game after all.

Lunch was a real treat for Robbie. His experience of eating out was generally a McDonald's or KFC, not decent pub grub like this. Fair enough, he'd still chosen a burger, but this was no fast-food chain patty. This was a proper burger, and even the children's portion was enormous.

When the bill came, Pete wouldn't let Liam pay for everything.

"It's too much, son. It's over a hundred nicker. At least let me get the drinks." He wouldn't take no for an answer and chucked £30 on the table. Liam couldn't refuse. He didn't want his dad to think he'd got reckless with his cash and grill him on how much he'd actually won. If he began to question what the stake was and what odds he'd got, it could escalate from there. What had he actually bet on and why was it such a sure thing? Nah, too risky, so he accepted the gesture with good grace.

Walking out of the pub towards the Braemar end, Robbie was happy they'd be sitting in his 'lucky stand'. This was where he'd seen Brentford win for the first time, against Leeds. He was keeping everything crossed they could do it again today.

Once they were sat down, Robbie ended up in the middle, flanked by the two women, with their husbands on each side. Ripples of applause rang around the ground as the players came out to warm up. Cue Robbie telling his mum and grandma who they all were and which ones were his favourites. He knew so much already for a seven-year-old.

"What do you think the score is gonna be today?" his granddad leant across and asked.

Robbie considered this for a moment. "3-1 I reckon, granddad."

Liam understood his son's logic. In the three games he'd been to so far in his short life, Robbie had seen his team score three goals each time. He'd be happy with a scrappy 1-0 win, to keep their good run going. But 3-1? Yeah, let's do it Bees.

They didn't quite manage three goals this time, but the margin of victory matched Robbie's prediction. Two-nil was the final score, although it could've been more. It was a really confident display from Brentford, with a goal in each half. And when Jozefzoon scored the second in the 83rd minute, Robbie was beside himself.

"Mum! Mum! Look!" He was already on his feet, jumping about and cheering the scorer. He unzipped his jacket and tossed it back to reveal the number on the back of his shirt. By putting his age on his very first Brentford top, his aunties had unwittingly created a hero. And that player seemed more than capable of fulfilling that role. A hero to a little seven-year-old boy who was having the time of his life. Stood there under the floodlights. Three generations. Celebrating together. Magic.

Full time: Brentford 2 Sheffield Wednesday 0

-38-

"Thanks for dialling in, everyone. I just wanted to give you a quick update."

"I hope it's good news." The menacing one was first in with a comment to the chairman.

"Hmm. Well, we haven't yet tracked down the black book or any of the valuables."

"Doesn't sound like much of an update to me," voiced another of the callers.

With an air of annoyance, the chairman continued.

"As you know, our men have been trailing the builder that worked at Mitchell's house. They haven't seen anything to date to confirm our suspicion that he's in on the burglary. But they managed to carry out a thorough search of his house on Christmas Day. They turned it upside down and didn't find a single piece of evidence. No cash, no watches, no black book. Nothing."

"Could he have it all stashed somewhere else? A business address or something? A storage facility?" another of the callers chipped in.

"It's possible, of course. But there's no record of any business premises and he hasn't visited anywhere remotely suitable over the last few weeks. So we could be in the clear there."

That was the good news over with, thought the chairman. Now for the sticky part.

"However, we have had notification of a fairly sizeable bet on one of our results from the black book."

He paused, waiting for the abuse to pour in. To his surprise, it wasn't immediate.

"How much?"

205

"Three hundred."

Gasps.

"Thousand?"

"No! Three hundred pounds."

"For Christ's sake, that's nothing!"

"Well, obviously in our world it is." A murmur of derision came through the phone lines. The chairman continued, "but on a 40-1 bet, it's still fairly unusual."

"Can we get hold of them when they pick up their winnings?"

"It's already happened I'm afraid."

Murmurs again.

One of the callers spoke. "I'm not concerned about that level of betting. It could be anyone. Probably unconnected to all this."

"Maybe so and hopefully that's the case. But it was a London betting shop, so we shouldn't dismiss it completely."

More murmurs.

"Are we keeping up the surveillance of this builder?" another caller asked.

"I was going to stand them down. Unless you have any objections to that?"

"I vote we suspend the surveillance and keep a watching brief on any further betting activity. That should tell us whether someone really has the book and has worked things out."

"Ok, does everyone agree with that course of action?"

The chairman went through each of the callers in turn, with all in varying degrees of agreement.

"What do we think if this all dies down? Do we let it drop? Forget the money and the watches and just carry on as we were?" a new voice in the conversation piped up.

"It pains me to let them off, but I'd say yes. I'd be inclined to think we've got away with it."

"No thanks to bloody Roberts. If he's going to stay in the job, he's going to have to buck up his ideas."

"Yes, we'll address that issue as and when we get through this. Right, gentlemen, I'll be in touch when necessary. In the meantime, happy new year to you all and let's hope 2018 brings us health, happiness and a lot more wealth."

Sarcastic laughter from the other end of the phone.

The chairman hung up and let out a huge sigh of relief. They had a stay of execution. For now.

PART TWO

-39-

Liam had had his best Christmas in a long time. But 2018 began in the worst possible way when he was laid off. His company had lost a big contract and missed out on another, so they needed to make cutbacks. He'd only worked there for a few months, so there was no safety net, no redundancy payment. Just one week's notice. It would have been catastrophic, were it not for the stash in the attic and his recent betting activity.

Nevertheless, it prompted him to seek out the fence that Danny had suggested. He'd waited patiently, but it was now over a fortnight into the new year. He felt compelled to take action, to start turning his haul into ready cash. He needed the money.

So, a few days before he was due to place the second bet, Liam rang Karl and arranged to meet at a pub a few miles away. It was a pub that had seen better days. But from Liam's perspective, it was empty and non-descript. In other words, he could make sure he wasn't being followed.

He walked into the once-loved pub and ordered a pint. Sat at a table not too far from the bar. And waited.

He didn't imagine he'd be handing all the watches over in the pub. It was too open, too exposed. But he could give this guy the lowdown, show him the two he had on him and then show him the rest elsewhere. He wanted rid of them. They were so valuable and yet completely useless in his possession. They had to be worth at least half a million quid but he'd be over the moon to get twenty per cent of that. Anything more would be a bonus.

Liam was shocked when he saw Karl walk in. He was an ordinary-looking, middle-aged bloke, around five foot five, with a potbelly and a thinning scalp. He must have had a fair old fortune stashed away. But he looked more like a fat Ian Beale than a Phil Mitchell-type of character.

He comforted himself with the fact that Danny recommended him. He wasn't a fence through chance, he had to be good at it. So Liam had to trust him, despite first impressions.

Once Karl had sat down, and settled himself in, Liam calmly stood up and walked over to his table.

"Anyone sitting here, mate?" he asked.

"Nah, feel free," was the casual response.

He sat down opposite Karl, completely out of his comfort zone and yet, quite confident in what he was about to do.

"Jimmy, yeah?" Karl asked, making sure he was the person he was planning to meet. Although he was fairly certain that wasn't his real name.

"Yep." Liam had decided to use an alias. He didn't want his name being bandied around the underworld. Liam wasn't that common a name, so it wouldn't take a genius to join the dots further down the line.

"Karl. Good to meet." And then, dropping the volume down ever so slightly, he said, "So what have we got?"

"I've got 43 watches, different makes, all top quality brands. All genuine." Liam surreptitiously passed Karl a list of all the watch brands. Karl took his time to study them, keeping the atmosphere casual.

"Jesus, you've got quite a collection there. I could give you fifty grand."

"Get to fuck. They're worth more than ten times that. Even twenty. Get serious, or I'll go elsewhere."

212

"They might be, pal, but you have no idea how difficult it'll be to get shot of them. And how long it'll take. So that's all built into my offer. I'll give you eighty-six grand. Two grand a watch. That's a great deal."

"Fuckin time-waster." Liam stood up and looked to be on his way out of the pub.

"Woah! Don't be so hasty, pal." Karl looked contemplative. He blew his cheeks out. Thought about what Liam had to offer.

"Right. If they're all genuine, which I'll need to check out, I can give you a hundred and ten grand, mate. But that's my final offer. It's not worth the hassle beyond that, believe me. They don't sell for anywhere near their proper value. They're too hot for that. And I'm the one who'll be taking the heat."

Liam thought about it. Tried to disguise his delight at the level of offer. Stalled. Finally, a few moments later, sensing Karl was gagging for an answer he responded.

"They're worth way more than that, mate, but let's do it. I just want shot of them."

The two men shook on it. Inwardly, both were happy with the deal, but one was a sight happier than the other.

"Have you got a couple on you, like we spoke about?"

"Yeah." Liam took a small padded envelope out of his jacket pocket, placed it on the table and slid it across towards Karl.

"Right. I'll have a good look at these and get back to you in a couple of days. If they're good, we can sort out handing over the rest after that. But I'll still need to check them all before I give you the dough."

Liam looked hesitant.

"Don't panic, I'm good for it. A deal's a deal. If any of them are fakes, we can renegotiate the price, but if they're all legit I'll get you the money straight away."

~~~~~~

As soon as Karl realised the watches were genuine, he didn't hang around; he rang 'Jimmy' back the very next day. He hoped his keenness didn't betray him and that Jimmy wouldn't try to renegotiate. Karl could be on to a fortune if they were all high-end luxury watches like these two.

Luckily, Jimmy wasn't interested in bartering.

"I can meet up tomorrow, pal if that works for you?"

Liam was able to make the time Karl suggested and was ecstatic things were moving along quickly. He was eager to get rid of the watches. They were damning evidence and he had no desire to hold onto any of them. He was a little unsure about the location for the handover, an industrial estate near Wembley. It seemed a little risky. But he kept reverting to the fact Karl had so far been true to his word. And he'd been recommended by Danny. That was good enough for him.

As he pulled into the car park the following day, Liam spotted the battered blue Mercedes. Parked up in a secluded spot, far away from any CCTV cameras. There were no other vehicles in the immediate vicinity, so he pulled into the space next but one to Karl's car. By now, his heart was beating faster than usual; this was another thing way out of his comfort zone. He prayed that even if Karl did do the dirty on him, he would at least stop short of roughing him up. Not that he could do that himself. He didn't look capable of hurting anyone but a child, maybe a woman. But he was bound to have some heavies working for him.

He turned off the ignition and waited for the signal. Exhaling deeply, he grabbed the carefully packed cardboard box from the passenger seat and got out of the car. He tried to look casual as he walked across to the Mercedes. The back door was flung open from within and Liam ducked his head down to see inside.

214

"Get in."

Shit. He hadn't expected this. But he did as he was told.

"Don't shit yourself mate," Karl laughed, noticing the look of fear on Liam's face. "We just want to check it's all there and there's no sense in doing that in the open air."

He relaxed, jumped into the back seat and handed over the box. Karl was sat next to him, while his two strong-arms were in the front.

Karl opened up the box and was entranced by the contents, as a raft of high-value items shone back at him. He tried not to look too elated. He knew they'd be tough to shift, but he'd still got himself a bargain. In due course, he'd make a substantial profit on these beauties.

Having done a quick tally of the watches, he closed the box again and posed the question he'd been dying to ask.

"Where did you say you got them from?"

Liam squirmed. "I did a job in town. The owner didn't let on to the cops that he had them nicked, so I presume that makes your job easier getting rid of them?"

Karl was non-committal in his response. He didn't want to risk this Jimmy trying to up his price.

"There's a few out-of-the-ordinary brands in amongst this lot, to be honest. So that'll make it tougher. Plus the fact he hasn't reported them stolen probably means they're a bit suss. But let me check 'em out and I'll get back to you in a couple of days. Here's a down payment in the meantime."

Karl tossed a padded envelope in Liam's lap. Liam looked puzzled. They hadn't discussed this on the phone.

"There's ten grand there. I know the first two watches are genuine. So even if these are all fake, we're still good. Call it a goodwill gesture."

Liam was shocked. He hadn't expected anything today. He realised he'd been totally naïve, but more than anything he just wanted to be rid of the watches. Truth be told, he'd have given them away for nothing, as long as it meant he couldn't be found with them in his possession. Today was proving to be a massive relief in more ways than one.

"Don't look so shocked, mate. I told you, I'm good for it."

Honour amongst thieves, thought Liam. It probably wasn't that common. But it did exist.

"Right, we'll speak as soon as I've checked these out." That was his signal to get out of the car. As he drove off a few minutes later, Liam felt a huge weight lift off his shoulders. The watches were gone. Karl appeared to be an honourable enough bloke. He wasn't going to get the shit beaten out of him. The icing on the cake was that he'd soon have over a hundred grand into the bargain.

His heart sank slightly at that last thought. Unlike the winnings from his bets, this latest hundred grand couldn't yet be used to pay off his debts. It was just more paper to add to the paper in the loft. It had already lost its meaning for Liam. Save for the odd little spending spree here and there, he couldn't do anything particularly constructive with this dirty money.

He made a mental note to get in touch with the money launderer in a few weeks. He had to take action or he'd forever be on edge that, one day, he'd be rumbled and his world would come crashing down.

40

Liam was shitting himself. He had a hundred grand in cash in the boot of his car. If he got pulled over now, for any reason, he was fucked. Well and truly.

He'd met up with Karl earlier and picked up the rest of the cash. Now he knew the watches were authentic, Karl mentioned he'd already been putting the word out. Only around his trusted contacts, but he was keen to start flogging them and getting a return. What he didn't tell Liam was that he reckoned he'd shift a few really quickly; they were desirable makes. And he was selling them for way less than their real value but, even then, he'd make a stonking profit.

Liam would've headed straight home after the pick-up, but today he had something else to do first. He was driving out to a bookies in Burnt Oak to put his latest bet on. It was a bit of a trek, especially on a Friday afternoon, but Callie was adamant it couldn't be close to home. He wasn't going to argue.

He was going to William Hill this time. He'd looked at the odds for tomorrow's game and most of the bookies were much of a muchness. So it wasn't critical to shop around for the best price. It was one of those scores where it would be a shock, but it was still a two-horse race. So even the 14-1 he was expecting to get was generous.

He finally found a parking spot in a nearby side street after driving round about four times. Christ, there were so many double yellows around here, it was mental. The last thing he wanted to do was draw any attention from the law. He made sure he was parked legally, before jogging back to the shop on Watling Avenue.

He'd decided to put £500 on a correct score of Swansea 1 Liverpool 0. The Welsh side were bottom of the table and six points adrift of safety. Liverpool were in fourth but had beaten leaders Man City in an entertaining 4-3 win last weekend. That had kept their unbeaten run of fourteen games going. A win for Swansea was highly unlikely. To add to the improbable outcome, they'd lost all their previous eight games against the top six teams. The bookies would think he was mad, especially with such a large stake. He had his cover story ready.

As he crossed the busy road to get to the bookmakers, Liam could see there was nothing in the window for his game. It was no surprise. It had been switched to Monday night for TV, so all the posters were focused on the weekend's matches. He'd have to find out the odds inside.

He pushed the door and walked in, greeted by a friendly woman behind the counter. He scanned the other customers inside. One was sat on a barstool to the right. He looked around sixty, an obvious smoker from both sight and smell. He was thin on top, face like worn leather and shabbily dressed. He was completely engrossed in one screen, showing horse racing from Lingfield. The race hadn't yet begun, but the horses were going around the parade ring. Odds were appearing across the screen, going up and down in line with bets placed.

As Liam walked up towards the counter, he was able to observe the only other customer. He was sat down, coffee in hand, studying a copy of the Racing Post. Younger than the first guy, with one of those small pens in his hand, plus another one tucked behind his ear. Mid-thirties, better dressed in jeans, jumper and a puffa jacket, with white trainers. He was reading intently and every so often would circle a horse.

"Hiya, love," he said to the woman on the counter, Sheila she was called. "Do you have a betting slip for Swansea against Liverpool on Monday night?"

"I do. I'll just grab it for you. There you go."

"Cheers." Liam took the A4 slip from Sheila, grabbed a coffee from the machine and went to find a quiet corner. He wanted to be alone at the counter when he placed his bet. So, he pretended to study the multitude of options on the page. Despite the fact he already knew exactly what he was going for. It would've taken two seconds to place the bet. Even so, he bided his time, sussing everything out.

As he looked absent-mindedly at the sheet in front of him, Liam became distracted by the older man. He was getting more and more animated. The race was well underway and it appeared his horse was in the lead. The winning post was in sight, but it was building up to a tense finish.

"Go on, son. Go on!" he was out of his seat now, willing his horse to stay in front.

He let out a huge roar as Oregon Gift crossed the line.

"Well done, Ted. Makes a change for you to have a winner," Sheila joked.

A decent winner as well, Liam thought, as the prices flashed up on screen. It had been the outsider in a field of six, priced at 12-1. Not a bad little windfall, depending on what his stake had been.

Ted didn't collect his winnings straight away though. Liam concluded from Ted's demeanour that he'd probably be in there for the rest of the afternoon. So, with the coast clear for him to go up to the counter, he looked back at the betting slip and found the option he was after.

"Get in!" he thought to himself as he spotted that it was actually 15-1 for Swansea to win 1-0. That's another five hundred quid in the bag.

He wrote the stake in the relevant box, finished his coffee and approached the counter once more.

Sheila smiled as he passed her the slip and then tried to cover up a look of surprise when she noted the size of the bet. The ultimate professional, she didn't mention the stake out loud.

"Is that cash or card, love?"

"Er, cash please."

"You must be a Swansea fan or summat. I don't think we've had any bets on them so far," she chuckled, as Liam handed over the small wad of fifties.

Time for the cover story. "I'm not, but my boss is. He's convinced they're gonna win. So he's asked me to put a bet on for him, cos he hasn't got a clue what to do. He's got more money than sense!"

Sheila nodded, as if in agreement.

"Actually, come to think of it, can you stick a tenner on a Liverpool win for me? It'll make it even funnier when he loses all his cash."

He'd decided to add that last bit to make it more convincing.

Sheila grabbed another sheet and scribbled a £10 stake into the Liverpool win box. It was barely above evens, hardly worth doing for the return you'd get.

She popped both slips into the machine, as Liam whipped a tenner out of his wallet.

"Good luck. I hope he treats you if he does win mind," she said, passing him the receipts.

"No chance," he laughed. "Either of the win or him treating me. He's a right miserable git. Cheers, love."

Liam bid his farewell, nodded a silent greeting to Ted that said "well done, mate" and wandered out into the afternoon sunshine.

He dodged the traffic as he crossed the road and headed back towards the side street where he'd parked earlier. As he turned down the junction, his heart stopped. A policewoman was stood there. Right beside his car. The vehicle which currently had a hundred grand in cash inside it. From an illegal sale of stolen watches. And she was writing something in her notepad.

He took the bull by the horns.

"Hi, is everything ok? I'm not parked in the wrong place am I?"

"No. You've got a smashed brake light though. Gonna have to give you a ticket, sorry."

"Aw, no way. It's my wife's car. I had no idea it was smashed."

"Well, it's obviously not just been smashed, because there's no debris here," she said, pointing to the tarmac underneath the light.

"Honestly, I dunno when it would've happened, she never mentioned anything to me. So, what do I need to do?"

"I'm issuing you with a vehicle defect rectification notice. It means you need to take proof of the fault being fixed into your local police station. Within fourteen days."

"Ah, great. Not what I need. I lost my job a couple of weeks ago." He was trying to play on her heartstrings, but it wasn't working.

"Sorry to hear that, but I'm just doing mine. If I didn't issue this and my sarge found out, he'd have my guts for garters."

Fair enough, he thought. In fact, why the hell was he spending time debating this? He had money now. It was no longer an issue. Get the hell out of here!

"I understand. Ok, I'll get it sorted somehow."

He took the notice from the policewoman, jumped in the car and even waved at her as he drove off.

He realised he'd had a lucky escape. And he had. But he needed his luck to hold out a little longer if he was going to get away with all this.

41

"It does look like someone has the black book, sir and they may have worked out the code." The voice at the other end of the phone continued. "We've been notified of a large bet placed on the next match. What do you want us to do?"

"How much this time?"

"Five hundred, sir."

"And where was it placed?"

"Burnt Oak. William Hill."

"Hmm. Are we able to tell if it was the same person placing the bet as last time?"

"No, sir. The betting shop won't give us access to their CCTV footage. So unfortunately we have nothing to go on again."

"Goddamit, how much of a jobsworth are these people? What bloody difference does it make to them?"

Silence at the other end. Waiting for instructions.

"Right. Well, I'm inclined to believe this might be a hopeful punter this time. Let's hang fire for now. That builder had a watertight alibi, so I don't see how it could be him. Maybe it was an opportunistic theft."

The caller at the other end doubted it. All the evidence pointed to it being an inside job. They'd uncovered the builder's criminal background, albeit a long way in the past. Presumably, the police had too. Surely that raised some red flags with them? They'd been all too ready to give up on the break-in, as soon as the trail had gone cold. Lazy fuckers! Although, in their defence, they didn't know the true scale of what had been taken. And they didn't have any idea about the black book.

"Okay, we'll keep you posted if we receive any more intelligence, sir."

The caller at the other end hung up.

Billy had been keeping an eye on this Danny fella for over a month. Ever since that pussy had owned up to his paymasters that the black book had gone. Roberts had played down the robbery initially. He'd even lied about the amount of money and valuables that had been stolen. But after a couple of weeks, realising the implications, he'd crumbled. He came clean about everything. The wheels were put in motion to prevent their secret getting out.

That's where Billy and his team came in.

They were used to dealing with complications. Clearing up the mess. Whether it was caused by incompetence or external scrutiny. Anyone who stumbled on what happened at the top table had to be dealt with. More often than not, they could be bought off. Greedy fuckers!

Billy himself wasn't a football fan. Rugby was his sport. Much more of a man's game. None of that dropping to the ground at the slightest contact. Or rolling around in agony after a harmless-looking challenge. Give him proper men every day of the week. Shrugging off clattering tackles and battling through the pain. He was glad he wasn't a football fan. Now he knew what he knew.

It'd been around seven years now that he'd worked for his current bosses. Mostly the job was about security and protection. Mostly it was above board. But every now and again they'd have to do the darker side of their role. A bit of undercover work that inevitably led to the heavy stuff.

From the moment Billy tracked down Danny, he could sense his guilt. He'd hoped giving him that warning shot on the first day would have been enough to scare him off. Then a week later, they discovered a £300 bet had been placed on one of their matches. They didn't have CCTV coverage of whoever had placed the bet. But that amount of money on a 3-3 draw raised their suspicions enough to keep a close eye on future matches. And increased their mistrust of Danny.

When they saw Danny and his partner leave home on Christmas morning, it was obvious they were going away for at least one night. This was their opportunity to try and find the black book and see if they could locate any of the other loot while they were at it.

Billy and his men turned that house upside down on Christmas night. There wasn't an inch of the property that was left untouched. Yet they didn't find a single piece of evidence that Danny had been involved in the burglary. Billy was baffled and yet still convinced he was the man behind the crime. Danny was a savvy ex-con though. He must have stashed it away somewhere else, wouldn't have been naïve enough to keep the damning haul in his own house.

Over the next fortnight, they delved deep into Danny's background. They tailed him every day and tried to uncover any premises at his disposal he might use as a hiding place. But their enquiries proved fruitless. There was nothing to suggest Danny was concealing any ill-gotten gains. Or that he had access to the little black book.

Despite their concern over the missing book, even his paymasters began to think the burglar had simply discarded it. If it hadn't made any sense to them, they'd want to destroy the evidence of their crime. Focus on making the most of the obvious

225

valuables. There had only been that one bet before Christmas. That could've been a foolish punter who was prepared to lose a few hundred on an improbable result. Were they worrying over nothing?

By early January, Billy's paymasters stood him down from the surveillance. They convinced themselves they were in the clear. That should've been that.

-42-

The following day, Billy got word that a well-known fence was flogging some luxury watches. They didn't appear to be your typical Rolex knock-offs; they sounded like the real deal. And while there were some Rolex amongst them, there were also some less well-known brands. The sort of brands seriously rich people owned. If they were genuine, this was likely to be the haul from Roberts' house.

Billy hung up the phone and leapt into his car. This could be the breakthrough he'd been waiting for.

It didn't take him long to track down Karl; his snitches had done all the legwork for him. He found him in a rundown pub in north London that looked like it was no longer loved, at least by its owners. The carpet was sticky, the seats almost threadbare and the whole place had a musty smell from the moment you entered. A jukebox in the corner, playing 90s tunes, and the constant beeping from a fruit machine, betrayed the pub's otherwise traditional feel.

The place was fairly empty, even for a Monday lunchtime. There was a middle-aged couple sat at one of the tables and a loner stood playing the fruit machine. In the far corner, Karl was sat with another bloke having a whispered conversation.

Billy ordered a pint of shandy and sat down where he could watch them, waiting for his opportunity. He didn't have to wait long. Ten minutes later, the other guy downed his pint and walked out. Karl gestured over at the barman with his glass and said loudly "pull me another Guinness will ya, I'm just off for a wazz?"

Now was his chance. As subtly as he could, Billy got up and walked over to the toilets, following his target in. He didn't think anyone else was in there, but if they were he'd save this for later.

Coast clear.

"Wha......What the fuck?" Billy caught Karl completely by surprise. He'd grabbed hold of him, swung him around and thrust him against the toilet door. Hand tight on his throat, the fence was already struggling to breathe.

"I just wanna ask you a few questions. You give me the answers I need, we're good. But if you fuck me over, I'll fuck you over. Okay?"

Karl nodded, fear in his eyes. He wasn't a big man, except for his middle-aged belly, and he was far from a brave one. He'd spent most of his life on the wrong side of the law, but he steered clear of anything violent. If he needed protection from time to time, he knew who to call. He hadn't realised this was one of those occasions. He did now. He was gasping for breath.

"You've got a load of designer watches you're trying to flog?" Karl nodded again.

"Where did you get them from?"

Karl looked momentarily confused. He was trying to think amidst the fogginess, as the oxygen drained from his brain.

"I...don't...know," Karl choked, trying to buy some time. Hoping that someone would come into the toilets and disturb whoever this thug was.

The tactic didn't work. Billy simply tightened his grip, irritated by the delay.

"I said I'd fuck you over and I meant it. You've got exactly five seconds to tell me who you got them from or your face is gonna get pulped, mate."

228

Karl was no grass, but his assailant meant business. He had to do something to save himself. He was trying to tell him he didn't know the guy's real name, but he'd been put in contact with him by someone he knew. So he could only give him his name. He'd be able to track down the other guy through him. Unfortunately though, Karl didn't get the opportunity to expand on what came out of his mouth next. The extra pressure on his windpipe didn't kill him, but it did cause him to black out and collapse on the floor. Billy calmly walked out of the toilets, over to his table, sank his pint and left the pub. Right after Karl had begun his sentence.

"Danny…"

-43-

It felt like fate that Liam had chosen today of all days to place his final bet.

26th January 2018. Nine years to the day since they'd had their mortgage offer confirmed and their bid on the flat had been accepted. He knew the date off by heart, as it was so monumental in their lives together. The fact they'd managed to combine the two had been nothing short of miraculous. To achieve it all while Liam was on leave was a further indication it was meant to be. Their stars had aligned.

Nine years on, what he was doing today would help to secure their future. Hopefully.

The plan was to put two bets on at different bookies around ten miles apart. Each bet would be a £500 stake and he was hoping to get odds of 40-1 for this latest prediction. Chelsea were unbeaten in eight games and in third place in the league, while Bournemouth were two points off a relegation place. They'd only won two away games all season. The wager would be on Bournemouth to win 3-0 at Stamford Bridge. A freak result.

The match was five days away, but Liam wanted to get the bet on early, get it out of the way. He had a list of jobs around the flat to focus on as well as searching for new employment. Plus, he wanted to pick up the winnings from his second bet. He'd be driving all across London as a result, but it would be worth it. As much as the previous two bets had given him a real thrill as they came in, he was relieved this would be the last one. He was on edge every time he did it; couldn't help worrying that

230

someone was watching him. Waiting to nab him, lock him up, or worse.

The thought of risking £1,000 on a crazy scoreline also scared the hell out of him. He'd never have risked his own money on such a large stake, no matter how much of a safe bet it was. At least if he lost, in theory, he'd be no worse off than before.

Liam's first stop was Coral's in Neasden. He put his baseball cap on; an almost futile attempt to camouflage his identity for any CCTV coverage. Still, it was better than nothing and more sensible than a ridiculous disguise. He dwelt inside for the minimum amount of time but still took the same precautions as before. He didn't want to attract any unnecessary attention from either punters or staff.

By the time he was back on the road towards Burnt Oak, his paranoia was setting in, convinced he was being watched. There was no reason he would be. He couldn't imagine there'd been any links made between him and the burglary. He hadn't even been taken in for questioning, so the police hadn't found any connection between him and Danny. But he had this nagging doubt. His discovery of the book meant someone more sinister than the police could be following him.

So when he walked into William Hill's and saw Sheila behind the counter, he was mightily relieved. He could plough ahead with his plan.

As he closed the door behind him, he clocked another three people inside. They looked like regulars, settled in for the foreseeable. He recognised one of them from his last visit there. Ned? No, Ted, that was it. None of them were at the counter or even close enough to see anything that happened there. So he strode up to the desk, greeted Sheila with a friendly "hi there" and passed her two pieces of paper.

Liam had scribbled a note once he'd parked up, to pass on slyly with his winning betting slip.

Can I have a cheque for my winnings?
And any chance I can sneak out of the back door?
I think someone's following me.
Don't want to get jumped, even if I don't have the cash on me.

Having responded with a similar greeting, she looked down at the papers. A moment of confusion soon disappeared.

"Ah right, I'll sort your winnings out for you, love. Back in a sec."

An anxious few minutes passed.

True to her word, when Sheila returned she had a cheque in her hand, together with a receipt and another slip of paper.

She passed them all across to Liam, the extra slip folded on top.

He casually unfolded the note and acted on its instructions.

"Any chance I could use your toilet? I'm desperate."

"Yeah, no problem. As long as you put the seat back down. You blokes are a bloody nightmare!" she joked. She lifted the top of the counter to let him through via the back office.

In front of the other punters, she went through the pretence of showing him through to the toilet. Then, once out of earshot, she said, "Gawd, I hope you're okay. Is there anything I can do?"

"You've already done it, Sheila. Thanks a million."

"No worries. Go through there and push the emergency door. It says it's alarmed, but it isn't."

"Thanks again."

"You're welcome. You take care. Oh, and by the way, congratulations on the win!"

Liam held his breath as he pushed the emergency exit door and was again relieved Sheila was an honest soul. He looked up and down the back street, turned left and then swiftly headed back to the car.

Ten minutes later, his second mission accomplished, he drove south. He used the same modus operandi in Betfred, Southfields as he had earlier that day. The only difference was his attire; he changed his jacket and swapped the cap for a beanie.

There were no hiccups here. No concerns about being followed. He felt confident as he placed the bet and as he walked out of the front door this time, he had a spring in his step. That was it now. Other than picking up his anticipated winnings, he was in the clear, on the home straight. Two months on from that surreal night on Elystan Place, he had almost achieved his dream outcome.

It was both fateful and tragic that Liam had chosen today of all days to place his final bet.

~~~~~~

Danny was on his way to West Hampstead to price up what sounded like a decent, profitable job. A two-storey extension on the back of a large townhouse, together with a loft conversion. If he impressed with this, there was the possibility of several other properties. The potential client was seriously loaded. After the Mitchell Roberts experience, he'd sworn he wouldn't target the richer parts of town. But these people had got in touch with him. He'd decided to hear them out at least. What did he have to lose?

It was relatively mild for a late January afternoon. The impending darkness, even though it wasn't yet 4pm, betrayed the fact it was still the middle of winter. Danny knew he wouldn't get home until late tonight, by the time he'd gone through all the details with the owner's personal assistant. He'd still have to battle through any residual rush hour traffic. It would probably take him nigh on an hour to drive back.

He'd warned Tina he wouldn't be home until around 7pm, so she said she'd put a casserole in the slow cooker for dinner. He could almost taste it now, he was starving. He felt around on the passenger seat for a chocolate bar he'd bought earlier. That would have to keep him going for now.

As he headed into West Hampstead, Danny was impressed by the grandeur of the houses. The whole feel of the area was a step up from where he lived, as pleasant as that was. But even if he could afford it, he wasn't sure he'd want to upgrade to this. He was happy and settled where they were. Money wasn't everything.

It occurred to him it was just over a month since he'd proposed to Tina. The wedding plans were progressing at pace now. It wasn't going to be a big do. Danny had no family to speak of, so would be inviting a few of his mates, as well as the lads who worked for him. And Tina's guest list wasn't much bigger. Tom, Nat and the kids would be there, of course. Beyond that, there'd be a few of her friends and work colleagues, plus a smattering of close relatives. She had a brother and a sister, plus their respective partners. Together they'd reckoned on about thirty guests in total, assuming they could all make it.

Speaking of which, Tina had already sent out 'Save the Date' cards to their guest list. She'd even forced Danny to pass them on to the lads at work and his mates. Despite his protestations that he could just tell them when it was.

Truth be told, he was over the moon she was so excited about planning their wedding. He'd been so nervous on Christmas Day, in case the answer was 'no'. He knew their relationship was solid, but he hadn't been 100% sure Tina wanted to get married. Now the date was set and arrangements were being made, the two of them were like a pair of youngsters. In the first throes of love.

The wedding would be a simple enough affair. A ceremony at the registry office, followed by a reception at a local hotel, in a room overlooking the river. It had some outside decking they could all spill out onto for drinks and chilling out. Ideal for their intimate celebration. And while it wasn't cheap, they were more than happy to splash out on this aspect of their day.

Friday 20 April 2018. Just short of three months away. Danny looked at the chocolate wrapper he'd tossed on the floor of his van. Maybe he should start eating more healthily. He wanted to look good in his suit, it was so rare he ever wore one. Decision made. No more chocolate until after the wedding. Should he cut down a little bit on the drink as well? Hmmm, nah, that was a step too far. The chocolate was enough.

Ah, bugger, he'd missed his turning.

He switched off from thoughts of the wedding and focused back on finding this house. If he could get this job, never mind the related work, it would pay for the whole thing.

Having doubled back on himself further up, he'd now found the right street. He scanned the numbers on the left-hand side, counting them down. As he approached the house in question, a four-wheel-drive indicated to pull out. What a result. He flashed the driver and went to pull into the space he'd vacated, in front of a black BMW. It was a bit tight, but it didn't look like he'd get anywhere else remotely nearby, so he parallel parked and squeezed it in. He grabbed the pad and pen he'd left on the passenger seat, checked he had his phone and jumped out of the van.

As Danny walked up to the door of number 55, he didn't spot the figure at the first-floor window looking down at him. It wouldn't have made any difference. He would've thought it was another member of staff employed by his super-rich client. Not a million miles from the truth.

"Hi, you must be Danny," a warm smile greeted him.

"You must be Greg," replied Danny, popping the pen behind his ear so he could shake the guy's outstretched hand.

For the next hour or so, Greg went through the pretence. He showed Danny the fake architect's drawings and the mocked-up planning permission. Walked around the back garden to pace out the footprint. Engaged in friendly conversation with a builder he had no intention of employing. And even made coffee, to stretch out the time they remained downstairs. All the while he was watching the light outside turn from dusk to pitch black.

"Shall we take a look upstairs, so you can measure up for the loft conversion?" Greg said now, having decided it was late enough and dark enough.

"Yeah," said Danny, feeling queasy all of a sudden, but trying to fight the nausea.

Greg led the way up the stairs, chattering away about the house improvements and his mega-rich boss. Danny was struggling to hear him clearly now. His vision was impaired. He was starting to see stars. And feeling really, really nauseous.

He struggled to the top of the stairs, following Greg across the landing and towards the back bedroom. He couldn't keep up the pretence any longer. His legs were starting to give way. He'd have to tell Greg he was feeling rough and needed some water. Needed to sit down, clear his head. Christ, he felt awful.

"Oh, fuck."

By the time he walked into the back bedroom, Danny's eyesight was failing. But not before he caught sight of the two heavies lying in wait.

Waiting for him.

-44-

Tina was starting to get worried.

When Danny hadn't returned by 8pm, she'd texted him to see what time he'd be home. When he left this morning, he told her it shouldn't be much after 7pm, so she was ready for something to eat by 7.30pm. By the time it got to 8pm, she was starving. She hadn't received any reply to her text, so assumed it was taking longer than anticipated. No big deal. She dished up her dinner and turned down the slow cooker, keeping the rest warm for Danny's eventual return.

She wasn't concerned by his lateness, initially. He'd mentioned to her this could lead to other work and they'd be big, profitable contracts. The thought of it paying outright for the wedding appealed to both of them. So she figured he might be discussing the other jobs as well. Strange he hadn't responded to her text though.

By 9pm, she sent another text. This one was more demanding, asking him to let her know urgently he was okay, even if he was going to be really late. She only managed to wait ten minutes before she rang his phone, having still had no response.

Beep beep. Beep beep. Beep beep. Fleeting relief when she heard him speak. But it was his voicemail. She almost hung up in frustration, but held on and left a message.

"Danny, ring me as soon as you get this message, would you? Want to make sure you're okay. Thanks, love."

This time she managed to wait half an hour. Gave him a chance to finish what he was doing and give her a call. But as it was now approaching 10pm, Tina was getting concerned. It was unlike Danny not to get back to her if he was delayed for any reason. Even if it was a brief couple of words, to say he was fine.

She called again. Voicemail again. She left another message.

"Danny, love, I'm worried about you. Can you let me know you're okay? Call me, please. As soon as possible. I know I'm probably fretting over nothing, but I just need to hear from you."

Tina had a sinking feeling in her stomach. Why wasn't he getting back to her? Had he been in an accident? Had he crashed on the way home from the meeting? All sorts of scenarios flashed through her mind. None of them were positive.

She didn't know what to do. So she rang Tom.

He picked up on the third ring, pleased to hear from her, although a little surprised at the late hour.

"Hi, mum. How are you doing?"

"Oh, Tom, I'm okay. But I don't know what to do. Danny was due home shortly after 7pm from pricing up a job in West Hampstead. But he's not back yet."

"Ah, he's probably got talking to them, you know what he's like."

"No, it's not that, I'm sure of it. He's not replying to any texts. He's not picking up any calls. He's not responding to voicemails. I've got this horrible feeling something's happened to him."

Tom could hear his mum's voice beginning to break up. She could be a bit of a worrier at times, but she also had good instincts. And it did sound a little strange.

"What if his phone's run out of battery?" he suggested.

"I hadn't thought of that," said Tina. "It still doesn't explain why he's so late though."

"Mmm, maybe he's running late and can't let you know because his phone's dead."

It seemed a logical explanation. Though she was still concerned, despite Tom's efforts to reassure her. It didn't take this long to price up a job.

"Maybe his van broke down on the way back or something," he said, but with less conviction than earlier.

"Come on, son, that's quite a few things all going wrong at once. He hasn't smashed any mirrors you know!" She laughed, but as she said it she remembered that someone else had. A few weeks ago. In their house.

"Yeah, you're right. Listen, let me make a few calls and I'll come back to you. But let me or Nat know right away if you hear from him in the meantime."

"Right, love, thanks. Do I need to do anything else?"

"No. Get yourself a cuppa and try to stay calm okay, mum? I'll give you a call back in about half an hour."

She followed Tom's instructions or at least tried to. She managed to make a brew, but it was going cold as she watched the minutes tick by. Getting more and more worried.

As soon as he'd hung up, Tom had asked Nat to start searching online for any accidents on Danny's route home. He rang the police to make similar enquiries. They had no record of anything. He then rang the various hospitals in the area. In case Danny had been brought in following a medical episode or anything like that. Nothing.

Finally, he tried Danny's phone himself. Voicemail. He left a message, but by now Tom was concerned too. This was out of character for Danny.

"Have you found anything?" he asked Nat, who was still looking at her laptop.

"Nothing. Whoa, what are you doing?" she replied, seeing him grab his coat and his car keys.

"I need to get over to mum's. She's really worried and I have to admit, I've got a bad feeling about this too. It's not like him."

Nat didn't argue, although she hoped she was right in thinking he was over-reacting. Like mother, like son.

Less than five minutes later, he was heading out the door. He had an overnight bag in one hand and the words of his wife ringing in his ears.

"Keep me posted. And don't drive too fast!"

It was a forlorn request. Tom sped down the M1, praying the traffic stayed light and there weren't any traffic police en route. He'd slow down once he reached built-up areas, but he wanted to get there as quickly as he could.

His first call on the way down was to the police. He knew they wouldn't take it seriously until Danny had been missing for 48 hours. Even then, he was an adult, so he'd be a lower priority. Unless there was evidence of foul play. Nevertheless, Tom wanted to register his disappearance. Get the wheels in motion.

Next, he called his mum. He didn't mean to increase her angst. The very fact he was speeding down the motorway after 10.30 at night made that impossible. By now she sounded panic-stricken. He was pleased he'd decided to head down there straight away.

"I take it you haven't heard from him yet?"

"No, nothing. Oh God, I'm so scared, Tom."

"It's ok. I'm on my way down now. I'm only going to be another fifteen minutes." Fastest journey ever. "Listen, mum, I've reported it to the police. I don't think they'll do anything yet and

I don't want you to worry yourself anymore. But don't be alarmed if they make contact with you."

"Where is he, Tom?" Tina's voice was properly breaking up now.

"We'll find him, don't worry. Listen, I'll get off the phone in case he's trying to ring either of us, but I'll see you soon."

He didn't want to leave his mum on her own with her thoughts, but he needed to focus on driving. And keep an eye out for patrol cars. Because he was still speeding. Not as fast as earlier, but still fast enough to be pulled over.

Finally, he reached her house, found a parking spot and ran to the front door. It flung open before he could even knock and his tearful mum collapsed into his arms.

As he hugged her tightly, Tom gently manoeuvred his way into the house and closed the door behind him. The house smelt of home cooking; the aroma from the slow-cooked casserole hung in the air. As did the concern.

Tina looked up at him, her eyes were red with crying.

"I'm so worried, Tom. I've got this awful feeling. I can't shake it off."

"I know, mum, but let's not jump to conclusions yet okay? C'mon, let's sit down and have a cuppa. I'll fill you in on what I've done and then you can tell me what his movements were today."

It was after 1am by the time the mother and son made their weary way upstairs to bed. Tom had told Tina who he'd been in contact with and she, in turn, went through what she knew about his plans. She'd spoken to Danny while he was driving to West Hampstead, so she knew he'd made it that far. She didn't have contact numbers for the lads who worked for him. They'd try and get in touch with them in the morning. They'd chase up the police then too, assuming Danny hadn't turned up in the meantime.

Tina was so conflicted. She'd give anything for Danny to walk through that door right now. But if he didn't have a damn good explanation, she thought she'd probably wring his neck herself. All this worry he'd caused.

Despite the late hour, they'd agreed to get up by 8am latest and work out their plan of action for the day. Tom had already called Nat to update her and she was now anxiously awaiting news. She was kicking herself for her initial cynicism.

As it turned out, they were actually woken by a knock at the door at 7.30 that same morning. A Family Liaison Officer. The police had tracked Danny's registration number on ANPR and had some news.

Tina braced herself, fearing the worst.

~~~~~~

It wasn't quite the news she'd been dreading, but it was still devastating. The police had put Danny's registration into their database. A couple of cameras picked it up late afternoon driving around West Hampstead. By 7.30pm the van was flagged leaving the area. It was then zapped numerous times being randomly driven up to ten miles away. Its final detection had been on the A5, near a local beauty spot. One of their officers had checked out the surrounding roads. They found Danny's van, parked up next to Brent Reservoir. Close to the water's edge. Keys still in the ignition.

Tina was in shock, Tom was numb. There was still hope. They hadn't found a body. But was it a matter of time? Were they kidding themselves he'd be found alive?

The implication Danny might have killed himself didn't ring true with either of them. Why would he do such a thing? He had everything to live for. There were no signs, nothing. The opposite in fact. They'd heard relatives of suicide victims were often left bewildered. Not expecting it. Not realising their loved ones were going through such desperate times. The departed had put on a brave face, covered up their unhappiness. But Tina and Tom couldn't process that at all. It wasn't Danny. It wasn't. It couldn't be.

Could it?

-45-

The cellar was dark, damp and foreboding. Paint was peeling from the walls and mustiness pervaded its entirety. It reminded him of prison. With one exception. It was freezing. It was the middle of winter and there didn't appear to be any source of heat. Jesus, he was cold!

He assumed it was a cellar. There were no windows and it had a subterranean feel, but he could have been anywhere. He had no idea where it was. For all he knew, he could still be in the same house in West Hampstead.

His head hurt like hell. He could sense congealed blood at the back of his neck. He'd been smacked hard with a baseball bat after entering the bedroom of that beautiful townhouse. The house he'd been tricked into going to.

Danny realised what was coming before it happened, but by then it was too late. There was nothing he could do. He was close to losing consciousness anyway, thanks to the drug Greg had put in his coffee. The combination of that and the whack around the head would keep him knocked out until the following day. Although he'd come to wish he hadn't woken up at all.

Why hadn't he seen it coming? Idiot. He didn't even like coffee for fuck's sake.

He had no clue how long he'd been unconscious for. There was no way of knowing what time of day it was down here and he didn't appear to have his phone on him anymore.

Danny had regained consciousness a few minutes ago. When he first opened his eyes, squinting with pain, he thought he had the mother of all hangovers. Vowed he was never drinking again. And then it all came flooding back to him. A nightmare that was becoming reality.

He couldn't see much in the dark cellar, but as his eyes became more accustomed to the blackness, he sensed he was alone. Any thoughts of escape were dashed when he realised he was chained to the floor. The iron around his wrists reminded him of police handcuffs. Cold metal, rubbing against his bones, ensuring he wouldn't be going anywhere anytime soon.

His ankles were cable-tied together and, now he was awake, it was impossible to get comfortable. The beginnings of cramp were starting to tingle ominously in his hamstrings. Please, God, no. I'm in enough pain already, he thought.

In his solitude, thoughts raced through his mind. Who were these people? What did they want from him? He assumed it was to do with the burglary, but he had a rock-solid alibi. And he'd done nothing dodgy since that November night, to raise any suspicions. The police weren't interested. They'd given up on solving the crime. So who were these heavies and why were they holding him captive? And, more worryingly, what were they going to do to him?

As the hunger pangs twanged in Danny's stomach, another thought occurred to him. Would they leave him here to starve to death? Or freeze to death? Hard to know which would happen first. He shuddered at the prospect but soon realised it would be pretty pointless.

He sat there in the cellar, alone, for what seemed like hours. He racked his brains as to what they wanted from him, what they could do to him and whether he'd get out of this alive. His mind wasn't sharp enough right now to come up with a credible alternative of that night, in a way that didn't involve him. He could put himself in more danger if he gave them a bullshit story. So he'd deny all knowledge and plead his innocence; stress he'd been on the straight and narrow for fifteen years. Getting involved in anything like that would have wrecked the life he'd built.

He didn't hold out much hope of these thugs believing him. Even if they did, would they let him go? Or were these four walls the last he'd ever see?

He was about to find out.

Up above, to his left, he saw a chink of light as a door creaked open. A torchlight was turned on and a dark figure began descending the stone stairs. Danny could make out little in the dim light, other than his captor appeared to be wearing a balaclava. He registered even less when the man got up close and shone the torch directly in his eyes. He was blinded.

"He's awake!"

A muffled sound from upstairs. He couldn't make out what was said. His senses still hadn't returned fully. Not only was his head pounding, but the torchlight trained on his face was making him see stars.

"Just fuckin' get down here now. We've got work to do."

At the top of the stairs, the other person flicked a light switch. It turned on a single bulb, a dim glow, but another contrast for Danny to adjust to. As the second set of footsteps descended, he was concerned to see this one swinging a wrench. He saw the first guy more clearly now, wielding a baseball bat. It was probably the same one they'd used to knock him out in the bedroom.

"Danny, right?"

"Yeah."

"You've got something belonging to our boss. He wants it back."

"I dunno what you're on about."

The first guy swung the baseball bat, tapping it into the palm of his hand, indicating his impatience.

"Really, I don't. What is it you think I've got?"

"You did some work on a house on Elystan Place. And it got burgled a few weeks after you'd finished. We want what you stole."

"I didn't burgle that house!"

"Bollocks. With your record and the access you had, it had to be you."

"It wasn't. I swear on my life." An unfortunate choice of phrase. "I've been straight for the last fifteen years. I don't rob houses anymore. It wasn't me."

"Don't bullshit us. You knew he had a safe full of money, you knew his alarm code, you had the opportunity to get some keys cut. Shit, you probably knew his safe code, that guy is such a dumb bastard."

"The police know I didn't do it. I was away when it happened, up in Manchester."

"The police are lazy fuckers. They've given up at the first opportunity. So if it wasn't you, then it was someone you briefed. Tell us who that is and we'll set you free."

"I don't know anything about it," he pleaded. "Honest to God. Please, just let me go."

The guy swung his bat in frustration, but not at Danny. Not this time. He merely waved it around in the air and then walked away to the bottom of the staircase.

Danny could just about make out the muffled conversation this time.

247

"He told us not to rough him up too much unless we know he's got something."

"Well, it looks like we're gonna have to, to get it out of him doesn't it?"

"Not until he gives us the go-ahead."

"We can't keep him down here forever."

"Yeah, but we can't just do him in either. We've gotta wait for instructions."

"Fuck that. I reckon we waste the fucker."

He imagined they were talking loud enough to try and scare him into a confession. He hoped that was their tactic; the alternative didn't bear thinking about.

He had to stay strong though. He couldn't grass on Liam. It appeared they knew nothing about him. They hadn't mentioned anyone else and there was no trail leading to him. If only he could convince them he wasn't involved. He was beginning to feel it would be an impossible task. That this wouldn't end well.

A phone rang out in the eery silence that had descended. The first guy put his phone to his ear and spoke. A baffling one-way conversation ensued.

"Yeah, it's me. You what? Yesterday afternoon? Two this time? Whereabouts? Was it before we met him? So it could've been him? Alright, send me the addresses and we'll head over there now."

As he hung up, the heavy turned to his mate and said, "I'll fill you in on the way. This can wait. There's been a development."

Danny was terrified something had been linked to him or Liam had been identified. But he also had one other pressing issue on his mind right now. Especially if they were going to disappear for a while.

"Can I have something to eat and drink? I'm starving."

"Good! If it was up to me, I'd let you rot here. We know you're in on this."

"We need to keep him alive, for now. I got that tray ready. Let me grab it and then we'll get off."

The other guy agreed, reluctantly. Having slid a tray of curled-up sandwiches and a Coke can across to him, they were on their way. Danny had no idea how long they'd be gone. But there was one thing he'd picked up on in their conversation that was bugging him.

For now.

We need to keep him alive, *for now.* Danny had a feeling of inevitability about his situation. An inevitable bad ending.

As far as Tina was concerned, the bad ending had already happened. Because, unbeknown to him, police divers were at that very moment searching the reservoir. Trying to locate his body. They were under the misconception he'd taken his own life. Even though, right now, he desperately wanted to live. More than anything in the world.

46

27 January 2018
Brentford vs Norwich City
Griffin Park, London
Kick-off: 3:00 pm

The first time Liam bought tickets to take Robbie to the match was a mid-table clash at the end of January.

Since the last match they'd attended, against Sheff Wed, the Bees had predictably lost at Wolves but won their other two league games. The FA Cup was best forgotten. Brentford got knocked out by League Two Notts County in one of the shocks of the third round.

Today was a tough one to call. Norwich had been struggling of late but were still a strong team. They'd been relegated from the Premier League two years ago and missed out on the play-offs last time around. It didn't look like they'd be anywhere near them this season. They were almost as close to the relegation places as the top six. And yet, they still had some decent players. Brentford's win at Norwich before Christmas had been a cracking result.

At least Liam had his lucky charm with him. Robbie was still to see Brentford lose, after a draw and three great wins in his four matches to date. And a fair few goals into the bargain. How long would that luck last though, he thought? All good things come to an end.

Even bad things came to an end, eventually.

In recent weeks, Liam had made significant inroads into his debts. The credit card was paid off and the payday loan was down to £15,000. Once the third bet came in, he'd wipe that debt out and put the rest into a savings account. Most of the money from the watches had gone into the holdall in the loft. When it was feasible to do something with that, he'd use the money launderer to set them up for the future. They'd kept a couple of grand in their hiding place in the kitchen cupboard, for any day-to-day expenses. He was still out of work after all. But apart from that, life was good.

So buying them a couple of tickets these days was no big deal. What a difference from three months ago, when he was so broke he could barely afford a two-quid bus ride. Nowadays, the focus was still on paying off his debts, but there were occasional treats from time to time. Nothing extravagant, just the sort of things normal people enjoyed week after week. They'd spent the last year living such constricted lives. He'd only realised how limited their existence had become once the shackles were off.

The third bet was due to come in over the next couple of days. That was the big one. Assuming there were no hiccups, he stood to pick up a cool £41,000. Forty. One. Thousand. Pounds.

They were meeting up with the lads in the pub again before the match; Robbie was as excited as he was at the thought of that. A real chip off the old block.

First things first though, they made a quick detour. This time it was a new experience for Liam. Treating his son in the club shop. Everything up to now had been bought for him by family members. Today Robbie would have a whole £20 to spend, a reward for winning the school's prize for good citizenship. They were so proud of him.

Robbie spent an age wandering around, looking at everything. Liam kept an eye on him but left him to make his own decision. He was surprised when he finally came back to him and had three small items in his hands.

"Dad, I think I've got enough money for these. Can you check for me?"

He totted up the prices. A key ring, a mug and a Mother's Day card, with the sweetest message inside, 'Mum, you're the Bee's knees'. Callie would love that. Four, eight, three, fifteen quid in total.

"You've still got a fiver left over. Are you sure that's what you want?"

"Yes, please. The mug's for me, the card's for mum and I wanted to give Chloe the key ring."

Liam could've sworn Robbie blushed at that last point. Maybe Chloe had become the lad's first crush. But regardless, he was touched by his son's thoughtfulness.

Suddenly, a worried look crept across his face.

"Actually, dad, you can have the mug. I don't have enough to get another one, do I?"

Bless him, he'd realised he'd missed his dad out.

"No you don't, but I tell you what, we can share it. Is there anything else you want with your fiver?"

He shook his head emphatically. "I've already got all this," he said, pointing to his shirt, his scarf and his hat. "I just love coming to the match."

Liam cleared the lump in his throat and went to pay for the latest merchandise.

Ninety minutes later, after a few pints in the Newie with his mates, the group headed towards the ground. For the first time in as long as he could remember, he felt relaxed, happy and positive about the future. There'd been no stress about buying a round and he'd had a great catch-up with Steve in particular.

He guided Robbie through the turnstiles but, once inside, the young lad knew exactly where he was going. He followed hot on the heels of Steve, as they all headed towards the bar for one more pint before kick-off.

Refreshments in hand, Liam shuffled his way in amongst the group. As he rested their drinks on a shelf behind them, he began to eat his pie and opened Robbie's up to allow it to cool down. The filling was often hotter than the sun and, as he'd learnt previously, Robbie could be a clumsy eater. Best not to tempt fate.

Several TV screens on the concourse were relaying pre-match information such as team news and player stats. In between, an advert or news item would pop up on screen. An ad for a funeral director, a local printer, news about the endless Brexit negotiations. Yawn. Then a local news piece appeared, asking for information about a missing man. He'd disappeared yesterday afternoon according to the ticker at the bottom of the screen. His van had been found parked next to a local reservoir and police were concerned for his safety.

And then they brought his picture up on screen.

Liam stood frozen to the spot in shock. Thank God he didn't have his pint in his hand, he'd have dropped it like a stone. He must've gone ashen when he saw the photo. Steve noticed, saying, "Christ, mate, are you ok? You've look like you've seen a ghost."

He couldn't speak. He nodded until his voice returned. "Erm, yeah," he croaked initially, then cleared his throat, "yeah, I'm fine. Just thought I recognised that guy on screen, but can't think where from."

"I saw that on the news this morning," Si chipped in. "He went missing pricing up a job and then they found his van parked next to the water. Reckon he must have topped himself."

"Steady on, mate, you can't jump to those conclusions. Apparently, he'd just proposed to his partner over Christmas and there was no sign anything was wrong."

"There's rarely any signs, mate. Remember Robbo?"

The group looked wistful, remembering a mate who was no longer with them. Who'd appeared to be fine, yet all the while was suffering in silence. Not too dissimilar to Liam in recent months, but thankfully he'd been rescued by a good samaritan. He'd yet to confide in his mates, but at least his life had taken a turn for the better over the past few weeks. Until now.

As the conversation moved on to the match itself, he was left alone with his thoughts again. He was in purgatory. What the hell should he do? Was it connected to the break-in? It must be. It had to be. Did that mean he was in danger? Callie? Robbie too?

For the duration of the match, Liam went through the motions with the lads and Robbie. He managed to get through it all somehow, but his brain was frazzled. He was on edge the whole time, constantly looking around, searching for any signs that someone was watching him.

The match itself was almost a reflection of his state of mind. Norwich scored in the first few minutes. Despite a hatful of chances for Brentford, they just couldn't find the net. For the first time in Robbie's match-going life, his beloved team had lost.

In normal circumstances, Liam would look to cheer him up and give him a dad pep talk. How this was football and the good times felt so much better because of the bad times. And how, even if you supported one of the footballing giants, you still had to get used to losing games.

Instead, he said the bare minimum as they trudged out of the ground and back to the train station. He told Robbie he was ill and hoped it hadn't spoilt his day, but he needed his bed right now. Bless him, the youngster tried to make sure his dad was okay, asking if he wanted some of his water. And he was much more subdued than he'd normally be, even taking the defeat into account.

Callie came to pick them up from the train station, having had a text from Liam saying he needed to get home urgently. He'd had a bad pint, or eaten something dodgy. Felt like death.

Robbie perked up at the sight of his mum, chatting to her about the game, despite the pain of defeat. The few minutes in the car were mostly a blur for Liam in his current state, though he heard Robbie mention going to the pub with the lads. As if he was a hardened drinker. He smiled, amidst his anguish.

Luckily for Liam, Callie wanted to nip to the shop, so he leapt out of the car as soon as she parked up. He ran inside, pressed the up button over and over and prayed that the lift doors would open soon. Finally. He jumped in the lift and pressed 5, hoping no one else would get in, either here or on the way up. He desperately needed to get into the flat.

On the fifth floor, he sprinted out of the lift and across to their door. Fumbling with the keys, he almost dropped them. At last, he got the key in the slot, turned it and dived inside. He made it to the bathroom just in time. As he collapsed on the floor beside the toilet, he threw everything up from earlier in the day. There were several retches. And then, a few minutes later, he was done. He flopped back against the cold, tiled bathroom wall. Sweaty, exhausted and empty.

He didn't know what to do. Just as it seemed they could look forward to the future with optimism, everything had come to a crashing halt.

The goalposts had moved.

Full time: Brentford 0 Norwich City 1

47

After throwing his guts up in the bathroom, Liam managed to avoid Callie for most of the evening, until she'd put Robbie to bed. It was a Saturday night, so he'd been allowed to stay up until 9pm. All the while, Liam had hidden away in their bedroom, under the pretence that he was still feeling ropey.

Callie had given him some tablets for his upset stomach but then left him alone to rest. Despite feeling exhausted, rest had been the last thing on his mind. He'd spent the first hour on his phone, searching for any updates on local news sites. He'd already done some frantic surfing on the train on the way home. There was nothing other than more background on Danny. Still, he couldn't find anything more recent than what he'd seen at the match.

He prayed Danny was still alive. He hoped against hope that this wasn't anything to do with the burglary. He knew that was selfish but, if the worst had happened, he didn't want to be in any way connected with it. The bloke had always looked out for him. He couldn't bear the thought that he was in any way linked to his demise.

Eventually, he drifted off into a fitful sleep for an hour, the stress and sickness finally catching up with him.

With Robbie tucked up for the night, Callie crept into their room and laid down on the bed next to Liam. He stirred, briefly.

"Sorry, babe, didn't mean to wake you. Are you feeling any better?"

"A bit yeah, thanks." He was torn, knowing he had to tell her, but not sure how or when to broach the subject.

"Was it something you ate? D'you think Robbie will be sick too? Or was it a bad pint, d'you reckon?"

"No idea. Just came over, all of a sudden. I think he'll be alright if he's not feeling ill by now." He hated being a chicken. He had to tell her; he couldn't risk her finding out about things on the local news. Or worse, for something to happen to him in the meantime. Or much much worse, to her or Robbie.

"Ah, that's good. Robbie reckons you were ill because Brentford got beat, bless him."

He laughed through his angst. "As if I've not seen that happen many a time before!"

"Ha, exactly. Listen, I'm gonna join you and turn in for an early night if you fancy?"

It may have sounded like a proposition, but he knew Callie wasn't suggesting anything other than kip. Having sex with a guy who'd vomited everything in his stomach a couple of hours ago didn't appeal to her right now. But he couldn't bear the thought of going to sleep without telling her. He knew she might not sleep a wink, but he had to do it. He couldn't put it off any longer.

"I need to speak to you."

"Yeah, I'm gonna grab a coffee and bring it to bed. Do you want one?"

"Not right now. I really need to speak to you. It's important." Liam pushed himself up onto his elbows, looking serious. Callie was uneasy. She sat back down on the bed.

"Oh, God, what is it?"

He took a deep breath. He didn't want to say this. But he had to. His family could be in danger.

"When we were at the match today, there was a news thing that came up on screen about a missing bloke. It was Danny."

The last three words were said almost in a whisper. In disbelief.

"Missing?"

"Yeah. He went missing yesterday, apparently. They found his van next to a reservoir and now they've got divers searching in the water."

Callie clutched her chest. "Ah no, that's awful. Poor bloke. Has he been going through a rough time?"

"No, that's just it. He proposed to his partner at Christmas and he was really happy."

"Yeah, but they always say you can never tell."

"I know that but, it doesn't feel right. And, I hate to say this, love, but…" he paused, not wanting to say what he was going to say next. "…I think it's something to do with the burglary." There. He'd got the words out. He didn't feel any better for it though.

Callie didn't respond immediately. She was taking it all in. Thinking about it. And the more she thought about it, the more she probably agreed with Liam.

"Are you saying someone's got to Danny and they've done something to him?"

"That's exactly what I'm saying."

"But, why?"

"It has to be to do with the book I guess."

And then it hit her.

"Jesus, Liam, does that mean they're onto us?"

"I have no idea. But I'm not prepared to take a chance if they are."

Callie suddenly looked terrified.

"What are we gonna do?"

"I dunno. But I'm gonna make sure you and Robbie are safe, ok?"

"How can you do that?" She felt helpless. Scared. Angry. And then she spoke again, quietly. "So, this Danny then. He's been done in because of what we, what you, did?"

"Probably," he replied. He felt bereft. There wasn't much she could say to make him feel any worse.

Tears pricked Callie's eyes. Even Liam was feeling emotional.

"Right, I'm off work tomorrow. I'll ring Rach first thing in the morning and see if she can have Robbie for the day. If not, can we ask your mum and dad? And then we're gonna sort out our plan of action."

"Yeah. I just want you both to be safe, babe. I don't care what happens to me."

"Liam, don't talk shit, please. We all need to be safe. But we've got to start being a bit savvier, in case anyone's on to us, ok?"

He agreed. "I'm gonna grab a coffee. You still want one?"

Callie nodded. While the kettle was boiling, he looked in on Robbie. He was fast asleep. Next, he went to check the front door, made sure it was locked and put the bolt across. Finally, he checked and secured their balcony windows.

As he carried the mugs into the bedroom, he sensed Callie was pissed off with him. He could hardly blame her. They drank their drinks in near silence, the barest conversation passing between them. Finally, once they'd finished, Callie announced, "Right, let's try and get some sleep. I've got a feeling we might be missing some before too long."

~~~~~~

260

A few miles away from Liam and Callie, Tina was being supported by her Family Liaison Officer. Kept in the loop, albeit there wasn't much of a loop. The divers were still searching the reservoir, but nothing had shown up so far. It was a waiting game.

Waiting to find out that your fiancé was gone. Tina didn't want to hear that news. She knew she was being naïve and foolish, but she was praying with every fibre of her being that they never found him in that reservoir. She still had a little shred of hope that he was still alive. That somewhere, her soulmate was hanging on.

-48-

Billy was pissed off.

Every time they thought they had a lead, they'd hit a brick wall.

He and his sidekick had visited both of the bookies where the latest bets had been placed. Without a warrant card or legal documents, they were unable to access the footage. Once again.

He could threaten the shop staff all he wanted, but they stuck to the letter of the law. They wouldn't release CCTV files. Despite Billy saying he was working undercover and needed to see who had placed a particular bet. It was more than their job was worth. If he tried to use strong-arm tactics, inevitably they'd call the police. That was the last thing he needed.

He was racking his brains how to get around the issue. There was no easy answer. They could hack into the system; it was all digital these days. But that would take time and right now they needed to find out who'd carried out the burglary. Urgently. Because whoever did it not only had all that cash and a load of valuable watches, but they also had the book.

Already, the pattern of bets suggested they'd worked out what some of the content was about. As the stakes and the winnings increased, so did the likelihood of this person realising what else the book contained. And that was worth a damn sight more than a few grand. It was dynamite. They had to get to this person before the penny dropped.

Could it be this guy in the cellar? Even if he hadn't done it himself, there was a chance he'd passed on inside information to whoever had done it. Or had they got it wrong? Was he a victim of circumstance? Billy wasn't sure anymore. He had a nagging doubt, but he needed hard evidence before he took any drastic action. His paymasters were ruthless, but measured; they didn't like things getting messy. If there was any doubt about Danny's involvement, they'd have to let him go eventually. Without proof, he was an innocent man.

They already had a system that flagged up when a large bet was wagered on one of their matches. That had been in place for a while, due to the actions of the previous boss. What an idiot. A greedy idiot. Bribing him with millions wasn't enough; he had to get his grubby hands on more. He was lucky no outsiders had found out about the handful of bets he'd made before they rumbled him. He was quickly removed from office and another yes man put into the role. Eventually. It had taken a while to complete the appointment this time. Roberts had been read the riot act before his tenure was confirmed.

Truth be told, Roberts was simply a puppet for Billy's paymasters and the 'VIPs'. He could look good in front of the cameras, do all the media stuff and so on. When it came to the under-the-radar activity, he was like a rabbit in headlights. Billy imagined he was completely mesmerised when he was briefed about the safe and its contents. Which made it even more staggering that he'd been so complacent with his security. This was all completely avoidable.

Time to head back to the house. Play the long game. He'd have to rely on the hackers but, with any luck, this would finally lead them to the culprit. As he drove back, he set the wheels in motion with the computer whizzes. They reckoned it would take a few days to get into the various systems. The fact this guy had used four different locations would make it more time-consuming. And four different betting companies too. But they were hopeful, so long as the CCTV was working, they could identify their suspect. At last.

They'd been away from the house for most of the day. Billy knew their captive would be cold, starving and losing the will to live. That was part of his plan. He wanted to weaken him, make sure he had the upper hand when it came to the interrogation. He might start on that tonight. Or maybe he'd leave him to stew a little longer.

~~~~~~

Down in the cellar, Danny was exactly as Billy imagined. Freezing. Starving. And scared. Scared he wasn't going to make it through this ordeal.

Hearing the faint sound of his captors returning upstairs, Danny braced himself for what might happen next. He felt weak from the lack of food and drink. The sandwiches he'd been given this morning were rank, although he'd eaten them anyway. And one can of Coke in over 24 hours had left him dehydrated. The thirst it created made his head pound even more; not ideal, considering the state it was in right now.

Billy and his sidekick weren't the most caring of captors. They'd grabbed a Chinese takeaway on their way back and had tucked into that before even thinking about heading down to the cellar. Having demolished their own food, Billy popped his balaclava on. He opened the cellar door and flicked on the light switch, to check that Danny hadn't made an unlikely escape. And was still alive.

Seeing he was still breathing, Billy dived back into the kitchen. He grabbed the extra portion of chips they'd bought and took another can out of the fridge. He wasn't in the best of moods after today's frustrations. So, having walked halfway down the cellar steps, he simply tossed the carton of chips and Coke can towards Danny. Then went back upstairs and switched off the light, leaving him in darkness again.

Danny devoured the chips. They were a huge upgrade on the sandwich, despite being cold. He hoped they'd sustain him through the night, assuming it was now night-time. He'd wait for the Coke to reach room temperature, despite his longing thirst. Although room temperature down here wasn't much higher than the fridge it had come from. He was struggling, no doubt about it. He was a tough, strapping, hardened bloke, who'd gone through a lot in his life. But the wound to his head, the freezing cold and the lack of any real sustenance were all beginning to take their toll.

He thought about Tina again. She must be going out of her mind. She was a worrier in the best of circumstances. He hoped Tom and Nat were able to be there for her. He couldn't imagine what they'd be thinking. He just had to focus on getting through the next few hours. And then the next few. And then the few hours after that. Although tomorrow would mark the start of a change in tactics from Billy.

Tomorrow, the real interrogation would begin.

It was late morning by the time Liam returned home from dropping Robbie at Rachel and Matt's for the day. He found Callie waiting for him in the lounge, pen and pad at the ready.

"I've made us both a brew," she gestured towards the mugs on the coffee table. "We need to get cracking. I don't want Robbie to have a late night tonight or he'll be shattered for school tomorrow."

He muttered agreement and sat down on the sofa, unsure where to start.

Thankfully, Callie took the lead. They'd both been mulling things over this morning, but she had a clearer idea of what they needed to do.

"So, the way I see it, there are three things we've got to deal with. Firstly, will the police come round here, because of Danny's disappearance? Secondly, how do we get your winnings safely, assuming the final bet comes in? And thirdly, what the hell do we do after that, so we're not looking over our shoulders for the rest of our lives?"

Liam took a sharp intake of breath. He was confident he could address the first two, but the third one, that was tough.

"Okay, the first one's pretty straightforward. Nothing links me to Danny, beyond a bit of work here and there. That's no reason for them to speak to me. And it's been about six weeks since we were last in touch, so I'd be surprised if they did turn up on the doorstep. Although I wish we could do something to help. I'll never forgive myself if…"

"I know," she said, squeezing his hand.

They both sat in silence momentarily, thinking about someone who didn't deserve the fate it appeared he'd met.

"So," continued Callie, "you think the second thing is straightforward too?"

"Well, I don't think it's straightforward. But I reckon we can sort it."

"Okay. How?"

"Well, if Danny was targeted because of the bets I put on, then I assume picking up the winnings will raise alarm bells too. So, we need to synchronise collecting them and have a safe, quick getaway from each location."

She puffed out her cheeks and thought about what he was suggesting.

"Can we do that ourselves?"

"We could. But it'll be safer to do it in pairs."

"Wha… who are you thinking of? Won't that put them in danger?"

"It shouldn't put anyone in danger, as long as we plan it properly. There's CCTV in the betting shops, but they're not allowed to share the footage. Even if someone gets hold of it, as long as we have decent enough disguises, they shouldn't be able to identify people."

Callie looked confused until Liam explained. He'd been forming the plan in his mind on the drive back from Wandsworth.

"I think we should do the driving. I was going to ask Lucy and Michelle to go into the betting shops. I reckon we can use Michelle's make-up skills to our advantage. Between the two of them, they'd look totally different. Michelle's a bit of a tomboy as it is, so it wouldn't take much for her to look like a bloke.

267

Remember when she dressed up as David Brent for that fancy dress party a few years back? Christ, she was convincing! And we could get a long, dark wig for Lucy and some padding and stuff. It would change her appearance completely."

Callie was horrified. "We'd have to tell them everything. And I'd never forgive myself if it put them in danger."

"Why would it, if we do it how I said? Believe me, I'm not gonna let my sister come to any harm. But this is our one and only chance, Cal. We could take the risk no one's lying in wait and do it between us. But I'm not comfortable with that. We'd either be on our own or, if you drive and I go into the shops, we could be rumbled by the time we get to the second one. At least this way we could get it over and done with quickly."

She pondered what Liam was saying. It did make sense. It could work. Although she hated the idea of involving his family. Having to tell them what he'd done. What their financial situation had driven them to.

"Let me think about it. What about the third thing?"

He'd been dreading her asking that. He didn't have an easy solution. Although he did have an idea.

"I think I need to go away for a bit. And, I hate to say this, but I think you and Robbie should go and stay with your parents for a while."

"Do you really think we're in danger?"

"Honestly, babe, I have no idea. But I'd rather be safe than sorry. I can't get this whole Danny thing out of my head."

"Yeah, me too. Maybe they'll find him, you never know."

He doubted it. All the signs were bad. And the messaging from the police had an air of inevitability about it. They weren't searching for a missing person; they were trying to locate a body.

Callie caught the look in his eyes and filled up.

Liam switched back to practicalities.

"Listen, I've been in touch with Kev and there's a contract going up in the North East for a few months. I don't want to be away from you guys for so long but, in the circumstances, I reckon it'd help to keep you safe."

She calmed at the thought of there being a solution, away from all this. It gave her hope things might work out.

"Where would you live?"

"Kev said I can stay with them for as long as I need to. We won't get to see each other every weekend, but maybe once in a while, you and Robbie could come up? Kev's always banging on about how beautiful it is up there."

Callie nodded, seemingly content with his plan. Kev was an old army mate. Nowadays, he worked for an electrical company, so he'd be able to get Liam a foot in the door, even it was just temporary.

"It would mean me heading up there next Friday. I'll need to get sorted with a car and stuff over the weekend. Be ready for starting work on Monday."

"What are we gonna tell our families?"

Liam hadn't considered that.

"We'll have to come up with a cover story. There's no way I'm telling them the truth. The fewer people that know, the better. Keeps them safe too."

Callie looked anxious. "Oh, God, how did we get to this?"

"I know. I'm so sorry. All I ever wanted to do was get shot of the debt. If I'd known we'd end up like this, I'd never have gone through with it. But we're here now. We've gotta work our way through it. We can do this, Cal."

She was sceptical.

Whoever they'd upset, they didn't sound like reasonable people. She was trying not to show it, but she was scared.

~~~~~~

A few miles away, Danny was about to find out just how unreasonable these people were.

He assumed it was morning, though it was impossible to tell. He'd had a restless night. The pain in his head and the freezing, damp conditions didn't lend themselves to sleep. It was mostly due to sheer exhaustion that he'd had a few moments of respite.

He heard the cellar door creak. The shaft of light snaked across the staircase. The two men walked down together this time.

They both appeared to be carrying something. Even though the light switch had been flicked on, he couldn't focus. The dim light jarred with the darkness he'd become so accustomed to, confusing his vision.

And then he caught sight of what they were bringing down.

The guy at the back was holding a plate and a can. Another goddamn can of Coke. Who knew what delights were on the plate this time?

Meanwhile, the guy at the front was again brandishing a baseball bat.

Danny had been trying to work out what the one-way telephone conversation had meant yesterday. He had no clue what was going on. Maybe he was about to find out.

"Sit up!"

Danny heaved his aching body off the cellar floor and propped himself up against the cold brick wall. The metal hand restraints chafed against his wrist bones. They were cold and unforgiving. Like his captors.

The guy at the back slid the plate across to him and rolled the soft drink can. He was less than enamoured to see a couple of pieces of buttered toast on the plate. Even so, he wolfed it down, not surprised it was cold. No doubt deliberate. Right now, beggars couldn't be choosers.

The moment he'd finished eating, the first guy switched on his torch and nonchalantly swung the bat.

He shone the flashlight into Danny's eyes.

"We're not fucking about any longer. Tell us what happened. If it wasn't you that broke into the house, then who was it? Because we know you know who did it."

"I don't. I swear to God. I did some building work on the house. The guy who owned it was an utter prick and he tried not to pay his bill. I had to threaten him to get the money, but it was only what he owed me."

His throat was dry and painful. Every word hurt, but he had to plead his innocence. He had to get them to believe him. He feared his life depended on it.

"We don't believe you. It had to be an inside job. You're the only one who had all the info."

"Why? Why would I do that? I've been clean for fifteen years!"

"Because of what was on offer. You got greedy."

"I didn't think they took much? Not according to the police. Or the telly."

"Don't believe everything you see on the news," the second guy piped up this time.

"I've no idea how much. How could it have been me?"

The other two men were starting to have creeping doubts. So far though, there was no other suspect. Everything added up to it being Danny. Plus the fence had mentioned his name too. It was too much of a coincidence.

"You've been peddling some watches to a guy in north London. Deny that."

"I haven't. Really, I haven't. Why would you think that?" He was confused. He could only assume Liam had done something with the watches, but why would that implicate him?

"He gave us your name."

What the fuck? Danny was in shock. He'd known Karl for years. So it wasn't as if he'd get mixed up over who was who. Why the hell would he put him in it, especially when this time he was completely innocent? It didn't make sense.

"I swear to you, it wasn't me." Had they threatened the life out of Karl, he thought? Had he blurted out the first name that came to him? Christ, from his perspective that was the definition of misfortune.

"So, you admit you know him?"

"No. I don't know about any of this. Please, let me go. I won't say anything about what's happened. You've got the wrong bloke. Maybe it's someone else called Danny."

Billy lost his patience at this suggestion. He swung the bat and aimed it squarely into Danny's ribs, generating a yelp of pain as it connected with its target.

"So, someone else happened to have the alarm codes and access to the keys? They also saw inside the safe and got hold of the combination. They also happen to be called Danny. But it's not you? Fuck me, you've been unlucky here, mate. Should we just untie you now?"

He didn't respond to his captor's theoretical questions. The look of thunder in Billy's eyes stopped him in his tracks. Instead of thinking of a credible answer, he was praying that the bat wasn't wielded in his direction again. His ribs were still throbbing from the most recent blow. He hung his head, disconsolate, out of ideas on how he could escape this situation.

"Well then?" Billy's sidekick interjected once again.

"I know it looks bad, but I promise you, I didn't burgle that house. I haven't stepped foot in the place since the day he finally paid me. As far as I know, that was before it was robbed. Mitchell was there. I made sure he was there. I just wanted to be paid for the work I did. There's nothing more I can say, but I'm telling the truth." Danny was of course mostly telling the truth, but protecting the real burglar wasn't helping his case. He prayed it would be sufficient.

"Fucker!" Billy's frustration boiled over as he was unable to break Danny through the measured route. He swung the bat once more, this time crashing it into his shoulder. Another cry of pain echoed through the cellar.

And then they were gone. By the time Danny opened his eyes, squinting from the pain, his two captors were heading back up the stone staircase. The light was turned off and he was left alone, again.

The two men had given up on their interrogation. For now.

-50-

If only Liam hadn't decided to sell the watches so quickly. If only he'd waited a little longer. And if only he hadn't placed any more bets. Especially that, in fact. That was the real red rag to the bull.

The watches were incidental to the people behind Danny's kidnapping. They had so many of them. The cash was almost as irrelevant. Their wealth was obscene. The thing that mattered most to them was the book.

Danny's captors were still convinced he was to blame for the burglary. They hadn't broken him yet but, when they did, he'd pay. If he'd only stolen the cash and the watches, they would have warned him off, recovered the goods and moved on. But the disappearance of the book changed everything. Now the thief appeared to have worked out some of the codes, they were even more desperate. They had to track it down and get it back to its rightful owners. The consequences of not doing so didn't bear thinking about.

They'd already turned Danny's house upside down and failed to find a single piece of evidence linking him to the burglary. They hadn't located any additional premises he could've used to store his haul. Kidnapping him was the only course of action they could think of to find out what had happened to the book. Until they discovered its whereabouts, he wasn't in mortal danger. But the longer this went on, the greater the risk of something going wrong.

They needed to start getting results.

They were done with their threatening questions and a bit of a whack here and there from a baseball bat. Yesterday proved that he wasn't going to succumb to the odd smack. Today, they'd start to turn the screws. Literally.

If he wasn't the actual robber then they'd up the pressure every day, until he told them who did carry out the burglary.

They hadn't fed him at all today. All he'd had was a flat can of Coke, shaken up by being thrown across the cellar floor. Tossed in frustration more than anything else. But the lack of food was a deliberate tactic, aimed to weaken his resolve.

For the next hour, Danny had to endure the first crude methods of torture since he'd been imprisoned. Despite his injuries, starvation and sleep deprivation, Danny was remarkably resilient. He'd survived the beatings and the damp, freezing, stone floor of the cellar. He wasn't going to give in easily. He was terrified for his life, but he couldn't let them do this to Liam and rob a young family of its dad. If he could cope a little longer, they couldn't hold him forever.

The next day, the process was repeated. As was the outcome. Although it was touch and go. By now, Danny's wrists were bleeding, he was weaker than he'd ever felt in his life and his head was throbbing. He prayed the end of his ordeal was in sight, as he didn't know how much longer he could hold out for. And he prayed that the end meant he'd be set free. Not the alternative.

Five days on from his abduction, Danny had a fleeting moment of euphoria. His captors began to unlock his handcuffs. The elation turned to despair when he realised they weren't releasing him. Far from it. They were simply putting him in position for today's interrogation. He had no energy to put up a fight as they heaved his large frame upside-down, suspended from the ceiling.

275

This wasn't going to be pleasant.

For the next half-hour, they alternated between waterboarding and beatings. It wasn't the extreme form of waterboarding. That could have potentially drowned him. Even so, it was their most brutal treatment to date.

Still, he resisted.

Back upstairs, Billy updated his boss on the lack of progress. He didn't seem too perturbed. They had one final throw of the dice coming up. Tonight Chelsea were playing at home to Bournemouth. They already knew what the score would be; Alex and Petr had paid a quick trip to Stamford Bridge earlier. They'd ensured everything was in place. If the rat in the cellar wasn't their man, a 3-0 win for the Cherries would smoke their skunk out of its hiding place.

Soon, they'd snare their target. And revenge would be sweet.

~~~~~~

"Shhhhhhh! Shhhhhh! You'll wake Robbie."

"Fuck it, let's wake him. Let's crack open some Champagne. Fucking hell Cal, we did it!"

She laughed at his exhilaration and Liam shrieked once more. He hugged Callie like there was no tomorrow. Except there was. And it was the day they had to go through their elaborate plan. If tonight's result was going to mean anything. They weren't yet home and dry.

The realisation made Liam calm down.

He'd been caught in two minds when he first placed the bet for tonight. Was he best to pick up the winnings tomorrow, straight after the game? Or would it be safer to hold off for a week or so and hope that, if anyone was lying in wait, they'd lose interest after a few days?

The conclusion he'd reached was the sooner the better. Maybe it carried a greater degree of risk, but he couldn't imagine waiting. He didn't think his nerves would hold out, never mind what it would've done to Callie in that time. Besides, he no longer had a choice in the matter. By Friday morning, he'd be heading north.

It was now or never.

51

Danny turned his pounding head towards the chink of light at the top of the stairs. Not again. Please, no.

This time it was just one of his captors who came down the stairs. Instead of a wrench or some instrument of torture, he had a plate of food in his hand. Danny could've cried with relief.

The captor placed the plate on the floor and rolled another ice-cold can across to him. Without saying a word, he turned and disappeared back up the stairs.

Danny struggled to move his aching bones and sit up. Everything hurt. He was in complete agony, but the reward was food. His first in three days. He had no concept of timescales down there. No idea that February had crept in overnight. But the starvation was now so acute that he knew several days must have passed since his last meal.

Eventually, he managed to sit upright. It had taken a herculean effort and he was exhausted, but it was worth it. On the plate was a cold pasty. Cheese and onion. Normally he'd hate it. He was a steak bake sort of guy. Today he would savour the lot. Even the icy can was a welcome boost. He'd have given anything for a hot cup of tea. But right now, any liquid helped to keep him going.

He must have spent a good half-hour relishing every mouthful of his food and drink. He didn't know whether it was a good or bad sign that his captors had given him food after so long. If it was his last for a while, he'd enjoyed it like a gourmet meal.

As he swallowed the final morsel, Danny was unaware of the conversation taking place above him. The reason why today's torture session was on hold.

"You're in place then? Cos it could happen at any point from today onwards. If we catch anyone picking up the winnings, we've got 'em. Keep me posted. And don't fuck this up."

Billy hung up and tossed his phone onto the table. He and his sidekick were biding their time upstairs in the kitchen. Depending on how things turned out, they might not have to put the squeeze on their captive today. With any luck, they'd nab the thieving bastards at one of the betting shops and then bring them back here. It would soon become clear whether Danny was in on it all at that point. If not, they'd let him go. But if he was… Billy was looking forward to exacting some proper punishment.

Finally, the end was in sight.

~~~~~~

"Christ's sake, Liam, what the hell were you thinking? Have you lost your absolute fuckin' mind?"

Lucy's initial response didn't fill them with hope.

Callie recognised the reaction though. It had been exactly the same for her. It was *so* out of character for him. Once he'd laid bare the extent of their money worries, she'd realised why he'd acted so recklessly. In time, she hoped Lucy would develop that same empathy.

It had been a few days since they'd spilt the beans to Lucy and Michelle about the burglary. Lucy was heartbroken her brother hadn't been able to open up to his family. Why hadn't he asked for more help? Or been totally upfront about his financial situation? Listening to how much debt they were in and how it kept growing exponentially, she softened a little. She still wasn't impressed by his actions, but there were mitigating circumstances.

Despite Lucy's reaction at the outset, the two girls agreed to take part in their plan. Lucy wouldn't look at her brother again with the same unquestioning admiration, but she'd still do anything to help him out. As long as they did things the way they'd discussed, she was confident they'd all be fine.

Michelle was even more assured they could do this. She was a couple of years Lucy's senior and definitely the one who wore the trousers in their relationship. In some ways, she was looking forward to the thrill. She wasn't averse to a bit of danger in her life.

Today was the day.

They'd decided to execute their plan late morning. Callie was about to start night shifts, so she could have a few hours rest afterwards, while Lucy and Michelle had both taken the day off work.

Once Liam had dropped Robbie off at school, they drove to Lucy and Michelle's place in Brentford. They'd have no more than half an hour to run through all the arrangements again. They wanted to get to each shop well in advance, do a bit of a recce driving around and make sure no one was watching them. Every aspect was discussed. Parking, walking to the shop, what they'd do once they were in there. And of course, getting out afterwards. That could be the toughest part. Making their getaway.

Opening the door to them, Michelle provided everyone with a little light relief. Her costume was incredible. Not because it looked fake or over the top, but because it was so realistic. They initially thought a man had answered the door. Black jeans, dark green trainers and sweatshirt. An aubergine bomber jacket and baseball cap. They were the clothes, but the real genius was the short haircut Michelle now had. And the make-up that disguised the true contours of her face. She even had some authentic-looking stubble. Liam did a double-take, before realising very close up that it was expertly drawn on.

The looks of confusion on their faces made Michelle roar with laughter and it was infectious. Exactly what they needed.

Lucy came bounding down the stairs, keen to see what all the hilarity was about. She looked equally convincing. She'd been transformed from an attractive, slim, well-dressed woman with blonde shoulder-length hair. She was now a heftier, non-descript girl, with unkempt brown hair, tied up roughly. The look was completed with much more casual, almost scruffy clothes.

In different circumstances, Liam would have taken their photos for the family album, shown them to his mum and dad. And Robbie, who would have found it hilarious. This was not the time.

Half an hour later, having gone through everything several times, they were ready for the off.

The atmosphere in the hall was tense. The nerves were palpable. They all hugged, wished each other luck and then set off.

Liam was driving Lucy in her car to Southfields while Callie and Michelle headed to Neasden. They were both planning to get to their respective locations around 10.30am. They'd drive round for twenty minutes to suss things out. Then their partners-in-crime would stroll to each shop, aiming to enter at exactly 11.00am.

Neither vehicle spotted anything as they drove around. That didn't mean there wasn't anyone watching them. Or that there wouldn't be someone already inside the bookies. That was the scariest thought. What if Lucy or Michelle ended up trapped inside? Liam felt they'd skimmed over that possibility. The whole thing was starting to worry him now.

He glanced at the clock in the car. It was 10.45am.

"Lucy, give Cal a ring will you and tell her to park round the back of the bookies? I don't think you or Michelle should have to walk very far once you get out of the shop. It feels too risky."

She did as he suggested. His nerves were starting to rub off on her. Would there really be someone watching them? It all seemed a little too fantastical. Then again, Danny's disappearance was sobering for them all. They shouldn't take anything for granted.

"Sorted. Anything else, before I hang up?"

"No. Are they ok? Have they noticed anything suspicious?"

"No, they're fine. All ready to go."

She wished them luck and hung up.

"Right, you know exactly what you're doing and you're going to be mega careful aren't you?" Liam asked his unrecognisable sister.

"I'm good. And you're going to be as close to the back door as you can get?"

"I am. If I spot anything I don't like the look of, I'll text you, ok?"

"Ok. Don't worry, I'll be fine."

"You'd better be. Take care."

Lucy got out at almost exactly the same moment as Michelle was stepping out of Callie's car in Neasden. They were a few streets away from their respective destinations. By the time they'd slowly wandered around and headed into the bookies, it should be 11:00am on the dot.

Sure enough, like clockwork, they had a steady stroll, each looking in shop windows as they went. They were relatively inconspicuous, blending into the background. Normal people in a normal suburb, doing normal things.

And then they each reached the door of their betting shop.

No going back now.

~~~~~~

Michelle pushed the door open into Coral's and took a quick look around, as the entry bell sounded. There were four customers in the front section and a middle-aged man behind the counter. More than she would've liked, but she comforted herself with the thought of safety in numbers.

She focused on acting natural, in her usual environment. She glanced up at the screens and looked for a quiet spot. Somewhere she could spend a few minutes gathering her thoughts. Pretend to fill out a betting slip. Check out the other customers and get ready for the next step. Remember, she thought to herself, you're a bloke.

Having picked her table, she pulled out a chair, sat down and spread her legs. From where she sat, she could see all the other customers.

Two of them were in close proximity, looking like your average betting shop regulars. It appeared they knew each other, though they weren't sat together. Michelle contented herself they weren't waiting for her. Or at least, not waiting for someone picking up the winnings she was there to collect.

To the right of those two, a younger man looked to be studying the form in his Racing Post. Head down, very focused, betting slips laid out in front of him. Every so often, he'd circle a horse in his paper. He looked to be trying to give the impression she was looking to create. It unnerved her; was he trying too hard to fade into the background? Come to think of it, was she?

To the left, sat on one of the bar stools, was an older guy. He had an almost full pint of beer on the shelf next to him and a packet of yet-to-be-opened crisps. He was engrossed in the TV screens, having an on-off conversation with the bloke behind the counter.

She decided that, if any of them were interested in what she was about to do, it was the younger guy on the right-hand side of the shop. If she was to get away without arousing suspicion, she'd have to avoid his attention.

Time to move.

Taking her betting slip up to the counter, Michelle also grabbed two other pieces of paper out of her jacket pocket.

"Hi, mate, what can I do you for?" So far so good, Eddy, the betting shop employee was talking to her as if she was a man.

"Can I have a tenner on that, pal?" she replied, putting on her best deep voice, trying not to sound like a parody. "And that as well, please." She took a deep breath as she passed the winning betting slip across the counter. The hand-written note was on top, impossible to miss.

It was similar to the one Liam had used a few days ago.

Can I have a cheque for my winnings?

And any chance I can sneak out of the back door?

Please don't mention out loud that you're sorting out winnings for me.

I think someone's following me.

Don't want to get jumped, even if I don't have the cash on me.

Thank you.

Eddy had a brief look of confusion on his face, but looked back at her and nodded his affirmation.

"Any chance I can use your toilet, mate?"

"Yeah, no problem. I'll just get this bet on for you. It'll be ready when you come back out."

"Cheers."

Michelle paused for no more than a couple of minutes inside the cubicle. As she headed back out, she almost jumped out of her skin when the Private door into the corridor opened. It was Eddy. He had a few slips of paper in his hand.

"Here you go, mate. Go through that door there and you'll be out on the back street. Take it easy." Eddy's words were measured enough, but he sounded a little nervous, had a few beads of sweat on his forehead. He seemed eager to get back to the counter.

She pushed her concerns to the back of her head. Of course, he'd be keen to get back out front; the betting shop had a few customers in it. He couldn't leave it unattended for any length of time.

Eddy's reaction implied that it wasn't unusual to leave by the back door. Although it was probably more common for a successful punter to get their winnings in cash. The cheque served a double purpose for Liam though. Not only was it safer than cash, but he could prove where it was from when he deposited it in the bank.

She still felt on edge. She still had to go through that door, not knowing what lay beyond it. Still had to hope and pray that Callie was parked nearby. That some fate hadn't befallen her while she'd been in the betting shop. They weren't out of the woods just yet.

Michelle took a deep breath and pushed the exit door.

52

Ten minutes earlier, Lucy had been going through the same process, ten miles away.

There were only two customers in Betfred in Southfields. They looked on the surface to be regulars. They chatted intermittently with the young woman behind the counter. They seemed to have hints of an eastern European accent, Polish maybe? That wasn't unusual. And they looked interested in various races.

Lucy followed exactly the same procedure that Michelle had. She found a seat where she could view everyone. She casually took a betting slip and looked as though she was studying form. She filled out the betting slip with one horse's details on it. Then, she stood up and went to have the same secret conversation with the betting shop employee.

"Hi, can I put a tenner on that horse, please?"

She slid the three pieces of paper across the counter towards the young woman. Her name badge said Angela.

Can I have a cheque for my winnings?

And any chance I can sneak out of the back door?

Please don't mention out loud that you're sorting out winnings for me.

I think someone's following me.

Don't want to get jumped, even if I don't have the cash on me.

Thank you.

Angela was young, around mid-twenties. She looked startled at the note, not the reaction Lucy had been hoping for.

For one awful moment, she thought Angela might be scared this was a note from an armed robber or something. The panic on her face was tangible. She was now beginning to panic herself. What if she gave her away or refused to follow the instructions? What if she 'disappeared' like Liam's friend Danny had? She was starting to regret getting involved in this hair-brained idea. Stupid! How could she have been so stupid?

And then to her relief, she relaxed again and smiled at her.

"Do you have a toilet in here?" she asked.

"Yeah, through that door there. I'll sort your bet out for when you come back."

"Thanks, love. You never know when you'll get the urge once you've had kids. Jesus, I'm busting!" and with that Lucy winked at her and headed towards the toilets.

Angela had a quick glance up at the two men and realised they'd been completely disinterested in the woman. They were engrossed in an overseas horse race on the TV, which was reaching its climax.

She wrote a reply to the note and checked out the winning betting slip, writing a cheque for £20,500. She didn't know who to make it out to, so left that blank. After all, the clock was ticking.

As the two men were shouting at the screen, urging their horse to victory, she discreetly slipped away. Out into the back office, to the corridor that led to the toilets.

A relieved Lucy was waiting by the back door, eager to make her exit.

"Read the note. Be quick and please, stay safe!" Angela said to her, the urgency in her voice not escaping Lucy.

"Thank you," she replied, taking the papers from her grasp. She pushed through the back door, shoving the other pieces of paper safely into her jacket pocket. Quickly, she looked at the rushed, handwritten scrawl that had been scribbled on the back of her note.

Run! 2 men in shop are looking for the winner of this bet.
Will stall for as long as poss.

Shit!

The rear entrance led out into a small car park. Liam was supposed to be there, engine running, ready to go. But there was no sign of him. Jesus, where are you, bruv?

She ran, through the car park, straight ahead, towards the side road. There was no other exit available, apart from heading back towards the front of the betting shop. That was too risky. She hoped she'd made the right decision. Prayed that Liam was close by. And that he was safe.

Meanwhile, in the shop, Angela went back to the counter, her heart pounding, desperate to look as if everything was normal. She remained calm on the outside, pretended to carry on with her day-to-day tasks. The composure dissipated as soon as one of the men spoke.

"Where's that woman?"

"Ey?"

"The one that was just in here. She went to the toilet."

"She's probably still in there. Why?"

"You haven't done anything stupid, have you?"

"I've no idea what you're talking about," she feigned, convinced that the creeping redness across her face would give the game away.

"Alex, check."

No! she thought. Not yet. Please, not yet. That woman needed more time. As did she. Her boss was due in at 11.30am. Just a few more minutes and she'd have some backup. As it was, she was on her own.

She heard shouting in the rear of the shop as Alex discovered the woman was no longer there.

The other guy ran through to the back, turning only to hiss "you stupid woman, we warned you!". She was terrified. What would they do to her? It was true, they had warned her. But she'd made a moral judgement. She'd decided that they weren't who they said they were. They weren't on the right side of the law. Their veiled threat held too much menace in it to be legitimate.

And then she remembered something. Something that would potentially save her.

~~~~~~

Lucy was now on the side street, running towards the main road. She grabbed her phone, trying desperately to call Liam without dropping it or slowing her pace.

It went to voicemail. "Liam, where the hell are you?" she cried, panic-stricken down the phone. "They're on to us. I'm out the back. I'm heading towards the main road. Hurry! Please hurry!"

As she made it to the main road, she glanced behind. One of the men from the bookies was now hurtling through the car park. She was breathless, terror-stricken. Which way should she go? Left or right? She had seconds to make her decision.

And then a car sped towards her, braking at the last minute, screeching its tyres. No decision to make. She flung the door open and leapt into the passenger seat. Ready to murder the driver.

Meanwhile, Alex had made it to the side street in time to catch a glimpse of Lucy's small black car. It accelerated away towards the junction at the top of the street. He had no chance of getting the number plate. He could barely even make out the model of the car. By the time he'd reach the main road, it would be well gone.

Fuck! Fuck, fuck, fuck!

As Petr came racing up behind him, Alex had already turned to go back inside. He shook his head at Petr.

The two men stormed back into the shop, bent on exacting revenge. But they were stopped dead in their tracks when they got back inside. They weren't prepared for the sight that met them.

Angela had pressed the panic button and was wielding a baseball bat, extracted from below the counter. She knew she was no match for these thugs, but it would at least buy her a few precious minutes. Minutes that could save her.

"The police are on their way and it's all captured on CCTV. So don't even think of doing anything stupid. Just get out."

Angela was trying to sound brave. Inside she was a quivering wreck. The guys had faces like thunder.

The uneasy stand-off was brief and silent. Her aggressors glared at her, wishing her harm. Full of fury that she had helped their target escape. Their eyes were black and cold, seemingly void of any emotion, other than anger.

And then, just like that, they were gone. A threat was spat from their lips as they left, which would leave Angela with many a sleepless night. But she had, for now at least, escaped harm.

She exhaled, not realising that she'd been holding her breath all this time. And then, her heart leapt as she heard the bell go and the door opened once more.

"Hey, what the hell's going on?"

Justin. Her boss. Never had she been so pleased to see him.

Although he wouldn't be her boss for much longer. By the afternoon that same day, Angela had been signed off on the sick and had handed in her notice. She didn't intend to step foot into that betting shop ever again.

~~~~~~

"Where the hell were you?" Lucy asked breathlessly as she leapt into the car.

"Sorry. I'm so sorry. I drove round a few minutes ago and there was a delivery van blocking the side street. I couldn't stop cos I was obstructing the traffic, so I had to drive round the block again. I thought I'd never get back here."

As he sped to the end of the street, Liam looked in his rear-view mirror. No sign of anyone. At the junction, his luck was in. He managed to pull straight out, turning right, away from their chasers. Away from anyone clocking the registration number. On the road to safety.

He breathed a sigh of relief. It looked as though they'd escaped the clutches of whoever was on to them. But what of Callie and Michelle?

Liam hadn't heard anything from either of them for half an hour. He was desperate to know they were safe.

Once they were a few miles away, having checked for signs of anyone following them, he pulled into the industrial estate. It was due to be their rendezvous point, virtually midway between the two bookies. Assuming all had gone to plan, Michelle would jump back in with Lucy and Liam would drive Callie home.

As soon as he parked up, he called Callie's phone. Voicemail. Lucy meanwhile was trying to ring Michelle. It was a similar story. No answer.

Brother and sister looked at one another in silence. What the hell were they supposed to do now?

53

As she opened the back door, Michelle sighed with relief that no one was on the other side, waiting to nab her.

That relief didn't last long. Because Callie was also nowhere to be seen.

She looked up and down the back street. Nothing.

Her phone buzzed. It was a text from Callie.

Car won't start, had to abandon it!

Trying to grab a cab & will get to you asap

Just get away from there, quickly!

I've got a bad feeling, think someone's watching x

The ominous words struck fear into Michelle. She was already running before she'd even finished reading the final line of text. She made a split-second decision to go left. There was a bend in the road further up, which would hide her from view if anyone was to pursue her.

As she ran up the road, she glanced back. She wished she hadn't. One of the men from the betting shop had appeared at the back door. From this distance, she couldn't tell which one, but at the speed he was now running she may well find out soon.

She began to sprint, desperate to reach the end of the road, to have somewhere where she could take cover. Her lungs were now heaving, her heart was pounding and the lactic acid was starting to slow her down.

Another look back. He was getting closer.

At last, she came to the junction with the main road. No time to dither, she turned a swift left, glancing back one more time. He was quicker than her, catching her with every stride. She couldn't stay ahead of him much longer. She had to hide. But where?

Michelle ran towards another junction, frantically looking for somewhere she could blend in. Where? Think, think, think!

A solution came to her. If only she could get there in time.

There was a bus pulled into the stop ahead. But she could tell it was about to pull away. With every sinew aching, she forced herself to use the final drop of energy.

Please, please, not yet. Not yet. Soon, but not yet.

Finally, in the nick of time, she made it to the bus, leapt on and grabbed the rail, so she didn't fall backwards.

Made it!

Turning round to see where her assailant was, she was horrified to see how close he was to getting on the bus.

Pull away, pull away, she implored.

She scrambled further into the bus, not knowing what to do for the best. She pushed through several standing passengers, thinking she must be safe now. Surely they wouldn't do anything to her, even if they managed to board?

To her relief, the bus was now moving. Her chaser had lost the race, a fraction too slow to get on board. She strained her neck to see where he was, what he was doing. She could see him, almost bent double on the pavement, exhausted from his pursuit. Ha! she thought. Then to her dismay, as he straightened up again, she realised he was on the phone. He was noting the number of the bus, relaying it to someone. An accomplice. Maybe ready and waiting to follow her in a car.

Michelle jumped as her phone rang. She grabbed it from her pocket.

"Callie!" she gasped, trying to regain her breath.

"Michelle, are you ok?"

"I've just been chased. I'm on a bus." She looked up. "The number 112. No idea where it's headed. But I think they might be following me. What do I do?"

"Stay on the phone, ok? And stay on the bus for the time being as well. I'm jumping in a cab now. I'll get them to catch up with you. They'll know where it goes."

"Ok, thanks, Cal."

"Do you know where you got on at?"

"Erm, no idea. Let me ask someone."

Callie heard the sound of muffled voices in the background.

"Ok, it was Chartley Avenue and the bus is headed towards Ealing Broadway."

"Handy! Ok, I'll get to you as soon as possible. Stay with me, in case I need to give you any other instructions or if you're worried about anything."

"I will, don't worry."

Michelle spied an empty seat further up the bus, towards the driver. There was a sporty-looking guy sat at the window seat. He briefly acknowledged her as she sat down next to him. He too was wearing black jeans, but with white trainers, she noticed. She took her earphones out of her jacket pocket and plugged them into her phone. Slotting one of the pods in her ear, she'd be able to listen to Callie, as well as hearing what was going on around her.

As she sunk back into the seat, she tried to control her breathing. It was a losing battle. She'd been fit in her younger days, but that sprint was the first time she'd done any serious exercise in the last few years. She needed to focus. Breathe in, breathe out. Slowly. Count to five each time. It was beginning to slow her breath and clear her brain. The sudden clarity gave her an idea.

294

"You ok, mate?"

"Yeah, I will be. Just had a bit of a run-in with some guys back there. Bit of undercover work."

The stranger on the bus seemed intrigued and asked what the undercover work was. Michelle summoned her creative juices and made up a tale. Still, the stranger was interested.

"I've got an idea," she said suddenly.

His eyes lit up. Obviously a fan of Line of Duty and the like, Michelle thought to herself.

"Are you a fast runner?" He nodded, so she continued. "Why don't you have my jacket and baseball cap on when you get off at your stop? If it looks like someone's following you, sprint away from them as fast as you can. If they happen to catch you, just plead ignorance. That'll give me a chance to escape from them."

She couldn't believe he was up for it. She took off her jacket and baseball cap and then hunted in her jeans. Found a couple of twenties. She shoved them in his hand.

"Nah, I don't need paying for it. I like a bit of danger in my life!"

"Take it. And thank you. No, put the jacket on over yours, I think it'll fit." Plus it'll make you look bulkier, like me, she thought.

There were a few minutes to go before the stranger's stop. Michelle was trying to relax. But the adrenaline was pumping and it was all she could do just to get her breathing under control again. She briefly spoke to Callie on the phone, to check she was still there. "Erm, yeah. Jesus, Michelle, I heard what you're planning. Bit mental, but hope it works."

And then, suddenly, the bus pulled over and the stranger rose from his seat. As he squeezed past her, he patted her on the shoulder and said "Good luck, love. You might want to work on the voice if you're trying to pass yourself off as a bloke though!"

Michelle laughed and thanked him again. In all her panic, she'd completely forgotten to tone down the tenor of her voice. Lucky she'd given him that fabricated story. What an idiot she was!

She watched intently as he jumped off the bus. He played the part well. Using the cap to shield his face as much as possible, he looked up ahead and then glanced behind him. Initially, he began to walk at a normal pace and then, as the bus pulled away from the stop, her heart leapt into her mouth. She saw him glance behind once more. And break into a sprint.

A car had sped past the bus, overtaking as it was pulling out and then coming to an abrupt halt in front of it. The bus driver was forced to slam on his brakes.

Michelle was horrified to see the passenger door fling open. Her original chaser jumped out and began to pursue her decoy. But her man was a pro and had the advantage of local knowledge. He'd already got a head start and he was faster, much faster than she had been. The bus driver pulled around the stationary car, blasting his horn and shouting expletives. As he did so, Michelle saw her ally disappear out of sight. Relief swept over her, praying they would both escape from these men.

"Callie, are you there?"

"I am, we're not far away from you now. You should be able to get off in a couple of stops."

"Ok. I think we've lost them. For now."

A few minutes later, Callie told Michelle to get off at the next stop, walk in the opposite direction of the bus and then turn down the first side street. She did so, shaking with fear that her assailants would be waiting for her, ready to pounce.

Her fear made her pick up the pace and she was almost breaking into a run as she turned into the side street. She was startled as a car screeched up beside her. The back door flung open. She didn't have the energy to run, she was spent. Oh, God, she thought, not now, not after all this. I was so close.

A voice called out from the back seat.

"Get in! Quick!"

Callie! Callie! Thank Christ, thought Michelle, it's Callie!

She almost collapsed in relief, but came to her senses, leaping into the car and hugging her sister-in-law for all she was worth.

The private hire driver was bemused, wondering what on earth was going on with these women. They'd had the maddest dash to get here, chasing a bus of all things. But what the hell, this was going to be a decent fare, so he'd go with it.

Once they'd both calmed down and paused for breath, they finally remembered to hang up their phones. Almost immediately, they both beeped, numerous times. Voicemail after voicemail. Texts. Missed calls. Frantic, urgent, desperate contacts from Lucy and Liam. All as yet unanswered. They both looked at the time. They were almost half an hour late for their meet-up. And they'd been out of range all that time. Their partners must have been going out of their minds with worry.

"Do you want to ring them or will I?" she asked Callie, grimacing at the prospect. Michelle drew the short straw and had her ears pierced for the next few minutes. Lucy went ballistic with rage, fury and then finally relief.

The four of them had made it through their ordeal. They were now safe. *They* were. Unfortunately, someone else was about to bear the brunt of their chasers' frustrations.

54

In the grim surroundings of the cellar, Danny's mind was starting to drift into oblivion. Trying to detach itself from the pain he felt coursing through his body.

It was clear his captors were in a bad mood today. Their whole demeanour had changed dramatically from the day before. They'd come trudging down the steps earlier with their torture tools. If he could've seen their faces behind the balaclavas, he'd have known that today was going to be worse.

What had happened, he wondered?

Another half-hour of torture ensued. Another systematic session of waterboarding and beatings. And though Danny was now close to breaking point, he managed to summon every ounce of strength to resist. Determined not to let Liam become a victim of the same brutality.

His captors were exasperated.

"We're getting nowhere here," Billy said, stepping back from Danny as he looked to slip in and out of consciousness.

The other guy grunted in agreement. They released him from his suspension, re-connecting him to the shackles as he lay, broken, on the floor.

"I reckon we should finish him off."

"You know we can't. Not unless the big man gives us the go-ahead."

"Yeah, but…"

"Yeah, but nothing. We wait for our orders."

"He's gonna be well pissed off after today though, isn't he?"

"Not as pissed off as I am. To get that close."

The baseball bat was swung again, this time in pure frustration and against the wall of the cellar. The sheer force saw it splinter and cause even greater anger to rise in the belly of its holder.

"Fuck! Those bloody Neanderthals."

At that, Billy threw the weapon at the wall and made one final threat to Danny.

"You either tell us who did it, or you're a goner mate. Our boss has had enough. You got that?"

He was right in his face, his hand thrust around his throat, almost choking him. Almost ending his life there and then.

Weakly, forlornly, Danny's response was still the same. Quieter than it had been, his voice broken by days of starvation and maltreatment. "I…don't…know. Really… I…don't…know." He was on the verge of collapse.

Billy released his grip, throwing Danny's head back as he did so. He spat on the floor beside him as he stood and walked away. The two captors made their way up the stairs, plunging the cellar into darkness once again. Leaving Danny alone with his thoughts and his pain.

He didn't see them for the rest of the day and didn't receive any food or drink. He ached everywhere. His limbs were either stiff from the forced position and cold floor, or in agony from the beatings and torture. His spirit was almost broken now. He couldn't take much more of this.

He didn't know it was evening by the time he drifted off. His body clock was completely out of kilter, thanks to the lack of windows and natural daylight. But it was around 11pm when he finally gave in to the exhaustion. Every night now he was left wondering if it would be his last.

Upstairs, Billy had spent the evening defending himself to the big man. It had been a heated conversation. More than once, Billy came close to telling his boss where he could shove it. More than once, his boss thought about dishing out his own punishment to his heavies. But he knew that would be counter-productive. He needed these guys, even if they did mess up occasionally. And they knew too much.

Billy was fuming. It wasn't his fault directly, but they were his henchmen, so he had to take responsibility. He should've done the damn job himself.

The instructions from above were loud and clear; one more day. If he didn't break by then, he was probably telling the truth. They either got him to talk or they released him. Billy was still convinced Danny was in on it, but without any evidence, they were headed down a cul-de-sac. His bosses were right. Decisive action had to be taken.

~~~~~~

Across London, the Family Liaison Officer had left earlier that evening. She'd given Tina and Tom the same update as the previous five days. No news. No sign of Danny. No trace of him on CCTV. No body located in the reservoir. No cards used. No phone records. Nothing. He had simply disappeared off the face of the earth.

Finally, she shared the bad news. They were scaling down the search. They'd keep the case files open, but they couldn't continue looking for him. He either didn't want to be found or he'd drowned in the reservoir and was untraceable in such a vast expanse of water.

Tina was still recovering from that body blow when Tom hit her with a double whammy.

"Mum, I'm so sorry, I might have to go back to work next week."

He hated having to say this. He'd been dreading broaching the subject, but he'd already taken a week off and they were no further forward. He was in the middle of a big case and Nat also needed his help at home. Juggling her job as well as the three kids was a struggle, especially when they had no other family nearby. They could count on friends in the short term, but it was the uncertainty of it all. How long could they go on like this?

"It's okay, love, I understand. Really I do." The strain of the last few days showed in his mum's face. She seemed to have aged overnight.

"It's the not knowing, mum, you know?"

She nodded, her eyes filling with tears. The thing was, she wasn't sure whether she wanted to know or not. This purgatory was absolute hell. But once she did know what had happened to Danny, would it just confirm her worst fears?

55

It was the morning of the move.

As far as Robbie was concerned, these were exciting times, with lots of things to look forward to in the future. He couldn't wait to stay with his grandparents for a few weeks; it would be such fun. Gran and Granddad lived really close to Griffin Park too, so he might catch a glimpse of it every now and again. Maybe he'd get to another game soon as well?

For Robbie's parents, however, they felt as if their lives had become a whirlwind, turned on its head, spinning around, not knowing when it would stop.

Having such a short amount of time to make major life decisions had been exhausting for Liam and Callie. Over the last few days, they'd got the flat into as decent a state as they could. They'd had it valued by several estate agents and plumped for the one that gave them the lowest commission rate. It would go on the market in the next day or so and the agent would handle any viewings. In an ideal world, they'd have put more effort into getting it ready, to maximise the price. But this was no time for aesthetics. Even so, it was a far cry from when they'd looked around it all those years ago. Small and basic maybe, but at least it now looked like a well-loved home.

Earlier that week, while Robbie was at school and Callie was catching up with friends, Liam went back up into the attic. It had only been six weeks since the last time, but the holdall had collected dust in the intervening period. As he lugged it through the loft hatch, it made him cough. The weight of the holdall and the dust on his chest almost made him lose his grip, but he leapt from the ladders just in time. A feeling of déjà vu swept over him. Memories from a couple of months back, that felt like a lifetime ago.

He'd bought some plastic zipper bags, sturdy enough to withstand any possible water leaks. It must have taken him a good hour or more to do this particular job. His paranoia returned at the thought of being rumbled now; the booty on show for all to see.

He counted the money out once more and stashed it in the bags, focusing on all the batched notes initially. Six bags contained fifty batches, a cool £125,000 in each, while the seventh held the remaining eighteen batches. Finally, he gathered up the loose notes. Once he'd taken out about a dozen fifties, he put the remainder into a single bag. By his calculations, this had a similar value to one of the main batched bags. He'd taken some of these notes for bets and other expenditure but had then topped it up from the sale of the watches.

With the cash all bagged up, it was time to put the next part of his plan into action. They'd both agreed the safest place to conceal it while they were away was its original hiding spot. Liam removed the bath panel and pushed the bags into position. Now that he had time, he was able to stack everything in an orderly fashion, pushing it as far to the back as possible. He put an old towel over the top of it, quite why he wasn't sure. If they were burgled and the thieves ripped off the bath panel, it wouldn't make the slightest difference. But in his mind, it was a further concealment. Then he flattened out the holdall and placed it in front of the cash.

He chuckled at the thought of someone robbing this place.

A crummy, little flat in one of the less salubrious parts of London. Imagine, breaking in for a telly and stumbling on that!

Once the money was hidden, he had a quick scout around, making sure nothing else needed to go in there. Satisfied that this job was done, he put the bath panel back on. He had to make it as neat a job as he could, to discourage anyone fiddling about with it. Again the déjà vu made a fleeting appearance. How much things had changed in a couple of months.

~~~~~~

"Mum, mum! Did you pack my Brentford top?"

The minute she walked through the door after the first of her four night shifts, Callie was pounced on by her excited son.

"Of course I did! As if we'd leave that here," Callie smiled, relieved she could remember packing that at least. Anything with sentimental value had been removed from the flat. Just in case. In case those people tracked them down and ransacked the flat. They could take the money if they found it. Despite their predicament, there were more important things than cash. Their safety and personal belongings were what mattered most to them right now.

She found Liam in the kitchen, flustered. He'd made sure the breakfast dishes were washed up and put away. Nothing was out of place. It was the same throughout the flat. He knew Callie only had a matter of minutes before they'd need to set off. He didn't want her to have any stress.

"Hiya, babe," he kissed her, his lips salty with sweat. "How was your shift? Here you go, a couple of cereal bars and a flask of coffee to keep you going."

"Ah, you gem. I'm gonna need that on the way back from the station! Shift was ok. Nothing major. Thank God."

"You all set?" he asked, nervously.

"Yep. Let's do this."

It was nearly 8.20am, their cue to get Robbie off to school and then follow through with the rest of their plans.

"Robbie, are you ready? We need to go!"

Liam chivvied him up, grabbing his lunch box and stuffing it into his school bag. They were both taking him in the car today, so Callie could drop Liam at Kings Cross afterwards. Then she'd head over to her parents to unpack. And, more importantly, to sleep. Staying awake until then shouldn't be a problem. She found it difficult to switch off straight after a night shift. But the prospect of a safe, cosy bed in a couple of hours' time felt like the ultimate indulgence.

The boot was already loaded up, full of new cases and a few boxes of things they'd need over the next couple of months. They'd told Robbie it was only for a few weeks, while his dad was up north. In reality, this would be the last time they'd all be in their flat as a family. Liam would come back at some point and retrieve the money and Callie would pop in occasionally for the post. But they'd use a removal company to get the rest of the flat emptied. They wanted to spend as little time as possible there until they knew they were safe.

As they locked up, Callie and Liam exchanged a knowing glance. They both had a wistful look in their eyes. They were sad to leave their first-ever home together but happy to move on to a better life. Robbie was oblivious.

"Dad, are there any football teams in Durham?" he asked as Callie pulled out onto the main road.

"Not in Durham itself, but they've got Newcastle and Sunderland not far away. Why?"

He turned round to look at his son and noticed his eyes were wide with excitement. A smile was spreading across his face.

"Brentford are playing at Sunderland soon! Can we go?"

"Er…I'm…I'm not sure. We'll have to wait and see how things go." He was doubtful, although it did plant a little seed in his head.

"Brentford against Sunderland was the first game I EVER went to, wasn't it dad?"

"It was. Cracking game." So pleased that I was still around to experience that, he thought to himself.

They were almost at school now. Liam was dreading saying goodbye to his son. He'd spent so many years apart from Callie during his army days, but he'd never spent a significant period away from Robbie.

Callie looked at him and read his mind. She reached across and squeezed his hand.

"Won't be for long, babe. We'll get through this."

She thought she'd said it quietly enough for Robbie not to hear, but should've known better. His ears were like satellite dishes, picking up every sound. You always had to watch what you said around him.

"What's the matter? What do we have to get through?" His face was worried, suddenly.

"Ah, nothing, don't worry. Just us moving and your dad having to work up north for a bit. It's gonna be strange that's all isn't it?"

When they got to the school gates, Liam was struggling to contain his emotions. Robbie unashamedly gave him the biggest hug and kiss. He held him tight for as long as he could.

"Bye, dad. I'll miss you." There were tears in his eyes.

Liam wiped away the tears as they dropped onto Robbie's cheeks and reassured his son. "I'll miss you too, but it won't be long until I see you. You and your mum can come up for the weekend or I'll pop back down here when I can. And we can Facetime whenever you want. I do need you to do something for me though, but it's a secret. Can I tell you?"

The boy nodded, a little baffled.

He whispered in Robbie's ear, pretending he didn't want Callie to overhear.

"I need you to look after your mum for me. Cos when I'm not here, you're the man of the house ok? Do you think you can do that?"

Robbie responded enthusiastically. His own worries were forgotten, he had a job to do while his dad was away. He gave Liam a final, quick hug, turned to his mother and, to her surprise, hugged her too. Then with a "Best go or Mrs Simpson will tell me off for being late!" he was off and through the school gate without so much as a backward glance.

"Flippin heck, what did you say to him?" Callie asked, still rooted to the spot in shock.

"I asked him to look after you while I'm away, cos he's the man of the house."

She laughed, "God, he's a keeper, isn't he? Bless his future girlfriends!"

It was almost an hour later by the time they got to Kings Cross. Thankfully, knowing the traffic would be bad, they'd left more than enough time. So their own goodbye wasn't rushed, though it was just as emotional as the farewell at the school gates.

"Be on your guard, Cal. I hate to say that, but it's important to be sensible for the next few weeks."

"I know, I know. And you too."

"Not sure sensible will come into it, once I meet up with Kev again. It's been a while."

"Yeah, I bet," she joked. "But you know what I mean. Be careful. I can't bear the thought of anything happening to you."

"Don't worry, I can look after myself."

"So could Danny from what you told me. But right now, who knows what's happened to him?"

It was like being stabbed through the heart, punched and winded in one fell swoop. The thought of Danny and the part his actions may have played in his disappearance were tough to reconcile.

He squeezed Callie one more time, kissed her and then grabbed his case from the back seat. Not wanting to leave but at the same time eager to escape before his emotions broke through.

Twenty minutes later and safely in his seat, Liam's train chugged out of Kings Cross, passing the Emirates stadium on the right-hand side. It began to pick up speed as it headed through tunnel after tunnel. The reality of his situation hit home once more. Liam vowed to only dwell on his predicament until the train stopped at Stevenage. Then he'd force himself to put his earphones in, listen to some music and chill out. If he didn't, he felt as if the whole thing would consume him.

For the time being though, his focus was on his missing friend. Where the hell was Danny? Was he alive? Was it connected to the burglary? Or had he been going through a tough time that no one was aware of and this was all his own doing?

Liam dreaded the thought of both options, but either way, he was desperate to hear news of Danny. Something to shed some light on what had happened to him.

The news, when it came, wouldn't be good. In fact, it would be devastating.

56

Billy and his sidekick didn't bother giving Danny any food the following morning. The two of them were hoping to make the final breakthrough today. Food would only give him extra strength to put up a fight. To avoid answering the questions they needed answering. That they needed answering today.

He had to admit he had a grudging admiration for Danny's inner strength and resilience. Until yesterday that was and the thwarted attempts to snare his partner-in-crime. Now it was pissing Billy off big-style. Danny's bloody-mindedness was starting to put his own future on the line. His bosses wanted results and he wasn't delivering. They were used to getting what they wanted. No matter what.

They let Danny stew in the cellar for most of the day. The cold, dark and now stench-filled cellar, thanks to the rudimentary 'toilet' facilities. They let him think about what he'd be giving up if he didn't give them the information they needed. It was a tactic that had worked before. Although most of their previous victims had capitulated long before this point.

By late afternoon, they decided it was time. Time for one more attempt downstairs before they had to consider their last desperate throw of the dice. That really would be the final act, before setting him free. Unless he crumbled.

It would go one of two ways. They'd break him and be able to nail the real thief. Or, he'd stand firm, demonstrating his innocence. Either way, they'd set him free. It was simply a matter of timing. If it was the former, they'd hold onto him until they could nab the burglar, so he didn't tip them off. But if it was the latter, they'd let him go tonight.

If only Danny knew how close he was to freedom.

An hour later, following yet more extreme torture, it was clear they'd have to go for that final throw. He was still holding out, still denying all knowledge. Billy had to hand it to him, this was one tough motherfucker they were dealing with.

Once they were back upstairs, they discussed the plan for later that evening. Danny was a big bloke. It had taken three of them to carry him out from the house in West Hampstead. And that was when he was unconscious. This was a whole different ball game.

"I'll ring Alex, but we need to knock him out. There's no chance he's coming quietly."

"What if he doesn't come round for ages though?"

Billy paused. It was a fair point.

"Then we need something that'll keep him out for an hour, no more. Any ideas?"

None were forthcoming. So in the end they took a chance, put a fraction of the Rohypnol in Danny's tea and kept their fingers crossed that it would have the desired effect.

It didn't take long for Danny to blackout. He was on the verge of losing consciousness anyway.

By now, Alex had arrived and the three men wasted no time putting their plan into action. They hoped Danny wouldn't be unconscious for longer than an hour. But they didn't want him to wake up as they were carting him into the boot of the car or dragging him out of it at the other end.

The coast was clear outside. Rolled up in a carpet, the three men carried him out to the car and dumped his large frame into the boot. They travelled within the speed limits to get to their destination. It would be crazy to get pulled over by the police for something so trivial.

Forty minutes later, they'd reached their carefully chosen location. There were no CCTV cameras for miles and very few street lights. No houses nearby and not a person in sight. It was the epitome of rural. Except for the train tracks.

Their plan was working so far. All was still quiet in the boot. With headlamps on, they lugged the carpet out and dumped it on the ground. It unrolled as they did so, revealing the battered and bruised figure. A figure that was now beginning to stir, ever so slightly. Time to move.

As Billy kept watch, the other two dragged Danny on the carpet across to the bridge. They heaved him up onto his feet, just as his eyes were opening. There was panic and bewilderment on his face as he began to come to. He felt fresh air on his cheeks for the first time in almost a week. It was still as cold as the cellar had been, but it was pure and refreshing. But where was he? And what were they going to do to him?

The two men pinned him to the bridge. He could barely move, so struggle was futile. He was so exhausted, broken and beaten that he was almost ready to accept his fate.

Billy came into view. His face was right up against Danny's.

"One last chance, Danny. Tell us what you know or we throw you over the edge."

"I've told you. I don't know anything." His eyes were misting over now. He could feel the end in sight.

The men were only trying to scare him. Trying to force him into a confession, to tell them who'd burgled that house. They weren't intending to kill him. It was the ultimate scare tactic. No one wanted to be thrown in front of a train. Not anyone in their right mind anyway. It was a desperate way to go. You had to be at the end of your tether to even contemplate it.

They hoisted him up onto the top of the parapet. Suspended him over the edge, hoping the impending threat would finally break him. In the far distance, the sound of an approaching train could be heard. It was still some way away.

"I don't believe you. Who broke into that house? Who took the money? Who knows about the fucking scores?"

Danny was confused. His body and mind were broken. After seven days without proper food or drink. Being tortured, beaten and deprived of sleep. He had no idea what they were on about with the scores. He wouldn't for one minute give up Liam's name. But he was disorientated, bewildered. As his brain tried to compute what they were saying, he inadvertently spoke his thoughts out loud.

"Eh, scores? I... don't... know... what... you... mean. They... took...a...million...scores?"

Billy was suddenly incensed. In Danny's confusion, he'd let on that he knew someone had taken a million. A million in cash. And yet, none of the publicity about the burglary had said that. It had been covered up by Roberts, at the behest of his bosses. As far as anyone knew, the proceeds of the burglary had been minimal. The intruder had been disturbed before they could take anything substantial. So how did Danny know?

Seven days they'd wasted. Seven days trying to break this fucker!

In his rage, Billy darted forward, aiming a punch at Danny. The sudden movement took the other two by surprise. They lost their grip. They tried to cling onto his arms. But it was too late. He slipped from their grasp. He fell backwards. Backwards. Over the parapet.

For one blissful moment, Danny felt free. Free from the clutches of those thugs, free from pain, free to live his life again.

For a split second, the three men remaining on the bridge held their collective breaths.

The train was now approaching, fast. So fast, that as Danny fell, floating backwards, he was instantly wiped out. Smashed to pieces.

As the train screeched to a halt ahead of them, the men made a hasty retreat, scooping up the carpet and throwing it into the still-open boot. Then swiftly, stealthily, they drove away from the scene. The headlights were switched off until they were out of sight of anyone on the tracks. Once they were in the clear, Billy flicked the lights on and put his foot down. He had some explaining to do to his bosses once again, but for now, he needed to get them away from here. Fast.

Meanwhile, a few hundred yards further up the track, a driver in shock was doing his best to hold himself together. He'd already contacted his emergency hotline. The emergency services had been summoned.

The driver would never operate a train again. This was one of those things you couldn't unsee. The trauma it caused was immense and many a driver before him had succumbed to the same fate. How did you ever recover from seeing someone die right before your eyes in such a brutal fashion? Feeling responsible, when you could do absolutely nothing about it?

There was nothing the emergency services could do for Danny either. A mix of limbs, blood and organs were splattered across the tracks and embankment. Part of his torso was virtually impaled on the front of the train. No one would know straight away that this was the man police had been searching for, for the last week. He had no means of identification on him and his

313

vehicle had already been abandoned elsewhere along with his phone, rendered useless by his captors. It would take a while to identify the person behind the body parts. But when they finally did, the heartbreak would be immeasurable. And the repercussions would be felt far beyond his family.

If only Danny had known how close he was to freedom.

57

PC Jenna Jones loved her job, but it had its wretched moments. Today was one of them.

As a Family Liaison Officer, she enjoyed looking after people when they needed it. Her priority was keeping them informed about their loved ones, helping them cope when they had to deliver bad news. There was many a happy outcome when a missing person turned up and was reunited with their family. Or a badly injured victim survived against the odds. Although it was more likely she was brought in when something bad had already happened. Something final.

She'd been supporting Tina and her son Tom for the last week since Tina's fiancé Danny had been reported missing. They'd found Danny's abandoned van early on, but there'd been no sign of the man himself. Her colleagues were certain it was suicide and he'd drowned himself in the nearby reservoir.

Jenna's role also entailed gathering information from the family to help an investigation. So she'd developed strong instincts over the years. The more she'd got to know Tina, the less convinced she was that her colleagues were right. It seemed so out of character, without anything to trigger it. She knew suicide was one of the hardest things to predict. Even so, she had major doubts that Danny had killed himself.

Either way, he'd been missing for a week now and Jenna had to be realistic about the outcome. Whether it was of his own making or someone else's, it was likely Danny had come to harm. People didn't disappear into thin air.

She'd been woken by her phone ringing just after 2am. It was the British Transport Police. A phone call she'd been dreading. A white male had jumped in front of a train. There was no formal ID yet, but Danny fitted that description, so it was immediately flagged on the system. They wouldn't be able to identify him for a little while, due to the condition of the body. Or to be more precise, body parts. Whoever the poor man was, he was no longer in one piece. Far from it.

The news of a 'train jumper' might leak out in a few hours, so Jenna needed to get to Tina's house early that morning. She may as well have gone straight away, the chances of getting back to sleep now were minimal. Instead, she slept fitfully for the next few hours, finally giving up at 6am and heaving herself out of bed.

It was now 7.30am and she was standing on Tina's doorstep, about to ring the bell. About to deliver the awful news. It wasn't yet the worst news imaginable. It was still speculation. So the anguish would continue until the body was identified. But there was a strong likelihood this could be Danny.

Jenna pushed the bell gently, aware of the early hour. She prayed Tom was still here. He'd been talking about returning home in the next couple of days. Hopefully, he hadn't yet headed back up to Hertfordshire.

She waited, then pressed the doorbell again.

Jenna saw a figure appear on the staircase through the opaque glass panel of the front door. It was impossible to tell whether it was male or female. Another figure followed them down the stairs, just as the first person opened the door.

Tina gasped as she saw Jenna stood in the doorway, her hand automatically going to her mouth. Bracing herself for the worst.

"Hi, Tina, love. Hi, Tom," she acknowledged the second person as he reached the bottom of the stairs. "Can I come in?"

"Oh, God, it's bad news isn't it?" Tina blurted out, as she welcomed her into the hallway.

"Mum, let's just see what Jenna has to say. I'll put the kettle on, you go into the lounge."

"Thanks, Tom, I could murder a cuppa." She was relieved he'd saved her from announcing her update on the doorstep. But she had to stop using that expression. It was so inappropriate.

She managed to make small talk for the few minutes it took Tom to make a pot of tea. Asking Tina how she'd been, how her grandchildren were and so on. She knew Tina was itching to know why she'd turned up on the doorstep at the crack of dawn. But she didn't want to say anything until her son was back in the room. He was Tina's crutch. Whilst Jenna would be around to support her too, Tom would ultimately be the one to get her through this ordeal.

As he rested the tray on the coffee table and began to pour, Jenna cleared her throat, ready to reveal all.

"Thanks, Tom," she said as he passed her a cup. "So, I wanted to update you both with some news we had overnight."

Tina held her breath.

"British Transport Police advised us a white male jumped in front of a train in the Hatfield area last night. We don't yet have a positive identification, but we believe it may be Danny. Despite the fact it's quite a distance from where his van was found."

Tina burst into tears as Tom sat down beside her, gripping her hand and comforting her as best he could.

"Surely it could be anyone?" he asked.

"You're right. But there were some identifying marks on the man's arm. We think they could be one of the tattoos you mentioned to us. We won't know for certain until we carry out the autopsy and pull together other identifiers. But I didn't want

317

you to find out about the incident from the news and speculate on things."

"Yes, of course. Thank you. Really I mean that," Tom responded, looking devastated.

"Is there a chance it's not him?" Tina asked, almost whispering in her grief.

"There's a small chance, but I think you should prepare yourself for the worst," Jenna responded. She knew there was only the tiniest prospect this wasn't Danny.

Tina broke down again, burying her head into Tom's chest.

"I'm so so sorry. As soon as I hear anything, I'll update you. I wish there was a better outcome."

Tom peeled himself away from Tina as he showed Jenna out a few minutes later. At the door, he asked the question he knew his mother would ask.

"Is it possible for mum to see the body if it's definitely Danny?"

She made sure her voice was low enough so that Tina wouldn't hear.

"You wouldn't want her to see it, Tom."

He nodded as Jenna walked out, realising the implications of her comment. He shut the door behind her quietly, gripping onto the handle as he bowed his head in sorrow. He didn't know if he could cope with this, but for the sake of his mother, he had to be strong. He stayed there for a few more seconds, then stood up straight, wiped away a few tears and returned to the lounge.

Outside, PC Jones made her way to the squad car. She only just managed to jump into the driver's seat and close the door before her body crumpled in sorrow.

-58-

"Thanks for dialling in at such short notice, everyone. I thought it best to let you all know urgently about the latest update." The chairman sounded unusually morose. The reason why was about to be revealed. "I'm afraid our men had a little accident with the builder last night. Unfortunately, he's no longer alive."

"Fucking hell!" seemed to be the most common response from the phone lines.

The menacing caller was first to stand out from the wall of sound.

"How the hell did that happen? We're not in the business of murdering people!"

"Exactly!" another voice chimed in. "Put the frighteners on by all means. Protect our assets and keep things quiet. But murder?!"

"I know, I know. It wasn't intentional. They were attempting to scare him, by suspending him over a railway bridge. Something went wrong and he fell in front of an oncoming train."

"Jeeeeesus!"

"Will it come back on us?" asked another caller.

Straight in with the self-serving concerns, thought Roberts. He was listening in on the call in the chairman's office.

"I don't think so. Our men managed to flee without being discovered. The way they set up the previous scene means the police are likely to treat this as suicide. We could be in the clear."

"Thank God for that."

"There is one other thing," the chairman continued, pausing for effect. He hoped this would be taken as good news.

319

"Just before he fell, the builder seemed to suggest he was aware of what was taken during the burglary. It's the first time he admitted knowing anything about it."

"What did he say?"

"He let slip something about a million when the guys were asking him about the book. But no one knows how much cash was taken, apart from the thieves."

"So, that could be positive, if he's now out of the picture?"

"Correct. Although we still don't know the whereabouts of the book."

"On the other hand, if it's someone close to him, this could tip them towards spilling the beans to the authorities."

The chairman agreed. He let the conversation flow for a few minutes, to see what options they came up with.

"Depends which authorities they go to," said one caller, almost jokingly.

"Yeah. It's only the police we'd have an issue with. And we could probably get round that somehow."

"Hmm. We just need a fall guy to blame everything on. Take the bullet."

"Not literally," one caller said, as a few of them laughed.

"Poor taste gentlemen, in the current circumstances. But you're right. And, let's face it, we have the perfect solution. Chairman, did you say Roberts is on this call?"

"Yes, he's sat here with me now."

"Good. Listen up, Roberts," it was the menacing one again. "If the shit does hit the fan, you're the one going down, ok? We'll look after you in the long run, but you need to convince people that this is all down to you. I'm sure the chairman will brief you on everything once we've finished the call. But get yourself prepared. Let's face it, it's your own stupid fault for being so careless."

"Leave that with me, gents," the chairman interjected, satisfied at such a reasonable outcome, in which he would escape any sanctions. "I'll make sure Mitchell is fully prepared. In the meantime, we should all keep our fingers crossed that this might be the end of this whole sorry episode."

As he hung up the call, the chairman turned to Mitchell and said, "right, we've got some work to do."

Mitchell could've sworn he saw a glint in the chairman's eye. He'd been quite content to go with this solution as soon as it was aired. Mitchell knew he'd only got himself to blame. But it wasn't his idea to fix games, to fix the beautiful game. He was far from perfect, but these guys were self-serving beyond belief and their greed knew no bounds. He didn't believe for a second that no one else had been harmed if they'd got in the way.

Now, his boss had just thrown him to these wolves.

Mitchell had considered once again whether to tell them about the other thing. The thing he'd made, not only as an insurance policy, but also to help his useless memory. He knew it was only a matter of time before it was discovered. He was aware it would be the final nail in his coffin. Only now, he was beginning to worry that that could mean literally.

59

MISSING MAN CONFIRMED DEAD AFTER TRAIN TRAGEDY

Police have confirmed that the person hit by a train near Hatfield three days ago was missing South Ealing man, Danny Williams. The 58-year-old disappeared a week earlier, on 26 January, and his van had been found parked up at the edge of Brent Reservoir.

DI Craig Holgate advised "The whereabouts of Mr Williams in the intervening days are unknown, but it's believed he sadly took his own life. The family has been informed and is being supported by our specially-trained officers. We're not looking for anyone else in connection with this incident and offer our sincere condolences to all concerned."

Liam was reading the news item on the Evening Standard website in shocked silence.

As the awful reality dawned, the anger rose inside him.

Finally, having got to the end of the article, he spoke in a loud whisper.

"Fuck. Fuck. Fuck! You absolute murdering bastards." Hissing the words out. Trying not to disturb his friends or their kids, but incandescent with rage.

As he paced around the bedroom, his anger spilled over. He punched the wall, connecting with such force that he damaged the plasterwork. And almost broke his hand.

"Damn!" Pain shot through his fist. He looked down. There were scuff marks on his knuckles and blood was starting to trickle out from one or two cracks. But he felt like punching the wall again and again. Again and again, until the pain became too much to bear.

This was his fault. He was convinced of it. His fault for being such an idiot to get into debt in the first place. For being so greedy to take far too much from that safe. And then being so bloody stupid to arouse suspicions by putting those bets on.

"Fucking idiot. Greedy, stupid, fucking idiot!"

Then the sadness overwhelmed him. His body crumpled. His knees gave way and he dropped to the floor. Sobbing. Shaking. He wasn't a crier, but this time he didn't stop the tears. He let them flow.

He sobbed and sobbed until there were no more tears inside. He felt empty, spent.

And then the guilt returned. How dare he cry for a man that had died because of his stupid, greedy actions?

He jumped as he heard a knock at the door.

"Are you alright, mate? Has something happened?" It was Kev. He had the sensitivity not to barge right in, thankfully. Liam could only imagine what a sight he would be. But worse than that, he wasn't ready to explain things right now. Including the dent in his bedroom wall. Shit!

"I'm fine, bud. I'm sorry about the noise. I'll explain everything later, but I need to speak to Callie right now, if that's ok?"

"No worries, pal. Let me know if there's anything I can do."

"Cheers, mate, you're a diamond."

Right on cue, his phone rang. It was Callie. He heard Kev wander back down the stairs and answered, not knowing what to say.

"You've read the link I sent you?"

"Yeah." He was struggling to stop his voice from breaking.

"I was getting worried, you were supposed to call me as soon as you'd read it."

"Sorry. I'm just trying to take it all in."

"It's awful, isn't it? I can't imagine what his partner is going through."

"I know. I guess you never know for sure what anyone's thinking inside." His comment made Liam think of his own brush with suicide a few short months ago. Truth be known, he didn't think the same situation applied to Danny.

"So do you actually think he killed himself then?"

Liam couldn't keep the pretence up any longer.

"No way. Those bastards got rid of him. But, as much as I hate to say it, that means we could be in the clear."

"Really?" The thought of Danny coming to harm had simply increased Callie's terror. Their escape from those thugs' clutches a few days earlier was still fresh in her mind.

"Yeah. Something must've happened to make them think he was the thief. I still reckon we need to be on our guard for a while. But if everything seems ok for the next month or so, I think we can start to get back to normal."

He might have a point. Liam could sense the relief in Callie's voice as she replied, "Ah, babe, that's so good to hear."

"Listen, do you and Robbie fancy a trip up north next weekend? It'd be great to see you both."

"Hell yeah! I'm not working either, so it'd work out perfectly."

324

"Kev suggested it. He reckons he can get hold of some tickets for the Brentford match at Sunderland. They'll be in the home end, but I thought it'd be great for Robbie to go to an away match. And it's a pretty decent stadium."

"Sounds good. Will he be alright in the home end?"

"Yeah, shouldn't be an issue. From what Kev says, there'll be plenty of empty seats around us. They're shit apparently!"

"Kev would say that, he's a Newcastle fan isn't he?"

"Ha, you're right. But they're still shit. Hopefully, we'll get a win with our little lucky charm with us."

Callie laughed. "Can I come too? I really enjoyed that match over Christmas."

"I was talking about the three of us, you idiot, not just me and Robbie. I'll get the match sorted. You look into trains for Friday afternoon and I'll come and pick you up from Durham station."

"Cheeky bugger! Ok, I'll get onto it once we hang up. Are Kev and his family going to the match as well?"

"Cal, did you really ask me that? He said he'd rather walk over hot coals than go to the Stadium of Shite!"

They both laughed at the thought of Kev's indignation at being asked to go and watch his biggest rivals. It was good to have a bit of normal conversation. To escape the veracity of their current situation.

They ended the call in good spirits. He told Callie about his first day at work. Then suggested she treated herself to some new clothes for the Saturday night. The two couples were going to head out to Newcastle, while Kev's eldest looked after the kids. Something to look forward to for once. And a rare night out together. When was the last time they'd done that?

Once they'd hung up though, reality hit home again with Liam.

He was certain Danny's disappearance was connected to the burglary. That his ultimate fate was determined by someone else. Why the police were treating it as a suicide beggared belief.

He'd told Callie they might be okay because he didn't want her to worry. But what did this really mean for them? Would these thugs track them down? Had they already discovered who they were, where they lived? Or did Danny's death mean they were safe, as long as he didn't place any more bets or arouse suspicions elsewhere?

He was exhausted by it all, physically and emotionally. On top of the guilt, the circumstances of Danny's demise had stirred unwelcome reminders. It was so heartbreakingly like his own dalliance with death.

The memory came crashing back into his consciousness. How close he'd come. Liam was eternally grateful to his guardian angel for saving him that night. Gavin would never know how much he'd given back to him, simply by being in the right place at the right time.

Liam resolved there and then to get back in touch with Gavin once this whole thing was over. He could never thank him enough for saving his life, but he'd like to do something to convey his gratitude.

He thought about the business card Gavin had given him. Possibly the only one Liam had in his wallet. He didn't mix in the circles where you exchanged business cards.

Where had he put it again? Of course, it was in the change compartment.

He grabbed his wallet from the bedside table. God, when was the last time he'd been in this pocket? He didn't use cash much these days, other than those huge bets of course. So he wasn't in the habit of getting any loose change.

He saw the business card as soon as he popped the clasp open. He squeezed it out and looked at it, managing to reminisce for once without bringing the pain back. Hang on. What else was in there? Oh yeah, the memory stick.

The memory stick. The memory stick! Suddenly it came back to him. He'd never looked at it. He'd put it in there all those weeks ago and meant to take a look at it when he got access to a computer. He'd completely forgotten about it.

Jesus Christ. What was on there? In an instant, the exhaustion disappeared, like clouds dispersing from an overcast sky. The adrenaline was racing through his veins again.

He had to know.

60

"Kev, mate, can I borrow a laptop?"

"Aye, I'll get mine for you. Is something wrong?"

"Can I fill you in later? I just need to look at something that's all. It's really important."

"Not a bother."

Back in his bedroom, with the laptop all started up and ready, Liam's hands were shaking. He picked up the memory stick, flipped it open and slotted it into the USB drive.

The laptop flickered into life, as it registered the device.

He clicked on the icon and watched as it brought up the contents.

There were only three files in total; a Word document, an Excel document and what appeared to be an audio file.

He began with the simple ones and opened up the Word document, entitled Induction – Codes.

Surprise, surprise. The codes were all the teams he'd worked out, the matchday number, correct result or score, who the official was and so on. Then, at the foot of the last page, there was a paragraph entitled 'Email template', with examples of the codes being used. He should apply for the secret service, he thought. Although, he reckoned they dealt with infinitely more complex encryptions.

Next, he clicked on the Excel document, named Induction – Golden Circle. It was a simple enough file, just as well as Liam's spreadsheet knowledge was rudimentary. But there were a few tabs within it. There was a tab for each club, or at least for six clubs. A tab named Premier League. A tab called Officials. And a tab entitled Others.

As he flicked through the tabs, he saw names and contact details for each person. Nothing untoward there, he guessed.

He was starting to think this was just a random gadget that had been accidentally put in the safe. Its owner had meant to pop it back in a drawer, but inadvertently put it in a security vault with something else. Just like he'd unwittingly removed it when taking the watches. It didn't seem to be anything out of the ordinary.

He almost didn't bother to click on the audio file, but his curiosity got the better of him. What the hell, he thought, what have I got to lose?

He double-clicked. The file opened up and began to play.

A voice boomed, almost causing his heart to stop. Quickly, Liam went for the volume button. He turned it down to a more normal level, sliding it back to play from the start again.

"…What are you doing still tapping away on there, Mitchell? I said you shouldn't take any notes on this bit, just listen very carefully. We don't want any record of what I'm about to tell you, but this is one of the key parts of your role, ok?"

"Sorry, chairman. I'm all ears."

"Right. As discussed when you accepted the job, there are certain conditions attached to the role. This is completely confidential. It should not be discussed in any *circumstances with anyone outside of the 'golden circle'."*

"Yes, sir. And the 'golden circle' is the list you sent the other week?"

"That's right. So, first things first, your PA has already signed a non-disclosure agreement. She will be responsible for any digital communications. These are kept to a minimum but are necessary to communicate with everyone promptly. Once actioned, the emails are destroyed. But bear in mind that your PA isn't aware of what this is all about and she isn't one of the 'golden circle'."

329

"Why isn't she aware of anything? Has she been with the company for long?"

"She's been with us for about four and a half years. But we have a code. And the emails are ambiguous in how they're worded, so she has no idea what they're actually about. You'll need to learn the code, but we'll send that over to you later today, so you've got the standard format we use."

Liam looked at the time bar on the audio file. He was only about a quarter of the way through it so far. It wasn't the earth-shattering revelation he was expecting to find. It was even a bit tedious, the way they were going on. Codes, golden circle, emails, blah blah blah. Nothing was being revealed that he wasn't already aware of. And confidentiality in any business wasn't unusual.

He persevered though. He'd give it a little longer, before giving it up as a bad job.

"Now, the first scheme involves specific games. We have several Far Eastern and Russian betting syndicates who reward us for ensuring certain results. These are generally scores that are out of the ordinary, so offer much higher odds."

Bloody hell, thought Liam. Here we go.

"There are some match officials in on the action – only a select few – and in return, they receive cash or watches.

"No managers are in on this, so be mindful of that whenever you speak to them. Our initial scoping exercise revealed they have far too much integrity to be part of such a scheme. More fool them, it's easy money and it doesn't hugely affect the final positions.

Liam was now hooked. This is unreal, he thought. He was obviously aware there was something dodgy going on, but he had no idea it was this far-reaching. He continued listening, not even realising he was open-mouthed as he heard the next part.

"There are a few players from each 'VIP' club involved, but again nowhere near all of them. And then a sprinkling of players beyond that, to

help us towards that crucial correct result. Obviously, this means we have to have some dubious refereeing decisions, but we've got away with it thus far. The players get the same benefits as the refs. Though it's anyone's guess why they need their salaries topping up these days."

Indeed, Liam concurred. The wealth in the top league was eye-watering.

"There's no specific reward as such for these 'VIP' clubs. But if they don't engage in this aspect, they're not allowed to be involved in our second activity. And believe me, no one is going to miss out on that."

Liam paused the recording to take stock of what he'd heard. He already suspected they were fixing some results, which was bad enough. But this seemed more widespread than what he'd imagined. And there was more? He clicked the play button once again, bracing himself for what else he might hear.

"Although the first part is risky and can be tricky to administer, we have to manage it for the foreseeable future. Our syndicate partners have significant sums invested in us. So it doesn't bear thinking about what they'd do if we upset them. The introduction of VAR will make things easier in this respect."

"You think that'll come in as planned the year after next?" Mitchell was heard to ask.

"All being well, yes. We've got a few more things to iron out and then we'll trial it, but it should give us a bit more control over results."

Handy, thought Liam, you absolute bunch of crooks.

"You'll need to handle the payment of referees and players yourself, for obvious reasons. When you get the safe delivered, you'll have enough cash and watches to keep you going for a couple of months. We'll deliver extra supplies from our vault, as and when required. All you need to do is put the required cash and watches into an envelope for each person. Once a week, Alex or Petr will collect these from you. They distribute them to the recipients after each game."

"Why don't Alex or Petr just deal with the administration? Wouldn't that be easier?"

"Good God, no! We can trust them to deliver a few packages at a time and if any were to go missing we'd be able to flag it up straightaway. But to trust them with the whole lot? What are you thinking man?!"

By now the recording was still only halfway through. Liam wondered what was coming next. He was about to find out there was something much more shocking going on. Something even more bent than fixing an odd result here and there, for someone's financial gain. Something that shook at the game's very foundations.

"So, as you know, our second scheme is the auction, involving our 'VIP' clubs. It generates significant sums, which we use to deliver both schemes. Any money left over at the end of each season is a 'bonus' for us and is reallocated accordingly.

"This scheme launched in 2009, after the original one had been running for a few years. You're aware of who instigated it and it's gradually expanded to the current maximum quota of six clubs. The two Manchester clubs joined in 2010. The other two London clubs signed up the following year. And Liverpool were last to join in 2013.

"Each club bids on a top-four place, in a blind auction, at the end of each season. The clubs are advised whether they've been successful before the transfer window opens. So they can plan their activity accordingly. The two unsuccessful clubs don't have to honour their bids, but everyone is expected to achieve the place they have paid for. They can't sneak in without paying for it."

YOU WHAT?! Liam was now listening intently. Gob-smacked.

"As clubs can build squads based on their guaranteed position, this scheme used to be easy to administer. Throughout the season, we didn't have to 'tweak' too many games to reach the desired outcome. And often, clubs

were satisfied to settle for a top-four place. Swindling their accounts to hide a full title challenge was too much for some of them.

"However, it's become much trickier since the group was expanded to six clubs. In an ideal world, the Champions League riches would be available to all six, rather than the existing four places. I'm sure it would also benefit the English game as a whole if this were to happen. Anyone can see that the money would filter down the pyramid."

Liam felt like laughing out loud, the cynic in him thinking that would be the last thing to happen. But right now, he was still in shock at the revelations.

"As a result of this challenge, we have had major fallouts within the 'VIP' group over the years. The most serious was after just two seasons of the expanded alliance.

"All the clubs abstained from making bids and refused to participate in any way. They were no longer guaranteed a Champions League place you see. There was a very real threat of the scheme being disbanded. In the end, the clubs decided to let the season play out naturally, without any interference. You're obviously aware of what happened that season…"

After a few seconds of silence, the same voice continued.

"Anyway, that freak result acted very much in our favour. The 'VIP' clubs couldn't come back to the table quick enough and have been even more generous since then! So far, we've managed to keep out any non-'VIP' clubs too."

Liam was staggered. He knew what this guy was alluding to. He paused, took a deep breath and pressed play again. The recording came back on to the sound of laughter. Cocky, arrogant laughter.

"We'll fill you in on how the auction works later in the year so you're fully prepared for our end-of-season 'VIP' meeting. But in the meantime, remember a lot of your job is about keeping these clubs happy. Don't forget to give the impression you're working on behalf of the other clubs though! And

of course, you need to maximise the broadcasting monies. If we let that slip at all, the 'VIPs' will be on our backs big-style. It's a delicate balancing act, but we're confident we've chosen the right man for the job."

Liam listened to the last few minutes of the recording. Pleasantries were exchanged and the sound of what seemed to be a laptop lid closing.

Seconds later, the recording came to an abrupt end.

61

BREAKING NEWS...BREAKING NEWS...BREAKING NEWS... BREAKING NEWS...

"... Sorry, we need to interrupt this story with some shocking news coming in, about a match-fixing scandal in the Premier League. Over to our reporter at the scene."

"Thanks, Sarah-Jane. I'm outside the Metropolitan Police headquarters on Embankment. An unnamed ex-employee of the Premier League is apparently still giving evidence. It's believed they're revealing details of match-fixing during the current season. And I understand this has enabled several Far Eastern and Russian betting syndicates to generate huge wins."

"This story, if true, is going to rock football to its very core isn't it, Jim? At this stage, do we know who is likely to be involved from a Premier League perspective?"

"Well, I'm hearing rumours this could go to the very top, as in the Premier League CEO himself, Mitchell Roberts. It may also involve key people at the clubs involved, including players. Though we have no confirmation of that yet. Shockingly, even some referees as well. This could absolutely devastate the top division in English football. It has massive implications for anyone who's associated with this scandal. Once the truth comes out, I'm sure the football authorities will hand out huge sanctions. This strikes at the very heart of the game."

For the next few days, the story grabbed headlines around the world and helped UK broadcasters fill their schedules. The shockwaves rippled across the land. Football and non-football fans alike discussed likely punishments for the guilty parties. For once, the nation seemed united in wanting to root out this corruption. To ensure the national game was free from sleaze.

Meanwhile, Liam watched the story unfold from a smart detached house in Durham. He was stunned and yet not surprised. Who the hell had leaked this scandal? And why were they only on about the result fixing and not the league placing collusion? That was even more damning, in his opinion. Rigging a few results here and there obviously had some impact on the league table and was unethical in itself. But fixing who finished in the top four? And denying everyone apart from six clubs that opportunity? That was bloody mind-blowing. Completely anti-competitive.

It had been a week since he'd listened to the recording on the memory stick. He was still taking in what he'd heard. He had no idea what to do about it. When the news broke about this betting scandal, he thought he'd been spared the trauma of having to report it himself. Saved from the inevitable danger it would place him and his family in. He waited for them to break the full story. There wasn't just a betting scandal to uncover; this corruption went far, far deeper. When they didn't, he began to get a really bad feeling. Did he need to go to the police after all?

Liam began thinking about his mates, relatives, colleagues. Yeah, his close mates mostly supported Brentford. But he knew people who supported teams across the country, throughout the divisions. They put their heart and soul into following their club. Spent a fortune. Made huge sacrifices. Lived and breathed their team's fortunes, or misfortunes. They didn't deserve this deception.

Then he thought about the people he knew who'd won those titles in that time. Imagine. Just imagine being one of those fans, who thought they'd won the league fair and square. Or qualified for the Champions League. Or any massive win during the season. Imagine taking those moments of joy away from them. God, it was sickening.

He considered how they'd feel if he went to the police with his evidence. If those titles were taken away. How the hell would that work? What would it do to the official records? It would devastate those fans *and* their clubs. Nah, bollocks to that. They deserved to get relegated for what they'd done to the game; punished in the strongest possible way.

And then he remembered Callie and how adamant she was that he didn't do anything to risk their safety. He was in such a quandary.

What the fuck was he supposed to do?

-62-

Liam was a melting pot of emotions. He was ecstatic to be spending the weekend with Callie and Robbie. But he was so conflicted about his latest discovery. The contents of the memory stick, when combined with the black book, were damning evidence of the extent of corruption at the highest level. If he went to the authorities, who would protect them from these people? They'd already shown their ruthlessness with Danny. He couldn't put his own family in that sort of danger.

Still, he kept coming back to the whole ethos of the game. How could anyone trust anything if he let this go? His own son was becoming fanatical about Brentford. Would they ever suffer because of this deception? Would they be denied success in the future, because certain people at certain clubs wanted all the riches for themselves? It stank. But the more he thought about it, the more demented it drove him.

On top of all that, he'd been presented with the opportunity of a longer-term contract. It had made him think about whether they should consider moving up north. Could that be the answer to their prayers? Would it make them safer? Would Callie be up for it?

As he waited on the platform on Friday night, it brought back memories of his army leave. The gaps between visits were shorter, but it was still difficult being away from his loved ones. They'd only been apart for a fortnight, but it had felt like much longer. He couldn't wait to see them.

It was after 8pm by the time their train pulled into the station. Darkness had descended long ago and it was already past Robbie's bedtime, so Liam was expecting his son to be half asleep. Callie would probably have to rouse him as they approached Durham, whilst she gathered all their stuff together. He could picture the chaos now, as the train slowly ground to a halt.

If he had been half asleep, it didn't show when Robbie leapt from the steps onto the platform.

"Daaaaaaaaaaaad! Dad!" he sprinted towards him, completely forgetting about his mum. Callie was struggling off the train with their suitcase, her handbag, his backpack and their coats. For a brief moment she fumed at being left on her own to carry everything. As soon as she saw her son and husband embracing, any annoyance disappeared.

A few seconds later, Liam had caught up with her, squeezing her tightly and helping her with all the baggage.

"Sorry, mum!" Robbie said, suddenly realising he'd left her floundering on her own in his excitement.

"It's ok, son, I know you couldn't wait to see your dad." The three of them joined in a group hug, as Liam hoisted his son up in the air.

"Are we still going to the match tomorrow, dad?" Robbie's eyes were wide with excitement and he was jumping up and down on the spot. The thought of an away game had him enthralled. He'd come close to it before when they'd seen the players arrive at Loftus Road. Although it didn't really count. It was virtually round the corner from where they lived and they didn't stay for the match. This was *miles* away, the furthest away game there was from Brentford. He couldn't wait.

"We are, son." Liam noticed Callie shivering all of a sudden. They hadn't had time to put their jackets on before getting off the train. "Right, let's get back to a nice warm house, ey? And you need to get to bed. Or you won't be fit for any match."

Robbie stayed up for another hour as a special treat that night. Kev's children were funny, friendly and chatty, like their parents, so they were made to feel at home right away.

Once the younger kids were in bed, the two couples cracked open some beers and a bottle of wine and got reacquainted. Liam and Kev went back years, but their wives had only met on a few occasions. Basically each other's weddings and the odd get-together. Callie found herself chilling out for the first time in forever.

"Karen, I was gonna ask, is it possible for me and Robbie to stay until Wednesday? I've taken a couple of days off work and it's half-term at Robbie's school, so I thought we'd make the most of it. I don't want to put you out. I know Liam will be at work during the day, but we can occupy ourselves. We won't get under your feet."

"Ah hey, that's no problem at all, pet. It'll be great to have some company. It's half-term for our lot too. We can do some stuff together during the day if you fancy?"

"Thanks, Karen, sounds brilliant."

Liam shot Callie a questioning look. She hadn't mentioned anything to him. He was pleased, he'd get to spend more time with both of them, but why hadn't she told him in advance?

When they went to bed around midnight, he got the opportunity to ask her.

"How come you managed to swing some time off?"

"Actually, I've been signed off with stress."

He was shocked. He pulled her towards him, waiting for her to explain.

"Work have been really understanding, actually. They've realised all that stuff last year is still affecting me." He could see tears springing to Callie's eyes. With everything else they'd been going through recently, it occurred to him he'd neglected his wife's mental well-being.

"I'm so sorry, babe. I've put you through so much. And you don't need it right now, on top of everything else."

"Liam, I'm not angry with you anymore. I feel much safer since we've been with mum and dad. And I can see a brighter future for us too. I've been looking forward to these few days away. It's like a little holiday. A break from reality. And I don't even need to tell you how excited Robbie is!"

Despite Callie's other struggles, they had a perfect end to the night. It had been the first time in a while.

~~~~~~

The next morning flew by like it always did in a house packed with two families. Breakfast was a long-winded affair. Kev and Karen made sure they had a cooked meal to keep them going until their dodgy burger at the match. It was obviously a rare treat for their kids too. Their eyes were on stalks at the feast of bacon, sausages, eggs, tomatoes, beans and even black pudding.

"God, Karen, this is an unbelievable spread," said Callie. "I can't remember the last time we had a full English."

"Me either," said Liam, as he squirted tomato ketchup across his plate, then did likewise for Robbie.

"Well, don't be getting any ideas, babe. It's back to cereal when you get home!"

"You might get a bacon butty if you're lucky in the morning. But same here," Karen laughed, quick to manage the expectations of her own family, as they devoured the food.

Kev and Karen were going to nip into Durham while their friends were at the match. They had to take their little ones along, as the eldest was on babysitting duty this evening.

"We're off, mate. Make sure you all get a shower when you get back. Wipe that sh… muck off you from that place," Kev laughed, correcting himself in front of Robbie. "And I hope you slaughter them."

"I reckon it'll be a 2-2 Uncle Kev," piped up Robbie. He was completely focused on the afternoon ahead. Already wearing his Brentford top.

"That'll do, keep them in a relegation spot," he replied, smiling.

"What did you mean about the muck?" an enquiring Robbie now asked.

"Ah, just that it's a horrible place, with a horrible football team."

"Kev man, we all know you hate them, but you don't have to make Robbie hate them an' all y'know." Karen admonished her husband, giving him a playful punch in the arm.

"I've not forgotten what they were like when we went down that's all. It would be mint to see them relegated to the third division. Again!" He roared with laughter, as they made their way out of the door, waving backwards at Liam and Robbie.

"What was all that hilarity about?" asked Callie as she came down the stairs.

"Kev, hating on Sunderland as per usual," Liam replied.

"Yeah, we've got to get in the shower when we get back, cos it's really dirty and horrible."

342

They both laughed at their gullible child, hoping he wouldn't repeat that out loud once they got to the stadium.

Liam parked up a fifteen-minute walk from the ground. Kev had told him which pubs to avoid, but they weren't bothered about staying in any pub for long. One drink was plenty to soak up a bit of the atmosphere.

It was friendly enough in the Wheatsheaf, amongst an atmosphere of doom and gloom from the home fans. Most of the chat was about where they were in the table. And lots of moaning they should be fighting for promotion not battling relegation. Another supporter said they needed to nail the three points today, to build on their result last week.

"Dad, was it Man United they beat last week?" asked Robbie. He was confused by the merging of two conversations, including one he'd overheard back at the house.

"Shhhh, no, that was Newcastle. Don't be mentioning them around here whatever you do."

Having sunk their drinks, they took a leisurely walk towards the stadium. Robbie was already getting excited as they strolled across the railway bridge, seeing the ground rise up in the distance. It was huge in comparison to Griffin Park. Liam wasn't a big fan of newer, purpose-built stadia. He felt they didn't have the soul of the old grounds. But, in the glorious winter sunshine, even he had to admit it was an impressive sight.

"Wow!" Robbie exclaimed.

He wasn't wrong. Liam had a strong affinity for Griffin Park, but you didn't get this sort of view there. At Brentford, the ground was embedded in the houses around it, quite literally attached to its residential neighbours. Apart from a row of turnstiles here and there and the floodlights over the top of the stands, it merged into its built-up landscape. In contrast, the

343

Stadium of Light was a beacon, standing proudly on its own, a few monuments dotted around the exterior. Monuments that had meaning to this particular club, this area, this community.

They had time to wander around the stadium, taking it all in. First, they headed down towards the Bob Stokoe statue, commemorating Sunderland's famous FA Cup win of 1973. Robbie hadn't known too much about last season's FA Cup Final, but Liam imagined he'd be keen to watch this year's. Something else that had lost a bit of shine, he thought ruefully. Jesus, he was turning into his dad, with all this nostalgia!

They walked through the car park, pointing out a huge Davy Lamp on the roundabout near the main entrance. The structure stood proudly as the reason behind the stadium's name. Admittedly, most opposition fans saw it as a blatant copy of Benfica's home ground.

As they circled around the ground once more, they came across another nod to the mining heritage of the area. The pit wheel that came from the old colliery on which the stadium was built.

The red ironwork structure poked out of what might be suspect ground. Bit ironic thought Liam, dodgy foundations, grabbing Robbie before he clambered all over the exhibit. They watched their son's perplexed, bewildered face as they told him about mining, coalfields and pits. Callie tried not to laugh. It was so far removed from their own environment. Expecting a seven-year-old to comprehend miners and working underground was stretching his imagination.

"Enough of the history lesson, who fancies a look in the club shop?" Callie had never been one to dwell on the past. Always looking forward. It was a good trait to have, although she would never stop Liam reminiscing.

"Meeeeeeeeeeeeeee!" came the reply from an excited Robbie. He'd stood in awe looking around the outside of the stadium, but now that was done, he was ready for the next adventure. And he'd already spied the shop, together with his mum, up ahead.

"There won't be any Brentford stuff y'know?"

"I know that, dad. But it looks so big, I wanna see inside."

Memories of that first game came flooding back. He'd had to budget so tightly that day. It was only due to his parents' and in-laws' generosity that Robbie was able to buy something on that first visit. The day had been so special. And yet, he almost wasn't there. Bloody idiot. He'd made some mistakes over the last few months, but that one would have been the worst by far. What the hell was he thinking? Look at them now. Look! Look what you'd have missed out on.

Deep in thought, he put his arm around Callie's shoulders and gave her an affectionate squeeze.

"You ok?"

"Yeah, just thinking about stuff. And I was remembering his first match. It was against these lot."

"Ah, I can still see his little face when he came running in the flat afterwards. Grinning from ear to ear. They didn't even win either!"

Robbie spent a good twenty minutes wandering around the club shop, looking at all of the shirts. Red and white stripes, like Brentford's, though he definitely preferred his own. There was so much to see. Callie had to keep hold of him. Otherwise she'd have lost sight of him amongst the throngs of people and rails upon rails of merchandise. After all that time, he decided he only wanted a programme as a memento of his first away game. It didn't seem right to get something with Sunderland on it.

The tickets Kev had managed to get were in the North West corner of the ground. Liam was relieved to see they were in the lower tier. He liked to be close to the action if possible. The thought of being up in the gods with the away fans didn't appeal, other than the atmosphere. They'd not be too far from them though, up in the top tier of the North stand.

They all grabbed a bite to eat once they were inside and then Liam noticed Robbie itching to get into their seats. The players would be warming up soon.

He gestured at Callie to watch their son as they led him up the steps. They approached the top of the staircase, their eyes fixed on his. Sure enough, it was a sight to behold. The mouth gaped open, the eyes wide with delight, speechless and in awe. And then just a single word, elongated with wonderment. "Wow".

"Got to say, I'm pretty impressed myself actually," said Callie, so pleased they'd been able to come up this weekend.

The sun was shining, the pitch was perfectly green and smooth like a snooker table. The stadium was huge, much bigger than anything Robbie had ever encountered. To a seven-year-old boy, getting into football for the first time, it was just… stunning.

"Beats the pants off Griffin Park, ey?" he asked his son, who was still stood there, drinking in the view.

"It's amazing, dad. But we've got a better team haven't we?"

And he was right.

Brentford dominated the first half, scoring their first goal after thirteen minutes. When the second one followed on the half-hour mark, a section of Sunderland fans walked out in disgust. Liam was shocked. In all his years following football, he'd never known fans leave a game that early on. Ah well, he thought, who cares. This is brilliant.

It was a tougher second half, the home team had obviously endured a half-time rant from their manager. But Brentford held firm and claimed the three points. It was another nail in Sunderland's coffin, as they slid further towards the trapdoor to League One. Not that there were any home fans there by the end. The ground had only been just over half-full anyway. By full-time, it was purely the Brentford fans who remained in their pink seats. Plus, a little family in the North West corner, of course.

Another great result for Liam's lucky charm. And Kev would be ecstatic.

Full time: Sunderland 0 Brentford 2

63

"Thanks for coming, everyone. We'll get onto the usual matters after coffee, but in the meantime, as you know we have our emergency agenda to deal with."

"We're not going to raise suspicions by being here today?"

"No," the chairman responded. "This is our scheduled meeting after all."

"What a week," said one of the men around the boardroom table.

"What a week indeed," the chairman replied. He looked as though he'd aged considerably since their last face-to-face meeting.

"I'm surprised you're in the meeting, Mitchell?" the menacing one asked, glaring towards Roberts.

The chairman responded before he could muster a reply. "Well, he needs to hear what we've got to say. Then I'll fill you in at the end of the meeting about what's going to happen with him."

The men nodded, grim-faced. Mitchell was only just behind Emma as public enemy number one right now.

"Right," continued the chairman, "onto business."

The men sat upright, ready to hear the latest update.

"So, we managed to hack into Emma's laptop and place some malware on there, which destroyed all the evidence. From our understanding, the police have some written notes about various files and some of the names. But now that the hard evidence has gone, chances are they won't have a case against anyone named in the files."

"I don't like leaving things to chance," the menacing guy interjected.

"I'm afraid that's the best we can hope for at the moment. We should be in the clear once our plan for Mitchell is actioned." Mitchell shifted *uncomfortably in his chair at the mention of his name. He'd been trying to avoid eye contact with anyone.*

The chairman moved on to the next point.

"I've been in touch with our syndicate friends and explained we have to call off any bets until the end of the season. We need to minimise any suspicious activity, as the eyes of the world will be on us for a while."

"I bet they were easy conversations. Not."

"Quite," the chairman responded, raising an eyebrow. "But they do understand this is best for us all in the long run."

"How the hell did she work out what was going on?" one of the men suddenly exploded into life.

"Maybe she was in on the burglary? Maybe she has the book?"

The thought created consternation around the room. If the police had the black book, there was nothing they could do from the outside to wipe its contents. They were done for.

"She may have been involved, but we can only assume at this stage that she doesn't have the book. The enquiries from the police don't indicate there's anything other than what was on the laptop. In fact, the book may have been destroyed."

The group mulled over the chairman's words before the menacing one chipped in with "What, to protect the person who's been placing the bets? After what happened to the builder maybe?"

"Could well be. We've had no bets flagged up for almost a month. And once we start getting different results from what's in the book, it'll help to put us in the clear. But we'll still keep a watching brief on any suspicious betting activity, so we can bring back the surveillance if necessary."

"Do we know if they've rumbled the auction?" The chairman was inwardly amused by this question coming from this person. It was no doubt caused by the fact that they wouldn't be in the top four again this season. Their purse-strings had tightened over the last couple of years. He couldn't help but feel they wanted to get back to doing things the old way. Either that

or they wanted to explore another alternative, where they could still fix things, but they'd **all** benefit from the big money. Six into four just didn't go.

"We don't believe they have any information on that yet. The code on the emails is pretty robust. So there's no reason Emma would've either known about it or been able to work out what was in the book. If she even had that. I think we're pretty safe as far as our auction goes."

"Just as well. We'd all be up shit creek if that came out," came a more nervous-sounding voice around the table.

"So," the chairman began again, "that leaves us with the little matter of what we do next."

Mitchell squirmed in his seat and looked down at the table, waiting for the executioner's blade.

The chairman continued. "Mitchell is going to resign from his position at a press conference tomorrow morning. He'll state that he alone attempted to instigate a programme of match-fixing, on behalf of overseas betting groups. But he'll claim the other parties refused to participate. Following that, he'll hand himself in to the police voluntarily. He'll plead he was coerced into doing this under threat of violence."

"At which point he'll be interrogated," pointed out the menacing one.

"Yes, he will. But he won't implicate any of us and will put forward a 'no comment' response to every question, on the basis that he fears for his own safety. Assuming he gets us through this unscathed, we'll pay him his full salary for the next two years as severance. Plus an unofficial bonus of course for maintaining his silence."

"Can we trust him not to spill the beans to get himself off? He could shaft us all, in return for immunity from prosecution and police protection." It was the menacing one again. And his eyes were piercing Mitchell's scalp.

"He'll have our lawyer in there with him," revealed the chairman. "So we'll know exactly how he answers the questions. Worst-case scenario, if he gets sent down, we'll compensate him for his sentence. And of course, we'll make sure he's safe in prison."

Ah, that last sentence. It was the final warning shot for Mitchell. Do as we say and you'll be looked after. Otherwise, the consequences are much more dangerous.

The group absorbed the details.

"*Never mind the police interrogation, the press pack will eat him alive when he makes that statement," one of the men suggested.*

"*Mitchell will only speak to make his statement. It'll be made clear that I'll answer any questions following that. There won't be any cock-ups."*

"*For a change."*

The laughter following this jibe was unfriendly at best.

"*Ok, Mitchell, I think we're done with you now. I'll see you later today, so we can prepare for the morning. Make sure you're available whenever. Right gents, shall we reconvene after coffee and we can discuss the latest on VAR?"*

64

BREAKING NEWS…BREAKING NEWS…BREAKING

LIVE - PREMIER LEAGUE PRESS CONFERENCE: MATCH-FIXING ALLEGATIONS

"Good morning, everyone," the chairman welcomed a packed media room. "Our CEO will read out a short statement, then I will answer any questions you may have."

"Thank you, chairman. In light of recent allegations, I have today tendered my resignation to the Board, which has been unanimously accepted. I would emphasise I worked alone to try and instigate a programme of match-fixing, on behalf of overseas betting groups. The other parties named within this action refused to participate. This is a testament to their integrity and the ongoing integrity of the Premier League.

"I am extremely ashamed of my actions. In mitigation, I was coerced into this under threat of violence. Nevertheless, I accept I have brought the game into disrepute. My position is untenable. I will be surrendering to the Metropolitan Police immediately after this press conference. I will, wherever possible, co-operate with their investigation."

BREAKING NEWS…BREAKING NEWS…BREAKING

The ticker message changed following the bombshell announcement.

PREMIER LEAGUE CHIEF RESIGNS IN DISGRACE

After Mitchell's statement, the press room descended into utter chaos. Reporters were clamouring to get their questions answered. Photographers were manically clicking away on their cameras. The broadcast media closed in on the culprit, scanned the room and then focused on the next person under the spotlight.

"Chairman," the first reporter permitted to ask a question began. "Surely the evidence suggests that more than one person is involved in this scandal? Are you trying to say no results were actually affected?"

"This is still part of an ongoing police investigation, so we're unable to expand at this point. However, we are hopeful, based on our conversations with Mr Roberts, things did not progress any further than an initial attempt at fixing."

A loud murmur carried around the room.

"Does it not concern you that the evidence handed over to police has been tampered with and wiped out? Does this not suggest that the match-fixing had already been taking place?"

"We can't comment on police procedures I'm afraid. There's no hard evidence any results have been influenced. Or that anyone apart from Mr Roberts has been involved in any wrongdoing. Until we are advised to the contrary."

More murmurs of discontent.

"Chairman, will the Premier League be carrying out its own investigation into this whole sorry saga?"

"Yes, we will carry out a full inquiry in conjunction with the police investigation. We are determined to ensure that the integrity of our competition is upheld. Our league is arguably the best in Europe and we are committed to keeping it at the top. However, I must stress, we don't believe this is an issue across the organisation or beyond. Just one rogue individual with some outside influences."

"With respect, chairman. Surely the evidence points to an ongoing, systematic programme of match-fixing already being in place? Maybe even before Mr Roberts was appointed. Does this not strike at the very heart of the game?"

"No, no. As far as we're aware, nothing suggests that that is the case. But rest assured, if it were, we would get to the bottom of it."

The press conference continued for another forty-five minutes, in much the same vein. Questioning the chairman about the extent of the corruption. At each turn being told it was all down to one man and hadn't actually occurred as yet. The cynics in the room, about 99% of attendees, didn't seem to be buying it, but couldn't get much change out of the chairman.

Eventually, the conference came to a natural end. The world's media spent the rest of the day reporting on the event, picking over its bones, analysing what was said. The higher-end print media began probing suspicious results, questioning outside influences. The tabloids thought up lurid headlines and created caricatures of Mitchell. They tried their best to turn the narrative into 'foreigners' trying to fix our beautiful game.

There was one common consensus, however.

Mitchell would inevitably end up behind bars.

PART THREE

65

BREAKING NEWS…BREAKING NEWS…BREAKING
MATCH-FIXING ALLEGATIONS:
EX-PREMIER LEAGUE CHIEF CHARGED BY
POLICE

"News just in. The Metropolitan Police have charged former Premier League CEO, Mitchell Roberts, with three counts of fraud. It's believed the case will come before the Crown Court in November this year. The Premier League have so far declined to comment."

The following day:

BREAKING NEWS…BREAKING NEWS…BREAKING
COMING UP –
PREMIER LEAGUE PRESS CONFERENCE:
MATCH-FIXING ALLEGATIONS

"Just a reminder that the Premier League has called a press conference for 11:00 this morning. They're expected to give an update on the match-fixing allegations, which have rocked the game since the news broke in February. We'll head straight across there as soon as it starts."

Callie's dad had flicked over to SkySports News as Liam popped his head into the lounge. The content of the 'Breaking News' ticker stopped him in his tracks.

Harry noticed his son-in-law's interest in the story.

"Bloody disgrace innit?"

"Yeah, but I bet nothing comes of it."

357

"Always the way. Bet you're glad you're a Brentford fan? I reckon you're pretty safe from any of this rubbish."

"Yeah, always the ones at the top. They get greedy, don't they?" And if I told you the full story Harry, you wouldn't believe it, he thought.

"Game's gone, son. It's been heading this way for years. It's all about money these days."

Harry was a bit of an old cynic, but Liam couldn't argue with his current view. For all he knew, he could've stumbled on the tip of the iceberg. What he'd discovered had been shocking, but what if there was more he didn't know about? He felt so out of his depth. It was also making him question his love for the game. Brentford were a proud club and big on integrity. There was little likelihood of them being involved in anything dodgy. But how far *did* this corruption go? Was it just the self-proclaimed big six or did it go beyond that?

"Give us a shout when the press conference comes on, would you? I'd like to watch it if you don't mind?" he asked Harry.

"Will do. That looks heavy. Do you need a hand?"

"Nah, I'm fine. Cheers, Harry."

Liam had just got back from the flat and was desperate to get the holdall upstairs out of the way. The removal men were due to come in tomorrow and Liam had decided to leave them to it. He'd given them clear instructions and labelled everything. He'd taken what he needed, surprised it was still there. The fact it was gave him a renewed sense of hope for the future. They could be in the clear.

During his week off work, the three of them had already stayed with Liam's parents for a few days. It had been good to spend some quality time together before they moved. They'd exchanged on the flat and were due to complete next week. Now they were back at Callie's parents' house for their final couple of days and the joint family meal tonight.

Callie was in the bedroom, packing their clothes into cases, wanting to get most of it done by this afternoon. She was conscious it would be a whirlwind from this evening onwards. Before long, they'd be packing the car up again and heading off to their new life. It was a wrench to make Robbie go through a school move in the middle of term, but they knew this was the right decision.

"Got it," Liam said, as he walked into the room, lifting the holdall up slightly so she could see it.

"Brilliant. I had visions of us getting robbed while we were away. Would've been typical," she laughed.

"And bloody ironic," he replied, relieved to see her relaxed mood. "How are you getting on here?"

"Almost done. I've left all our clothes for the next couple of days in the drawers. Everything else is pretty much packed," she said, reaching to pull the lid over and see if it would close. Just. "All our toiletries are still in the bathroom. Other than that, we're good to go."

He knew she'd miss her family, but he could sense the positivity from her over the last few weeks. He felt the same. Ever since they'd made their decision, the world seemed a brighter place. He hated to break the good mood, but she'd find out anyway. Might as well get it over with.

"There's a news conference coming up on TV. From the Premier League. About the match-fixing."

To his surprise, she didn't seem fazed.

"I bet nothing else happens. That guy's taken all the blame so far, hasn't he?"

"Yeah," he replied. "Y'know, I checked some of the results over the last couple of months and they're different to what was in the book. Must be running scared."

"LIAM!!! It's coming on any second."

The yell from downstairs took them both by surprise.

Callie looked confused.

"I asked your dad to let me know when it was coming on. Fancy watching it? We can compare thoughts afterwards!"

"Yeah, let's see what these crooked buggers have got to say."

BREAKING NEWS…BREAKING NEWS…BREAKING LIVE - PREMIER LEAGUE PRESS CONFERENCE: MATCH-FIXING ALLEGATIONS

"…over to Premier League headquarters now for their press conference."

A swarm of cameras were taking photos of the Chairman sitting down and readying himself. Flashes were going off left, right and centre. He waited until the camera noise subsided and allowed an inquisitive murmuring to die out by taking a sip of water. As the room fell silent, he began.

"Good morning, everyone. I wanted to update you following the fraud charges brought against Mitchell Roberts. Over the last couple of months, we have worked closely with the police to help with their enquiries. We have simultaneously carried out our own comprehensive internal investigation.

"We have found no evidence of any further wrongdoing. This has led us to conclude Mr Roberts was acting alone. Although there were intimidating circumstances, this is no excuse for his conduct. We have therefore taken steps to summarily dismiss him from his role and rescind his prior resignation. This means he will not receive any further remuneration from the Premier League going forward."

At a smart townhouse in West London, a glass fell to the slate floor and shattered into a hundred pieces. Those last two sentences had caused more of a shock than the previous day's news. "You bastards!" Mitchell said out loud. "You lying, conniving, corrupt bastards." He held his head in his hands as the conference continued.

"This episode has proved to be extremely sobering for everyone involved at the Premier League. Whilst we appreciate Mitchell was coerced, there is no defence for his actions. As guardians of the top level of football in England and a beacon for the game around the world, our stakeholders deserve complete trust in us. I can only apologise to the clubs, players, fans, officials and everyone who has an interest in the game. Integrity in sport is paramount and Mitchell has fallen far short of the standards we expect."

Liam glanced across at Callie and raised his eyebrows, staggered by the hypocrisy.

"We are reviewing our governance procedures to ensure nothing like this ever happens again. We'll take our time to appoint Mitchell's successor. In the meantime, I will take on the role of acting CEO. I hope this draws a line under the whole sorry affair and that we can focus again on being the best league in the world. One man's actions should not detract from our global appeal."

The press pack clamoured to ask questions following the end of the Chairman's statement. How could they be sure no one else was involved? Were there any results that appeared to have been fixed? Did any players, clubs or officials fall under the spotlight? What would they do to ensure nothing like this would happen in the future? Had any sponsors pulled out as a result of the scandal? And so on. And so on.

The Chairman answered each question calmly and concisely. He was well-rehearsed and seemed transparent in his responses. Every time he was asked about others being involved, the reply was a firm **"No evidence whatsoever."** He then moved swiftly on to the next question.

"Load of bollocks!" Harry commented, as the press conference drew to a close. "Right, I'll leave you two to it. Gonna get the lawn mowed before it gets too hot. No doubt your mum will want us to have some drinks out on the patio tonight, in this gorgeous weather." He tossed the remote over to Callie as he left the room.

They looked at each other.

"Jesus, it's all been swept under the carpet. How have they got away with it?" Liam was incredulous.

Callie was shocked, but not surprised. She'd seen it coming.

"Told you. They're point-blank denying anyone else was involved. Making out they're squeaky clean and it was only that guy you robbed."

"It must be true, that rumour that the laptop was wiped remotely," he mused. "I mean, other than that guy confessing to it all, I guess they didn't have the evidence anymore."

"Yeah, it's amazing what you can do when you've got money," she laughed, sarcastically.

He felt a pang of guilt. "At least we did what we did to make a better life for our family," he said.

"Hmmm. Still doesn't excuse it. I'll never feel totally comfortable about it, but I know we've got to move on and get on with our lives."

He looked away. Focused back on the TV screen, thinking about what he'd just heard, trying to take his mind off what he'd done.

"So, if these guys are still in charge and still as greedy as ever… How the hell do we ever rely on things not being fixed in the future?"

"Don't, babe. Don't even think about it." He could sense Callie's mood changing as she said it.

"Don't worry, I'm not gonna do anything. But the evidence I've got is enough to implicate all of them."

"Probably. But I don't want to live in fear for the rest of our lives. I want us to live a normal life and bring our kids up in a safe environment. I don't want to be looking over our shoulders, worried that someone's after us. We're just ordinary people. We can't bring these guys down. Money gives you power. Even with what we've got now, it's not enough to take them on."

"I know, I know. But it pisses me off these greedy bastards have ruined our game."

"You've still got Brentford. That'll never change. I know you'll only see them occasionally, but you'll always be able to rely on them."

"I was looking forward to taking Robbie to every game," he said, a hint of regret in his voice. "I wanted to buy us all season tickets."

"One day. We might be back here someday. You're still sure about moving though, aren't you?" Callie was holding her breath as she asked the question. She was sure. Liam *had* to be. There was another reason now.

"I am. To be honest, I can't wait. I know we're gonna miss everyone, but it all just makes sense. It's like fate."

"It is," she agreed. "In fact, you know when I came up to see you the second time when we decided what we were going to do?"

"Yeah," he was wondering what direction she was going in.

"Well, the fates obviously collided then." Callie slipped her hand into the back pocket of her jeans and pulled something out.

Liam looked at what she had in her hand, confused at first. And then the penny dropped. He saw the two lines. Remembered the last time. Without warning, he pounced on Callie and enveloped her in the biggest hug. It was the best news. A little brother or sister for Robbie. Completely unplanned. Only this time, there'd be no money worries.

~~~~~~

Up in Manchester, Superintendent Mark Yates had also been watching the press conference with interest. He'd followed the saga over the last few months, intrigued by its developments. His instincts told him there was more to it than they were letting on. One man acting alone. Really? It seemed disingenuous. He listened to the Q&A session at the end. He was about to switch over as it became tedious. Different journalists asking nuanced questions over and over.

And then he saw them. To the side of the conference desk, blending into the background. At least trying to. But Yates had spotted them. Yates had recognised them.

It was the men from Old Trafford, almost exactly twelve months ago.

66

21 April 2018
Brentford vs QPR
Griffin Park, London
Kick-off: 3:00 pm

It was another scorcher of a day in Brentford, as the family group set off from Clayponds Avenue. It was only a fifteen-minute walk, but the heat was already getting to Liam. His head was still pounding from a few too many beers last night. When would he ever learn?

It had been a great night, both of their families all together, good food and plenty of alcohol to wash it down with. Except for Callie and Robbie of course. But the others more than made up for their abstinence.

They'd managed to have everyone outside up until it got dark around 9:30pm. The sunny, warm weather helped them cope with the numbers. Eleven people sat down eating and drinking could be a bit of a squeeze in their cosy, semi-detached house. But spilling out onto the patio made for a much more relaxed affair.

If there was one saving grace for Liam, it was that it hadn't been that late a night. His mum and dad, Lucy and Michelle had all left around midnight. They were sharing a taxi home and none of them wanted to be too late when they had the game to look forward to the next day. Along with more eating and drinking.

Robbie had been allowed to stay up until the darkness took hold. He was reluctantly packed off to bed as the adults settled indoors. Despite his protestations, he was fast asleep within minutes, worn out by all the excitement of these few days. Today had been his last day at school and his friends had made him cards and given him gifts. He'd been made to feel extra special and Callie had seen him tear up in the rear-view mirror as she was driving home. She spotted him as he looked back at the school one more time. She prayed he'd soon settle into his new one and make friends as precious as those he was leaving behind.

Once he was tucked up in bed, Callie and Liam made their special announcement. Under normal circumstances, they'd wait until their first scan. But they didn't know when everyone would be together again, so it seemed like the perfect opportunity. They wanted to give them some happy news, in amongst the sadness of them leaving.

"Shhhhhh! You'll wake Robbie!" shushed Callie, as the family members screamed in delight at the news. "We need to keep it secret from him until we know everything's ok. We just didn't want to leave without telling you all."

"I thought you seemed a bit sober, Cal!" Rachel suddenly realised.

"Yeah, I've been drinking tonic all night. Fooled you all!"

Rachel and Matt were staying over with Callie's parents too, so they could both have a drink. It would have cost a fortune for taxis and they were going to the match the following day as well. So their final couple of nights would see Robbie bunking in with Liam and Callie in their room. It was a bit of a squeeze, but they didn't mind. Callie's family had been so supportive over the last few months. Not to mention all the help that Rachel had given over the years, looking after Robbie for them.

Matt grabbed another beer or two from the cool box once Liam's family had departed. Harry and Margaret had headed upstairs as soon as they'd said their goodbyes. Rachel and Callie sensibly seized the opportunity to retire for the evening. They knew what their partners could be like given half a chance.

Left alone with their beers, Matt suddenly blurted out, "I'm made up for you, mate. About the baby. And everything. Just don't be strangers. We're gonna miss you all, but Rachel's gonna be lost without Robbie. They have a special bond."

"I know," Liam responded. "It's only up the country though, it's not another planet."

"Feels like it at times!" Matt laughed.

It was after 1:00am when they decided it was time to hit the sack if they wanted to feel at all human tomorrow.

The plan hadn't worked.

As Harry asked what everyone wanted to drink in the Griffin, Liam and Matt exchanged a look. The latter puffed out his cheeks as he contemplated the best option, the former turned a shade of green.

"Sod it, hair of the dog," Matt jumped in first. "I'll have a pint, Harry. I'll get these though, you looked after us all last night."

He looked at Liam, roared with laughter and gave him a hearty slap on the back. "I'm getting you the same, mate. It'll sort you out."

Liam's queasiness brought back memories of the last time he'd been at Griffin Park. The day he saw the news about Danny's disappearance. When he threw up his guts back at the flat. He began to feel the bile rise in his stomach again at the thought of how things had panned out.

"You ok, babe?" asked Callie, noticing that he'd turned a strange colour.

"Yeah, I think I just had a bad pint last night. I'll be back in a sec."

He dived into the toilets, doing the only thing he could do right now. Better to get it up and out of his system. Thankfully, this time he felt better for doing so. As he splashed his face with cold water, the colour began to return to his cheeks.

Whilst the nausea had created flashbacks of a shocking few days, he told himself that he had to deal with it. He had to bear the burden and carry on with life for the sake of Callie and Robbie. And today, just like last night, was going to be a special memory for them all. He wasn't about to ruin it by overthinking the past.

"Lightweight!" Matt called over as he headed towards the tables they'd reserved.

He resisted the urge to tell him to fuck off, due to present company. But the joking look he gave him whilst mouthing the words got the message across.

Liam's family joined them all once again for a pre-match meal, a replay of the previous night's get-together. It was a happy occasion. He was relieved he'd got over his earlier sickness. The hair of the dog had worked its magic. He looked around the tables and felt genuinely happy. God, he'd miss everyone, but he couldn't wait to start afresh up north.

On their way to the Griffin, Liam had glanced towards the New Inn as they turned to walk down Ealing Road. Many a happy time in there. He'd loved to have nipped in and seen his mates, tell them his news, but the fewer people who knew they were moving the better. He'd catch up with them next time he made it to a game.

Lunch over, they had one more thing to do before heading into the ground. The club shop. Another memory that seemed like a lifetime ago and yet it had only been six months since Robbie's very first game. The contrast between those times was stark. Liam felt like buying most of the shop this time, compared to the tight budget they'd been on back in October. He felt guilty for taking his son away from here. Like he had all those years ago, Robbie had fallen in love with the Bees and was already an ardent fan. Christ, Liam hadn't even left yet and he was already feeling homesick.

Robbie was confused. He couldn't think of anything else he needed. He had his Brentford top with number 7 and his name on the back. He had a Brentford scarf and hat, although he wasn't wearing either in the sky-high temperatures today. And he had his Brentford sports bag that he'd be using at the first opportunity at his new school.

And then he saw it. What his parents had come in for. Result!

"We thought you'd like this in your new bedroom when we get sorted with a house," Callie said. She was holding up a duvet set.

"Really? For me? My very own Brentford bed? I LOVE it!" At that moment, Robbie realised his life hadn't been complete. Now it was, though. Wow, moving somewhere new wasn't so scary after all.

The family of three headed into the ground, catching up with the others, who'd gone in ahead. Everyone had tickets for the match, but they wouldn't all be sat together. Brentford had gone on another decent run and weren't that far off the playoffs with only three games to go. Today was a sell-out, their biggest crowd of the season and another derby into the bargain. So the chances of getting eleven seats all together were nigh on impossible. But at least they were all in the Braemar Road stand.

There was a buzz around the ground as they took their seats a little later. If they could get three points today, they stood a real chance of making the playoffs. Jesus, thought Liam, what if they get to Wembley? And getting into the Premier League didn't even bear thinking about. That would be typical, he thought. He was moving to the other end of the country as his beloved team were on the up.

Today had an end-of-season feel to it, even though their final home game wasn't for another fortnight. Not the kind that had players' minds already on their holidays, playing like they had their flip-flops on. More like the crucial, everything hinging on this game, whole season boils down to this, type of atmosphere. Liam loved being at the match in this weather and Griffin Park was bouncing in anticipation. It was still only April and yet it felt like summer already. The sun was blazing and the mercury was blasting through the mid-twenties.

The players more than lived up to the fans' expectations. It was a cracking, hard-fought derby, with most of the twists and turns taking place in an eventful first half. Brentford scored in the 13th minute through Sergi Canos, ramping up the atmosphere. Cue Robbie hugging both of his parents in sheer delight. Then a couple of minutes before half-time they were awarded a penalty. The goalie was injured in conceding the penalty, but should've been sent off. To rub salt into the wound, he got up from being treated and made a great save from the wronged party, Watkins.

And then, in first-half injury time, Rangers left Bees' fans seething as they snatched an equaliser. Shit! Liam thought. Not today. He was desperate for Brentford to win, to give Robbie the perfect send-off. He glanced across at his son, who looked desolate.

As the half-time whistle blew, everyone leapt from their seats to meet up in the concourse. There were varying reactions to the closing stages. Some were fuming, others more relaxed. It was clear that each and every one of them were enjoying the game.

"What d'you reckon Robbie?" Pete asked his grandson, keen to hear the oracle speak.

"It's a brilliant game isn't it granddad? I think we're gonna get at least another goal, probably two. I'm going for 3-1."

Pete smiled to himself. That seemed to be his favourite score. Maybe he wasn't a prophet after all. Maybe he just picked that score and hoped for the best?

Again, Robbie didn't get the actual correct score, but it was another win for the Bees. The second half wasn't as good as the first, but Brentford made their pressure count. And in a fitting finale, who better to get the winner than Jozefzoon?

Robbie was ecstatic when the goal went in. The number on his shirt meant so much more than his age. It couldn't have worked out better if they'd deliberately chosen a player.

"You ok, babe?" Callie asked as the roars of the crowd were beginning to die down a few minutes later.

"Yeah, just got something in my eye," Liam responded. And a big huge lump in my throat he thought, as he fought his emotions.

Football could get you like that.

They stayed a while at the end to applaud the players off and allow the crowd to filter out ahead of them. Soaking it up one more time. Taking it all in. Today had been nigh on perfect.

Could this be our year, thought Liam? They were now in a great position to qualify for the play-offs. Knowing what he knew, he was in a quandary as to whether he wanted Brentford to go up. In amongst all that greed and self-servitude. All the corruption, fixing, deception. He had to put those thoughts out of his mind. Brentford could soon be up amongst the big boys if everything went their way over the next few weeks. It's what dreams are made of. I should have a little wager on them, he chuckled to himself.

His phone buzzed as the buoyant families walked back to Callie's mum and dad's after the game. Robbie was walking up ahead, hand in hand with Lucy on one side and Rachel on the other. Liam let go of Callie's hand as he reached for his phone. The text was from Kev.

Great result for you guys.

Have a safe journey up tomorrow.

And what a fuckin result for us!

Followed by a load of crying with laughter emojis.

Liam was momentarily confused. He flicked to the scores on his phone. Newcastle hadn't played today. He switched to the football headlines. Scrolled. And scrolled again. Ha! There it was. Now he understood the message. Sunderland had lost at home to Burton. In injury time. And they'd been relegated as a result. To League One. No wonder Kev was in stitches.

He smiled. The pangs of sadness at leaving London were mixed with excitement at what the future held. For them all.

And no doubt Kev would have the mother of all hangovers when they arrived tomorrow.

Football could get you like that too!

Full time: Brentford 2 QPR 1

67

Tina heard the letterbox rattle and a thud on the doormat. It had been a while since the mail had made any noise dropping on the floor. A couple of months almost. Since the sympathy cards had stopped.

In amongst the bills and the flyers, there was a padded brown envelope. About A5 size. Small enough to fit through the letterbox without the postman having to disturb her.

She peered at the postmark. Peterborough. No idea what it could be or who it was from.

She walked into the kitchen and dropped it onto the worktop. She'd look at it later. Probably. She wasn't feeling that motivated today.

It was a few days since what should have been the happiest day of her life. Instead, it had been one of the saddest days.

Tom, Nat and the kids had been down to stay with her for the weekend. She knew why, although the topic hadn't been mentioned excessively. Just a few kind comments about Danny, sporadic tears here and there and some tighter than normal hugs. It had been wonderful to see them and it had given her a bit of a boost. But the joy of the weekend had elapsed, now that they'd returned home. Her house was empty again and she felt lonely, bereft and so utterly heartbroken.

A few hours later, she finally opened her mail, albeit with no anticipation or enthusiasm. She reached into the padded envelope, tipping the contents onto the kitchen worktop as she did so. A memory stick dropped out. In her hand, she was holding a black, hard-backed notebook and a few pieces of notepaper. She peeked into the envelope to make sure she'd got everything.

Still clueless as to what it was and who it was from, she noticed her hands shaking as she began to unfold the notepaper. Grabbing her mug of coffee for moral support, she took everything into the lounge.

Dear Tina

I don't write many letters and I've thought long and hard about whether I should write this to you. But I would never forgive myself if you were left to think that Danny killed himself. Because he didn't.

She dropped the letter in shock. What on earth? She wasn't sure if she could continue. She sipped on her coffee as she mulled things over, as memories came flooding back. The caffeine gave her clarity. Tina decided she had to know what it said, no matter how difficult it was to read. She took a deep breath and picked up the notepaper once more.

I've known Danny for a few years and he was an absolutely sound bloke, one of the best. I was devastated to hear about his death. But because of what I know, I don't for one second believe he killed himself.

Last year, I was in serious financial trouble and everything got on top of me. I could see no way out, no possibility of ever paying off my debts. It got to the point where I tried to end it all. Thank God, someone was there to stop me and I'll be eternally grateful to them for saving my life. Danny wasn't aware of that last bit, though he did know about my money problems.

He tipped me off about a house he'd been working at, which was an easy target for a break-in. He'd seen there was a large safe inside, with enough cash to end my financial worries forever. Danny said the guy who owned the house deserved it, as he'd had to resort to threats to get paid. He'd been an 'obnoxious git' (or words to that effect) the whole time he was there. I don't think he'd have even considered it if the guy hadn't been a jerk.

Even so, no matter how desperate I was and how straightforward it was to break in, there is no excuse for what I did. If I could turn back the clock, I would.

I saw Danny a couple of times after the burglary. He never told me about any threats he'd had or anything he was worried about in connection with the break-in. If he had, I'd have done whatever it took to make sure he was in the clear. Since he disappeared though, I've seen evidence myself of dark forces. I've had to make some life-changing decisions to get my family away from all this.

The last time I spoke to him, Danny told me he'd proposed to you on Christmas Day. He was really looking forward to getting married. It's been obvious over the years how much he cared about you and your family. I don't think he could believe his luck to be honest, after everything he'd gone through in his younger days.

Anyway, I didn't just take cash from the safe. There were loads of expensive watches in there, as well as the two things I'm enclosing with this letter. Danny had no idea who the house belonged to, as he's not a football fan. But the guy was actually in charge of the Premier League. I say 'was' because he's about to go to prison on corruption charges.

This corruption goes <u>much</u> deeper than the current investigation suggests. And implicates a lot more people. I've agonised over whether to take the evidence to the police. But after what happened to Danny, I can't put my own family in any more danger. Besides, I came to the conclusion that the choice should be yours. I've taken a copy of everything for safe-keeping, but I won't do anything with it unless it's absolutely necessary. The ones enclosed are the originals. It's your decision what to do with it all.

If you go to the police, please send the evidence anonymously for your own protection. If you decide to get rid of it, then dispose of things carefully. Don't throw them away where they could end up in someone else's hands. These items and the evidence they contain are most probably why Danny was murdered.

I appreciate you'll be angry with me when you receive this, but my sole intention is for you to know the truth. And to know that Danny would never have killed himself. He had too much to live for.

I'm ashamed of what I did. And, knowing that it most likely had something to do with Danny's disappearance will haunt me to my dying day. I'll never forgive myself and I'm so so sorry that my actions have robbed you of your future together.

Please forgive me.

The letter was unsigned. No name. No address. No way of knowing who it came from. But it sounded sincere. It appeared to be genuine.

Tina folded up the notepaper, quietly and calmly placing the letter on the coffee table in front of her. The tears that had been blurring her vision throughout the letter reading were now in full flow. She was heartbroken, angry, sad, raging and yet slightly at peace. It appeared Danny hadn't killed himself after all. Her instincts were right.

She was still sobbing two hours later.

~~~~~~

That same morning, Gavin answered the door to the postman, surprised to see him holding a large jiffy envelope. He wasn't expecting any deliveries today.

He took the padded envelope into the kitchen so he could carefully cut it open. When he saw what was inside, he did a double-take. What? What the hell?

On top of the main contents, he spotted a letter. This one was much briefer. No need to go into any explanations about the burglary, the corruption, the guilt in this letter. Nevertheless, it still shocked the recipient.

And caused them to sob their heart out too.

Dear Gavin

Last year you saved my life. I can never thank you enough.

I had a financial windfall recently, which has set me up for life. I wanted you to have some of it, so you can buy that camper van. Go travelling with your wife and Jack. Make some special memories.

Life is too short, it's true. But thanks to some of the best people in this world, my life still has a long way to go. I can never repay you for what you did. Hopefully, helping you to live your dream will go some way towards that.

Wishing you every happiness. You're one of the best, mate.

68

14 May 2018
End of season auction
Secret location
By invitation only

"Good evening, everyone."

The acting CEO greeted his most important stakeholders warmly as he stepped onto the boat. He always enjoyed this event, the first half at least. Wining and dining on the finest of everything. Money no object. Mainly because the newly-crowned champions would be footing today's bill. That was an unwritten part of the agreement.

They'd arrived earlier today. Private jets and limousines had whisked them here. Almost as soon as the final ball had been kicked and the celebrations began to peter out. It would be a glittering end to the season.

The superyacht sailed out to sea, as they sipped on 1959 Dom Perignon Champagne. It tasted exquisite. So it should, at thirty grand a bottle. None of that tacky Cristal that the players so famously devoured. This was quality.

It had been a tough season, all things considered. But things were looking up again. They were in the clear with the police. Their syndicate friends were back on board for next season. And now, they knew they could carry on with their auction. Without any chance of being rumbled.

The reason? As the acting Chief Executive delighted in telling them earlier, they had finally tracked down the genuine burglar. They'd never got hold of any footage from the betting shops. It was either too secure for them to hack in, or such poor quality that they couldn't make anything out.

But by a stroke of luck, they'd stumbled across some CCTV from the night of the burglary. A nearby street. A silver van. A white male. Carrying an enormous, heavy holdall. After a little investigation, they even found a link between him and Danny. They'd now traced him. They knew where he lived. After the hassle he'd caused, he would soon be dealt with. Permanently.

The sun was setting as they finished their food. They'd dined on lobster and caviar, followed by Kobe steaks. Washed down with several bottles of Petrus, a stunning red. Dessert, cheese and some of the finest Cognac in the world completed their feast.

Now for the second half. The blind auction.

This was always a tense affair. There was no love lost between the guests. Theirs was an alliance for financial reasons only.

The VIPs made their secret bids. It was a fine balance between how much they wanted to splurge and what it would cost them in transfer fees as a result. It had to look genuine, after all. But this was rarely about the football; this was all about the money they would rake in from their guaranteed positions. The beautiful game had become consumed with greed.

The acting CEO smiled as the call came through. Just in time. He'd been expecting it sooner, but at least it meant the auction could now be ratified. They were home and dry. Presumably.

He walked out onto the deck to take it. He wouldn't be long.

"It's done. He's eliminated."

He hung up, without any response. That was all he needed to know. He was smiling broadly as he sat back down at the head of the table. What a great end to a fantastic evening.

Time for him to divulge the result.

He looked through the bids, hidden from the others' view. Wondered how he'd spend his bonus this time. A bonus which was increasing year on year on year. His VIPs waited with bated breath. He raised an eyebrow at the outcome. That should make for an exciting title race, he thought.

And then he cleared his throat and revealed next season's top four…

379

EPILOGUE

"What the hell…….?"

PC Joe Devlin pushed open the splintered door of the flat. It had obviously been jemmied open.

His jaw dropped at the scene that lay before him. A trail of destruction everywhere he looked.

He didn't think there was anyone inside, but he shouted out anyway. No response.

He surveyed the mess, checking each room in turn. Making sure no one was ready to jump out at him. Or that someone else hadn't already succumbed to that fate.

In the living room, he was shocked to see what looked like brand-new furniture, completely destroyed. Everything had been systematically tossed, slashed or wrenched open. Not a care for any damage being caused. They'd even slit the back of the sofa's upholstery and the underside of a chair.

In both bedrooms, more brand-new furniture had been wrecked beyond redemption.

He walked into the bathroom. The toilet and sink had been smashed up. The bath panel wrenched off.

They'd even been up in the loft space, judging by the ladder still hanging down.

Whoever lived here had clearly upset someone. It looked like pure wanton vandalism. Or they were searching for something.

Nothing had been left untouched. Nothing.

The call had come in earlier from a concerned neighbour. They'd heard a commotion from the neighbouring property.

They didn't want to put themselves in any danger, so they'd rung the police. They thought someone may have come to harm.

Devlin was baffled now. Was this a burglary gone wrong? Or just some kids with nothing better to do than smash up other people's belongings? Either way, he'd love to get his hands on whoever had done this.

He shook his head at the senseless crime as he wandered into the kitchen. The cupboard doors had all been flung open, one or two were even ripped off their hinges. Frustration? Or anger? The contents lay strewn across the worktops and the floor. Coffee, tea bags, cereal, pasta. Everywhere he looked was a total mess.

He began to radio in, as he wandered across to the balcony windows.

"Hi, reporting in from the earlier call-out. There's obviously been a break-in here. The place is a mess, but there's no sign of the homeowner. I'll make sure the property is secured and leave them a card to get in touch with us."

"Ok, have you spoken to………?"

"*WHAT THE FU….?*"

At that very moment, Devlin heard a shocking scream from a property nearby. He opened the French window, noticing some patches of blood on the door casing.

As he stepped out onto the balcony, he spotted the origin of the scream. A neighbour from the adjacent apartment. They were looking down. Five floors below. To where a crumpled body lay prone, surrounded by a huge pool of blood. Obviously expired.

"Shit. I think I've just found the homeowner. Best get the coroner round here, sharpish."

"Can you confirm the address?"

"Yes. It's Hanover Court. Hanover Court, Uxbridge Road."

Acknowledgements

I've always wanted to write a book. Like most people, I never got round to it. Everything else always got in the way. Until now.

In November 2020, I decided to join Michael Heppell's Write That Book Masterclass. One of my best decisions, I have to say. Not only has Michael developed a brilliant resource for budding writers, but my fellow aspiring and now-published authors are some of the most amazing people I've encountered. Their feedback and encouragement has been phenomenal.

And so it began. The Big Fix – under a different name – was born.

It's been a mix of emotions along the way. Fulfilling, exhausting, frustrating, exhausting, educational, exhausting, inspiring, exhausting, exhilarating, exhausting. I'm sure you get the picture. I wouldn't have made it to this stage without a lot of support, help and expertise, beyond my book buddies above.

I'll kick off by thanking my husband, David, for his wavering *and* unwavering support throughout all of this. I know you had your doubts as to whether I'd finally make it. So did I, but I did it! Granted, I have to give you credit for the initial idea, one that you've had for years. The storyline I developed from that is all my own. And you may not agree with how it pans out, but you can always change that when you write the screenplay for the film. (Yes, he's retained the film rights!)

To my sisters and my wider family and friends, thank you for always being there for me. I really couldn't wish for better. Although I do wish my parents were still alive to see this day. I hope they'd be really proud, even if they might not approve of some of the language (sorry, Aunty Christine!).

A special thank you to some talented friends who have helped immeasurably in certain areas. Rob Townsend for my website and related aspects, including your never-ending patience with my technical limitations! Paul McNally for the cover design and supporting marketing materials. Rob Allen for being my last-minute beta reader. And Roger, Hannah, Vic, Kerry, Jenny, Matt, David, Richard and my sister Julia, for your feedback on various chapters.

I'm grateful also to a couple of sense-checkers on certain aspects. Without your input – Ged and Jeff – I might have missed some details in areas like policing and train incidents.

Something else that helped me towards this goal was a fantastic programme called Visionary Women. You know who you are and why I say that, Toni, Lesley, Kate, Sarah, Harriet and Camilla.

My book includes a couple of issues that were hard to write about, but I felt were important to cover within the storyline.

With regard to Grenfell Tower, the TV pictures are still vivid in my mind and my heartfelt sympathies go to anyone caught up in this tragedy, including the emergency services. I went to great lengths to ensure these particular characters were not factual in any way.

In addition, the topic of male suicide is intrinsically linked with the world of football. The #BeAGameChanger campaign is just one example of the work being done right now to help anyone, not just men, struggling with their mental health. If my book makes just one person think twice, that's worth more than a million book sales.

Speaking of which (I haven't sold that many yet, obviously!)…

To you, the reader, a huge thank you. For buying this thing that I've always wanted to write. For investing in me. And for making all those very late nights writing it, editing it and perfecting it worthwhile.

To each and every one of you above, thank you for all your support.

And, finally, a note to football fans far and wide, no matter who you follow. To coin a phrase, we all have more in common than the differences that separate us. Don't let greed and corruption destroy the game we love. And remember…

Football without fans is nothing.

Follow me on social media:

https://twitter.com/jmorrisauthor
https://facebook.com/jillmorrisauthor
https://instagram.com/jillmorrisauthor